For my parents,
Kay and Al Castellana
Thanks for never clipping my wings too close
I love you.

Special thanks
to
Bounty Hunter Bert Leydee
one of the last of a vanishing breed.

DANGEROUS DESIRE

"Ignore me, I won't go away," Chris said. "Deny what we feel, it'll still be there in the morning." His voice lowered, almost threatening. "And if you run, I'll follow you."

Victoria shook her head. "You can't."

"I will. You're not getting away from me. I can't let you, Tori. You're already in my soul."

She blinked, momentarily stunned by the heat in his eyes, the depth of his certainty. "You just want—"

His mouth slashed across hers, cutting off the remark. He caught her wrists, pulling her arms around his waist. She pounded him there, except she kissed him back, opening her mouth wide, devouring him. She gripped his waist, her fingertips digging, then she drove her hands up his chest to catch his jaw between her palms, imprisoning him.

And the kiss became hers—liquid fire and untamed passion. Hungry. Wet. Possessive.

Books by Amy J. Fetzer

MY TIMESWEPT HEART

THUNDER IN THE HEART

LION HEART

TIMESWEPT ROGUE

DANGEROUS WATERS

Published by Zebra Books

DANGEROUS WATERS

Amy J. Fetzer

Zebra Books
Kensington Publishing Corp.
http://www.zebrabooks.com

ZEBRA BOOKS are published by

Kensington Publishing Corp.
850 Third Avenue
New York, NY 10022

First Printing: December, 1997
10 9 8 7 6 5 4 3 2 1

Printed in the United States of America

Chapter One

Victoria Mason hunted killers for a living.

And this one was the worst of them—a homicidal maniac in an Armani suit.

"Got a bead on him, Samurai?" she whispered into the headset mic.

"Yeah." Deep, masculine and annoyed. "Jesus, it's dark."

"You think, maybe, because it's night?"

"A hundred comedians outta work, and you gotta be a smart ass."

A brief smile tugged her lips as she rested her head against the wall and stared at the stars. "Ivy League knows we're here, Cole."

"How you figure?"

"Has he looked behind himself?"

"No."

The bastard had confidence, she'd give him that. "Lit a smoke yet? Using that gold cigarette case like a mirror?"

"He is now."

"Stay back!" she snapped, holding the thread mic closer to her mouth and hoping he wasn't within striking distance.

"I'm a big boy, Vic." Testy, soft. "How'd you know he would?"

"I don't know. I just do."

"Jesus, woman, you give me the creeps sometimes."

"Yeah, and you give me the hots."

His soft chuckle, knowing and male, soothed the unintended insult. He'd meant it as a compliment, left-handed as it was. Cole was a P.I., blonde, brawny—and her best friend. They'd tried being lovers, once, and tried was the optimum word, because all they did was laugh, never making it beyond a little heavy groping. They'd settled for friends after that, closer than most, but friends.

"We gonna take a vacation after this one?" she said after a moment. God, she could use one.

"Depends."

"On?"

"Do I get to see those legs in a skirt?"

"You've seen all I've got, Cole, so what's the difference?"

"Allure," he whispered huskily and she smiled, shaking her head.

She had all the feminine allure of a slick doorknob, and they both knew it.

"He's just smoking, Vic. No, he's moving, unlocking the trunk, bending. Oh, God."

"What is it?" she hissed, looking left and right before moving in closer and wishing she'd taken out her night vision goggles.

"It's a kid. Shit, she can't be more than eighteen."

"Blonde?"

"Yeah. She's gagged and tied." She heard another curse laced with a plea to God, and then, "It's Sgt. Allen's daughter."

"Don't move in yet, Cole." She inched toward his locale. "If she's bound, she's got to be alive."

Please be alive, she thought, her stomach rolling. Allen was the cop who'd collared the perp in the first place. He had found the three small town murders that linked with the others. Eleven women left dead across the country, with no connection except the manner of their deaths. A serial killer and her *defendant* had been charged with number twelve. Only number twelve. But this morning some slick-ass lawyer convinced a judge he wasn't a flight risk and he'd walked. She'd trusted her instincts, not lawyers, and followed, his previous moves reeking of suspicion and finally, bringing them close to the county border. Fat Jack's a fool for putting up the bail, she thought, even if he provided only a hundred thousand of the million five bond. Ivy League could easily afford the whole enchilada, and she figured he dealt with a bondsman just to satisfy the court. Regardless, she and Cole had trailed him here, to what she hoped was his souvenir burial ground. But if they didn't do something quick, preppy-with-a-weapon would add another trophy to his collection, a young bride of no more than two years.

Victoria wanted to do him, now.

But her conscience wouldn't allow it and she side-stepped against the wall of the dilapidated building. It was an abandoned stock yard at the base of a mountain, littered with rotting wood and shadows.

"Cole?"

No answer

"Cole!"

"I'm here."

"Jesus, don't scare me like that!"

"Gosh, *pumpkin,* didn't know you cared."

"Where is he, *jerk face?*"

She could almost hear him smirk.

"Setting the stage. I'm going in for a closer look."

"No!" He didn't respond and her temper rose. "Back off, pal. He's mine." Her voice chilled through the tiny mic.

"I'm not going to provoke him."

"Being here will provoke him."

"We're covered."

"Just because marshals are within radio distance doesn't

mean we're safe. This guy is slick and fast and you could be his next victim.''

She heard him grunt.

''I am.''

''Cole?''

A crash and she felt the impact of his body hitting the wall as sound banged against her ear drum.

''Cole!''

Victoria immediately yanked her hand radio from her jacket pocket and called in the police, then took off, moving as fast as she could in the dark, sliding up against the crumbling wall, her gun close to her body.

''Answer me, damn you,'' she hissed over and over, but she knew. Oh, God almighty, she knew. A gurgling came through her ear piece, amplifying his lungs working desperately to draw in air. It sounded wet and spongy. *He's taken it in the chest.* ''Hold on, Samurai, I'm coming.'' She imagined his pain, his lungs filling with blood, foaming from his lips, lips she'd kissed. And her heart shattered.

A shot fired, soft, whizzing. Cole. He always used a silencer; said the usual noise made civilians panic. ''I'm coming, pal, hold on.''

''Wounded . . . him,'' came between a faint shuddering gasp.

''I'll see you get a medal.''

Through the highly sensitive mic she caught the faint uneven thump of footsteps and Victoria quickly slipped into the building, circumventing the room as she stepped over fallen beams and shattered furniture, her eyes constantly checking for Ivy League, her back always facing the wall. She headed to the rear entrance, silver gray moonlight from the alley spilling over the half-reclining body slung across the doorway.

Oh God.

Victoria checked the alley, her back, then knelt. ''I'm here, Samurai. Don't cut out on the party now.'' He was sweating; a stream of blood, black and shiny in the dark, trickled from the corner of his mouth, stained his shirt just below his heart, and she covered the bloody hole, her hand trembling. He struggled for one more breath before he went still.

She blinked, stunned. "Oh Jesus, Banner, don't do this, don't. Help's coming!" It was too late. Even in the dark she could see his pupils were dilated, his pale blue iris's swallowed up with black. She slammed her eyes shut, stinging grief and guilt and rage clawing through her. She clung to it like talons to fresh meat to keep from crying. If she did, she'd never stop. Never. She drew a deep breath, letting it out slowly, purposely. Later, she thought. Dropping a kiss to his still lips, she closed his vacant eyes, then stood, slipping her flash light free and stooping low to search the ground for a show of blood.

Come on, Ivy League, bleed for me.

She scanned the ground around Cole's body, littered with trash and soda cans and splintered wood someone used for target practice. Rotten place for such a good man to die, she thought, then tried to imagine the struggle, examined the angle of the foot prints, then noticed the blood on Cole's jeans. His killer's blood. Point blank, she decided, dropping the beam to the area beyond Cole and picking up the shiny splatter. The slim flash light wasn't very strong, but gave enough light to find the direction. She followed it, wishing again that she had her night vision goggles so her flash light wouldn't alert him, wishing she'd taken point instead of Cole. Police sirens ripped the stillness somewhere far behind her and she hoped Cole's killer would lose his arrogance and run.

And bleed.

Yeah. Do us all a favor and die for me, you son of a bitch.

The darkness hampered her, stealing precious time, but his blood trail wasn't going anywhere. And neither was she.

His bounty just went up.

A half hour later, she stared at the mountain rising up before her like Jabba the Hut and faced the fact that no matter how much she jiggled the flashlight, she wasn't going to get anymore power. Behind her, the blue and red lights of squad cars lit the

darkness as they overtook the long twisting road to the stockyard. Decision made, she tied her dead Mag-light to a dry bush
and headed back, mentally listing everything she'd need to
track, not even conscious of the tears rolling down her cheeks.

With her shoulders braced against the wall, Victoria watched
the men zip her best friend into a black body bag and lift the
girney into the coroner's wagon almost in synch with a stretcher
being lifted into an ambulance. Paramedics worked over the
comatose young woman.

At least she's alive.

And she was an unfinished kill for Ivy League, a break in the
ritual. It would make him angry, she supposed, and hopefully,
sloppy. That the kidnapping was motivated by revenge was a
new facet to consider. Shrugging deeper into the fleece-lined
suede jacket, Victoria took a drag on her cigarette, blowing out
the smoke in a sharp stream and eavesdropping on the police
chatter while she waited for a friend to bring her a horse. She
sucked another toke, raked her hair off her forehead, then dug
the heels of her palms into her tired eyes and prayed for an
attack of patience before she strangled someone. What's taking
so damn long? Her heart felt numb, impatience riding just ahead
of her emotions. She needed to get moving, before the FBI
Special Task Force showed up and flexed its muscle, before
the sweep of deputies, highway patrol and volunteers trampled
the grounds, obliterating the trail. But she was forced to remain,
letting precious minutes tick by while she gave her statement.
Damn paper work—if she didn't get the go-ahead, she'd yank
a few chains and take it.

A man approached, his face weathered and familiar: Mark
Daniels, U. S. Marshal.

"Give this one up, Vic," he said, handing her Cole's headset.
"You've done your part."

If she had, Cole would be alive. "Not a chance." Stuffing
the set in her pocket, she flicked the cigarette into the air,
watching as it made a smooth arch of glowing red before hitting

the dirt. "Jack doesn't pay me to sit on my butt and mope," she said, pushing away from the wall and brushing past him. She headed to her car. Standing at the rear, she dug for her keys, staring at them briefly. Cole had driven tonight, and she'd had to search his body for them. They were still sticky with his blood.

Jamming the key in the lock, she threw open the trunk and shoved aside Burger King and Taco Bell wrappers to grasp her back pack, unzipping it and immediately taking inventory. Flipping her hair back over her shoulder, she checked her battered tackle box, the load of her gun, stashed an extra clip, a knife, a tazer, the pair of head mics, night vision goggles, a micro camera, maps, a couple of slim bottles of water and a rolled pair of jeans. Then from another duffle, she added a couple fistfuls of necessities—a thick envelope of back-files, two non-descript tee shirts and a plastic lunch bags stuffed with clean panties. A bra she could go without if she had to, but not food. She pushed energy bars and freeze dried *whatever* into every available space.

Mark stood beside her the entire time, trying to convince her to let them handle this one and give herself a break.

"You mean wait for the Feds?" That was not in her plan.

He shifted uncomfortably. "They're responsible for this case now."

She spared him a quick glance through a curtain of dark gold hair. "We all are, Mark. But he's a bailed defendant headed to the country border, the wilderness and that makes him mine." All accounted, she zipped the pack shut. "I have to move, *now.*" To prove her point, helicopters crossed overhead. They'll have thermal tracking equipment, she thought, and FBI field agents to destroy the trail.

"Should I swear you in as a deputy?"

She shrugged, still checking her trunk for equipment as he mumbled the oath. To cover his butt, she thought, throwing up her right hand.

"Yeah, yeah, save your breath—I do." She slammed the hood closed and faced him. "I'm losing good hunt time." She tossed the keys and he caught them. "Keep it." He frowned and she shrugged inside the bulky sheepskin. "Sell it, junk it, I don't care. I've got a feeling that I'm not coming back."

Panic swept his craggy features. "What!"

"This is my last one, Mark. Then maybe . . ."

Maybe what? Grow flowers? It wasn't like she'd planned for the future. Oh sure, bounties were high, but the courts got the forfeitures. She worked for Fat Jack, and her paychecks just barely covered her expenses. Hell, she didn't even have an apartment, having shared a house with Cole for over a year. Not that she was ever there. And now he was gone.

"Anything you need to know about me is in Cole's file cabinet under Pain-in-the-ass."

Mark smirked, his eyes sad. She was a skilled hunter, the best, with a tuning fork in her head about felons. That's why he wasn't going to stop her. Even if the area was sealed off so tight a fly wouldn't get through, they couldn't overlook her 100% recapture rate, or that she'd suspected the killer's move and his playground before anyone else. She lived for nothing beyond bringing in the bail jumper. And she was a master at making herself blend in enough to do it. Mark couldn't count the times he stood right beside her and didn't recognize her. But he'd known her for years. He was her training officer when she'd been a marshal, but the woman standing before him was nothing like he remembered—sharp edged and callous, about her job and her own needs. Hell, he didn't think she ever did anything for herself like other women did—date, shop, lunch with friends, maybe some pampering. Nothing but hunt.

"Don't say a damn thing," she warned, recognizing that pitying look. " 'Cause it won't matter."

"I wasn't. I know it won't, but one of these days I'll get you to wear a dress and date my little brother."

She blinked. "The fashion plate from L.A.?" He nodded. "Oh, we'd have just tons to chat about," she said, rolling her eyes and slinging her pack on her shoulder. A deputy called out to her and she turned, meeting him halfway and taking the reins of the horse. "Thanks for the loan, Kyle."

Kyle glanced briefly at the U.S. Marshal, about to put in his two cents, then thought better of it. It was personal now. "If you lose her, she'll just head home."

"How comforting," she said, then lashed her pack to the saddle, yet before she could climb on, Mark grabbed her, swallowing her in his beefy arms.

"Dinner with Janey and the kids, this Saturday," he said in her ear and Victoria nodded, savoring the masculine strength, a lump swelling in her throat. Family dinners, laughing kids, a home . . . *Don't! Don't weaken. Or Ivy League will eat you alive,* she thought, quickly pushing out of his arms and swinging up onto the animal's back. She guided the mare away from the bulk of police cars when Fat Jack Palau suddenly blocked her path. He grabbed the mare's bridle, scowling and breathless, which wasn't unusual, but the chopper in the distance told her he'd hauled that Hawaiian-printed bulk in a hard run to catch her.

Jack eyeballed her, her pack, and the determination in her gold eyes. "Firing you won't make a diff, will it?"

"You did that last week."

He snorted, glancing at the rolling coroner's wagon, then raising a questioning brow.

"That's Cole."

The color drained from his face and Jack glanced around, as if to make her a liar by spotting Cole.

"He was brain dead before I got to him." Her voice fractured when pain flashed in his eyes, and she told him what happened. Cole, the girl, the blood stains and the car were enough to indict, but they needed Ivy League—dead or alive.

"How much of a lead does that som' bitch have on you?"

She was relieved he wasn't going to fight her. Jack was a tough adversary when you pissed him off. "Better than two hours." Her expression blamed the Marshals, the local sheriff, and the heel-dragging paper work she loathed. "And he's booking it at five miles an hour, if I had to guess."

"Your guesses are Goddamn gospel." He let go of the horse. "Find him."

"I'll have daylight in a few hours," she said, controlling the nervous mount. "He's bleeding, bad from what I can tell, and he can't get that far with the old mining roads already barricaded, but that depends on where Cole wounded him." And if he even took the roads. She looked at Mark, a half dozen cops behind him itching to tear her from the saddle. "You swore me in to cover your butt," she said leaning down and plucking the star from his jacket pocket. "You can't stop me," she warned and cops grumbled, strapping on bulletproof vests. Hell, they'd spend the next hour deciding who was chief and who were Indians. "This area levels off til about five miles north to a forest, then a mountain that's rocky as hell, before sinking into a valley." She pointed west and Mark nodded, agreeing with her geography. "I suggest you get beyond it and I'll try to send him to you." Men with badges, all at once, tried destroying her strategy. "Listen up!" she said, her naturally deep voice cutting through the noise. "I tracked him for over a mile before you guys showed. My marker will be easy to spot with NVG's." She pulled the goggles from her pack. "If he gets into that valley, we'll lose him. Come in behind me. I don't care." She jammed her sweat stained cowboy hat on her head. "But at least give me a couple hours before your flashlight toting volunteers blind me."

"One hour," Mark conceded. "And you have to keep radio contact." Voices scratched over the hand set he offered.

"Forget it. What if he's got one tuned to your freque?" She kneed the mare, forcing them to back away or be trampled. "He's outsmarted the finest criminologist on eleven kills, and I'll be damned if I'm gonna get my throat cut because you want a pre-game report." She didn't give them anymore opportunities to delay her and sauntered around police officers hovering over grid maps. They were her friends and they were giving her this hunt time.

Staring at her retreating back, Mark opened his mouth to argue the risk, but Jack stopped him. "Trust my girl, Daniels. She can get into places your boys can't, and you know it. Vic won't let us down."

"She's just a woman, Palau."

Jack smirked. "Since when?"

She heard that and let the sting of it slide off like water, focusing on the hunt. The squawk of radios and rolling blue lights made the horse dance and in the dark, Victoria paused beside a black and white, staring down at the slightly over-weight officer as he lifted his gaze, his eyes rimmed red and swollen.

Sgt. Allen blinked, straightening. "You're going?"

"I let him get away, Randy." Her voice was flat.

He took a step closer, reaching for her. "I'm not blaming you."

"I know," came softly as she grasped his hand. She thought of sweet Lisa Allen and all who'd be destroyed if she died—this man here, his daughter's young husband and family, her friends. God, if it were me, no one would suffer. She leaned down in the saddle, pecking a kiss to his ruddy cheek. "I swear I'll bring him in," she whispered. "Dead or alive."

She let go and reined around, heading north, melting into the darkness with a psychopath on the run.

Chapter Two

1872
Colorado Territory

Marshal Christopher Swift caught the dirty twelve-year-old boy by the shirt collar, yanking him off the back stairs to the saloon. He let him dangle off the ground in sheer panic as he glared up at the painted half-naked woman standing on the landing.

"Ain't none of your business, Marshal." Her hand on her hip, her slippered foot tapped out her impatience.

Hell it was. "You ought to have enough sense, Dee."

She snorted indelicately and sauntered into the cat house, hips swaying as she half-heartedly dragged the dressing gown up over her bare shoulders.

Christopher turned his attention to the boy, shaking him once before releasing him. He smelled like old potatoes, his hair so filthy it stuck out around his head like tumble weed. The lad shrugged his shirt into place, his gaze darting beyond the marshal to the hulking deputy leaning against the support post, using an Arkansas tooth pick to clean his teeth.

"You ain't gonna tell, are you, Marshal?"

"I might."

Horror struck across the boy's face. And Chris sighed, wishing he could do something for this wild child. "If I see you within twenty yards of this place, I'll squeal to your Pa."

The boy blinked. "Then I can git?"

The marshal inclined his head and the boy took off like a pistol shot, and Chris watched him go.

Noble Beecham sucked his teeth, then said, "What'd you 'spect from one of Vel's girls?"

Only his eyes shifted to the deputy. "Not to offer to make him a man."

"Dang." Noble looked longingly toward the staircase. "I wish Dee'd give me a freebee."

Chris's gaze sharpened. "Take the walk, deputy, and check on the men."

With a lazy look in his direction, Noble flipped the long collapsible blade around and slid it into the sheath at his waist, then nodded and pushed away from the post.

"Can't Daddy them all, Chris," drifted softly to the marshal. "That's a boy without a Ma when he needs one the most."

"You're too soft," he murmured on the breeze.

Too soft. If he were, he'd have let the boy go with the whore. Striding out of the alley, Chris moved down the street, testing the doors of locked shops, peering in alleys. He and Noble traded *the walk,* a show of presence against any trouble, though he had fifteen deputies stationed throughout his town. His. What a laugh. He was no more a part of this city than if he'd been born here. Buggies and buck boards filled with families on their way home rattled down the street. Music colored the early evening air. The owner of the mercantile turned his key and jiggled the doors as two women, their purchases tucked against their chests, walked to their buggy. He tipped his hat in acknowledgement. They responded with only a giggle and a polite nod. He quit expecting more and strode on.

"Don't blame Dee, Marshal. She thought she was doing the kid a favor."

Chris stopped to look up at the robust redhead hanging out the window with damn-near everything else she owned.

Chris tipped his hat. "Evening, Vel."

"Hell if it is. Got three of my best girls up here bored enough to play cards!" she said with false indignation. Her smile was wide and inviting as her gaze raked his long body. "Wanna amuse them?"

"Not tonight."

"Like you ever have." She laughed, her plump breasts nearly spilling from the tightly laced corset. "You know, Marshal, gets mighty lonely with just that horse for company."

Chris glanced to the side, at the black beast waiting in the center of the street like an obedient puppy.

"I do all right."

"Then you got to have one helluva rock between those handsome thighs, honey!"

His lips curved. "You're shameless, Vel."

"Ain't a whore 'posed to be?"

He grinned, a flash of white teeth. She was honest and kind, and Red Velvet Knight made no bones about who or what she was. And she had to be the happiest harlot in the territory.

" 'Night, Marshall."

Lightly he touched the brim of his hat and moved on. He never patronized Vel's place, not that he didn't have the urge, but he believed he'd lose a whole lot of respect if folks saw the marshal with a whore. Besides, if he wanted to lie with a woman he rode to the next town, to the sweet Widow Bingham. Angela was his age, attractive, independent, and after fifteen years with an abusive husband, she wasn't ready to have any man in her life. They had an understanding—no ties, no future expectations, just polite conversation and discreet comfortable sex. But that was just it. It was blandly comfortable—no passion, no earth shattering kisses or sensual teasing. Only a release.

Chris wanted more, from himself and from a woman. And it made him ache. A lot.

Crashing glass cut through his thoughts, and he paused before the Pearl Handled Saloon. A bit noisy for the week night, and he noticed the heavy number of miners and cowboys fresh from the range, all drinking whiskey like water.

Damn.

He'd enough trouble keeping a lid on the tempers in the last week and didn't need his jail filled with drunk cow punchers. Better let Noble know, he thought as he turned back. He was in no mood to clean up this mess tonight.

With the leads in her hand, Victoria bent and gripped the leaf, rubbing her thumb over the membrane. Wet, tacky. She brought her hand to her nose and the metallic scent of blood filled her head.

Memories came, and with them, the rage.

It pushed her, fast and furious, ahead of the rest.

Straightening, she lifted the heavy cyborg looking night vision goggles to her eyes and scanned. The darkness brightened, but she knew she wouldn't see him. He was too far ahead, but in about an hour, she'd be climbing up his ass.

He was bleeding, bad, but she still couldn't tell from where. Obviously it wasn't enough for him to stop. She hoped it was his head.

I have to quit that. She was letting him get to her, pecking at her anger, clouding her thinking. But she kept remembering Cole, attractive, brawny, a girl's dream of a rescuer, and stone cold dead. *Must have pricked his heart to die that fast.*

Clearing the image, she focused on the trail. Tracking was slow, and she couldn't rely on a few blood stains. His bleeding would eventually stop. But the soft earth was enough to mark his staggering foot prints, a bent twig, a patch of over-turned pebbles. He'd stumbled here, she thought, going down on one knee, his depression like a skid mark in the dirt. It's amazing how distinctive a print Herme's shoes could make in the rich Colorado soil.

Rising, she continued, her marker nearly four miles behind her and dawn climbing over her shoulder, daring her to get ahead of the cops. He would be weak and need water, she thought, shrugging out of her jacket and tossing it over the saddle.

"Come on, girl," she urged, the horse obediently following, the pair heading north toward the trees sloping into a mountainside. Briefly, she glanced back over her shoulder, squinting at the cop cars still surrounding the stockyard, a line of men like a dark string on the horizon. The posse's coming, she thought with a small smile.

"We got to find him first, girl," she said to the horse as a chopper hovered over head. She made a circling motion, then pointed northwest. The craft rocked once, then headed off. Silently, she thanked Mark Daniels for the chance to redeem herself after screwing up and costing Cole his life. Her eyes burned suddenly and she shook off the grief, picking up the pace.

Water. He'll need water.

Victoria let go of the reins, allowing the horse to drink from the narrow stream as she strode up the bank, pebbles crunching beneath her boots. Ivy League was hurting, his wound either in his side or his leg, point blank, the bullet likely passing straight through. And now blood was filling his shoes. Picking her way over a low cluster of bolders, she put her hand out to brace herself and it immediately slid off the rock. She stared at her palm, coated with dark coagulated blood.

"Bingo," she whispered, a little thrill running through her. She stooped to examine depressions in the soft wet gravel, marking a path up the shore line, then she straightened, frowning at the small water fall, her gaze slipping beyond to the gray rock face surrounding the tongue of water. I don't remember seeing that on the map, she thought. Working her way closer, she found more stains, more black heel scraps and turned rocks. Her feet braced on a wobbly plateau of rocks, she stared a few feet above her head at the water fountaining into a river like a crystal petal out to catch the dew, arching slightly before falling straight down in a hard rush.

Okay, the stream could be just run off, but the National Park Service was better than Rand McNally at marking their maps. So why wasn't this fall on hers? And the mountain, a hill really, wasn't steep enough to generate such a strong spill. But hell if it didn't exist.

She jammed her hand beneath the flow, letting the cool water sluice over her fingers before she cupped her palms and drank, slaking a thirst she didn't realize she'd had. Drying her hands on her jeans, she maneuvered back down to the bank, covering the ground twice to see if he went in another direction. Sloshing into the narrow river, she waded to her hips, not trusting the soft bottom to be shallower than she suspected and checked the opposite bank. Unmarred, except for a few animal tracks.

Returning to the south bank, she retraced her path to the fall, certain his didn't lead anywhere else. He didn't climb over it or there would be at least blood or shoe marks on the jagged rock face. Then where the hell did he go?

She concentrated, imagining his desperation and pain and that he might try to hide and wait it out. Her gaze snapped to his tracks, following them *into* the fall. Nah, too easy, she thought, immediately unsheathing her knife. Steadying her feet, she moved sideways, her back flush to the rock as she inched toward the spilling water. Preparing herself for the cold shock, she put up her arm to block some of the flow and ducked into the liquid curtain. She blinked, scanning.

"Jesus Christ almighty," she whispered, then stepped forward, hunching to accommodate the cavern behind the fall, leaving her untouched by the flowing sheet of water. Inside, the rock gouge glistened with the soft back-spray, puddles of water marking the uneven floor. No foot prints. Sunlight and water cast a strange blue and yellow glow inside the cave. Must be quartz in the rock, she thought fleetingly as she swiped at the water dripping off her nose with her sleeve, then knelt, carefully studying the ground, the interior walls, her fingers grazing over jutting edges, then twisting them toward the light to see if she'd found blood again. The wet spray melted the stain on her fingertip to pink.

She smiled.

Flicking her soggy pony tail over her shoulder, she stood, strangely lightheaded as she took a step forward, knife out. Bright light suddenly showered over her, like a clicked on light bulb. Victoria stilled, frowning back at the water fall no less than a yard from her touch, then to the open terrain spread out before her. Impossible. And she turned back, retracing her steps. When she returned to the point where she entered the fall, her horse was there, munching on grass, Ivy League's blood smeared over the rocks and grass, vivid and running. Drenching herself again, Victoria re-entered the fall, matching her steps and still coming to the same conclusion. The cave opened into the mountain, like a passageway. But it wasn't deep enough.

And it dropped sharply.

She did a quick scan before she skidded down the hill, scattering dirt and pebbles, the immediate area unusually dry and dusty. She searched the ground, expecting to see more of his foot prints or a blood trail. But there was nothing, dammit. She dropped down on a bolder, her clothes giving off steam in the scorching heat. This was not good, she thought, pulling off her Timberline boots and pouring out water. Her wet jeans felt as heavy as her disappointment and she wrung out her hair, pushing aside confusion to logical thought. He came through the water fall and vanished. How? When? And if he was only a few hours ahead, where were his tracks? The wind couldn't have obliterated them in such a short time, aside from the fact that there wasn't much of a breeze.

She glanced around, her gaze honing on the shape of the tree line, sparser than she first imagined, the jagged terrain stretching untouched for miles to the south down the mountain. She squinted, the sun's glare nearly blinding. It hasn't rained here in a while, she thought, shielding her eyes to look where she'd come. The gray mountain appeared as if a huge fist had slammed down on a giant pile of stone, leaving scatters of bolders and small rocks. There was a strange familiarity about the area that she couldn't place. Then her gaze lit on a dry mud smear on the stones around her. Frowning, she went down on her knees and gently scraped the rocks with her knife, then slid her finger carefully across the blade. The substance was black and brittle, and she lifted another sample from the dirt. She sniffed, then sanded her fingers. It powdered and using the water dripping from her hair, she wet it, smudging it between her fingertip again. Oxidized, but it was blood.

Uncaring of her stockinged feet, she searched on, bending over to the ground and picking up anything suspicious, examining it carefully before discarding it. The under brush was dry, catching her clothes and when she turned to release her sleeve she found what she needed. Tiny bits of charcoal gray thread meshed over a short bush. And then she saw his foot prints, dragging.

Those damned thousand dollar shoes, eh, Ivy League? Can't do a crime without them.

Herbs, pungent and wet, hung thickly on the evening air, the steaming swirl of their fragrance permeating the natural shelter of stone. A small fire hissed and popped, sending glittering sparks high into the trees. The creatures of the night painted the air with their calls, but Swift Arrow heard none of it, his body cradled on the skin of Mother Earth and his mind caught in a deep familiar dream. Sweat sheened his bare flesh, his breathing rapid with the wonder and confusion of sensations, the smells and textures of reality heavy in the story of the sleeping.

He stood on the edge of his father's camp, his path barred to his family's lodge, a line of silent painted warriors shielding entry. His demands went unheeded and, outnumbered, he turned away and went home, to his place in the white world.

But there, too, his way was blocked. He turned from street to alley, each path barred by men and women. He tried another path, but without success, then another and still another. He could see his valley, his home in the distance, painfully empty and unreachable.

A mountain lion, a cougar, appeared at his feet, circling him, baring its gleaming fangs. It reared before him, matching his height and swiped the air with a clawed paw, cutting three lines across his heart before the creature settled. Blood drenched his skin to his waist. The animal took a step away, stopped, then twisted its proud head to view him, before proceeding, the people parting for the great cat.

The man-hunter led him, taking him home.

The dream shifted suddenly to the mist of the dense forest, heavy and wet, a shimmer of unearthly light haloed in the distance. He heard strange sounds, like the whirl of a Spaniard's bolo, the constant rush of water and the call of distance voices.

The tree rustled softly, but Swift Arrow did not move, poised for attack, his bow primed.

The cougar appeared through the mist, its walk slow and lazy. The animal's coat was wet, each step was cautious and measured. And silent. The hazy air clouded around the beast, enveloping it, and its gold eyes rimmed in black kept him rooted where he stood. He felt no fear, not for his life, and he sensed a definite feminine presence as it neared. And then the cougar's body shifted shape, growing longer with each stride, paws lifting and changing slowly to slender hands, hind quarters to long slender legs until the cougar was walking upright as a woman, tall, sleek and strong with muscle.

But the eyes were the same.

She stopped before him, her gold eyes infinitely sad and needy. She didn't speak, her image hovering between the mist and the elusiveness of reality as she lifted her hand and covered the scratches on his chest.

Swift Arrow experienced the sudden hot jolt of her touch before she tumbled back into the mist, the night swallowing her in a hauntingly liquid darkness.

He reached for her, but could not move. His heart ached with a pain so terrifying that he thought it would destroy him.

He felt his eyes burn and looked down at his chest. The bleeding cuts were healed.

Swift Arrow jolted awake, blinking, then turning his head. His gaze scanned the area before he sat up, swiping the sweat from his forehead. He cradled his head in his hands, part of him trying to draw back the image and part wanting it to stay away and never return. Three times in two days he'd had this same dream, coming in increments—until tonight.

He had not lived in the white world so long to dismiss such a vision and the Cheyenne blood running through his veins warned him to accept this dream as a prediction. But Marshal Christopher Swift didn't need the path of his life changed, and he'd be damned if he'd let a cougar who walks like a woman do it.

"Kyle insists you'll go home, so I'm trusting you. Girl stuff, you know." She stuffed a note in the saddle bags, loosened the cinch a little, then slung her heavy pack on her shoulder, slapping the mare's rump before heading into the fall without a backwards glance. She didn't have any thoughts about the police a mile behind her or the choppers overhead, only that Ivy League had found a way to escape and she was going after him. Poised before the crystal arch of water, she lurched into the fall, catching her balance and shaking water off her hair like a puppy. Dizziness, heavier than before, spread roughly through her, the air feeling like mercury sliding over her skin. She ignored it, and two steps brought light and warmth. Victoria skidded down the incline, hungry for the hunt and unaware that behind her, the flow of cool water was growing thinner.

Chapter Three

Victoria rolled around, gun in hand and came face to face with a . . . an Indian?

She blinked, looking him over.

He wasn't two feet from her, squatting. And he hadn't so much as flinched.

In fact, he was incredibly still, not even his bare chest moved with his breathing. Only his dark eyes shifted, sliding once down to her boots, then snapping up to prowl over her hair, her face, before meeting her gaze again.

He didn't give the .45 cal Barretta a second glance.

The warm breeze caught the flap hanging between his thighs and feminine instinct admired the smooth corded muscle, before quickly taking in the over-the-knee deer skin moccasins, plain, unadorned, a bow and quiver of arrows lay beside his right foot, the razor sharp tips gleaming in the light. Strung game lay inches away. His elbows were braced on his thighs, hands clasped, hammered silver cuffs circling his wrists. But it was his face that held her interest.

Like carved bronze.

Aristocratic, strong. Almost beautiful.

With the body of an athlete. Bet he stopped a few hearts in their tracks.

"What do you want?"

No answer.

"Great Spirit got your tongue, Tonto?" She didn't feel threatened and lowered the barrel. "Hungry?" She gestured with the gun to the half of a squirrel lying near her dead campfire.

Still, he stared at her, dark strands of hair ruffling in the wind and she wondered if it was as soft as it looked.

"What is a woman doing in the wilderness, alone?" he said suddenly. She liked the sound of his voice—deep, like wood smoke.

"Gee. My prone position give you any clue?"

There was a hint of a smile behind that stoic look, she thought, and eased the hammer down before rising up on her elbow. The motion put her face inches from his and her hair spilled over her shoulder. She could hear him breath now, almost feel his pulse. He looked fierce, angry.

But he has gentle eyes.

And she wanted to drown in them.

Jesus.

No time for that.

And Victoria immediately laid back down, turning her back to him and resting her head on her pack. She sighed and closed her eyes, hoping he got the message.

Chris easily read her dismissal, but what the hell. He was impressed. She had no horse, could snare game, handle the strange looking gun, and was utterly fearless. Not even for a moment did it waver. Yet there was something else about her he'd never seen in a woman—savagery. She almost dared him to test her. Her senses were acute, more than he'd expect in a woman, especially a white woman, and he wondered if she knew he'd watched her for nearly a half hour before approaching.

She has a mouth made for slow wet kisses, he thought.

But it was those eyes that speared him, conjuring hazy images and an undeniable heat.

He looked her over again, liking what he saw in her long slender shape, her unusual coloring. He'd never seen hair quite like that before, mostly a dark brownish gold, thick and richly streaked with shades of red, pale blonde and brown, but darker around her face and underneath. It gave her a wild look, coupled with her tanned skin and dark arching brows . . . and the eyes, gold, flecks of black edging the iris.

Everything about her was sultry, mysterious. Predatory.

His brow knitted, a cool ripple over his skin. Her? Was she the cougar . . . ?

Slowly, he reached out to touch her hair, then caught himself, instinctively resisting the connection he experienced from the dream.

Hell. She'd likely shoot him in between yawns. And here he was in the forest, having notions about a perfect stranger, who was obviously not intimidated nor interested in even a conversation.

But God, she was tall, legs went on til Sunday.

He smiled when she continued to ignore him, though he knew she wasn't asleep, and left her to her nap.

Victoria sensed his sudden absence even though she didn't hear him leave. She almost called him back. It had been too long since she was in the company of anyone who wasn't a bondsman, a criminal, or a junky looking to score a few bucks with some information. Not that she ever had any offers for much else.

Besides, she was exhausted, so much that she lost track of Ivy League's trail twice. She only needed a couple hours and it was killing her to stew that long. But she knew from experience that exhaustion bred dangerous mistakes.

And she couldn't afford even one.

Or someone else would end up like Cole—with a twelve inch razor thin stiletto shoved through their heart.

Beneath a canopy of trees, Victoria sat huddled behind rocks and shrubery, studying the town—a town that wasn't on her maps. A large town that shouldn't be here. That there were no telephone lines, electrical cables or even a satellite dish was one thing, but not a car or truck moved through the city. Everyone mobile was either walking, on horseback or in buggies or wagons. No choppers swarmed overhead, no police rode across the terrain in land rovers. It made her nervous, since they should have caught up with her hours ago. It was just too quiet.

Frowning, she slumped back against the rock, winding a lock of hair around her finger and sifting through her options, formulating a plan. If Ivy League came this way, which she was nearly certain he did, he either stopped there, or skirted the town and kept running. But he was wounded. And likely thought that if there were no phones, he could get help without alerting the authorities. She doubted that cellular phones would work out here.

He was counting on that, and if he was smart, he'd keep moving. Ivy League was lethal, cunning, and likely feeling feverish and in desperate need of a transfusion. She'd have to see if there was a doctor in this town first. At sundown. Less conspicuous. Less people. Got to keep a low profile. Very low.

Sighing, she scrubbed her hands over her face, then raked her hair back. It would take at least an hour to prepare herself, maybe more, if it got dark quickly. And she couldn't afford to use her flashlight or make a campfire, not if he was near and had doubled back to get her. It's happened before, and she wasn't going to suffer the price of underestimating this creep.

She'd done it once already.

Damn you, Cole. Always got to play the hero, huh?

Her eyes burned, her throat tightening like a clenched fist. She was going to miss the hell out of that man. Swallowing repeatedly, she fought off waves of grief, tears lurking just below the surface and scrounged in her back pack for a cigarette. Finding a crushed pack, she slid the slim filter between her lips, flicked her Bic and drew, inhaling deeply.

Cole hated that she smoked, even though it was only when she was upset. Another resolution down the crapper, she thought, yet still dragged the smoke into her lungs. Only had a few left anyway, and as she glanced over the rock at the city, she had a feeling the last thing she was going to find in that town was a fresh pack of Virginia Slims.

Christopher stepped into the coolness of his office, his gaze going to the sullen cowboy sitting on the edge of a cot, fiddling with his wedding ring. Serves him right, he thought, shutting the door with enough force to get his attention. The young rancher leapt to his feet, nearly over turning the cot and gripping the bars.

"Did you see her, Marshal?" He dragged his hat from his head. "Did you talk to Millie?"

Chris eyed him for a moment, recognizing eagerness and a healthy dose of regret. "She was more worried about your safety than anything."

"She said that?"

Chris tossed the keys to Noble. "Let him out," he ordered, then moved behind his desk, taking a holstered gun from the rack. He faced the young rancher. "Talk to her next time, Boyd, instead of heading to the nearest saloon and busting up the furniture."

"Yes, sir." Boyd accepted his gun belt, strapping it on, then waited for the marshal's permission to leave. Chris inclined his head toward the window. Boyd followed the direction of his gaze, his face lighting up at the sight of the young woman perched on the wagon seat, then just as quickly it wilted as he jammed on his hat.

He strode slowly out the door, closing it behind him and Chris remained where he was, watching as their eyes met and she tilted her head. He said something to her, and she responded with a subtle nod. Boyd rushed to the side of the wagon, gripping the sides and staring up at his wife with the adoration of a man deeply in love. She touched his cheek, tears in her eyes, and Chris didn't doubt she assured her husband of her love, because the cowboy smiled, dragging her from the wagon and into his arms. Unashamed, they kissed and kept kissing until a passerby startled them.

Only after they were nothing more than a cloud of dust in the evening light did Chris realize he hadn't moved from the spot near the cell.

"Shoulda let him stew overnight," Noble said, returning to his seat behind his desk across from the marshal's. A flick of his wrist sent the ringed keys spinning through the air to hook on a peg.

"He's in love and hurt that she was upset enough with him to tell him not to come home, that's all."

"You sure as hell know a lot about marriage and kids for a fella who ain't got neither."

Chris stiffened, his hooded gaze slicing to Noble. "Your point?"

"Damnation, I'da never married Willow, or Red Elk, or Little River, if I waited 'round in this town."

"I could remind you that you met those women while you were a prisoner of their fathers," he said, ignoring the hint. "And you outlived all three of them." Which meant Noble was as alone as his boss.

But the grizzly man only sighed pleasantly, his big chest rumbling with quiet laughter. "Least they died with a smile on their faces."

Chris shook his head, his lips curving in a rare smile. Noble never held onto to vengeance, grief or love. He simply let it pass and went on. Chris supposed living in the Utah mountains virtually alone since he was a kid had a lot to do with it, for emotion would eat you alive if that's all you had for company. Sighing, Chris was just lowering himself into his chair when the door banged open, a child of no more than eight skidding to a halt inside.

"Got trouble, Marshal."

Cursing softly, Chris left the office, swinging up onto his horse's back and heading in the direction the boy pointed. The Pearl. Even as he rode, he could see three miners facing off with one man and the entire episode was over in seconds. The loner, unarmed from what he could see, simply waited for the first to approach like a man courting death. A red-headed cowboy swayed before he charged the loner. Loner stepped out of the way, slapping a hand to Red's back and sending him flying past, skidding down the street on his face. No sooner than Red landed in the dirt, a brown haired man hopped on the loner's back. Loner grabbed the hands circling his neck and the brunet howled as his opponent ducked, tossing the brunet over his shoulders and dumping him on his rear. Loner instantly spun round to face the third.

But he didn't move. Bigger, wider and with less liquor to dull his senses, he circled the loner, shrugging his sleeves back, fists primed.

"Them's my friends."

"Idiots travel in packs then?" came from the loner, deep and raspy.

Loner kept his eyes on the big one, yet his right foot snapped out, as high as his shoulder to connect with the brunet's face, who was about to blind side him. The big guy charged like an enraged bull, drawing back to swing, but the loner blocked it with his forearm, landing a solid punch to Big's gut, a left to his jaw, then spinning around, his leg flying out and contacting with Big's face. As Chris approached, the big man hovered on the edge of consciousness, then dropped like a wet feed sack to the ground.

The brunet was on his feet, prepared for a second chance.

A pistol hammer clicked. "That's enough, boys," came with deadly calm.

The three left standing turned to face the marshal, two swearing and groping for their hats. The loner didn't even look winded.

"He started it," the redhead said, pointing to the loner. "He was walkin' inta town, real suspicious like. Hanging back in the dark, over yonder at the mercantile, like he was studying the place."

"And he ain't got no horse," came from the brunet. "What kinda man ain't got a horse?"

"Ever think it might have gone lame, or shot out beneath him?" The red and brunet men flushed, looking sheepish, yet as defiant as they could muster being bruised and bloody and covered with dirt. Chris dismounted, his gun aimed as he strode forward to check on the big man. He grabbed a handful of hair, lifted his head and scowled at the blood and teeth pouring out the man's mouth. He looked up at the loner and Victoria stared into the compelling eyes of her Indian.

So much for a low profile.

"Who are you?" he demanded.

Her gaze dropped briefly to the huge gun he leveled at her chest. "Mason." It should have been her first clue—the gun, and the signs posted near the bar door, *Firearms prohibited inside the city limits.* Or the lack of mechanization. Everything about this place blared like a broken siren. Nothing was right, not in the way she knew it.

"You going to tell me what happen? The part I didn't see, I mean."

Victoria tugged her cowboy hat down and clamped her lips shut, not offering a response. Her wisest tactic would be to listen and observe first, then talk. These yokal's attacked without provocation, and she was furious that they'd forced her to defend herself when she wanted nothing more than to slip into this bizarre town without notice. But her presence stirred up more suspicion than it ought, and she suspected Ivy League was the cause. If he was around, he'd be easy for the people here to recall, since a stranger caused this much commotion. And she was fairly certain he wasn't lying dead around here anywhere. She'd checked the circumference of the town as much as she could before showing herself.

The long trek made her wish she had a horse.

For there wasn't a car or truck or a gas pump, not to mention a paved road or even a train station around. But there was a coach station, an actual pulled-by-horses stage coach. Talk about backward and isolated. And she considered that this tow~ could be like a tourist town, where it was their job to re-ena~ the past, down to the last detail. *Just like a western movie* she thought and half expected Sam Elliot to come sauntering around the corner with his Sackett brothers.

Too real.

Except there were no tourists, or souvenir shops and it wasn't on any map. But nothing stunned her more than to see *Tonto*, dressed in black and wearing a badge. Or the accusing way he was glaring at her now. No, at *him*. She'd drastically altered her appearance, with a short dark wig, colored contacts, facial latex, makeup, and a little body padding. She looked every inch a homely young man, slightly Mexican. The thin mask glued to her skin thickened her forehead and broadened her cheeks and jaw, besides giving her the scars of acne. That made the seams easier to hide. Regardless, Tonto saw only a man. A plus, for this guy was sharp, his dark gaze assessing her too thoroughly.

But by now, the streets were filled with curious spectators, period dressed spectators, and she studied each one, searching for him, congratulating herself on blowing her plan right out of the water as two men wearing badges, pushed through the crowd. They came to the marshal's side and handed over a jangle of metal.

"Seth, take him to the Doctor," Chris said, nodding to the big one still lying in the dirt. "Angus, lock them up." The red-headed and brunet men sullenly proceeded the deputy down the street at gun point as Seth helped the big man to his feet.

Victoria made a mental note of the direction Seth headed.

"Show's over, folks," Chris said to the crowd and people shuffled back the way they came. He turned his gaze to Mason, the gun spinning on his fingers and sliding into the holster. At least he didn't wear a gun, Chris consoled, yet reached forward to remove a large knife sheathed at his waist. He could have used it and didn't. Didn't need it, he corrected, silently admiring his ability. Yet from the look of that nose, he wasn't always successful.

"Charges, Marshal?" He grabbed her gloved hands and tened on the crudest pair of handcuffs she'd ever seen.

"Disturbing the peace, brawling in the street, and intent to do bodily harm."

"It'll never stick," she said, her stance wide, arrogant. "Self defense." She'd *had* to win. One punch would have torn her face off, literally.

"Not after what I saw."

Victoria met his gaze, the chain between the cuffs chinking as she smoothed the artificial moustache with a thumb and forefinger in a purely masculine gesture. Her opinion of the marshal slid into the gutter. *He means business. Placate him—until you can figure out where you are.*

But she'd studied this area, and this town wasn't supposed to be here. Mentally, she retraced her steps back to the fall, to her last fresh blood trail. The most outlandish thought rocketed through her brain, cut short when he barked, "Move it."

He nodded in the direction he'd come.

Hunching her shoulders, Victoria strode ahead of him, catching him murmuring something to his horse. The black stallion's big head ducked and bucked before the animal swung around and trotted down the street. There were white hand prints on the horses rump. War paint? She cast the marshal a quizzing glance, yet when he simply stared at her with the same unreadable expression she'd seen in the forest, she faced forward.

"I'm not the perp. Or has accusing strangers obliterated that small fact?" she said back over her shoulder.

"Perp?" His brows drew down, his gaze raking her before returning to her face.

"Perpetrator," she tossed with a glance. "You know, the one who *commits* the crime."

A black brow shot up. It was a reasonable monniker, he decided, trying to pinpoint what was familiar about this man. "Just what are you doing here, Mason?"

"Looking for work, enough to buy a ride and get lost." She gave him her back, recognizing the absence of the usual bright lights in the homes and businesses, even in a city as backw as this. And there were no street lights, only tall torche flame surrounded by paned beveled glass. A chill skittere her shoulders and down her spine. This is not good. People whispered as she passed, doors slammed shut, locks thrown, and even a mother grabbed her child away from her. Creepy.

"You need to be lost?"

A citizen called out from his window, asking about his prisoner, but the marshal didn't respond.

She lengthened her stride. "What exactly is going on here, Marshal?"

"You. Disturbing my peace."

"I didn't throw the first punch, so don't lay that crap at my feet. Got enough of my own to deal with." Hoping to see something modern, she glanced at an undraped widow, catching a glimpse of a woman lighting an old fashioned oil lamp. Was there really no electricity at all?

"And just what is your problem, Mason?"

It took her a moment to recall what he'd asked. "I told you. I'm broke without transportation." She didn't want anyone, even the handsome marshal, to know why she was here. She didn't need his help, nor his interference. Stepping onto the porch, she paused, taking in the split rail for tying hoses and the polished wood sign set into the brick work, which read Territorial Marshal. How quaint, she thought, pushing open the door to the jail. Victoria strode directly to the double cell and pulled the heavy door closed behind her.

Chris simply stared. Noble glanced between the prisoner and the marshal.

"Oh, you might want this." She bent, removing a knife from beneath her pant leg, then tossing it through the bars. It clattered to the floor at his feet. "Wouldn't want to be accused of harming such a paragon of police work."

His features tightened, his eyes gone hard as slate, and Victoria felt a small measure of apprehension as they pierced and robed her face. She'd just made him look incompetent. Dan-rous move. But there was more than false arrest going on —a lot more. Aside from the fact that everyone acted bingly natural about all this, the tension in this town was enough to cut steak, and her nerves yanked when he scooped up the knife, then flipped it back over his shoulder. The tip stuck in the wood of his desk like a pencil, vibrating for a moment before it went still. He advanced, without a sound, and with a key, unlocked the cuffs, and Victoria noticed he kept a safe distance from her, making her stretch to him as he threaded the heavy iron shackles through the bars before dumping them in a wood box with a dozen others. It was a typical police move, protective. And it magnified the idea that what she'd assumed wasn't at all what was truth.

Backing away, she turned to the small barred window, peering at the darkness lit with porch lamps. In scant seconds, she searched for signs of modernization—a false wall to the neighboring buildings, wires, an electrical outlet neatly disguised, anything remotely contemporary, but found nothing. Victoria dropped onto the cot, uneasiness creeping heavily beneath her skin. *This is all too pat to be scripted.* And she laid back, stretching out her legs and folding her arms beneath her head, her insides jumping uncharacteristically as the deputy who'd escorted her attackers, stepped into the office from a door adjacent to the double cell. More cells beyond the wood door, she assumed, if the barred window was any indication.

The deputy nodded to the marshal and hastened out the door and as Victoria's gaze followed his retreat, her attention caught on a poster on the wall, no bigger than a standard sheet of paper. Wanted, Dead or Alive. And the sketch of the man below resembled her, or rather her masculine counterpart. Charged with cattle rustling.

Oh, right. Like cattle were easy to stuff down your shirt and make a run for it? That she'd discovered the reason behind her arrest, which was watery at best, fell away to finally taking a decent look at the office. Bars picketed the windows, and with the exception of the cell, which was concrete, the walls were red brick, the floor thick slats of wood, slightly uneven. A pitcher and bowl sat on an antique mirrored washstand in the corner like something out of *Victoria* Magazine, a row of pegs above it. A book case sectioned with cubby holes and filled with holstered guns rested beside it. Big, long-barreled pistols.

Shit, not even Dirty Harry carried cannons that big. Beyond the marshal's desk and against the brick wall was a heavy cabinet racked with rifles, each one tagged.

But it was the newspaper the linebacker-sized man behind the opposite desk was reading, that grabbed her sudden interest. She rolled on her side, squinting at the headlines. *Apache Wars Raging. Mahloon Loomis of Washington, D.C. awarded patent for first wireless telegraph.* Has to be fake, like those places where you can get the paper printed with your personal headline. Her dad had sent her one when she'd graduated. Yet she couldn't keep her gaze from following his movements as he closed the paper and tossed it on the desk. It slid to the floor and she leaned up to glimpse the date. July 20th, 1872.

Nah. Not possible.

But a horrible sickening sensation rode through her stomach on waves of uncertainty.

What if it is?

"Gonna let 'em sleep it off."

Chris wrapped three gun belts around their holsters and shoved them in a cubby hole. "Send someone out to their homes, tell their wives. I think having to be brought home by the ear ought to do it."

Victoria leapt to her feet. "Jesus Christ, you might as well just slap their hands."

He made her wait for a response as he poured himself a glass of water. "I might," he said into the hollowness, then drank. His prisoner didn't know he arrested this threesome at least a dozen times a year when they came into town for supplies.

"Do I have to barf up a lung for you to be satisfied it was self-defense? Open this cell, Marshal." She shook the bars, unaccustomed panic destroying her usually controlled composure. "I'm not your goddamn cattle rustler." She gestured with her chin to the poster.

Chris' gaze traveled slowly over the man's denim shirt to the gloved fists gripping the bars. He noticed the leather band circling a too-slim wrist and knew wristwatches were expensive and had only in larger cities. Where did this man get the money for that if he didn't have enough to buy a horse? He glanced at the wanted poster, frowning before his eyes shifted to his prisoner. "Who do you work for?"

"Fat Jack Palau. Who do you work for?"

A single black brow shot up. "The U.S. Government, the people," came sarcastically.

"Well this *people* is doubting it." *God,* was she doubting it. And everything else around her. "Who's Brad Pitt?"

"How the hell should I know?" He finished off the water and turned the glass rim down.

"Who's Bullwinkle's partner?" Now *that* was reaching, she thought dizzily.

"Bullwinkle? Hooey, Marshal! That a new gang we ought to look out for?"

Chris slanted Noble a butt-out look, then stared at Mason. "Where'd you have a job last?"

"Dallas. I saved Kennedy." She watched his eyes for the truth, the fraction of humor or even anger. He looked only tired.

Chris combed his fingers through his hair. "Are you ever going to give me a straight answer?"

"Are you?"

He folded his arms over his broad chest. "I'm not the one behind bars."

"A mistake and you know it," she sneered. "Remind me to cross your fair city off my travel plans in the future." She thrust away from the cell door and dropped onto the cot, stretching out and fixing her hat over her eyes.

Outwardly she appeared the profile of a lazy prisoner, inside she was running a mile a minute. Calm down, she repeated in her head. This isn't happening. There is a logical excuse for this. Isn't there?

Chapter Four

But there wasn't. Not sane-type logical reason, anyway. In as much as she didn't want to believe it, she was definitely in another world, another century. By way of the water fall. Chasing a killer had taken her through a rip in time, a passageway into the past—probably lying dormant til Ivy League found it. Lucky son of a bitch.

Christ.

Time-travel.

A quantum leap.

Once she let it congeal in her head, everything explained itself, easily, simply. She snickered to herself, drawing the marshal's attention. Easy, huh? Try to make bail without currency from this century, girlfriend. That she was on her own, totally, didn't bother her. She usually worked alone, yet needed to get back to the fall in a hurry, to confirm her theory, to be certain that when she caught Ivy League, she could take him back for trial. Nothing mattered, but seeing he paid for his crimes. And slowly.

An eerie calmness settled over her. *I can handle this. I can.* Time-travel meant only one thing to her now. Ivy League was free. No cops on his butt, no choppers to spot him. He was unrecognizable to anyone, except her. He could slide into this society and start all over again, and even as cute as the marshal was, she doubted he'd ever pit himself against anyone like a 20th century psychopath.

The danger was imminent, because Ivy League didn't think anyone was after him. No threat. No panic. Maybe he would take his time stalking. Maybe he'd simply walk down the street and into her possession? Fat chance, girlfriend. Since you're locked up and he's not.

The adhesive beneath the mask itched, but she didn't dare scratch or she'd come apart at the seams and really scare the hell out of everyone. For about two seconds she considered stripping it off and confiding in the marshal, then dismissed it.

If she did time travel, her being here did something to history. What exactly, she'd never know til she returned to her time. *If* she could. Scary thought.

Cramming her anxiousness over the possibility that she just might be permanently stuck here in 18-whatever into a corner of her mind, Victoria did what came naturally. She planned out her next moves, considering every angle, filtering through every scenario Ivy League could possible try. He'd get comfortable, be as slow and methodical as always, insinuating himself into this town, unnoticed, like he had eleven times before. Then he'd stalk. *If* he was alive. He definitely wouldn't go back when he knew there was a three state man-hunt underway just for him. She had to find him. She was the only one who could and there were no if's about bringing him back. She sure as hell wasn't going to stick around in the 19th century.

The metal-to-metal clank startled his prisoner and he sat straight up, swung his legs off the cot and left it to face him. He was never asleep, Chris thought, twisting the key in the lock and opening the door. Mason stood back, his broad brows pulling down in question. Chris looked him over and not for the first time noticed the square toed work boots. Something about this man wasn't right.

"Telegraph came this morning." He inclined his head to the spot where a wanted poster had been. "Got shot in Tucson a week back."

"Why didn't you just say that's why you wanted to hold me?" Not that it would have mattered.

"I don't have to."

"But I had the right to know." Did civil rights exist? Or did she? In this century?

"Not in my town, not this week."

"You either got a lot of trouble or someone's greasing your pockets, Marshal."

Chris's gaze sharpened like a razor against a whet stone.

"Not full enough, I see," she sneered. She didn't like the way this guy ran things. He kept too much of the law clenched in his fist. But what did she know about 19th century rights. "My knives."

Chris went to the desk drawer and took out the weapons. He'd examined them last night, noting the numbers on the handle, the fine workmanship. Noble, who produced some of the finest knifes in the territory, couldn't have done better and said as much when he'd seen them.

He handed them over and Mason immediately shoved them back into their perspective sheaths. "Don't go beating the tar out of my citizens," Chris warned as Mason paused at the door.

Victoria looked back at him. "Hey, if they don't fuck with me, I won't knock them into next week." He didn't blink at her harsh language and she didn't care. She was supposed to be a man and acting like one called for walking and talking differently. Just wait until he gets a load of her bag lady get up, she thought, then left, trying to keep her pace next to normal. She was glad the town wasn't awake yet. It gave her a chance to examine it in the dawn light—the horse troughs, the stage station, a couple of drunks sleeping in the alley. *It's really real.*

Another chill spilled over her spine. Reality check, she

thought as she passed the telegraph office and briefly considered trying to send one. But she didn't have any money. Not the 1872 kind. And no one she knew was alive—yet. And everyone she loved was dead.

Kelly Galloway was dead, and the last time she was seen alive, she was with a slim man with a moustache. That description and the wanted poster made Chris wary enough to hold Mason. The man might not be a cattle rustler, yet without evidence to connect him to anything else, he had to release Mason. As he stepped out of his office, Chris still couldn't shake this feeling they'd met before. He's moving fast, Chris thought, propping his shoulder against the porch post to watch his retreat. His gaze scraped across Mason's back, his straight body down to his feet. He straightened. Small feet. Even in those boots. He'd taken a half dozen steps toward him when someone called out and he stopped, twisting to see the first shift coming in on horse back. Chris flicked a glance in Mason's direction, but the street was empty and early morning quiet. It made him feel as if he'd let the wrong man walk. Turning his attention to his deputies, he decided he'd take reports and then go after Mason himself.

The emotion she'd shut down in the jail, to logic, to survival, raced out of control, reaching out to snag her by the throat as she ran as fast as she could with the thirty pound pack smacking against her back. Dirt from when she'd buried it crumbled off the nylon as she scrambled up the incline, losing the pack at the entrance and ducking inside. Her heels dragged, and she ignored the heaviness in her legs, attributing it to the dead run of better than three miles. Still in disguise, she kept her hat on and used her arm to deflect the rushing water as she leapt into her century. Her horse was still there, chomping on grass. She took off her hat and gave it a shake, sending a shimmer of water across her already soaked clothes.

Okay, okay . . . everything's the same.

No.

Something's not right, she thought instantly.

The sound of chopper blades slapped the air, several jeeps and range rovers headed her way, kicking up clouds of dirt. They should be closer, yet the mare was still there. So much for Kyle's four-legged homing pigeon. Assured she could bring her bounty back, but not wanting to risk waiting for help—not that a soul would believe her story—she turned, about to leap into the fall when she noticed the horse again.

It hadn't moved. In fact, it wasn't moving, jaws open to chomp. All sound ceased. Even the birds were silent. Frowning, she donned her hat and turned to the fall, ducking in, yet out of the corner of her eye, she saw the horse shift. Risking ruining her disguise forever, she stuck out a foot, propping herself directly under the pouring water. The horse moved, yet the instant she stepped further in, the mare froze, in motion, a foreleg lifting enough for detection.

Time stood still on her side.

It should be twenty-four hours later here, not seconds.

Feeling it was a now-or-never thing, she leapt into the fall, her movements suddenly stagnated, as if wading through gel. Not good, this is *not* good, she warned herself as she struggled, bursting into the light and tumbling ass over belly button down the incline. She just sat there, wet and dirty and mad as hell. Time moved on this side, but not in hers. Great. No telling how much of a lead those few hours gave Ivy League. Days? Weeks? Maybe even months.

He isn't a stranger to this town. I am.

Ivy League was freer than free. He'd committed no crime here, had no record, no indictment, no connection. The dockets and bonds giving her the right to hunt were meaningless, especially when she'd need them most, proof she had the power to take him out of the city.

I have nothing, no authority, no warrant. No reason in 1872.

She couldn't just search and apprehend, couldn't take him out with a tazer and drag him back. She'd end up in jail for kidnapping and assault or worse, hung by a lynch mob. She had to make a case, uncover indisputable evidence. And the marshal would be watching—Mason. Easy to enough fix that, she thought.

Resolutely, she trudged up the incline, slinging her pack over her shoulder. Her boots squished as she headed to town. She never made it.

Half way there she sat down to rest and fell asleep.

And she woke to a gun nudging her awake.

"Where's the owner of that pack?"

Victoria blinked, the contacts stinging her eyes as she tried to focus. Hell. He could have shot her in her sleep, and she wouldn't have known it. He was squatting beside her, looking like a giant vulture hovering over a fresh kill.

The cobwebs of her ill-advised nap still clinging, she climbed to her feet, ducking her head to fake a cough and run her hand over her face to be certain her hop through the fall hadn't loosened the mask. She could feel it coming away from her skin, making ripples. She hoped he didn't notice.

"What's your problem, Marshal. Got no one to pick on today?"

He wasn't amused and leveled the gun as he straightened. "The owner of that pack, where is she?" His tone clipped with impatience.

So, he was worried was he? "I don't know what your talking about."

He didn't respond and instead, advanced on her. Victoria didn't budge, hooking her thumbs in her belt loops. "I didn't kill her." He wasn't convinced. "Look. She's probably long gone." Instinct warned her not to say it, not to goad him. " 'Sides, finders keepers."

His expression turned black with anger and Chris grabbed him by the shirt front, yanking Mason up to meet his face. He pushed the gun beneath a stubbled chin. "I'm used to getting answers to my questions, Mason."

He meant business with every syllable and she could see her

downfall in his jet black eyes. "You're not a patient man, are you, Marshal?"

His brows drew tighter. "What happened to your voice?" It was softer, not the gravely rasp and the sound of it drove through him like a splash of ice water, catching him in places it shouldn't. Like a perfume or a caress. And where was the accent?

Victoria cursed her slip. "Let me go." She didn't know what to make of his expression, the boiling black eyes. "Take my knife if you want." She jabbed it in his side, smirking at his startled look. "Not as stupid as I look, huh?"

He didn't move, his breathing non-existent, his body tense as an iron door. She could feel it, feel him. It was like being too close to a fire.

"Go ahead, then. Blow my brains out. Won't solve anything."

"A rancher's wife was killed by a man answering your description."

"It wasn't me."

"Prove it."

She couldn't. Not unless . . . damn. There was no way around this. She couldn't stab a lawman, not this one, and she didn't have much of an escape, except through heaven. And she'd lost the advantage of voice.

"Back off and I will."

With calibrated moves, Chris released Mason, keeping his gun aimed. As promised, he handed him the knife, bent and gave him the one strapped over his boot. That this drifter got the jump on him infuriated the hell out of Chris and he'd about ten seconds worth of patience left this morning.

"Well?"

Victoria hesitated, aware she couldn't use this mask again if she didn't take it off with the solvent, but letting him see inside her back pack was too risky. She didn't know what damage her presence was already doing to history, let alone allowing him to see her cache of high-tech toys.

"You're not going to like it," she said, then carefully felt for the separation in the hair piece. With both hands she peeled her *scalp* apart, removing first the larger wig section, dropping it on the pack before she grasped the remaining bit of artificial hair and latex tacked at her hairline and tugged, peeling it slowly down, working it free from her eyes and lips, and praying it wouldn't be totally destroyed.

"Great father in—!" Chris stumbled back. "What the hell are you doing?"

"Proving my innocence." She eased the mask from her jaw and throat and couldn't help checking the *skin* for tears before laying it aside.

"A woman!"

She met his gaze and felt it roam over her face still studded with bits of adhesive. "Yeah, sort of a rush, huh?"

He was scowling like a madman on the verge of a fit.

"Not enough?" She plucked the bobby pins from her hair and Chris's heart picked up pace as he—she shook out a mane of dark golden hair.

He'd never forget that color. "You!"

"Nice to know you remembered, Tonto."

The sound of her voice rocked him down to his boot heels. "But—" His gaze dropped meaningfully to her body.

Glad she'd at least worn a tank top beneath her clothes, Victoria unbuttoned her shirt, flipped open her belt buckle and unzipped her pants, trying not to laugh at the marshal's expression. His eyes were as wide as cue balls. She slipped her arms from the sleeves, then loosened the padding from her waist that gave her the straight lines of a man, before reaching over her shoulders to grasp the foam. She worked the sculptured rubber vest off over her head.

Chris stared, speechless, then dropped back against a tree. "Damn." Her body was beautiful, stealing his breath, a piece of a heart beat, then his gaze flicked over the papery mask she'd laid carefully across the satchel, shaped and molded like her face on the inside, yet craggy and scarred like the prisoner he'd arrested, on the reverse. Anger and absolute humiliation warred inside him. A woman! *That* woman. He would have never known, never suspected something wasn't right ... except the feet. Her feet were too damn small for the rest of her—him—her—shit! Chris was seeing red and something else when she unwrapped a binding across her chest, heard her moan softly before adding the beige bandage to the pile of wadding. No, not wadding. It was smooth and looked spongy, shaped like shoulders and arms, sculpted, muscular. A man's body. Was this how the killer got close to his victim? Disguised as a man? He didn't want to believe that of her, not of the face that haunted his dreams, not the wild eyes—

"How are your eyes a different color?"

Victoria she bent over a touch, propped one eye open wider and squeezed off the soft contact lens.

Chris inhaled when she straightened. She had one gold eye and one dark. Oh Jesus, he thought with a look down her body. He hoped to God nothing else came off.

"What the hell are you?"

Disgust rang in his voice, and it stung more than it ought to. Even though the cops, bondsmen and lawyers who worked with her often pricked her thick skin with veiled digs, not one of them doubted she was female.

"I'm a woman, Marshal, or did the breasts escape your attention, too."

No, they didn't. How could they? But his anger—at failing to recognize the disguise and the feeling he'd been made an utter fool by this annoyingly competent female—manifested in a cruel twist of his lips, his dark eyes racking her critically from head to toe.

Victoria stared him down, no emotion, no reaction. She knew she wasn't a knockout and his look confirmed it.

"Who are you?"

"Victoria Mason. I—" Victoria clamped her lips shut, forgetting for a moment where she was and *when*. Bounty Hunters were not highly respected in this era, no better than hired guns. Dead or alive meant just that, and anyone with a gun and a wanted poster could hunt. In her century, she was a part of the judicial system, freeing up cops and FBI to bring back bailed felons. But here . . . Suddenly he was inches from her, grabbing her upper arms and tugging her close to meet his face. His eyes bored into hers.

And every sense she owned jumped to life.

"Why did you come into my town like *that?*" Again the disgust.

"Take your hands off me, Marshal." A quiet warning.

He ignored it, shaking her. "Tell me!"

She brought her arms up between them, batting his hands off and in quick precise moves, shot a cross to his jaw, a knee to his stomach, yet when she went to catch him in the groin, he clamped his legs around hers. He gripped her arms tightly. She twisted, hooking the back of his knee. Balance vanished and they hit the ground with a lung crushing jolt. Immediately, she pushed herself up, hands braced on his chest and realized her leg was caught between his thighs. Tightly. Purposely. She stared down into those dark eyes, wishing she had the leverage to belt him and desperately trying to ignore the waves of warmth ripping over her, tearing through her blood.

Everything went still, her breathing, his, the sounds on the breeze.

Her damp hair floated past her shoulder in a lush curve.

His fingers flexed on her arms. His gaze darted over her face.

She looked every bit like a wild cat, wickedly feline, the fall of her hair covering her *dark* eye. He had the irresistible urge to strip her naked and see if she had fur. He jerked her down to inches from his face, felt her fight, heard her hiss and waited to see fangs, waited for her to acknowledge the unspeakable heat burning between them. He lifted his head a fraction, her moist breath dusting his lips and he waited to hear her purr.

It had been so long, she thought fleetingly, gazing into his eyes. So long since any man looked at her like that. And she ached, everywhere, everywhere they touched, from the press of his muscled thighs around hers, the hardness of his broad chest beneath her palms, his buckle, his gun, his—she scrambled off him, raking her hair back and glaring at him as he came slowly to his feet.

"I think that about answers your question, Marshal." She gave him a half-lidded stare and wanted to smack that masculine I-know-you-felt-something look off his handsome face. She didn't like feeling *like that* around him. Because right now, he was her adversary. "I wasn't pestering anyone, and I was attacked. Imagine if I'd come in dressed like a woman, alone. Instead of trying to whip the crap out of me, those drunks would have pulled me in the nearest alley and raped me." Unnerved by the riot going on in her body, she scooped up his hat and sailed it to him like a frizbee. "Leave me alone, Marshal." He caught the Stetson. "I do just fine that way."

With great care, he settled it on his head. "I'll be watching you, Miss Mason."

"You do that," came dryly, her lips scarcely moving. He'll *never* recognize me.

He started to walk away.

"And Marshal." He turned slightly, that arrogant brow lifting, and she had the urge to shoot it off. "It's just Mason." She didn't want him giving her up accidently. "No miss."

His gaze slicked over her before he scoffed. "That ought to be easy enough."

Her eyes flared, then cleared. "Just who the hell did I meet in the forest?" she demanded.

He studied her briefly before he answered. "Swift Arrow."

The corner of her mouth quirked, showing off a dimple he hadn't noticed before.

"Well, I liked *him* better."

Chris stared, then turned away. After a few steps, he smiled.

Chapter Five

Christopher swung up onto the saddle and looked in her direction, half expecting her to evaporate into smoke before his eyes. But she was still standing beneath the shade of trees, her shirt hanging from her pants, that heavy chemise or whatever it was, outlining the ripe contours of her torso. Her hands rested on her trim hips, hips cocked at a defiant angle, and he noticed the definition of twisting muscle running the length of her shoulders and arms. So different from any woman he'd ever met, he thought, unconsciously rubbing his jaw. Though instinct told him to make certain she was protected, he didn't have any reservations about leaving her in the woods alone. She was more than capable of defending herself—even against the desire they just shared.

Desire? Eruption was more apt. His body still bore the imprint of hers, the solid feel of her hips against his. God. He never wanted to open his jeans and pound into a woman as much as he did in those too short moments. It was lust, pure, unexplainable, and he admitted he never felt so much reined power in it before, not *that* much at once. Yet he doubted this woman would be any more receptive than she was five minutes ago. The only thing soft on her were her breasts.

It'll take a chisel to crack that shell, he thought, touching the brim of his hat before reining around, and still not knowing what to think of her. She talked different somehow, clipped, sarcastic, yet to the point. And he admitted his heart hadn't stopped pounding from the moment she peeled away her face, the sight of it as horrible as it was fascinating. What was that mask made of, to stretch like that? And look so real?

Her deception was nothing short of incredible.

He rubbed his side, the sting of her knife pricking more than his skin. But the memory of her body draped so deliciously over his, the brush of her breath, her breasts, wasn't going to leave, and Chris resigned himself to riding back to town with a crowd in his jeans.

Victoria watched him ride away, ignoring how good he looked on a horse and remembering his unflattering comments—another digging reminder that the only men in her life were informants, cops, and bondsmen. It was clear he thought her edges too rough. Oh well. He's a nineteenth century man and used to a totally different woman.

Big deal. It was her job not to look good, not to stand out. Just become the furnishings, the background, blend in. She was an expert at hiding behind the norm. So why consider otherwise now?

She shoved her hair back off her forehead, holding it at her crown. Damn it. She hadn't felt desire like that since she was a teenager, when her life was uncomplicated. And anger built in her, for the femininity she'd lost and at him for making her feel it again when she didn't have the time to explore it.

Her roles as bag ladies, gang members or prostitutes weren't glamourous—and not that she could remember the last time she ever had a real date—she wouldn't know how to behave like a lady, seductive and soft and gentle, if her life depended on it. Oh, she could mask it, assume the personality of her characters, but not herself, not *Victoria Mason*. Over the years, that side of her had simply been ground away.

Quit whinning.

No one's around who gives a damn, so give it up.

Find Ivy League. Find the evidence.

Stick to what you know.

And she needed two things to do it. A job and fresh clothes. Nineteenth century clothes.

Shaking off the ungratifying moment of self-pity, Victoria stared down at the mask and padding, then hunkered down before her pack, unzipped it, removing her gear box and taking inventory. Marshal what's-his-face could watch her all he wanted . . . *if* he could find her.

Christopher stepped into the coolness of the livery, waiting for his eyes to adjust to the darkness. The beckoning ring of a mallet to metal took him to the back of the stable. "Clancey?"

"Hey-yah, Marshal." The thick armed smithy didn't look up from his work, slamming the hammer a few more times, sparks flying like fire flies, then shoving the glowing metal into a barrel of cloudy water. The liquid boiled around the new horseshoe, steaming the warm summer air and Clancey looked at the marshal through the fog. "What can I do for yah?"

"Caesar threw a shoe. Got time?"

"Sure, lead him into the second stall."

Chris looked back over his shoulder at the black stallion and said, "Get in number two, boy," and the horse softly walked into the appointed stall.

Clancey shook his head and smiled. Like a dern child, he thought, then let loose a bellow that made Chris wince.

A low call answered from the depths of the stable, beyond hanging tack and rental carriages.

"Got another assistant?" Chris saw the figure of a slim young man, further down in the row of stalls.

"Yeah," Clancey remarked. "Just a drifter, but Jake's a damn hard worker."

Jake finished the job, set the pitchfork aside and sauntered toward his boss. Chris watched the youth, but Jake didn't look him in the eye.

"See to the marshal's mount, son. Clean his hooves, check for another loose shoe."

Jake bobbed his head, shoving the round spectacles up his nose. "Yessir." He glanced at the huge black beast, then slid his gaze to the marshal's. "He gonna bite me?"

"Not unless you bite him."

Jake smirked, then moved off toward the horse. A strange sensation rippled over Chris's shoulders as he watched the kid's long easy stride.

"You sure about him, Clance? Caesar might act docile, but he'd—"

"He'll be all right," the blacksmith interrupted. "Ain't afraid of nothin'. Just quiet, is all." Clancey shrugged thick muscled shoulders. "Likes working at night."

Chris shifted his gaze to Jake and though he couldn't see much beyond the slats of the stall, he could hear the low soft murmurs as he spoke to Caesar. Least he wasn't spooked by the animal's size, he thought, then took a step away.

"Oh, hey Marshal, got that pipe you wanted."

Chris crossed to him, accepting the crooked length, examining it with a skilled eye before nodding his approval. He paid Clancey.

"What you gonna do with all this pipe?"

Chris grinned. "Make it rain," he said cryptically. "Give a holler when he's done being pampered." Chris slipped between the wide open doors and into the night.

A few moments later, Jake poked his head out of the stall, then crossed the hay covered floor to Clancey. "He's cut back and ready, Mister O'Brian. Shoes are good."

The smithy nodded, smiling. "Go git yerself some supper, son." He tossed him a coin and Jake caught it in his gloved fist, his expression solemn. "You can finish up the Delaney's rig when you get back." Jake nodded, then left, pocketing the coin.

Outside, Victoria took a deep breath of the night air, pleased that the marshal, Marshal Christopher Swift she'd discovered, hadn't recognized her, nor had he when she passed him on the street two days ago. That was courting madness, but his biting words still stung, enough for her to be smug about fooling him. She'd taken the livery job for quick money paid at the end of each day, for she needed clothes and a way to gather information. But beyond who needed what repaired and a few drunks looking for a place to sleep it off, she hadn't discovered much that wasn't unsubstantiated gossip. Until this morning, when she'd altered her appearance and landed a job as a maid. She didn't know which was harder work, hauling hay or hauling dirty sheets, but the hotel position gained her much more information—a description, though vague, but enough to start. And tonight, she was going to see an honest-to-God 19th century saloon for herself.

Checking her funds, she dug her hand into the pocket of her new button fly jeans and stared at the coin. A silver cartwheel. God, what this would be worth in my time, she thought. She didn't have money to waste after buying a woman's outfit and a used satchel to hide her back pack. That set her back a day's pay, since women were expected to wear a hell of a lot of clothes beneath a simple blouse and skirt. She'd bought the garments as *Jake*, claiming they were a gift for his sister, even had it wrapped so it wouldn't appear suspicious. Dowdy Clara the maid and quiet Jake were wall flower types. She couldn't be seen, ever, as herself. That was against the rules; never show until the cuffs are on and the cell door slams shut.

Show time, she thought, tucking her shirt in the back of her pants and hunching her shoulders before she strode across the street, dirt puffing with every step. She was nervous, and though she'd gone searching often enough in bars, she prayed she didn't stick out simply because of her century.

Pushing through the bat wing doors, Victoria saddled up to the bar in her best cowboy walk, propped her foot on the rail and tried not to gawk.

Too cool.

The noise was deafening, laughter and conversation beating a hum around her. Round tables filled the room, polished to a bright shine and ringed with green padded chairs. Most of which were occupied with gamblers, cowboys, and dirty miners with tiny sacks of silver dust. Smoke hung in a gray haze at eye level, fighting with the dim light of chandeliers and the gleaming gilt of the framed paintings lining the walls. A man wearing a derby and garters on his white sleeved arms played an upright piano with more excitement than necessary, and several extravagantly dressed women loomed in the back-ground, one smoothing her hand over a gambler's shoulder. He shrugged her off and she huffed indignantly and moved away, finding another tired soul to tease. There must be a whorehouse in here, too, she thought, then slid her gaze to the door marked private, then up the long staircase behind her and to the left, leading to a balcony, with several doors lining the walk. The tiny, fragile-looking blonde leaning over the rail and fanning her nearly bare breasts confirmed her suspicions.

Victoria let her gaze slide down, wander, then come back to her hands resting on the bar. Her stomach grumbled, but she wasn't hungry enough to eat. Not that this place didn't have some decent food, if the way the miners and trail dirty cowboys lining the wood bar and steadily shoveling food in their mouths was any indication. But she didn't want to spend any more time in public than necessary and kept her head down enough to watch what was going on around her, catching most in the mirror hanging over the bar.

The bartender finally drew himself away from a conversation with a plump smiling redhead and acknowledged her with a nod, his rag making a slow circle across the bar as he neared.

"Beer," she murmured, slapping the coin on the wood counter.

"How old are you?"

"Old enough." The bartender chuckled, reaching beneath the bar to slide a wet one across the wood. She caught it, tilting her head back enough to meet his gaze. She waited for her change, staring at him, aware that the pale blue contacts made her eyes look almost white. His features tightened and Victoria heard the rattle of coins before he dumped several on the counter. She dragged them back and into her pocket, then dropped her attention to the long neck of her beer.

She shoved the specs up her nose and drank, taking a long pull and trying not to choke on the harsh lukewarm taste. Definitely not a Coors, she thought, stealing another look at the saloon. She backed away from the bar, moving slowly, avoiding a glance at the card players. Might make them jumpy, she thought, and headed toward the piano, her ears tuned to conversation.

Cattle thieves plagued the ranchers. Lost one man to a skirmish.

An acting troupe was reported heading this way.

Doc Maclaren's office was busted into for the second time.

And how come the Irish were everywhere? That brought several heads around to glare at the tubby speaker.

And what did Sam somebody-or-other think about poor Kelly Galloway?

Damn Irish, another commented. *Serves 'em right.* Victoria could feel the tension mount in the room. The other woman did, too, and fled, casually, quickly.

A solemn man at a corner table, red-eyed and drunk as hell, she decided, murmured something that brought a few customers to their feet. Victoria took a last sip of beer and plunked the half empty bottle on the nearest table, determined to get out before a brawl erupted. She was just at the bat wing doors when she heard a voice, clear and amiable.

"Gentleman, gentleman. Relax."

Her stomach wrenched in painful knots.

Ivy League.

She didn't look, waiting for more, waiting for the handsome boyish face to form in her mind, to remember the exact tone of his voice and make a match.

"No need to get your feathers up tonight. God knows, I can't afford the damages." Chuckles melted through the massive room and Victoria's skin shifted on her body. "Drinks are on the house."

A cheer shivered the beamed ceiling, and she forced herself to turn and look back over her shoulder.

Her heart slammed to her knees and she gripped the winged door. She was hoping she wouldn't find him here. Hoping he'd run for the hills and died from exposure. But he was smiling, his gate dragging a little as he strolled among the patrons, tapping a walking stick and acknowledging his generosity. He was dressed in somber dark blue, refined and elegant for the times—a white shirt, string tie, brocade vest, gold watch fob—Goddamn perfect, down to the blaring sheen to his snake skin boots. His sandy brown hair was longer, combed straight back and showing off the G.Q. looks that won over eleven unsuspecting women.

"Congratulations on winning the Pearl," a man said from his seat at a card table, a stack of chips before him. "Never seen her look this good."

"Thank you sincerely, Ezera." Ivy League grasped Ezera's shoulder, giving it a rough manly squeeze as he flashed that thousand dollar smile. "Then this means you'll come back and spend money so I can pay for it?"

Smooth, she thought, like the slide of a razor against tender skin.

The customers laughed, and Victoria wanted to put a bullet between his bright smiling blue eyes.

Algenon Becket.

Millionaire and murderer.

Cole's killer.

And he was no stranger. He was the owner of a nineteenth century saloon.

And responsible for the deaths of twelve innocent victims.

Ivy League, she thought, was here to stay.

And prey.

Chapter Six

The saloon suddenly wasn't big enough, the air not clean enough and Victoria shoved open the door, stepping onto the covered walk. She drew a deep breath, forcing the beer to stay where it belonged and tripped down the stairs, brushing shoulders with a pedestrian.

"Sorry, pal," she murmured and kept going.

"Too much to drink, Jake?"

Victoria stopped in her tracks. Oh God. Not him, not now, she thought and schooled her features before cocking a glance over her shoulder. Damn, he looked good tonight, fresh, his white shirt stark against the warm bronze of his skin.

"Nah, just stuffy in there is all?" She half turned toward him, shoving the specs up her nose. Did he have a date, she wondered, then dismissed the idea. It was none of her business.

Chris frowned, glancing beyond to the Pearl, then back to Jake. He got an uneasy feeling about this kid. Like he did with Mason, before he knew he was a *she*. And he cursed the woman for making him so damn suspicious about every new face.

Victoria rubbed her nose with a gloved fist and pushed her

hands into her jean pockets. "Well, I gotta git back to work," she drawled, then walked briskly toward the livery.

"I'll walk with you," he called, forcing Jake to slow his steps. "I need Caesar." He planned to take a trip out of town and look for Mason. Knowing where she was might ease his mind. He still didn't trust her.

Victoria yanked up the bar on the door and swung it open. "Mister O'Brian's home," she said when he frowned into the dark. Victoria moved with counted steps to the lantern. She'd tripped enough in two days not to have this place down to a science. From a dented cup she took a match and struck it to the lantern, praying she didn't singe her face off. Adjusting the flame, she walked the few feet to the second stall, catching the lamp handle on a nail.

"Wake up, pal." She unlatched the low gate, swinging it open. "Daddy's here."

Chris smirked, giving Jake a quelling look. He knew the townfolk took amusement in his horse, but the embarrassment meant little. Caesar had saved his hide more than once. Chris clicked his tongue and Caesar swung his magnificient head around, snorted, then came over to the gate. Instead of Chris, the horse went directly to Jake.

"Boy," Chris warned. The stallion didn't take well to anyone but him, usually greeting with a few teeth marks.

Victoria stared blankly at the beast's black eyes, prepared for the unpredictable. Caesar stepped and nudged her shoulder. "Don't have anymore treats," she hissed.

Christopher arched a brow and Jake looked at the hay strewn floor, scratching his arm.

"I gave him sugar," the lad confessed. Caesar lipped Jake's hat and the young man scrambled to keep it on his head, glaring at the animal. "Go home, you brat," he said, then headed to the open door, obviously in a hurry to get rid of him. Chris clicked his tongue and Caesar followed, pausing when he did at the door.

And Victoria thought for a moment she'd been made. "Pay Mister O'Brian in the morning, Marshal. I'm sure you're good for it." She didn't want him to know she still hadn't figured out the money. It all looked fake to her, like something you'd get at the Pirates of the Carribean in a fishnet sack.

"Where are you sleeping, Jake?"

Mentally she groaned, wishing he'd leave and quit playing the concerned father role so she could get to more important things, like some sleep before watching the son of a bitch across the street.

Jake inclined her head to the back of the barn and Chris saw a bedroll and leather satchel tucked against the tack room wall. He returned his gaze to Jake. Kid's damn shy, Chris thought, counting him to be no more than nineteen or twenty with that scarcely shaven skin and shock of white blonde hair poking out in all directions from beneath the brown hat. And he needed a bath.

"It's dangerous, even for a man."

"I ain't afraid, if that's what you mean," she snapped, hoping she sounded like an indignant cowboy. "But I ain't gettin' any sleep standin' here being a damn door stop."

Chris smiled, a smile that nearly knocked her back, the flash of white teeth and sparkling dark brown eyes making her heart stumble wildly, and she couldn't help but return it. But she knew he only saw a young man.

"I get the message. 'Night, son."

Victoria closed the door, dropping the heavy bar into place before taking the oil lamp with her to the back of the barn. She spend a half-hour refitting the new brake to the rig O'Brian had assigned her, then deciding nobody was going to get killed from her handiwork, she arranged some hay in an empty stall, then shook out a blanket. Dropping to the cushion, she set her wrist watch alarm for four hours. Ivy League was a control freak, that much she knew, and he'd control his saloon as well as his kills. She didn't anticipate him leaving his roust to go hunt, but he liked living on the edge, doing it with people close by, close enough to get caught. It was that above-the-law attitude that made her furious, as well as the murders.

And as she stretched out, tugging her hat over her eyes and

sliding her tazer beneath her right thigh, she drifted off to sleep, the image of dark eyes, crinkled at the corners with an easy smile, joining her dreams.

Victoria shifted her elbows and brought the binoculars to her eyes. From her vantage point she could see into the Pearl, the bartender sweeping up, the drunks lazing outside on the walk. Through the lens she studied each window; upper level, back stair exit as well as through the staircase, the ladies rooms, and from the look of it, business was booming and bumping. But the lower far left level captured her interest now, and she focused on the open undraped window and the interior beyond. Facing the street, the office was too visual to risk breaking in to do some heavy searching. She didn't think a second thought about doing it, if she could. Bounty hunter's had rights cops didn't.

Not that it would matter a hell of a lot in 1872.

She lowered the binoculars, a shiver simmering down over her spine. Since she arrived, she hadn't taken much time to consider where and *when* she was, who she was talking to every day. And what part of history she might be screwing up. *These people are all dead in my time, this town is nothing but wood scraps and rusted metal.*

And what about Marshal Swift? Would she find him in the history books when she went back? Did he live to a ripe old age or was he shot in the street by some gunslinger refusing to give up his gun to the town policy? She didn't want to know and focused on the room.

It was large, its interior door opening inside the saloon, to the right and beneath the staircase, she deduced. The door marked private and likely kept the noise of the customers from disturbing his peace. Just prior to his private door was a store-room, adjacent to the south wall, the section behind the bar itself.

Her surveillance arena was excellent.

He was sitting in the room, alone she could only assume,

since the light was too dim to see much beyond his figure in a chair, feet propped, a snifter cupped in his palm. Instead of a lamp, three candles rested on the table in a cluster. She watched him, a part of her Marine training recognizing how strategic a sniper shot this would be from her position. He tipped the glass, staring at the liquid, and she saw his lips move, a slick smile gracing his lips as he addressed the corner.

He was talking to someone.

And when a dark figure moved in front of the window to set a matching glass on the table, she realized it was the marshal.

Immediately, she rolled away from the loft window, breathing deeply.

Okay, okay. Becket isn't a criminal here. But what would the marshal be talking to him about at two in the morning?

Her heart sank to her stomach. Was he on the take? Was he friends with Ivy League? A horrible thought occurred to her. What if he told Ivy League about her? Not that Ivy League had ever seen her face, or the masks she was using now, but if Marshal Swift mentioned finding her in the woods, near the dry fall, would Becket be alerted? Her only chance was that Becket thought he hadn't been followed, that he was free to move around at will. And get careless.

Lifting the glasses to her eyes, she watched Becket as he doused the lamp, the moonlight offering only his shadow as he opened another door. Light sliced from the room and she deepened her focus lens. There was a woman in his bed and just as he closed the door, she wondered where she'd seen her. In the saloon, she realized, the one who'd touched the gambler. At least he wasn't too perfect, Victoria thought as the marshal appeared in the alley. Caesar trotted over and he swung up onto his back. No saddle.

He made no effort to hide his presence.

And she settled easier when a man approached, the star on his chest catching the moonlight. A deputy. She couldn't hear them, but Christopher was gesturing to the saloon and the drunks sleeping on the porch. The other man nodded and Chris rode off slowly, ducking to look beneath surrey rigs and wagons, into alleys and unshaded windows.

Making his rounds, she realized, utterly relieved.

He was thorough and she leaned out the loft, nearly falling in her effort to see which way he went. Was he going home? To a wife?

He *had* to be married. He was too handsome not to be.

And why, a voice pestered, does that bother the hell out of you?

Victoria was on her feet by the time the second pounding-whatever smacked the door. She ran to the far end, lifted the bar to incessant pounding and jerked open the door, prepared to rip the intruder a new asshole when she stared into the dark eyes of the marshal.

"There's been an accident." He was breathless, sweating, his white shirt dirty. "I need Clancey's mallet and chisel." He didn't wait for the fog of sleep to lift and pushed past her to the rack of tools beyond the furnace.

"What happened?" She rolled down her sleeves to cover her watch.

"A kid sleeping in the back of wagon. It cut loose, rolled, and it's wedged against some rocks. His leg is caught."

Before he finished she'd opened the first stall and lead a horse out, slipping on a bridle, then using the stall slates to climb on its bare back.

"I'm coming," she told him when he scowled at her. He nodded curtly, leaving, throwing the locks before swinging onto Caesar. Chris lead the way, and all Victoria could think of was the frightened child, alone and hurt and thinking he'd been abandoned in the dark. It was a wrenching sensation.

Chris bent over his horse's head, whispering, and the beast lurched, their wild ride stirring the still sleeping town. Hooves clattered on the only paved street and deputies called out, threatening to shoot before recognizing the rider. One deputy mounted up and followed behind Jake. And though Chris didn't think the young stablehand could be much help, he was glad for the extra pair of hands.

They rode, passing homes and businesses until they came to the edge of town where the earth sloped into a valley. A drop off and in the dawn light Chris could see the edge of the half shattered wagon, hear the soft whimpers of the boy. He reined back, Caesar protesting at the poor treatment and Chris slid from the mount, pushing the horse aside and moving down the hill.

Jake was behind him.

"Jesus Christ," Jake whispered and Chris stopped, glaring at him. Their fear wouldn't help Lucky. Then he saw it, schooled features, a hard look before he side stepped down the incline toward the wagon. Jake followed, scattering pebbles and dirt.

"Marshal?" Lucky cried, trying to sound brave.

"Here, son. Told you I'd be back." Chris was thanking any God who'd listen for not letting the wagon take him over the cliff. The bolder was the only thing keeping him there. Lucky was pinned beneath the debris and Chris could have pulled him out if his leg wasn't caught in the spokes of the wheel, the metal pressing down on the limb. And the cracked half of the wagon kept shifting, threatening to take rubble and child over the side of the ravine.

Chris slid down the sharp incline, chunks of earth tumbling toward the cliff. Lucky lay head first toward the ravine and his only hope was to bend the metal back and chip away the wood, let him slip his leg out, then pull him to safety from beneath the wagon. But it was unstable.

Victoria laid on her stomach beside the wagon, reaching a hand out to Lucky. "It's going to be all right, pal," she murmured to the boy, his wide eyes striking a stab of painful memory through her. "I'm not going to let you go."

Chris inched closer, the avalanche of rocks and caving earth terrifying them. "Stay back, Seth," he called to the deputy.

"And get a rope and see if you can secure this thing somehow," Jake ordered in a tone that surprised Chris, if he had time to think about it. Seth obeyed as Chris positioned the chisel between the wood and metal and raised the mallet.

"Are you crazy?" Victoria hissed. "One jolt and we both go. You're going to have to either take the wheel off or bend the metal back."

Chris's gaze narrowed, though he wasn't going to argue. Jake was right. He slipped the chisel into the loop of the carter pin, first trying to pry the rusted metal loose, then gently tapping. Lucky winced with every jolt.

The wagon shifted, spilling rocks and broken planks over the cliff and they all froze. It was a few seconds before they heard a responding crash.

Chris turned his attention to the pin, trying to concentrate as Jake spoke to Lucky, never stopping the silly chatter, asking the kid all sorts of questions.

About a minute into the conversation, Jake met Chris's gaze and Chris knew he'd realized Lucky had some problems, aside from being alone.

A lasso whirled through the air, catching around the wagon's tongue and Chris worked frantically to loosen the pin. Finally it gave.

"Don't let it up, deputy," Jake called out as the line went taut, then looked at the boy. "I'm going to let go now, Lucky."

"No, no, no!" came in a high-pitched scream as he grappled for her hand.

The wagon scrapped against the bolder.

"Lucky," Victoria said firmly, bending closer. "Look at me." The child lifted teary eyes to her and her chest tightened. He was terrified and not understanding any of this. "I'm going to come under there and hold you."

"Jake!"

Her head snapped around and she sat up, her white blue gaze clashing with his. "Have Seth tie the lasso to Caesar. It will brace the wagon. You work the wheel off the axel and I'll hold onto him. As soon as the axel's free, cut the line to the wagon."

"Hell no, I won't. You'll both go over!"

"Not if you rope my legs." His expression told her he thought this a lousy idea. "He's terrified, Marshal. He'll panic, try to help you get the wheel off. It's the only way we can do this."

She didn't wait for him to argue, tossed her hat up the hill, then called for and caught the extra rope, knotting it around her calves. She crouched, slipping through the narrow gap beneath the wagon as the marshal tossed the second line to Seth. God, she hoped this worked.

Caesar backed up, tightening the wagon line as the deputy secured Jake's leg rope to a saddle. Chris rose up carefully and grasped the bent wheel. He tugged, shifting it left and right and the instant it started to move, Lucky shook his leg, whimpering, as if trying to shoo off a bee. But Jake talked to the boy, murmuring softly, holding his leg still and cradling him against his body, preparing for the moment when the weight of the broken half of the wagon was going to fall.

Then it happened.

The wheel hub popped free of the axle and Jake rolled on top of Lucky just as wagon dropped. "Cut it! Cut it!"

The line whipped free like a curling snake, the abrupt release springing the fractured wood up and over the cliff.

Jake and Lucky went, too.

Chris grappled and the line on Jake's legs snapped tight. The horse reared in protest. Seconds passed before the wagon hit bottom, the sound of shattering wood like a gun blast.

Chris pulled on the line while Seth shouted at the horse, waving his arms to force it back. Caesar stomped. And Chris's hands burned against the rope, his booted heels digging into the dirt.

His heart thundered in his throat, fear racing through his blood stream.

If the rope cut on a rock—he heaved, his muscles screaming as he yanked the dangling weight up the cliff. He saw boots soles and the wheel first. They were on their side, Jake's arms and legs clutched tightly around the boy, the wheel spokes no more than misshapen scrap metal. Chris pulled harder and dragged the pair onto firmer ground.

He rushed forward.

"Jake?"

Lucky lifted his head, smiling his innocent smile and Chris had to pry him from Jake's arms. He handed him up to Seth and the boy clung to the deputy, allowing him to bring him away from the edge and take up the challenge of removing the metal bracelet.

Jake lay perfectly still.

"Jake?" Chris touched his shoulder and he flinched. "You all right?"

"Give me a minute," came a dry croak.

"Why did you do it? You could have been killed."

"He's just a baby. What was I supposed to do?"

It was another moment before Jake pushed himself up, backing up the hill on all fours, then sitting back on his haunches.

Chris frowned at him, then stood, moving over to the boy. Lucky showed off his freed leg as if it were a new toy. It was bloody, Chris thought, but not broken.

"Take him to Abigale," he told Seth. "She'll see to him."

Seth nodded and he and the boy departed. Lucky chattered about the pretty sunrise and what Abigale might cook him for breakfast, telling Chris the near death experience was already dismissed from his fragile mind.

Jake dropped back on his rear, bracing his forearms on his bent knees and finally catching his breath.

Chris stared for a moment at his back, then scooped up his hat and crossed the distance, squatting beside Lucky's true rescuer.

"Christ, I'll be bruised for a month," Jake said tiredly and Chris whipped out a knife to sever the ropes.

"Thanks."

Hands pulled away the scraps.

"You're bleeding."

"And you're something else, Victoria Mason."

Victoria's head snapped up.

He grinned.

She groaned.

"Damn. How did you know?"

Lightly, he tapped the hard soles of her work boots with the blade. "Your feet are just too small for a man."

Chapter Seven

She chucked a stone over the ridge. "Rats."

"Well, that's about the cleanest thing I've heard out of your mouth lately."

She glanced to the side, her gaze suddenly caught on the chiseled curve of his mouth. "Appearances are deceiving, Marshal." Her gaze flicked to his. "Vic and Jake have an entire repertoire I haven't begun to scratch."

It's like acting to her, he thought. "And what about Victoria?"

"Depends on my mood." Which wasn't great, she thought, then flopped back on the dirt spread eagle and sighed. She'd hoped to keep up the disguise for a while, but now that she'd been made, she didn't know how to explain it. Damn boots. No one had ever noticed her feet before. And she couldn't afford any that fit with the *times*. Her gaze slid to his, but he was looking over her clothes, lingering at her breasts hidden beneath Ace binding, foam padding, a dirty shirt and a short leather vest.

"Yes, it hurts," she said to the question in his eyes.

His skin darkened a fraction as he settled beside her.

Damn, but the woman was blunt. "Then why do you insist on masquerading this way?"

"None of your business." Being rude looked like the best way to get out of this right now.

Chris didn't take offense. She was stand-offish from the start, yet he was naturally curious as to why. Victoria Mason was hiding more than her gender behind the masks and padding.

"I can see where you might feel safer," he said, contemplating the sunrise. "Though you certainly smell bad enough to keep people away."

She shoved his shoulder and he glanced back, smiling. Like he meant it, she thought, something warm springing in her chest. "How'd you find Lucky at this hour?"

"I was heading home and heard him talking to himself. He would have never called out, he was just entertaining himself until someone found him."

Learning disabled, she realized. And he was alone. God, what opportunity did kids like him have in this century? "He doesn't have any family?"

Chris drew up his knees, propping his forearms there and shook his head. "Some people said he was dumped from a wagon train, but I don't know. He just turned up, alone and hungry." Chris remembered the day he found him, his ribs cracked from being kicked around by some bored drunks like a bothersome dog. "He wasn't treated well, not that he'd know the difference."

"He knows." She sat up, selecting pebbles to hurl over the ridge. "He just buries it to where he feels safe."

Chris sensed sudden pain and turned to look at her profile, a little shock running through him, for she'd discarded the raspy masculine voice to her own softer normal tone. It was hard to look at her like this, knowing what was beneath the paint and mask. But *who* was it hiding?

"You act like you know him."

"I know children like him, Marshal. He's—" she glanced down at the dirt between her boots and if Chris didn't know better he'd swear she was holding back tears. "Special. Very special. Needs a lot of patience."

"That's if he'd stay put long enough." He joined her in flinging rocks. "I've tried to find where he hides, but the kid's too fast."

He loves the boy, she thought, swallowing the rock climbing up her throat. It warned her not to get involved, with anything but Ivy League. You're leaving, a voice reminded. You can't stay. You're from another age, another life.

Right.

What life?

"So where's home, Marshal?"

Chris nodded to the ravine and she came to her feet, dusting off the seat of her jeans as she walked several yards along the ridge until she could see the area without threat of falling off the mountain.

She whistled softly, planting her hands on her hips. "Now that's what I call paradise." She didn't see Chris smile, her gaze on his home, a lush green tree-filled valley, a winding narrow river cutting it in half, and on the right side, *their* side, was a ranch, a couple thousand head of cattle meandering where they pleased, two barns, a paddock, corrals, and horses shifting and stomping off the cool morning dew. The quiet peaceful surrounding stole her breath and she wished she had binoculars, yet even from the distance she could see Seth, Lucky perched before him, the pair riding up the dirt road to the loveliest house she'd seen in ages.

She never imagined him in a place like this. But then, she'd never taken a moment to consider where he lived. Suddenly, a woman came flying out the door and off the porch, heading straight for the boy and the muscles in her chest squeezed down on her heart. Victoria didn't want to examine her feelings or thoughts and walked briskly to her horse.

"I have to get back to making myself smell even worse," she said, leading the horse to a decent sized rock so she could climb on to the animal. Chris was there, offering a leg up and she accepted it, swinging onto the animal's back.

She stared out over the ridge, adjusting the reins in her gloved hands. He was still there, beside her, moving closer and laying a hand to the horse's coat near her thigh. Victoria could feel the heat radiating from his skin, yet he never touched her. The closeness made her insides shift and hum.

"Victoria?"

The sound of her name on his lips stabbed her. She lowered her gaze and could see he was trying to pry beneath the disguise.

"Am I ever going to see the woman in the forest again?"

She almost laughed, a nasty bitter laugh. Who was he fooling? There was nothing remotely enticing about her, the *normal* her, and she knew it. Her job was who she was, a hunter, a vigilante of the court system. Half the time she walked the thin side of the law and in her darkest dreams thought herself no better than Becket. Christopher Swift didn't need to know her. This kind, gentle man didn't need his life complicated by the horrors that cloaked her.

"Don't be curious about me, Marshal. You have no idea what your messing with."

The brush-off made him angry. "Why don't you just tell me, so I'll understand?"

"Not a chance in hell." His features darkened and before he could speak she said, "Go home, Marshal Swift. To your ranch, your family, and stay out of my way."

"Goddamn it, woman—"

"No." She backed the horse up, breaking his hold. "There's nobody home, so quit knocking."

Christopher stepped out onto the porch in front of his office, leaned back against the support post, then fished in his shirt pocket for papers and tobacco. He rolled a smoke, watching the traffic on the street. Two boys teased a dog outside the dry goods store, a carriage rolled past, its driver having trouble keeping the rig steady. Nothing was unusual and without pause, his gaze slipped to the livery. He'd been tempted to go see her, to demand why she was masquerading as a man, for he wasn't dumb enough to believe it was simply for safety's sake. Women were basically narcisstic. At least most women he'd encountered—selecting and enjoying dresses and perfumes and the feminine frippery to entice a man to madness. Trap him into feeling wanted. Except Victoria. And he wondered why.

Good God, that's all he did where she was concerned.

Wonder—why she talked strange? Why she was downright rough, which he felt was intentional—to keep him or anyone back? How she could disguise herself so meticulously, without a shred of recognition? Where did she come by the mask and fake hair in the first place? What was in that knap-sack she refused to let him get close enough to see? Had she been raised by men without the touch of feminine presence? God knows she had the steel nerve of any man.

He'd been shocked to his boot heels when he realized Jake was Victoria. And he recalled his uneasiness around the young man—the woman—ah, shit! He slid the cigarette between his lips and struck a match, cupping his hands and dragging heavily on the smoke. His brain ached and trying to dismiss the cause, he blew out a gray stream, made smoke rings and watched as they were erased by the breeze before he bent his knee, propping his boot sole against the post. Citizens nodded as they hustled past, shopping, urging children and Chris thought of Lucky. Abigale had bathed him, bandaged his wound, filled his belly with food and put him to bed in one of the guest rooms. And he'd vanished. Chris knew he'd turn up somewhere, probably in trouble for stealing food, but it worried him, gave him sleepless nights knowing the innocent child was running around without anyone to care for him.

He'd have to remind his deputies to keep a lookout for the boy, he thought, turning back to the office and pitching the cigarette in the dirt.

He glanced once more over the street, his gaze slipping past, then returning sharply to a woman, her head bowed, her stride so long it kicked her dark skirts out enough to show her petticoats.

He smiled, his gaze dropping immediately to her feet. The boots.

She slipped into the dry goods store, yet Chris remained on the walk, considering his next move and wondering why the hell he was so damn pleased to see her again. Even if it was in another disguise. He smiled hugely and crossed the street in a casual pace, watching her through the window as he approached and stepped inside. He ignored the surprised glances from the customers, his gaze roaming over her.

That has to be the most unattractive hair style in creation.

Her hair, now a lackluster brown, was scraped tightly against her skull, covering her ears and knotted in a fat bun. Her cheeks appeared puffed and the spectacles perched on the end of her nose made her look pinched, like a tall squirrel, the gray throat-choking blouse and brown skirt doing nothing to enhance her figure. She's padded her waist, he realized, and bound her breasts again.

He strode close. "Well, this is an improvement at least."

Victoria's head jerked up, her features pulling tight, stretching the artificial scar on her cheek. "I beg your pardon?" she murmured, pushing up the spectacles, then casting a glance at the other customers. They all seemed unnaturally interested in their conversation.

"But that scar *has* to go," he spoke softly, folding his arms and leaning his hip against the counter. He gave her his full attention. Victoria tried to ignore him, staring ahead and handing the remainder of her list to the proprietor.

"If you'll excuse me," her gaze dropped pointedly to his badge— "Marshal. I have work to tend."

"Is that so?"

"It is." Victoria straightened her spine, hoping she appeared every bit the prim spinster. God knows she was old enough to qualify.

He tugged on her white apron and she batted away his hand, sending him a scolding look. He grinned. She leaned over the counter to arrange the cleaning products and linens. "Please don't," she hissed under her breath.

He inched closer, sinking down onto his elbow, and the scent of his cologne, something woodsy, filled her head. It made her think of how wonderful it would be to hold him against her, taste his bronzed skin and when he spoke, his voice was low and private.

"You're going to fess up, Victoria. Soon."

She tossed him a half-lidded stare, brown-green eyes bright with anger. "Clara, sir. Clara Murphy."

His smile widened, dark eyes dancing with the threat of mischief, and she wanted to see just how many of those perfectly white teeth she could loosen with one punch. He was going to blow it for her! Gossip would bring attention.

"Any relation to Jake, over at the livery?"

Victoria fumed, gathering up her parcels and addressing the store keeper. "Mrs. Fotheringham asked that you put this on her credit account."

The storekeeper nodded, and beyond him, she noticed the other women in the shop staring at Chris with a mix of fear and fascination.

"Would you care for some assistance?" Chris offered.

"Thank you, but no. I'm quiet capable."

His expression fell a little, his smile appearing forced as he tipped his hat and left.

Victoria bumped the counter, unaware that his closeness affected her so much until he was gone. Her heart beat pushed against her throat, the fabric of her blouse suddenly too tight in several places.

"Oh dearie, are you all right?" a woman rushed over, patting her shoulder.

"Imagine him, talking to you!"

"How dare he!" came another voice.

She blinked, her gaze passing over the bonnet-tucked and bustle-bunched women.

"How dare he what?"

"Why, speak to you like that? So intimately," came on a stage whisper.

Okay, she thought, morals were high in 1872, but this was ridiculous.

"What's so bad about it?"

They huffed like disturbed hens.

"Didn't you know? Why, he's a savage!"

Victoria turned her gaze to the window, watching Christopher's determined stride, his incredible behind tucked in snug jeans and she wanted to know just how *savage* he could be, then realized they meant his heritage.

"I am aware of it." She met their inquiring gazes. "And I don't see a problem."

"You must not be from around here, ma'am." This, from the shopkeeper. "Indians is nothing but trouble."

"But he's the marshal."

They responded with a collective shrug.

"Oh, I see," came with a icy bite. "He can uphold the law and keep peace, even die defending *your* personal safety and *your* property, but because of his bloodlines, he isn't good enough to be accepted as one of you?"

They examined the floor boards, the air gone out of their indignation.

"Lucky man."

A half dozen pairs of eyes jerked up, and Victoria's expression turned thoughtful as she addressed a redhead with green eyes. "You're Irish?" Redhead nodded. "A Mick." Redhead gasped, glancing at her friends for support, but Victoria went on without mercy. "And you, I'd say English and maybe Scots." The pale skinned woman nodded, frightened by what would come next. "A limey and a pinch-penny."

Feathers ruffled, wings flapping. "How dare—"

"I'm fat and scarred," she interrupted. "What do I care?" Victoria shifted her packages, giving them the once over. "Doesn't feel good to have people look negatively at your heritage and not consider the person, huh?" She headed to the door, pausing on the threshold to glance back over her shoulder. "And I don't have to be from around here to know not one of you *purists* can count your own lineage as far back as he can."

Victoria left, fury stinging through her so hard she didn't see the tall barrel-chested man slip from behind a rack of rifles, watching her through the store window as she moved down the walk. His face pressed the glass, eyes straining, he smiled.

But as Victoria stepped off the walk into the street, she fought down her scathing temper, wanting to tear those prejudiced narrow-minded whiners to shreds, yet too aware that it wasn't in her power to change centuries of lousy upbringing. But God it felt good to get in those shots! And she didn't know what made her angrier, the corset-laced toads or the man she defended. She'd just made enemies and stirred up gossip, but the eruption was hot and fast and *blessedly* easy. She didn't like what he made her feel, like a part of something. She couldn't be, not here in this time, not with Becket on the loose.

Damn. Damn, damn!

This was getting too personal.

Catching herself before she sharpened her tongue on some unsuspecting bystander, she took a deep breath, striding slowly into the Hotel Excelsior and offering the supplies to the manager. Immediately, she went back to her duties, the side trip more of a surveillance tactic than a favor. The hotel was three floors with twenty rooms and she thanked God her portion was the first and second floor. The steep steps in full 19th century female battle gear—bustles and petticoats and corsets and just too much crap—put StairMaster to shame and each bed she changed looked more inviting by the minute. Even though a small room at the back of the hotel on the ground floor came with the job, she hadn't slept in the narrow bed once and she was exhausted, having stretched herself thin. But she needed the money. She couldn't maintain the charade wearing the same clothes every day and not be noticed by the wrong people, Ivy League included. Besides, washing wasn't a twenty minute task here. Wishing she could find a job that gave her access to the saloon, yet knowing the only position that paid well required her to lay flat on her back, Victoria dismissed that consideration and conceded that other than a teacher, housekeeping was all she could do here, as a woman, without references or suspicion. But becoming Jake again didn't sound so inviting.

She rapped on a numbered door, called out, then opened the

lock with her master key. The odor hit her first and she caught her breath, forcing herself not to vomit. The room was in absolute shambles, curtains torn, crockery smashed, the contents of an up-ended chamber pot soaking the carpet, and she groaned, sagging against the door, her chance of an early get-away for some sleep vanishing beneath the food littering the floor and redecorating the walls. Looks like a rock band partied here. Now she'd have to go straight to the stable and change, replace her face and perform her duties there while watching over Ivy League.

She caught one of the servants delivering a service of coffee and gestured to the room. "Who stayed here?"

The boy shrugged, then stared horrified at the destruction. "Some real tall skinny fella, sniffed a lot."

"Sniffed?"

"Yeah, like he had a cold. Did this." Demonstrated by pinching his nose several times and Victoria frowned.

"Tell Mrs. Fotheringham about this. I'll be awhile."

"Want me to bring up some hot water and buckets, Miss Murphy?"

She smiled at the offer. He was a cute kid, about thirteen, and at least he wasn't offended by her *scars.*

"Thanks, pal."

He nodded, heading off down the hall and Victoria went about the room, searching for a clue. And when she found who did this, she'd dump him in the nearest sty—where he belonged.

Chris stared across the horse's back, waiting for her to lift her gaze from her currying. She knew he was here. Hell, there wasn't much she missed.

"I like Clara better."

"That so?" Her voice was Jake's voice, like a scuffle through gravel. "Perhaps you should go tell her yer smitten?"

She wasn't giving him an inch today, or yesterday or the day before. He walked around the animal to face her.

"Why, Vi—?"

Her gaze flew to his, knifing off his words. She glanced around her, releasing a breath only when she was certain they were alone. But they wouldn't be for long.

"If you don't quit visiting me, people are going to talk."

"About what?"

"That you just might be a little strange." She let her wrist go limp and pouted her lips.

His features tightened. "Ladies aren't supposed to know about things like that."

Her gaze held his, briefly, before returning her attention to the horse. "Guess that proves I'm no lady, huh?"

He caught a sadness in her tone, unsure and almost timid. Chris shook his head, certain he'd imagined it. Not this bucket of nails.

She squatted, brushing the coat down to the hooves, and the big animal nickered softly. "You like that, don't you, baby," she murmured in a husky voice that stole through Chris like smoke, whispery and warm. It wasn't a voice she affected for her personas, but her voice, the one he'd heard in the forest, low, throaty—utterly feminine. He went down on one knee beside her, taking the brush from her tight grip.

She looked at him and he saw boyish features, white-blonde hair and pale ice-blue eyes behind spectacles. But beyond that, he saw her.

"Have dinner with me?"

She blinked. "What?"

"Without this." He gestured to her disguise and couldn't hide his distaste.

"No."

"No to dinner? Or no to the disguise?"

"I said no."

He glanced around the darkened barn, assured of privacy before he grasped her hand. Instantly, she struggled for freedom, her eyes darting about, yet he slid the glove off and captured her hand in his.

"God, your skin is soft," he whispered and Victoria squeezed her eyes tightly shut, unable to move. There was a power in his touch, she thought, reckoning, frightening. And he tormented her by leaning closer and she could smell him, clean, earthy. A fraction of memory flooded her mind—the forest, the feel of his body taut beneath hers, the flawlessness of his amber skin, the seething power beneath his motionless body. God. His very presence commanded, smothering sensations battling beneath her clothes and she wanted to rip off the mask and padding the very instant she gazed into his eyes. *Can't you see*, she wanted to shout at him, *I am nothing you want, so stop looking at me like you'll find a princess beneath the frog!*

Her hand trembled, and Chris felt it shiver over her body.

"I'm not having dinner with you."

"Yes," he growled. "You are."

Her breath quickened, and for a fraction of a moment, she wanted nothing more in her life than to be the woman he imagined. It hurt to know she'd never measure up, for any man, ever. A tiny sound worked in her throat, so foreign, and Chris knew she was weakening.

"Or I'll reveal your impersonation."

"Bastard." She hissed softly and angrily as she twisted from his grasp. He was luring her into revealing her purpose. She should have known better. "You have no idea what you'll be jeopardizing."

She was spitting mad, he realized suddenly, as she straightened, grabbing back her glove and pulling it on. He stood. The curry brush was still in her other hand.

And if her posture was any indication, she was going to throw it at him any second.

"What am I jeopardizing?"

"My life!" She thumped her chest.

His brows drew tight. "Who's trying to hurt you?"

"No one, if you keep out of it!" Her feet shifted in the hay. "Christ, do you think this is a game?" She waved to her clothes. "That you can blackmail me and I'll just take it?"

"No, goddammit, but is it—" he lowered his voice suddenly, realizing he was close to shouting. "Is it too much to ask for an explanation?"

"Yes! That I'd go to this extreme ought to give you a clue, *Marshal.*"

"Woman," he said for her ears alone. "I haven't got one about you."

She stared at him, yanking the curry brush off her fist and somewhere in the recesses of the massive barn she heard footsteps, a door close, hooves stomping.

"You aren't going to butt out of my business and leave me alone, are you?" her voice stole across the short distance like a whisper of dry wind.

Slowly, he shook his head, his look saying the situation was too interesting.

She sighed, her arms loose at her sides as she stared over the horse's broad gleaming back. He stood to the left of her, close. She was messing with history, his history, but the need, dormant, yet now stirring to life wanted to know this man, wanted to spend even a few moments with him.

"I'll meet you at Duckett's in an hour."

His handsome face split into a wide grin. She didn't have to see it to feel it.

And she knew her next words would destroy it.

"Jake will."

His dark eyes flashed with irritation, like shaved onyx against moonlight.

"Take it or I'll go so deep under, you'll never see me again." She didn't have a choice.

Chris gazed at her for a long moment, a voice inside him warning him not to let this extraordinary woman get away, that when she wanted, she *would* vanish.

He couldn't let her go. He'd never felt so drawn to anyone before.

Not even Camille made him feel this wild brand of excitement.

And he was going to marry her.

Chapter Eight

Duckett's was cheap and hearty in the way of food, and what it lacked in decor, it made up for it in comfort. Several tables lined an open veranda facing the street, the cool breeze sliding off the mountains offering a relaxing atmosphere to the small restaurant. The assortment of patrons were the working class, cowboys mostly, the local laundresses, postmaster, dairymen, and an abundance of weary miners hungry enough to leave their claims. No one was turned away if they had money and even some who didn't. Not from Sal Duckett's kitchen. Chris enjoyed the solitude of the veranda's corner and one of Sal's best ribeye steaks. He shoved a forkful of meat into his mouth and glanced at his dinner partner. He'd plied her with questions, and she stoically refused to answer. It was an uncomfortably silent evening, except for her drilling him about Lucky, his whereabouts and how come even his Cheyenne senses couldn't find the boy. She made him feel negligent, and he regretted forcing her into this. She'd agreed only to appease him, but he wasn't backing down, either. One way or another, he'd get her to confess why she needed to look like a man.

"Hey, Marshal."

Chris looked up from his plate as Velvet Knight sauntered over to him, her full dark red skirts rustling and drawing an eager look from every man in the room.

"Evening, Vel."

Chris rose from his chair, as did the man opposite him and Velvet smiled at the gesture. Marshal Swift was always a gentleman, even to a whore.

"Set that cute bee-hind down, mister," she drawled, a southeastern twange to her accent.

"Velvet," he scolded, smiling, ignoring Victoria's snicker as he offered Vel a chair. "Take a load off."

"And ain't it a big one," she chuckled meatily, settling her bulk into the seat. "Got the night off from keeping the city safe?"

"No, but I'd ask the same of you."

Cutting her steak, Victoria watched covertly as he leaned back in the chair, propping his arm on the back and giving the cathouse madam his attention.

"Nah, just a break." She waved off a waitress before the tired girl got to the table. "Mister Becket's a real caring man."

Victoria's eyes sharpened on her, and though Vel didn't notice, Chris did.

"Like him, do you?"

She seemed to struggle with her next words, then finally said. "Yeah. Had the Doc check out all the girls, makes 'em use skins, though most of the customers whine, and he watches my girls close."

That bothers her, Victoria thought.

"If he had the notion, I 'spect he'd stand over 'em to be certain they was having a good time." She chuckled to herself. "Not that it would matter none to the boys lookin' for a piece." Her attention slid to the young man and Velvet gave him a bold once over, even leaning out to inspect his hardware. She flashed an impatient look at the marshal. "Gonna introduce me?"

Chris could hardly contain his amusement. "Ah, um,

Jake—?'' He met Victoria's gaze, not knowing which last name she used.

"Farrell, ma'am." Victoria nodded to the redhead, shoving the wire rimmed spectacles up her face and maintaining a shyness that didn't invite questions.

"Velvet Knight." Vel's carefully pencil-arched brows knitted. "I've seen you before."

"Maybe." Victoria stared at her plate and forked a chunk of potato, eating. She knew who Velvet was the instant she walked to the table, yet she'd hoped her visit to the saloon had gone unnoticed.

"In the Pearl."

Victoria's gaze shifted upward to Chris, then the voluptuous woman. "Yes'm," she said around the food. Thinking before she spoke made her appear a bit slow-witted, but she didn't care. Slow was better than dead. And she was suddenly glad she'd been a John Wayne fan as a kid and made a convincing cowboy.

"Well, when you come into the Pearl, ask for me. Any friend of the marshal is, well—" her smile widened, "—a good lay for me."

Victoria sputtered, grabbing her glass of milk and drained back the food threatening to choke her.

"I like 'em shy," Vel whispered, reaching under the table to squeeze Jake's thigh, her hand running higher.

Victoria plunked the glass down and shifted out of Vel's grasp, but the woman wasn't offended, glancing at Chris, who was struggling to keep his laughter under control, then shrugging her bare shoulder.

"Eat up, honey," she whispered silkily. "Need lots of energy to keep up with me." The young man was devoutly more interested in his meal than sex, Vel thought, turning to the handsome marshal and leaning forward, availing him with an unobstructed view of her bosom, which she hoped was spilling from the low cut red satin dress.

And he looked, bless him, lavishing her with his dark fathomless eyes.

Victoria grit her teeth. Hookers were so obvious.

"Found out who killed that sweet Kelly Galloway yet?"

Pulling his gaze from Victoria's, Chris features sharpened a little. He was trying to keep it quiet until he uncovered more evidence. And word around town was accident, not murder. "How did you know about that?"

Her smile was soft and sexy. "When a man wants a tussle, he'll tell a girl just about anything."

"My deputies?"

"Nah," she waved. "They know you'd likely kill 'em." Her expression turned sad. "Sean Galloway was in the Pearl, drinking up a storm, itchin' to beat the hide off of anyone who'd tangle with him. Lucky no one would," she told him, frowning briefly at Jake, then looking at Chris.

"You'll let me know if you hear something?" Chris said, his voice low, almost intimate.

Victoria felt her jaw would snap any second. Did his eyes have to keep straying to those plump breasts? Velvet might be a large woman, but she was undeniably beautiful, with her light red hair, green eyes bright with humor and fire, and a lush rubinesque figure like an hour-glass. She was a real woman, generous where it counted, so obvious with the stares her presence garnered. Her face wasn't garishly painted, but soft and enhancing, her hair swept high and curled meticulously. Rubies and diamonds sparkled from around her peaches-and-cream throat and wrists. Gifts from satisfied lovers? Was Chris one of them? She looked more like a queen than a madame, and Victoria decided that if she didn't have to hide behind Jake, and the object of Vel's immediate lust, they might have been friends.

Her attention jerked to what Vel was saying.

"Sean doesn't believe it was an accident."

Neither did Chris, but he couldn't say.

"I'll find out what happened, Vel. I promise."

She reached out and patted his hand. "I know you will." Then she came to her feet, cocking her hip and planting her hand there before leaning down. Victoria's gaze flickered to their surroundings, then between the two as Vel whispered, "There ain't a thing that moves in this town that I don't now about or find out sooner or later, Marshal."

She was offering her service and Chris shook his head. "Too dangerous."

"I like livin' on the edge, honey." Her gaze slipped over his broad shoulders and wide chest and she sighed regretfully. "My offer still holds."

His eyes danced with amusement. "Go make some lonely cowboy happy."

She grinned, turning her gaze to Jake. "When you're lonely, Jake honey," she said on wink, then slipped away, and Victoria watched as she paused at a table full of miners and saying something that made them burst with laughter.

Chris rested his forearms on the green table cloth. "It's good you can't see a blush beneath all that stuff," he said softly, fighting a smile.

"You knew she was playing with me under the table?"

He laughed shortly, and she liked the sound of it. "You're lucky she didn't grab your—" he stopped himself but she finished.

"—crotch?"

His lips twitched maddeningly.

"Got socks in there."

"Jesus."

Victoria shrugged. "She's not the first woman to try to cop a feel when I've been like this."

So she does it often, he thought. "How did you get your hands to look like that?" She'd been eating through his conversation with Vel, and if anyone watched close enough they could tell her movements were feminine. But her hands were bony, heavy knuckled and bigger. "They're like gloves," he realized.

Victoria took a last bite, wiped her mouth, careful not to tug the latex into ripping and sat back. "Yes." He'd quizzed her for an hour before Velvet showed, and Victoria was fast running out of evasions. She didn't think he believed a single one, anyway.

"You get them hot, real hot, and slide them on. They cool, they shrink." He gazed at her hands and she tucked them under the table. His eyes shot to hers, narrowing and she felt suddenly on edge.

"What happened to Kelly Galloway?"

His look was closed and it rankled her.

"You accused me of killing her—"

"I accused Vic Mason, a very suspicious man who answered the description," he justified.

"I'm not going to get into false arrest discussion with you, but what's so odd about this murder that you won't let the townspeople in on it?"

He took up his utensils and attacked his steak. "You ask a lot of questions for someone who won't answer any."

"Think of me as an uninvolved point of view. I don't know anyone or the situation."

"Why should I confide in you?" he said, then took a bite of meat.

Her smile was benign. "No reason whatsoever."

His gaze lifted, searching the ice-blue eyes for the incredible gold hidden beneath as he chewed and swallowed. "Why are you interested?"

"I'm not."

"Liar."

"Killjoy."

He leaned across the table. "Woman."

He gave her a look that spoke volumes, tons, that he knew what was beneath the mask and he wasn't having trouble remembering.

Under the table, she kicked him.

He grunted, yet his expression remained unchanged but for a painful flicker in his eyes and the tightening of his grip on the fork and knife.

"A man doesn't look at another man that way, Marshal. You get my drift?"

"Shit." His features stretched tight and he focused on his meal, covertly glancing around. No one had noticed and Victoria was amazed and a little flattered that he chose to see the woman and not the young man everyone else did.

"Okay, how 'bout a trade? Vital statistics, for the scene of the crime info."

Damn. She was back to the Galloway killing. "How vital?"

"If you get too personal, I'll tell you."

He eyed her for a moment then said, "Are you married?"

"No." Her gaze wavered unexpectedly.

"Were you ever?"

Briefly she toyed with the handle of her coffee cup before answering. "Yes. He was killed before he could divorce me."

His brow flicked upward and he stared intently. She blames herself, he thought sadly.

She didn't care for his pitying look and suddenly straightened in her chair, pushing the plate aside and leaning forward, hands folded. "Let me save you the trouble. I'm twenty-eight, five foot nine, one hundred forty-five pounds on a good day. When I can, I run two miles just for the hell of it. My best friend was a man, now dead. I had a daughter, also dead. I consider cooking torture, sewing something someone else does so I can buy it, and right now I'd kill for a cigarette."

Chris gazed across the table. Even within the gravelly voice of *Jake* he heard bitterness—and anger. For the deaths of everyone she loved or her vulnerability because of it, he didn't know. But he wanted to find out, wanted to seek what made such a sharp, intelligent and undeniably beautiful woman so rough and secretive. Slowly, he set his fork down before reaching into his shirt pocket to bring out papers and a small half empty sack. Swiftly, he rolled her a cigarette and handed it across the table. She stared at the crimped white cylinder and he could see the moisture collecting in her eyes. She sighed, looking fragile even beneath the padding as she took the smoke, lighting it off the small lamp resting between them.

She drew lightly on the filterless cigarette, avoiding his probing gaze.

Chris picked up his fork and focused on his dinner, then set it aside, deciding his appetite was gone. Signaling a waitress, the service was cleared, her coffee refilled, and a beer set before Chris.

He made designs in the mug's perspiration.

"Kelly Galloway is—was—a rancher's wife, young, pretty, very kind and generous. Sean owns a small spread about ten miles east. He came from a good family, ranchers, but he wanted to mine silver. He struck a vein, bought the ranch and sent for Kelly. They had it good, but Sean didn't want to mine the *Dublin's Heart* anymore, said it made him crazy to live in the dark. He took what the mine gave him and didn't go any deeper." She frowned, confused. "With miners, they play out a strike until it's gone. All gone. Sean just sealed his up, but he wouldn't sell it either."

She paused in bringing the smoke to her lips. "Who'd he piss off?"

It was his turn to look confused for an instant. "Miners, the Flat Pick Mining Company. They want the *Dublin,* but to work it they needed the land surrounding it, too."

"And Sean wasn't going to sell his what? Prime grazing land?"

Chris nodded, taking a sip of his beer. "He built the ranch around the mine, or rather, below it."

"And they'd have to level the ranch to do anything." He nodded, agreeing. "You think someone from the Flat Pick killed her?"

"Too obvious." He shook his head, the lamp light shimmering over his coal black hair, and she wanted to touch it.

"How did she die?" Victoria took a drag, afraid to hear it.

"Trampled by half their cattle, a hundred yards from her house."

She blew out a straight stream, relieved. It wasn't Ivy League, unless he suddenly changed his M.O. "Were there any other wounds? Any signs of rape? Did you take bl—" She clamped her lips shut. He couldn't take blood samples or anything else that needed a lab to define.

"There wasn't much of her left, *Jake.*"

She didn't miss a beat. "What was she doing outside?"

"Sean thinks she heard something."

"Where was he?"

"Asleep."

"And he didn't hear what she *might have* heard? She didn't wake him?"

"No. He said he heard her get up and leave the house and thought it was to relieve herself."

"Isn't that what chamber pots are for?" Just the thought of those things disgusted her. Yet she could see she had him thinking, she decided, tossing the cigarette over the veranda into the street. "Let's say she was using the facilities, how far is it from the house in respect to the barn?"

"About twenty yards both ways—what are you getting at?"

"Noise. Tramping cattle make noise, a dying woman makes noise."

"Yes, and the bray of cattle is nothing new to men like Sean."

"Humor me a sec," she said, briefly putting up her hand. "What good would it do to kill her? Who'd profit? She didn't own the land. He did. Killing her wasn't going to get Sean to sell. If anything, he'd hold tighter. So, unless the mining company is run by incredibly stupid men, rule them out for now. Was she faithful to her husband?"

"As far as I know."

"Did you ask if they were having problems?"

He scowled. "That's personal."

"So is murder," she hissed sharply, hating to think how many murders went unsolved because police didn't want to delve beyond some Victorian code of propriety. "Perhaps they'd had a fight and she went out to cool off and he saw an opportunity to end it all?"

"She loved him, *Jake,*" he gritted through clenched teeth. "I've seen them together."

She scoffed. "Anybody can fake affection." Victoria thought of her husband and the look on his face every time she came home from a hunt.

"You heard Velvet. He was at the Pearl looking for a fight. Does that sound like the man you're painting?"

"Maybe he regrets it now?" She shrugged. "I don't know. But a happy woman doesn't go out in the middle of the night, in the middle of a ranch and get trampled by steers who are supposed to be peacefully grazing."

"Wolves spooked them." His voice was clipped. "Sean said he heard the howl."

She wasn't buying that. "If he heard, why didn't he get up to protect his beloved and his precious ranch. Perhaps she was meeting someone? Perhaps she was trying to save her livelihood without bloodshed? Had there been any threats to the Galloways?"

"No, just insistent pressure to sell."

Her brow arched at that.

"More money than the place was worth." Perhaps someone knew something about the mine that he didn't, Chris reasoned, admitting she had several valid points. She was far too insightful about all this, for a bystander and a woman, and it chiseled at his pride.

"But those are the only threats you knew about."

"Yes, dammit."

Her forehead knitted. "Don't you want to find the truth?"

"Of course I do!" he hissed, his eyes, black and hard as wet pebbles, pinned her to the seat.

"You just don't want *me* approaching your territory, huh?"

"You don't have the authority. And I'll tell you, Sean and Kelly were happy, about to have their first child."

Beneath the mask Victoria felt the color drain from her face.

"Sean is rich enough, probably better than most around here. Maybe someone thinks he can get rich off the Galloway mine," he said, his temper rising, his voice harsh. "I don't know, it isn't a closed case, but I'll be—"

"Be damned if you'll let a woman help you?" He opened his mouth and she snapped, "Don't bother. I get the message."

She showed no outward signs of anger, slumping in the chair and drinking coffee as if waiting for the sun to rise. But Chris could feel it, a tight coil of every muscle in her body as if she were naked and not padded down like a mattress.

She met his gaze and quirked her lips wryly and Chris experienced a wave of resentment he couldn't charter away to reason. God, he was beginning to really loathe that disguise and wished she'd trust him. But before Vel showed, he hadn't been able to get a morsel out of her.

And after the conversation they'd just had, he didn't like what he was thinking. That maybe she was right? a voice pestered. *That maybe she's better at this than you.* The emasculating thought had his mind shifting on a another path and he considered she might work for Pinkerton, or the government.

Victoria glanced to the side, then returned her gaze to the horse walking down the street, leads dragging. Caesar. He paused, raised his head, obviously sensing Chris, then turned toward the veranda. For a moment Caesar stared, black eyes unblinking, then he snorted, nodding his head and nudging Chris's shoulder.

"No. It's mine."

Victoria looked to Chris. His expression benign, he ignored the horse.

The stallion nudged him again, so hard he nearly fell out of his chair.

"Dammit, Caesar." Resolutely, Chris slid his beer across the table, within Caesar's reach and Victoria watched in amazement as the animal opened his mouth wide around the mug, tipped his head back and drained the beer.

"Don't toss it!" Chris snatched the glass, plunking it down on the table. "Had enough?"

The horse burped loudly and Victoria laughed. Chris's gaze jerked to her, a flush creeping up his neck. But her laugh was a woman's laugh and dammit, he wanted to see *that* female.

Suddenly he stood, and she looked up as he tossed a few coins on the table.

"What's the matter now?"

"Be ready at sunrise. I'll take you to the Galloway place and we'll test your theory."

It sounded like a threat, a challenge.

"I'm not saying I'm right, Marshal, only that there are other possibilities."

"Oh, I'm open to possibilities, *Jake,* just not all of yours." He strode away and she watched his long legs eat up the floor.

"That was damn sexist," she said, stunned that he would say it. She looked at Caesar, his head hanging over the low porch wall and caught his bridle, bringing the smooth black face up to meet hers. "Didn't that sound like a sexist remark to you?"

Caesar snorted.

"Yeah, I thought so."

Nothing, absolutely nothing, got her ire up than to be treated as if she didn't have a few brain cells to rub together.

Chapter Nine

Christopher cut through the kitchen, not giving the startled employees a glance and headed straight for the back door. He stepped into the alley and drew a deep breath. The woman was going to drive him stark raving mad. He couldn't imagine trying to explain his feelings to her or himself. How could he gaze into those pale blue eyes knowing they were some fake glass over her own and still get aroused? She looked like a man, for Christ sake!

But he could *feel* her, the woman beneath, the strength and confidence. And though he couldn't pinpoint it, it was all he could imagine when he was near her—the woman from the forest—the wild mountain cat with a strange gun and a fleeting moment of vulnerability. He wanted desperately to catch her alone, without the disguise.

A sound drew his attention and he looked down the alley toward the street. Caesar stood in the entrance, his big body blocking the lamp light. The horse snorted, jerking his head.

"Yeah, I'm coming," Chris mumbled and strode to his animal. He didn't mount up, walking the two blocks back to his office to check in with Noble.

"Keep an eye on the Pearl. Sean's been there the past three nights, so it wouldn't surprise me if he is again."

Noble frowned over the edge of his newspaper. "Dinner that bad?"

Chris stilled in thumbing through the mail, not looking up. "No, it was fine."

"Jake seems like a nice kid."

"He is."

"Mebee we ought to take him on as a deputy?"

Only Chris's eyes shifted up. "No."

"Why not? It ain't like we couldn't use another—"

"Not that one."

"Somethin' about him bothering you?"

Yes, he thought, Jake's a woman with warm skin he wanted to taste and a lower lips so full and lush he could nibble on it all night. "I'll figure it out," he said cryptically and Noble smirked, shaking out his paper and focusing on the print.

"See you got a letter from Camille."

"You're a nosy son of a bitch."

"Yeah, and if I could spend ugly, I'd be a rich man, too."

Chris blinked, then chuckled shortly, shaking his head as he crossed to the pot bellied stove and flicked open the tiny door. He turned the envelope over in his hands.

"Ain't cha gonna read it?"

He responded by tossing the perfumed letter into the embers, then propped his rear against the edge of the desk, watching it catch and flare. The frying paper reminded him he shouldn't try to understand women nor trust them. Camille was proof that they said one thing and meant another. Except Victoria— she'd warned him to stay away, flat out told him to lose interest and get lost or he could get her killed. The latter was an exaggeration, he decided. But he ought to listen to the voice of reason. God knows he'd been burned enough already.

But she'd risked her life for a troubled boy she'd never met, had a husband and a child once, ticking off their deaths like a grocery list, but the quiver in her gruff voice made him believe she wasn't as tough as she claimed. Was she looking for their killers? Was that what drove her to such extreme measures? Hell, half the time he didn't know whether he was talking to a man or woman. Her viewpoints were far too objective for anyone with an ounce of emotion under that strange skin—not that he could see any of it well enough to gage.

Yet his own distrust clouded the possibilities she'd outlined at dinner. Sean Galloway was a good friend, an honest man who loved his wife and unborn baby. But even Chris remembered seeing Kelly talking intimately with Raif Dunkirk the week before she died. And Raif was Sean's best friend. But talking didn't make her an adulteress, and Chris was going to sadistically enjoy watching Victoria try to prove it. Or anything else. He wouldn't give her an inch. He'd already said too much. But as he left the office and mounted Caesar, a part of him hated her for being so damn capable.

Victoria rehashed their conversation over and over in her head, wondering if she's acted superior and finally deciding if she had, it was the hundred twenty five years separating their attitudes and approaches that did it. Yet it steamed her to no end that he couldn't see her point simply because she was a woman, but then, he didn't know she'd been second guessing perps for years. Deciding she needed to concentrate on her hunt and not bother with his, Victoria recklessly stepped into the Pearl, close to ten o'clock, where the pleasures of the 19th century were in full swing. Vel's girls were draped over the laps of cowboys and miners, smoke graying the light, and a piano player tapped out a lively tune she couldn't name. She walked in her best lazy saunter over to the bar, ordered a beer and hoped Vel didn't make a pass at her as she shifted to the far corner where the long marble top curved at the end. She braced her back against the wall. From her position, she had a perfect view of the entire saloon.

The Pearl had a regular crowd, she realized, the same customers as the first time she'd been inside, the same as she'd seen through her binoculars every night since. Ivy League didn't come out until late, gracing the underlings with his presence. His pattern of routine was confirming itself with each passing day. Sunday the saloon was closed and that would be her chance to see him in action and every moment she dreaded that he'd kill someone before she could get evidence on him.

She scanned the drunken crowd, recalling Vel's comments and drawing on her memory as her gaze lit on an exceptionally handsome man. She recognized him from the other night. Plunked in a corner, his long legs propped on the table, he rested a half empty bottle on his stomach. Sean Galloway? Dark reddish brown hair curled and tumbled over his eyes, intense green eyes, and even at this distance she could see his body was lithe and muscular beneath the chambray shirt and worn jeans. And he looked as if his world had come to an end. Regrets or remorse? One thing was for certain, Christopher Swift and Sean Galloway were friends and Chris didn't want anyone, especially her, defaming his friend's honor and raising suspicion.

Anymore than he wanted her help.

She turned back to her beer, groaning to herself when Velvet Knight headed in her direction.

Vel smiled, sliding against the bar toward Jake. Her gaze slid admiringly down over his body, to his cute rear, then back to his face. Spectacles rested on the end of his nose. So studious. "Feelin' lonely?"

"Lonely? Yes. But I got a girl back in Denver, Miz Knight." That ought to do it, Victoria thought.

Disappointed, Vel nodded. "I understand." She sighed forlornly. "Lucky gal."

"Should I be insulted that you gave up so easily?"

"Makin' you betray your woman ain't my style."

Jake arched a blonde brow.

"Even a whore has standards, honey."

Jake nodded, smiling slightly and pushing his spectacles up his short nose. "That Sean Galloway?" he asked, inclining his head to the corner.

She glanced and her expression saddened. "I think he's trying to drown himself to death."

"Him and everyone else." Jake nodded to the sandy haired man on the opposite side of the room, slunk in the chair, his head bowed and a drink cupped in his hands. Much like Sean. He glanced up only long enough to look at Sean, then focus of the liquor, shoulders hunched, long fingers gripping the glass.

Vel frowned, her gaze shifting between the two men. "That's strange."

"How so?"

"Sean and Raif are good friends." At least they were, Vel thought. "I'd have thought they'd cry in their beers together."

"Why you figure they're not?"

Vel shrugged, winking at a potential customer. "Maybe Raif's too torn up to console him."

"Did he have an itch for Kelly?"

Vel scowled at Jake, looking older, harder. "Not like you're implying." Jake's expression remained impassive, waiting for her to continue. "Raif only recently met her, about a month or two before she died." Jake's eyes flared and Vel warmed to the story. "See, Raif and Sean mined the *Dublin* together. Sean owned it and gave Raif half the profits for helping him out, then scaled it up. Raif left the territory for a couple years. In the meantime, Sean worked his ranch and married Kelly."

"And Raif?"

Vel signaled the bartender. He automatically poured her a flute of champagne and brought it to her. "He didn't have much luck with his place," she said after a delicate sip. "Flash flood or something. Sean comes from ranching stock, knew the business better, I guess." She stared into the mirror, her gaze on the reflection of Sean Galloway. She could feel his despair from across the saloon. "He'll never recover from this. Kelly was his life."

"Did you know her?"

"Everyone did. A pretty little blonde who could sew like a dream." Velvet smoothed her stays, remembering Kelly's meticulous work on the gown. "She was very kind, even to me."

Jake nudged her. "It's hard not to be, Vel."

Red Velvet Knight, the most sought-after harlot in the territory, actually blushed.

"But what I'd like to know is what happened to the twange in your accent?"

Vel blinked, then laughed to herself. "Shoot," she said, shaking her head, then draining the champagne. "Don't miss much do you, honey." Jake shook his head slowly. "Heck, I was even married once, you know." Vel didn't know why she was telling him a damn thing, but it just seemed easy. Sakes. A man who listened! "But the Apache wars killed him and the Indians burned everything we had. I had to resort to *other means* to feed my baby."

"Baby?" Jake said so softly that the ears around them wouldn't hear her business. The consideration warmed Vel's heart.

"I couldn't take care of her, not living like this." She flicked at hand to encompass the saloon. "It wasn't right for her to see her Momma servicing men who weren't her Pa. I had to give—" Vel bowed her head, her throat working furiously. Her heart broke every time she thought about her little girl.

"Gets lonely, doesn't it?" Jake covered her trembling hand, giving it a squeeze. "With no family."

Vel's painted lips curved. "You aren't supposed to be so smart for such a young man." The bartender refilled her glass and she was about to bring it to her lips when she frowned at the mirror. "Well, it looks like old friends are still friends," she said, then drank.

Victoria turned to see Raif, slim and tawny haired, cross the room to Sean. Galloway didn't look up, taking a swig of whiskey, ignoring him, ignoring the world. Then the blonde spoke, and Sean's head jerked up, his eyes narrowing to mere slits as he listened. But Becket entered the saloon from his offices just then, capturing her attention. Several men twisted in their seats to greet him, and Victoria's teeth set on edge as he offered his hand and that million dollar smile to his customers. He checked his appearance in the mirror with a discrete glance. How vain. Black suited him, she thought morosely, her gaze shifting over his clothes, the red brocade vest beneath the coat. Perfect. Clean. But she could feel the slime on him twenty clicks away. Doesn't matter how hard you scrub, she thought, the blood still drips from your hands.

Her gaze jerked to Galloway as he suddenly shot out of the chair, his fist connecting with Raif's face so hard he toppled back and hit the ground like a felled tree. The entire room was still for several seconds, every pair of eyes on Sean. But instead of taking his pound of flesh, he tossed a coin on the table and stepped over Raif, staggering out the bat wing doors. Raif stirred, moaning, rolling onto his side before pushing himself to his knees. He spat blood, tongued the inside of his jaw and then climbed to his feet, shoving off helping hands. Victoria tensed as Becket approached him, murmuring something she couldn't hear, then patting him on the shoulder. Raif nodded and left. Victoria didn't think he'd make it beyond the porch steps before he passed out in the dirt.

Becket shook his head and signaled the pianist to continue playing and the noise heightened almost instantly. Victoria turned back to her beer, taking a gulp and feeling Becket closing in behind Velvet.

"Everything all right, Miss Velvet?" he said grasping Vel's hand and bringing it to his lips for a kiss. Vel smiled at him and Victoria's stomach rolled. Couldn't she see the predator beneath all that refined crap?

"I thought we were going to have a whopper of a brawl there for a second."

Becket's blues eyes slid past Victoria as if she wasn't there to the door. "A tragedy," he murmured. "It's a shame they can't help each other." He sighed, then smiled at Vel. "How is Dee?"

"Feeling better, still tired."

"She has an appointment with Doctor MacLaren tomorrow. I trust you'll see she makes it?"

"Sure thing."

"I knew I could count on you." He pecked her cheek and ordered another glass of champagne for her. "Let me know the results and Vel?" He waited til she lifted her gaze to his. "Think about my offer."

"I will, Algenon. I will."

He left and Victoria let out her breath, glad to be rid of him. "Offer?"

Vel gave her a silencing look, then leaned close. "He wants me to come in as a partner. Imagine me, owning a place like this?"

"It'd be great, if you could." What was his motive for being so generous? Vel didn't fit the profile of his kills, so it wasn't to ingratiate himself. He was always around her, therefore deleting his chance to stalk. Or was he handing over the responsibility so he *could* stalk? Victoria hung around until he bid his customers good night and disappeared beyond the private doors. So punctual, she thought, glancing at the talk clock outside his door.

Saying good night to Vel, Victoria left the Pearl and headed down the boarded planks. Two men rushed past her with a shove, knocking her off the planks. But she let it pass, in no mood to bust heads tonight. Her bed was calling for her. She could almost feel the cool clean sheets against her bare skin and quickened her pace. A groan, long and pained drew her to a stop. She frowned, waiting for it to come again, then followed the noise, crossing the street to the livery stable. Inching along the narrow alley way separating the barn from the small horse pen, Victoria squinted in the dark. She could scarcely make out a figure, crumpled against the wall, but she recognized the shape of a gun.

The sliver gleam of nickle plate gave it substance in the dark as a broad hand brought it upward and for an instant Victoria thought she'd be the target, til the clouds blocking the moonlight shifted. She heard the click of the hammer drawing back and saw the long barrel he pressed against his temple.

She lunged. *"No!"*

Chapter Ten

This ranked up there with the time he and Hunter McCracken charged a rebel patrol with only eight bullets between them.

Dumb, motivated by emotion.

And Chris spent half the night cursing himself for allowing his own to get to him, enough to challenge her sharp mind and take her to Sean's ranch. She had no business sticking her nose in an investigation, even if she did have some valid points. And as Chris covered a yawn and rolled his shoulders, he watched her inspect the area where Kelly Galloway died. Though there wasn't much to inspect except broken wood and gutted earth.

Yet down on one knee in the mud, she poked the earth with a pencil she'd swiped off his desk at dawn this morning. The cattle pen a few yards before her was empty, the gate and fence rails shattered like twigs, unable to halt a thousand tons of angry beef.

Carefully, she straightened, something dangling from the pencil's tip.

Chris frowned.

"A piece of her nightgown, I guess."

She dropped it into a small sack and Chris wondered why the hell she was keeping the bloody scrap. She checked her watch, then made a wide birth to the barn, kicking at the splintered gate. She picked up a short plank, examining the end, using the pencil to pry and prod for a few moments before leaning the wood against the barn wall.

"No one's been in here since?"

Chris shook his head, scowling. What could she possibly find that he didn't? "We couldn't even get her from Sean to bury her. He'd picked her up and carried her into the house, then locked himself in. When we he finally let us in, she was prepared as best he could." Chris stared at his boots, remembering her lovely face crushed, her horribly mangled body even the fresh dress couldn't hide. "The ranch hands have been off looking for the steers since."

"When did this occur?"

He met her gaze. "Two days before I locked Vic Mason up."

No wonder he was so hot on her trail, she thought, glancing back at the deeply trampled ground.

A shot rang through the morning air and instinctively Victoria ducked behind the open barn door. Chris hadn't moved, but now he strode toward the house. Sean Galloway stood on the porch, his legs braced wide and a rifle cradled in his arms like the baby he'd lost.

"Get off my land, Marshal."

Chris put up his hands. "Take it easy Sean. We, or rather Jake," he inclined his head to Victoria, "thinks he knows what happened to Kelly."

Victoria caught the doubt in his voice and it made her more determined as she moved around the wood door. Sean's gaze narrowed on her and she felt ripped in half by the sorrow and resolution in his eyes. She prayed she was right about this. This man didn't need anymore pain.

He left the porch, walking toward Chris, pausing to speak briefly to him, then continuing on his way. He stopped a few feet from her, his hard gaze raking over her like beef at an auction.

"Where's your dog?" Chris had said he had one.

"Buried with Kelly."

Just to say it caused him pain, she thought, then pushed aside her sympathy to business. She'd already marked off the trek from the house to the privy to this area. It took Kelly no more than three minutes total, she decided, a theory gelling in her head. "Now correct me if something sounds out of place to you."

Sean shouldered the rifle, his hand on his hip and Victoria was certain she had his full attention.

"Kelly got up to use the facilities and let the dog out. But when her pet—"

"—Atticus."

She acknowledged the correction. "When Atticus didn't answer her call, she went to look for him." She shrugged. "Nothing unusual there. This was her home, why should she be afraid?" She glanced at the barn, then to Sean. "Marshal Swift said you heard a howl?"

Sean nodded, his gaze piercing her like a branding iron.

"Could it have been your dog and not a wolf?"

Sean arched a russet brow, considering her more closely. It made her sweat beneath the mask and padding. His green eyes were bloodshot and his handsome face hadn't seen a razor in days, but he was still a powerful presence.

"It's possible," he finally said. "I got out here just as the herd bolted. Sounded like squealing thunder. I had no idea what happen until—" He took a breath, deep and slow and for an instant broke his gaze. "Atticus was beside Kelly when I found her." She could see detachment in his eyes, a closed hardness that would either help him get through this, she thought, or destroy him.

"I think she heard it, came to investigate, certain you'd follow. But she wasn't alone." She squatted and pointed to the foot prints near the barn and gate. "See. These are square toed." She gestured to the ground close to the fence. "Then there's her prints, just a couple, but enough to know she walked along the fence line before stepping out into full view.'' She indicated the area where the body had been discovered. ''I found only one of Atticus's, over by the gate.'' She glanced up to see Sean and Chris leaning over, gazes combing the area. ''Your boots are pointed, the marshal's, too. Mine rounded.'' She straightened and moved to the barn, picking up the plank. ''Atticus likely snooped out whoever was here and he killed the dog with this,'' she hefted the two-by-four, ''to shut him up. That was the howl.''

''How do you know that for sure?'' Chris snapped and she frowned at him. Why was he trying to shoot her out of the water?

''Atticus was white and brown, a long hair?'' she said to Sean.

''A collie.'' A fracture of awe in his deep voice.

''Blood and hair are caught deep in the splinters. The rest,'' she waved to what was left of the gate and fence, ''are broken from the cattle stampede, except this one.'' She tossed the club to Chris and he caught it, peering at the bloody tip. ''It's not the same wood, probably picked up when the perp realized the dog might be out.''

Sean's brow furrowed deeply and he glanced at Chris.

''Perpetrator. The criminal,'' he interpreted before Sean returned his gaze to Victoria.

''While looking for Atticus, Kelly must have seen them opening the gate. She caught someone in the act of releasing your assets and was shocked, so shocked that she was immobile, but by the time she regained her senses, the gate was swinging open and the cattle moving. I think she was trapped between the gate and the fence and called out to the intruder, which brought you out of the house. But when the perp realized she was there, in the path of steers, he tried to get to her. By then the herd was wild enough to storm the fence. It was hopeless.''

Sean mashed a hand over his face, then speared his fingers through his hair. His sorrow was palitable.

"I'm sorry, Mister Galloway. From what I've heard, Kelly was well loved."

He nodded gravely. "But why was she so stunned? Kelly had backbone," he said, then looked at Chris. "You know that. There wasn't much that scared her, besides snakes."

Chris looked at Victoria, his dark scowl implying that she'd better have satisfactory explanation for dragging his friend through this.

"*Who* was trying to destroy your business was what shocked her, Mister Galloway. Because it was a friend."

"Raif," Sean hissed, gripping the rifle.

"I found him last night, after you punched him in the bar. He was in the alley, beat to near death, but he didn't get there on his own." She met Chris's gaze and could tell he was pissed she hadn't come to him with this earlier. "Two men bumped into me last night, real hot to get lost. I think they did him, just then." Her eyes shifted back to Sean. "Maybe looking to blame you, since damn near everyone saw you hit him and you left the Pearl at the same time. When I got to him he was putting the gun to his head."

Sean took a step. "Is he dead?"

She shook her head. "I left him with Vel."

He sighed, relieved she thought, and Victoria hoped, for Sean's sake, he could get past his pain.

"Why would he do this to me?"

"He owes money."

"Christ, Raif knows I would have given him my last nickle!"

"His pride wouldn't let him, I guess. You'd already given him part of the *Dublin*'s silver."

"He earned every ounce of that!"

"Maybe, but he told me he owed the Flat Pick for equipment. When you wouldn't sell the mine, I think they used him to get to you. Losing all the cattle, you'd have to sell the *Dublin* to stay afloat. Kelly just got caught in the middle."

"What proof do you have?" Chris said. She couldn't decipher his withering stare.

"Beyond footprints and Raif's mumbling? Or this?" She

lashed a hand to the prints and the bloody club. "None. Raif said he didn't mean for her to get hurt." Her raspy voice lowered to a whisper. "So much that he wanted to die."

Sean stood there, tense as barbed wire, his finger flexing on the rifle's trigger. He wanted to kill Raif. She recognized the look before—in herself—once. "He's tied up and going nowhere, Mister Galloway."

"Good," he growled, lifting his gaze to hers. "He'll be an easy target."

"No!"

He scowled and she realized she'd lost her masculine voice, but Sean strode past them to the barn.

She turned to Chris. "It was an accident. Raif was black-mailed. Stop him!" she shouted when he simply stood there.

"He won't kill him, _Jake._"

Suddenly she was up in his face. "Don't you see? If I hadn't bumped into those two guys, if Raif had pulled that trigger, Sean would be in jail for his murder. They were setting him up to cover their tracks!"

"I'm aware of that." A dull red crept up his neck, his lips a tight line.

"But what if I'm wrong?"

"You're not and you know it."

She shook her head wildly. "We have to check his boots, his alibi for that night, question him. It's not iron clad! We have—"

"_We_ don't have to do a thing," he bit off, then brushed past her to the barn where Sean was saddling a horse. He grabbed Sean by the shoulder and spun him around, his fist connecting with his jaw. Sean went down hard.

"What the hell did you do that for?"

He stood near his friend, feeling Victoria move up behind him. "Saves me from shooting him. No! Leave him there," he said when she bent to shake him. "When he wakes, it will give him time to think clearly, and I can get Raif behind bars."

"What about the creeps at the Flat Pick?"

"Don't question how I do my job, Vic—'' He dragged his gaze from his fallen friend to her. *"—Jake."*

Bitter anger laced the single word, the name, her other personality. He hated it, and was despising her for it, too, she realized. He tied Sean's hands to give himself more time, then mounted his horse, not bothering to wait for her. Men, she decided, were pride-packed, hard-headed chauvinists who needed to get in touch with their feminine sides. If they did, women wouldn't feel rotten every time they used their brains.

She'd ridden back at a much slower pace, almost dreading seeing Christopher again and made certain there was at least an hour separating them. God, he looked ready to chew her butt off and she didn't doubt whatever he was holding back was in that knock-out punch he delivered to Sean's tender jaw. He hated her disguise and her secrets—and yes, mostly his pride was in tatters because she'd figured out *a* method of the crime before him. Well, too bad. She had one hundred twenty five years of experience on him and wasn't about to make excuses for who she was.

If he couldn't handle it, then tough. She had a job to do anyway, and was doing him a favor besides.

He'll never see it that way. He's 19th century, you're 20th.

Hardly matters. She wasn't sticking around to find out otherwise. Reining up before the marshal's office, Victoria slid tiredly from the saddle, slapped the reins over the rail and stepped into the coolness of the office just as Noble slammed a cell door shut. He turned, grinning when he saw her.

"Damn good investigatin', Jake." He crossed the room and pumped her gloved hand as if it would give water.

"It all sort of fell in my lap, Mister Beecham," she said and beyond him saw Raif, his adjoining cell occupied by two members of the let's-pulverize-the-locals gang. Victoria didn't want to be around when Sean showed up.

"Well, with Raif in custody, didn't take much arm twistin' to get the truth outa Pike and Deek."

Owners of the Flat Pick, she wondered, recognizing one as the man who'd plowed into her last night.

"All we have to do is round up their boss," Beecham added, glancing between the marshal and Jake.

Her gaze shifted to Raif and he met her stare accusingly, as if keeping him from killing himself was a crime of nature. "I was right, with all of it?" she said, cocking a look over her shoulder at the marshal.

"Hell yeah," Noble said before Chris could respond.

Feeling uncomfortable with Chris's dispassionate glare carving holes in her back, Victoria adjusted her hat and headed to the door. "Got a job to do," she muttered and grasped the knob. The door flung open, a young woman about twenty-five rushing in. She halted abruptly and remembering she was clad as Jake, Victoria stepped back, allowing her to proceed. The woman flashed her the brightest smile, sweeping inside with an elegance that defied logic. Victoria envied that every man around leapt to their feet, including prisoners, at the sight of her. She waved them back down and addressed the marshal and Victoria folded her arms over her chest, leaning back against the door to watch and listen.

"So sorry to disturb you, Christopher." British, Victoria thought, trying not to envy the woman's gown. Girl clothes.

Chris expression drooped. "Tell me it didn't happen again?"

"Afraid so. I'd hired a man to keep watch, since Reid is out of town. But the poor dear ended up getting beaned on the head."

"What was stolen this time?"

She fished in her reticule and pulled out a slip of paper. "Laudanum, poppy extract and mesquite, enough for several doses in stoppered dark glass bottles."

"Somebody's either dying or havin' one hell of a good time," Noble said from his seat and Victoria realized this woman was a physician. She was impressed, considering the year.

"Excuse me, doctor?"

Jenna MacLaren turned toward the man near the door. "Yes?"

"Jake Farrell, ma'am." Victoria touched the brim of her hat. "I was wondering what all these drugs would do?"

"Why make one oblivious, I'm afraid. I use them only for severe pain and of course, during surgery."

"All anesthetics?"

Jenna nodded.

"What else was taken?" Victoria could feel Chris's butt-out glare as if he'd jabbed her with his elbow.

"Some very expensive laboratory equipment."

"And before?"

"They hadn't the chance. I came in upon them and scared them off."

"Doc Jenna's dang accurate with a knife, Jake."

Doctor MacLaren flashed Noble a brief smile, a blush stealing into her cheeks and Victoria wished she still had the innocence to do that.

"If someone were to use these drugs, what's the manner and effect?" Victoria could feel her century creeping up on her.

"Well, assuming it's the same person, they'd likely distill the ingredients and either dry them to a power or inject them directly into the vein."

"Jeez-zoo! Who'd want to get stuck with a needle ifin' they didn't have to."

"An addict," Victoria and the doctor said at the same time. Poppy was opium, Victoria remembered, the base of heroin and morphine. And deadly in unrefined doses. Great. Users and losers here, too.

A memory surfaced and she focused on Christopher. "Clara Murphy, over at the hotel—" He smirked nastily but she went on "—said one of the guests last week was a tall thin man, who kept pinching his nose, snifflin'. She found some stuff like the Doc mentioned. Empty vials, spoons with a residue."

"The distilling!" Jenna gasped, glancing at the marshal.

"He also left the room in a wreck. Like he'd been oblivious

to anything for days. The servant, a young boy 'bout twelve can describe him.''

"Do you think he's still there?'' Jenna asked anxiously, her gaze slipping between the man and the marshal.

"If he broke into your place last night, he ought to be close, or even passed out somewhere, enjoying your opium,'' Chris said. "I'll post a deputy in your area again, Jenna. When is Reid due back?''

She smiled that light-up-the-room smile. "Any minute now.''

"Well, that makes me feel a little better about leaving you alone.''

"Oh, for pity's sake, Christopher! I can very well take care of myself. It's the drugs in the wrong hands that has me worried.''

"Yeah, well, it's what Reid will do to me if you get hurt, that has me worried.''

She laughed, a soft delicate sound that made the men smile, but Victoria stiffened when Jenna rose up on tip toe to peck a kiss to Chris's cheek. Jenna murmured something to Chris in a language Victoria had never heard before and he responded in kind. It made her jealous. The doc could speak Cheyenne.

Pressing the list into Chris's hand, Jenna crossed to the cells and questioned Raif about his injuries. She looked at Chris.

"Have this man in my office today, Christopher. He needs medical attention.''

"You know I will,'' he replied.

She headed to the door, acknowledging the men standing for her departure. Jake opened the door for her.

"Thank you, Mister Farrell. You've been most helpful.''

Victoria nodded as any *man* would to a lovely woman and Jenna swept out the door. She watched her, wondering how she could walk with such dignity in all that hardware and wishing she had an ounce of the doctor's femininity. Yet she lost every bit of it when a man astride a gorgeous Palomino skidded to a hard stop in the street and slipped from the saddle. With a happy squeal, Jenna ran to him, launching into his arms and kissing him soundly. He was a giant, honey blonde hair and shoulders big enough to block out the sun, but it was the long braid, reaching nearly to his waist that surprised her. And intrigued her.

"Well. Looks like ol' Jake's been more help than hurt, marshal. Solved two crimes in one day."

"Yes," came in a steely tone. "Congratulations, Jake."

Bet it killed him to say that, she thought, tipping her hat before shoving the spectacles up her nose. "Just tryin' to help." She smiled at Noble, scratched her arm, then left and was half way across the street when the marshal called out to her.

Victoria stopped to face him.

"Are you real pleased with yourself?"

"Excuse me?" She didn't like his tone. "Oh, I get it. You can't handle that I figured out who killed Kelly before you. Or that I happen to be working in the hotel when a drug addict puked all over one of the rooms I had to clean."

"What kind of person knows about murderers, hair and blood remains and how opium addicts make their drugs?"

"An informed person."

"Not good enough."

"Too bad." She turned away, taking several steps before he caught her arm and wrenched her around. "Unless you want your nuts kicked up to your throat, Marshal Swift, let go."

His features pulled taut. "Is there anything you can't do better than a man?" He leaned closer and spoke in a malicious voice thick with revulsion. "Christ—" his dark gaze scraped over her body and she felt her skin ripple beneath her disguise "—is there even a *woman* in there?"

Victoria went still. Deathly still and Chris thought he held onto a statue instead of human tissue. Her features slackened, icy-blue eyes clouding with a pain so deep and vivid he felt it slam into him, gouge him in places he swore were too hard to penetrate.

Oh Jesus.

Then she wrenched free. "Apparently not."

Chapter Eleven

He might as well have slapped her. It stung that hard, bit that closely and she lowered her gaze, a lump swelling in her throat and threatening to choke her. She wasn't woman enough. Wasn't anything. It wasn't her choice, it just happened. And she let it go on and on until she couldn't blame him for feeling like a jilted bridegroom. She'd left him standing before his friends and took off with the prize. But it didn't change the fact that he was once remotely attracted before and obviously, wasn't anymore. She knew she shouldn't get so involved. And though she'd no one to blame for destroying their friendship but herself, the loss of it, of having grasped the silken edge of some small pleasure and have it ripped away, left her achingly hollow—without a place to fall.

Her head down, Victoria bit her lip, holding back the tears threatening to spill. She turned away. He didn't call her back. And the tiny fracture in her heart split a little wider. Victoria didn't think she could still feel pain any more, not after her life had been ripped apart five years ago. But she was wrong.

God, was she wrong.

Striding briskly to the back of the barn, she started to open a wood storage box, then fell back against the barn wall, sniffling, closing her eyes and forcing the tears back. *Damn him*, she cursed, then rolled around and tugged open the lid, pulling out the satchel concealing her back pack, then heading to the outhouse to change her disguise. It was difficult in the cramped smelly cubicle and perspiration ran in rivulets between her breasts by the time she slipped into her room at the hotel to afix more spirit gum on the seams and pockets of her pudgy mask. She thanked Alexandria again and again for making the things strong enough that she could re-use them so often, but her skin showed signs of irritation. She'd have to give her complexion a rest soon, though it wasn't in her plans just now. Her skirt was sadly wrinkled, but she covered it with a fresh apron from the hotel's supply, then stored her pack in her bleak little room, wishing she could climb into bed and forget about Christopher Swift and his devastating words.

So she concentrated on Ivy League.

And with him seeking a partner for his business, she knew he was up to something nasty.

At least maybe Chris would back off now. He saw her for what she was. Too rough to want, too smart for his century. It's all for the best, she consoled with a residual shudder. She wasn't here to find relationships and make friends. She was here to hunt.

And take *her* prey back home.

He was a jack-ass.

The instant she strode away he knew he'd been acting like prime mule stock since dinner yesterday. But it irritated him to no end to look at her and know there was a woman beneath. A woman, who, for some reason, like hiding behind a mask. God, she never slipped, even when the doc showed up. She never cared what he thought. And she made him feel vastly incapable.

Was that really it? Was that the reason he felt so danged useless around her? He'd admired it at first, when he saw her in the woods, when she risked her life to save Lucky, but why did it set his teeth to grinding now?

Combing his finger through his hair, Chris adjusted his hat and sighed. Pig-headed jack-ass. Victoria was a woman, no matter what she looked like on the outside, and he'd been cruel and mean and waited arrogantly by for her to fall on her adorable rump so he could pick her up, hold her, kiss her, and maybe feel like she needed someone.

You?

After that? He'd be lucky if she didn't fill him full of bullet holes. Turning back to the office, he flung open the door and moved to his desk, dropping into his chair. Noble had moved the prisoners into the rear cells and Chris was grateful for the solitude. He didn't like the way he was feeling right now.

"What'd you say to that young fella?" Noble accused.

"Now who sounds like he's mothering the strays?" Chris snapped without looking up from the stack of files.

"He's a good kid, and you ain't got no cause to be angry over what he done."

Chris's jaw tightened. His guilt was heavy enough as it was. "Go get some breakfast and sleep, Noble." His tone dismissed, and Noble cast him a half-lidded stare, tossing the keys and not bothering to see if they hooked the peg.

"Don't forget to take Raif to see the doc, this afternoon."

Chris glanced up, his scowl still firmly in place.

"Her husband's home. Give 'em some time."

Husband. Wife.

Just the thought of the happiness Reid and Jenna MacLaren were experiencing soured Chris's mood even further. How could he keep blaming women for their fickledness when he'd managed to destroy two relationships in one year.

Chris stood outside the hotel room, the heavy scent of lye and the sound of scrubbing drawing him further inside. She was on her knees in a cloud of dingy brown skirts, her hand circling over the same area so hard she was going to wear the wood into a gulley.

He cleared his throat.

"Yes?" She kept scrubbing, not looking up.

"Victoria."

She stilled for a moment. "Go away, Marshal. I'm busy." Her brush scoured.

"We need to talk."

"You said quite enough the other day."

He winced, dragging his hat from his head. "I wanted to apolo—"

"Don't!" She scrambled to her feet, tossing the bristle brush into the bucket. Water splashed the floor as she faced him. "Don't say what you *don't mean* just because you think my feelings are hurt. Well, they aren't. I've been called a lot worse by people who know me a hell of a lot better. I know what I am *exactly,* and I don't give a crap what you or anyone else thinks. I have a job to do and nothing more. Get that? *Nothing more.*"

Her tone set an axe to the words, severing anything they might have shared. And Chris hated that she could be so controlled about this. Damn if he was.

"What's the job that threatens your life and keeps you looking like that?" He gestured to the wet drooping skirts and theatrical face.

She stared at him, hurting to look into his sympathetic eyes and for a split second thought of fending off her accidental slip by referring to this job, then decided the best way to get him gone was to disgust him into leaving.

"I'm a bounty hunter, Marshal." She let that sink in before she added, "And it comes as natural as breathing."

She wasn't the student, he realized, but the professor. Yet there was more to it, to her background, and he didn't bother asking who she hunted. She'd never tell him, anyway. There were thousands of criminals out there with a price on their heads. But that she'd stoop to taking cash for dead outlaws speared through his gut like a belly full of rancid meat. He never imagined she'd be like that, deep down, but he'd just scratched the surface of who Victoria Mason really was. And if the past two days were any indication, she wouldn't let him get any further. He supposed he deserved it. No, he *knew* he deserved it, and as she grabbed the mop leaning against the dresser and swabbed the floor, he saw her in a different light, her movements in the past days panning out to explain themselves. Almost. She rung the string mop out in the bucket, her hands red and rough and strong as she twisted. She ignored him, and he felt the valley between them widen.

A bounty hunter.

He should have known.

Victoria peered at the posted advertisements, searching the want ads. She had one more mask to alter her appearance and she was determined to get a suitable job and vanish. Chris wouldn't back off as she'd hoped, showing up every day, sometimes twice, trying to talk. She didn't see the point. Her leaving was inevitable, and he'd live out his life with some rancher's daughter and have kids and a home while she returned to her century and watched Ivy League be injected with a lethal dose of drugs. She preferred seeing him hang for his murders, like they did in this century, or a firing squad, but since that wasn't possible, she'd settle for cyanide burning through his veins.

She rubbed her temple, the heat and the heavy latex making her feel as if she were suffocating. Her head throbbed, and she knew the combination with so little sleep since she'd arrived left her open to mistakes she couldn't afford.

An ad snagged her attention, and her brows shot up at the location, yet before she could read the qualifications she experienced the sensation of being watched. She cast a glance about her, her heart sliding down to her heels when she saw Chris. She felt trapped in his gaze, unreasonably vulnerable to his silent plea. *I could pick him out of crowd anywhere,* she thought and spun away, moving down the walk, his hasty pursuit bringing attention. The knock of his boot heels against wood drove into her like a mallet and she quickly slipped into the hotel, immediately hustling to the back. His heavy determined steps muffled on carpet, scraped on wood, then came to an abrupt halt. Yet she didn't look up, couldn't, as she donned her apron and took up fresh linens.

Coward.

Yet she could feel him behind her, the breeze from the open supply room door bringing the scent of his cologne straight to her head. Closing her eyes, she gripped the folded cloth, holding onto the pain of his insults and praying he'd leave her alone so she wouldn't feel anything for him. Ever again. Then the sensation vanished and she glanced back to find the doorway empty. But somehow she wasn't as relieved as she'd hoped.

"Angus needs to get his reports in sooner, and for Christ sake, teach the man to write legibly!"

"Yessir!" Noble's biting reply was lost on the marshal as the man hovered over paperwork, his elbow braced on the desk, fingers rubbing his temple as he scribble. He tossed the paper into a stack and snatched up another.

"Did Seth get back from the territorial prison yet?"

"Do you see him standing in here?"

"Just answer the question, Noble," Chris snarled. "And what the hell is taking him so long?"

"I 'spect he wanted to sleep or take a piss somewhere's between there and here."

Chris snorted. "Not until this case is closed does anybody rest."

The door opened and a young man about twenty-five stepped in. "You're late for your shift. Go relieve Tomas before the man dies of hunger."

The deputy backed out of the office so fast he stumbled.

Noble made a sound of disgust. "I'm 'bout sick 'a you barking at me and everyone else around here!"

Chris's head jerked up, his dark eyes narrowing to mere slits.

Noble brushed the silent warning aside and spoke his mind.

"I don't know what the hell's got you so snippy, but you're gonna find yourself without a staff dang soon. Either go get yourself laid or shut the hell up!"

Only Noble could speak to him like that and still keep his teeth, he thought. For about two seconds, Chris considered riding over to Angela's, then dismissed it. It wasn't Angela he wanted. But Victoria wouldn't give him the time of day. Hell, she wouldn't even look at him.

"Go home, Chris," came in a friendlier tone.

Chris rubbed his hands over his face, then shoved back the hair falling over his eyes.

"When's the last time you slept good?"

Before I met her, Chris thought. Tossing the pencil on the desk, he leaned back in the leather chair, the springs creaking as he laced his fingers and tucked them behind his head.

"That long, huh?"

"Yeah." He flexed his shoulders and glanced around. "This place looks like a bunk house."

"I got someone coming to clean it, so go home and pester Abigale."

Chris lowered his arms, rubbing his hand over his stomach as it growled with hunger. Maybe that's what he needed. The solitude of his house and Abigale's cooking.

Leaving the chair and snatching his hat off the peg, Chris headed for the door, his mouth watering at the thought of Abby's Thursday night apple cobbler. A soft rap rattled the door and he waved off Noble, pushing it open.

Chris swallowed. Victoria stood there. Or rather Clara, dowdy and scarred and immediately dropping her gaze to the floor.

Chris clenched his fists, itching to say something to her, itching to rip the mask and wig off, and she finally lifted her gaze, pounding him into jerky with her withering stare. There was hurt in her eyes that even the strange glass couldn't hide and he felt like an even bigger cad.

Noble frowned, his gaze dancing between the two. He squinted at Clara as Chris stepped back and allowed her to enter. Their bodies brushed and she inhaled, but Chris didn't move, wedged in the doorway with her.

"Excuse me," she muttered and forced her way past.

Chris nodded to Noble, who was staring at Victoria with the strangest smile on his face, then left.

Victoria lifted her gaze and smiled with the appropriate amount of shyness. Noble was an intimidating man, rough but with a gentle humor wrinkling around his eyes.

"What would you like me to do, Mister Beecham?"

"Just make this place look like men ain't the only ones comin' through here." She nodded. "And call me Noble. Ain't never had enough stiff in my starch for Mister," he said as he returned to his desk, rummaging through a stack of papers—messages to the circuit judge, official warrants and the lawyers writ after the marshal closed down the Flat Pick and their lawyer seized all files. But they forgot one thing—the marshal was a trial lawyer, too. And a danged lonely one, Noble thought as Clara swept around him, collected trash, washed out the cells and even left flowers floating in a cracked bowl of water on the stove.

"It will get rid of the staleness in here," she said when he asked and he nodded approvingly.

Pushing her spectacles up her nose, she scratched the inside of her arm and looked for a chore undone. Noble's features suddenly pulled taut, his gaze raking her as she completed her dusting. He watched a moment longer, then with an agility that startled her, he left his chair and went to the stove, pouring a cup of coffee. "Set a spell, girl, you look exhausted."

Victoria groaned, gratefully taking the coffee and chair he offered. "Thank you, Noble," she said with feeling. "I am a bit . . . fatigued."

"I 'spect so."

"How's that?" She blew on the liquid before taking a sip.

"I mean with you tryin' to be Vic Mason, Jake Farrell and Clara Murphy all in one week."

Victoria sputtered, then quickly caught the drip of coffee trickling down the side of her mouth.

"Why whatever do you mean?" She hoped she sounded like an indignant spinster.

He leaned closer, grinning a huge self-satisfied smile and she noticed he had a gold tooth. His eyes slipped over her before he caught her wrist, examining the watch. Victoria wrestled her arm free.

Noble sat back, sucked his teeth and studied her. "I don't know how you do it, but I know it's you, *Jake.*"

"I beg your pardon?"

He chuckled, a rumble of warm thunder, his barrel chest shaking like Santa on Christmas. "Aside the specs and the way you scratch yer arm now and then—"

Her Norplant, she realized.

"The height and walk did it. I didn't outlive three wives not to be able to spot a woman tryin' to pass as a man, darlin'."

"Three wives?"

He folded his hands on the desk. "Ah-uh." He shook his head. "You ain't goin' nowhere, nor are you changin' the subject."

Victoria felt cornered by a bear and stared unblinking into his eyes. But when his moustached mouth spilt into a wide grin, she gave up and sighed, resolute.

There was always one in the crowd she couldn't fool. No matter how hard she tried. She'd been so intent on Ivy League and avoiding Chris, that she forgot about the watch, the spectacles. God, the history she was screwing with, being here, was unimaginable.

"He knows, huh?"

She nodded, setting the cup on the desk.

"He don't like it much, neither."

That's putting it lightly. "No. Now ask me if I care?"

He chuckled. "Don't 'spect so, since no one's seen you as anything but," he waved at her face, "this."

She leaned forward. "Can I trust you to keep this to yourself?"

This means a lot to her, he realized. "If'n you tell me why?"

She groaned, sinking into the chair. Here I go again. She

could have said she was a method actress, researching a role, but she didn't take Noble Beecham to be as dumb as he was big.

She told him. He didn't bat an eyelash.

But Noble understood why the marshal was in such a sour mood. Imagine a danged bounty hunter, a woman hunter, solving a crime, tying it up in a neat little bow before Chris could get his feet wet. But that twanged his strings a bit. "Now you got me *real* curious, little lady, as to what you look like under all that muck."

"Nothing special, Mister Beecham," she said dispiritedly, looking at her lap. "Trust me."

If it wasn't special, Noble thought, then Christopher Swift wouldn't be tearing his hair out over you.

Chapter Twelve

The kid gave her a do-you-really-think-that's-going-to-help look as his gaze swept her cream-covered face. She smiled benignly, touched her towel-wrapped head and stood by the door, half shielded by the wood as he dragged the copper tub from her darkened room, the metered scraping drowning out his mutterings. Teenagers, Victoria thought, pressing a coin into his hand before shutting the door. She leaned back against the wood, smiling, massaging the alpha-hydrox cream into her abused skin. She didn't doubt she'd scared the pants off him when she'd answered his summons, but the dimly lit room and thick cream were necessary to hide her lack of disguise.

She needed this break, and as she crossed the room to the commode, she stripped off the heavy robe, flinging it on the bed. It felt good to be clean and free again. And wearing a man's chambray shirt, the only clean one she had left and costing a whopping thirty cents, she peered into the small mirror, wiping away the cream before dragging the towel from her head. Her hair was still damp and she toweled it dry, then snatched up her brush and let the cool evening breeze coming through the window do the rest. Bent over at the waist, she brushed, pausing to stretch her tired muscles.

I haven't work this hard since boot camp.

Cleaning ten rooms of the hotel and just as many stalls in the livery had taxed every unused portion of her body.

Then it took her over an hour to bathe, wash her hair, rinse, discard the water, the tub, and she wondered how any woman managed to get a damn thing done in this century. She glanced at the door, her Clara/Jake clothes hanging on a pair of hooks to dry. She was beginning to hate the false identities and couldn't use them much longer; the masks could be removed only so many times before they lost their resilience.

You're lying to yourself, she thought, straightening, dropping her head back and dragging the brush through her hair. It was because of Christopher.

Pain streaked through her chest at the thought of him, his snarling words and, oh God, the despising look in his eyes. She swallowed repeatedly, fighting the boiling swells of loneliness. Then, suddenly, she turned toward the tall dresser, tossing the brush onto the scarred surface and resting her elbows there. She cradled her head in her hands, fingers sinking into her hair. Her eyes burned. Her throat tightened with misery. Rejection shouldn't hurt this much. She didn't want it to.

But it does.

And she hated him for making her feel . . . ugly.

A sob caught in her throat and she swallowed it back. Crying was for babies and spineless wimps. Blinking rapidly, she sniffled, raked her hair back and damned herself for allowing everything about that man to pierce her hide like his razor sharp arrows. It wouldn't be so bad if she didn't like him so much, respect the man he was. A chill rippled over her bare skin beneath the simple work shirt and she slapped her hand over her gun and spun about, arms outstretched, finger hooking the trigger.

"I was wondering when those keen senses were going to notice me."

Every muscle in Victoria's body clenched. She could see the

outline of a figure, a man, a man she'd recognize in her sleep, tucked lazily against the dark corner beyond the bed, arms folded, shoulder braced on the wall as if he'd all the time in the world.

"Move." She indicated to the right with a flick of the silver barrel and Chris pushed away from the wall, emerging out of the shadows and rounding the foot of the bed. His gaze shifted to the long naked legs exposed beneath the shirt, to the small gun she pointed at his heart, then to her incredible face. Something hot struck him square in the chest at the sight of her eyes, *her eyes,* gold and black, piercing, and red from tears.

I've done this to her, he thought.

"You going to shoot me?"

"Don't tempt me." God, he looked sexy—the pig. "I thought I made myself clear."

"Call me hard-headed."

She snorted indelicately. "Get out, Chris." It was the first time she'd said his name and she spat it like a curse.

"No." His gaze never left hers as he advanced, slowly.

"I'll shoot."

"No," he growled softly. "You won't."

"You sure?" She flipped the safety off.

"Yes." Her hands were shaking. And when he stopped before her, the cool barrel pressed to his chest, she still didn't move, and he swore she wasn't breathing.

"Go away, Chris. Please." Her voice broke and she hated it. "There's no point in this."

"There is. And you know it."

He stared.

She stared back.

His expression softened.

And she hardened herself against the beauty of it.

"Victoria."

The heat, the determination in his dark eyes, seared and simmered through her. No man ever spoke her name like he did. As if he could taste her on his tongue, his lips.

Victoria pointed the gun to the ceiling, flipped the safety and tossed it on the dresser. It spun for a second, toppling a plastic bottle, then stilled, yet Chris never took his eyes off her, drinking in the simple act of seeing her without mask and paint.

"You have the most incredible eyes."

"Go to hell."

A raven black brow arched.

"Don't try for flattery, Marshal. I've been on the receiving end of about all I can take."

"Victoria. I'm sorry."

The sincerity in his tone nearly broke her. Nearly. She looked away, staring at nothing, a cascade of honey dark hair partially shielding her face. "Fine. Good. Now go."

He took a step, and she retreated, scowling like a wary cat about to scratch. He advanced, a slow prowl, forcing her to either retreat or touch him. Then she had nowhere to go as her back pressed to the hard wall.

He flattened his palms on the wood, just above her shoulders.

"I never thought I would see you afraid."

She gazed unflinchingly into his dark eyes. "I'm not."

"Then why are you trembling?"

"I'm resisting the urge to belt you where it counts."

"Liar," came in a dark whisper as he leaned closer, his face coming within an inch of hers, and he inhaled deeply, catching the exotic scent of cinnamon and ginger. His breath fanned her jaw, warm and intoxicating, as he tilted his head, inhaling, exhaling, absorbing, drinking in her fragrance and Victoria splayed her hands on the wall, determined not to touch him.

"Are you really going to hit me?" he murmured, then leaned back a fraction, briefly catching her gaze.

"If you go now, I might reconsider it."

The corner of his mouth quirked, yet he continued to absorb her, like an animal scents its prey for life, his face coming closer and closer, letting her feel his nearness, his breath against her hair, her ear, the curve of her throat. "But I don't want to leave." A smokey whisper, caressing.

"What *do* you want, Chris?" A breathless plea, a nerve stretched taut, and Christopher knew she was experiencing the same incredible burning as he. Like gunpowder about to be lit—even if she tapped every resource to quell it.

"I want you to see what I see."

She stiffened. Hurt speared through her gold eyes, and Chris regretted his choice of words.

"I already know that." Bitter, cynical.

"No, Victoria. Even I didn't."

A dark amber brow rose.

And his outstretched arms bent, his long leg shifted, knee insinuating between her thighs. But never touching. It was like standing too close to a fire. She could feel the heat of him. Naked skin to black jeans. And Victoria closed her eyes, fighting him, fighting her intense desire for the pressure of him, long and hard, against her. Her body knew his, the sultry air between them like a thin cushion laid to her skin, defining the width of his chest, mapping every curve and contour down to his lean hips. And the masculine heat between. Oh God, she wanted to touch him.

"I see strength and beauty, Victoria." She opened her mouth to protest and he hushed her, the soft sound spiraling through her like a silken ribbon. "I see a vibrant woman, trapped behind a painted mirror." His lips grazed her chin, her throat, then his head dipped, his mouth brushing over her collar bone. A tiny moan, almost lost in their breathing, came from her.

Chris retraced the contours of her skin, the flesh layered over bone and muscle. "I've never known anyone like you. I've never seen anyone so determined and angry."

"I'm not angry." She swallowed, her head back. "Except with you."

"I know and I'm sorry." His words imprinted her skin, hot and liquid. "But I need to see the woman."

"I can't give you that."

"Yes, you can," he whispered in her ear, sending a chill over her skin. "She's there. I felt her in the forest. In the stables." His voice lowered to a husky pitch. "I'm feeling her now."

"Chris." She bit her lower lip and squeezed her eyes shut.

His lips touched her skin above her breast and her heart shot up to her throat. Her nipples tightened, stinging with need, to have him touch her there as his one hand slid down the wall, slowly, tightening her nerves, and he brushed the fabric off her shoulder. He kissed her there.

"You have the most beautiful shoulders," he murmured, dragging his tongue around the scented flesh, his movements lusher and deeper than before. "They should never be covered."

Her chest rose and fell rapidly. His hands on her shoulders felt like strands of hot lead, branding her skin. Between her thighs dampened, and she tried to ignore it. But wave after wave of sensation roared through her, viciously pelting her body with feelings she never thought she'd experience again. She was on fire for him, his tenderness and patience ripping a tear in her shielded heart and Victoria shivered from the force of it. She couldn't kiss him or she'd be lost again. And she had to leave him. But God . . . it had been years since any man kissed her, *really* kissed her, and he made her feel so sleek and sexy that she hungered for more, for a single brief moment to find what she'd lost.

"Look at me, Victoria."

Her lashes swept up and he saw the faint sheen of tears. His heart fairly lurched out of his chest. She was so vulnerable—the guard dropped and the scared woman revealed.

"Why are you doing this to me?" A soft wail, wounded.

His expression saddened. "To prove what we have is real."

"Chris—"

"God, can't you feel it? It's like a razor between us."

She squeezed her eyes shut, then opened them slowly. "I feel like I'm on the edge of a cliff," she gasped.

"I swear, Tori, I won't let you fall."

His hands slid to the wall, both scraping up to rest above her, the motion arching his back, drawing his body closer. Her breasts, the hard tips hidden behind chambray cloth, grazed his chest. She gasped at the delicious friction.

And he covered the sound with his lips. She flinched, shock

upon shock ripping and tearing between them. He moaned and sank into her mouth as his body sank against hers, grinding her to the wall. His thigh pushed up between hers. She whimpered. Nerves danced. Her womanhood moistened, warming his skin through his heavy jeans and Chris strained, fists clenched against the wood as he kissed her and kissed her and kissed her, his mouth liquid heat and rolling, his tongue parting her lips and driving inside. Her reaction was wild, savagely raw, undoing his restraint. Victoria couldn't get enough. Liquid fire seared in her blood, her legs gone boneless, her breasts throbbing and swelling and aching for his touch.

Her nails clawed the wood wall.

"Touch me, Tori. I need you to touch me."

When she didn't, his hands slid down the wall and swept beneath her shirt, cupping her bare buttocks. The contact made her flinch, but he didn't stop, shaping her hips, then driving up her smooth back and around to enfold her breasts. A little shriek spilled into his mouth and her control broke, her arms wrapping around his neck with desperate hunger. She arched, rocking his thigh as his thumbs circled and flicked her nipples. They ripened into his touch and he wanted to taste them, needed to, and he caught her shirt, flipping button after button, then spreading the fabric wide. He pulled his mouth from hers to look at her, naked to his gaze.

He swallowed thickly. "God, Tori." She was perfection, full pear-shaped breasts, paler, untouched by the sun, a stomach tanned, lean and flat and defined with muscle. His trembling fingers smoothed the clean line of skin rounding her hip and the delicate area between. It was incredibly erotic, the stark contrast, and the sight of her bare thighs straddling his robbed him of his breath. It took every ounce of control not to open his jeans and drive into her. But his hands wouldn't be still, sweeping up her body, wild images conjuring and calloused palms enfolded her breasts as his gaze climbed to meet hers. He recognized fear, her worthiness laid for him in the dim light. "Exquisite," he said and she knew he meant it. "Do you taste as good?" He dipped his head.

And Victoria breathed deep with exotic pleasure as he took one pink tip into the hot suck of his mouth. A low rough moan sprang in her throat. She drove her fingers into his hair, feeling its tickling softness, but her mind centered on the wet lips pulling at her nipples, first one, then the other, over and over until she thought she'd faint. No man had even made her feel like this, so precious, so sexy, and her body was without control, starving for him, writhing with pleasure as his teeth grazed the soft underside of her breast, experimenting with touch and taste and finding her most tender spots. His hand lowered to her spine encouraging her rocking against his thigh. It was wicked and sensual and she wanted more. Damn him. More.

He straightened, and she clawed his shoulders, clutching handfuls of his hair and holding him for her plundering mouth. Chris trembled, matching her fire. It was almost a battle to see who could force who over the edge. He was determined to win and shifted his leg, spreading her, and Victoria felt the cool air touch her femininity. Then his hand did, two fingers plunging into her softness and she cried out.

"Ahhh God, Chris."

"Let me, Tori. Don't fight it."

"I couldn't if I wanted to . . . oh, Chris."

His fingers withdrew and thrust again. He held her pinned to the wall and to him, an arm about her slim waist, his broad thigh hooking her leg. Her mouth was on his, tongue wielding honeyed fire. She clawed at his waist, his hips, one slim hand reaching between them and Chris thought he'd explode his seams when she boldly shaped his erection concealed in dark fabric, her gold eyes locked with his as he drove intimately into her softness over and over. He witnessed her climax, a darkening of her eyes, a tightening of her grip on his neck. For the length of a heart beat, she stilled.

A short ragged inhale. A shudder of pure feminine desire.

Then he thumbed the tender core of her and she flexed wildly, every muscle clamping tight and Chris buried his face in the curve of her throat, holding her as swells of thick opulent pleasure racked through her. He felt every breath she took, every ripple of sleek muscle, hard and soft, wet and musky against him. He wanted to be deep inside her. Right now. Slick and hard and sliding into heaven. But he couldn't—not this soon. She may have accepted his touch, but he'd no idea if she'd rip his face off in a moment for making her so vulnerable.

Ah, but she smelled so sweet.

He hadn't meant for it to go this far. He'd just wanted to kiss her. Apologize. But there was nothing simple about kissing this woman. Nothing at all.

She settled softly and he cupped her hips, rubbing her against his thigh, wanting her to remember how easily the fire blazed, wanting to feel her shiver and moan for his touch. He lifted his head and she kissed him, a warm slide of her tongue into his mouth, sensual, natural, and Chris thought he could stay here forever, just kissing her. She made him feel like a king when she did.

Slowly he eased his leg down, letting her foot touch the floor.

Her hands rested on his shoulders, then smoothed down the front of his shirt, muscles jumping to her touch. A faint smile curved her lips, the power she possessed freeing her in ways he could never understand. Briefly, she titled her head back and took a deep breath. She ought to be ashamed. Yet she was anything but.

"That was certainly an experience. But can't we get arrested for it?"

He quirked a smile. "The marshal has certain rights."

"Proving a point again?"

He heard the edge in her voice. "I wasn't proving anything, Victoria," he growled, sandwiching her to the wall. "We were."

"Do I get a chance?" Her hand slipped between them, firmly cupping his arousal and Chris flinched.

"Tori."

"Yes?" She smiled like a cat, her fingers manipulating him.

"Stop," came through gritted teeth, even as he nuzzled her throat.

"And if I don't?"

He jerked back, sensual pain etched on his handsome face. "Damn it, I didn't come here for that."

"What then?"

"At first," he looked sheepish "just to get you alone long enough to apologize."

She nodded thoughtfully. "Apology accepted, in case you didn't know."

Oh, he knew. "Then I wanted to kiss—"

"God, you're like a rock against me," she whispered suddenly.

He groaned. That's it, he thought, sweeping her into his arms and carrying her to her bed. A man can only be just so chivalrous. He laid her gently in the center, then settled to the mattress beside her, his body quaking and his manhood tight and straining his pants. He ignored it, deserving his suffering, and brushed tawny gold hair from her face, wondering how long he could take looking at her, knowing she erupted like a volcano when they touched.

She held his gaze, her hand riding his arm to his shoulder, branding him like a new born calf. He wanted her so bad even his teeth ached. Yet when she opened her mouth to speak, he leaned closer, brushing his lips over hers.

"Sleep, Tori. There is always tomorrow."

He leaned toward the table and blew out the lamp. In an instant she knew that he was gone.

And she missed him.

Curling to her side, Victoria reveled in the sweet ache simmering through her body. Tomorrow. She didn't have many of them. Not in this century. But if the rest of them could be like tonight? She squeezed her eyes shut, shutting out the need, the undeniable hunger she felt for him.

Victoria wasn't stupid.

Christopher Swift was a once-in-a-lifetime kind of guy. And even if this might be her only chance to feel loved, she couldn't hurt him.

No matter how much she wanted to love him.

Chapter Thirteen

In the darkness, Chris eased open his front door, shivering, his boots in his hand, and he stopped short at the unexpected burst of light.

"Well, it's a fine thing, comin' in this late . . . and why are you all soppin' wet, lad?"

"One does not pry in his lordship's affairs, Miss Abigale." Randel raised his oil lamp a touch.

Abigale, short, slightly round and cherry cheeked, snorted indelicately at the Englishman. "I diapered his bum, I'll stick my nose where I please." Randel sighed uselessly as she looked at Christopher. "Affair, it is?"

Chris's gaze shifted between the two, ending on the valet and imploring for some masculine support. Randel, clad in an impeccably pressed dark robe and not looking at all as if he'd just dragged himself out of a warm bed, gave his employer a bland look. His usual expression. No help there. Abigale, on the other hand, cinched up her ruffled dressing gown and studied him closely, her gaze drifting down to his stockinged feet, to the boots, then to his wet hair.

"In the river, were you?"

Great. Here comes the Spanish Inquisition. "Yes."

"Why, in the name of heaven, when we've got that new bathing room, with the heater and pumping water—"

Randel cleared his throat and shot her a quelling glance. Abigale returned it, searching his aged face. Suddenly her features tightened and she looked at the master, her brows high.

" 'Tis a *woman* who's set you to jumping in freezin' water?" came in a squeak.

She looked too damn happy about it for Chris's mood. Which was foul with unsatisfied passion. The swim did little to squelch his need for Victoria, except make it less obvious in his trousers.

Ignoring the unspoken question, Chris strode through the dimly lit foyer, dropping his boots by the umbrella stand and heading up the staircase toward his bedroom. He didn't get far. Not that he thought he would.

"Christopher Waythorne Swift!"

He sighed, dropped his head forward, then cocked a look over his shoulder. "Yes, Abigale. A woman." She beamed. "But don't get any ideas. I'm not."

"Oh, I wouldn't dream of it, laddie," she called sweetly as he mounted the remaining steps, but Chris recognized her tone. Abigale was plotting, or would be the instant she discovered Victoria's identity. He scoffed, pushing open his bedroom door and slipping inside. Abigale would be the last person to recognize Victoria, if she had anything to do with it.

But he supposed the old woman was repenting, since she'd encouraged him with Camille. A sudden dull ache worked in his chest and he rubbed it, crossing the room and stripping off his wet clothes. Camille McCracken. She'd insisted she loved him, agreed to marry him, then when he told her, merely to reaffirm his own skepticism, that he was half Cheyenne, she immediately broke their engagement.

"Just because I'm friends with Indians," she'd said in a condescending voice. "Does not mean I want to actually *marry* one."

She'd destroyed him with her carelessly chosen words, smashed his faith in women of her ilk—ladies, refined and gently reared, with compassion and understanding that only went as far as the eye could see. He should have recognized it, but he'd assumed. How could he not, her relatives were Sioux, for Christ's sake. Venting his old anger and new frustration on his clothes, he tore at the fastenings, slapped wet garments over the back of a chair. It crushed his fierce desire for Victoria, but in the same instance, it made him remember. Everything. Her scent, her taste . . . her eruption. And he stilled, his breathing labored. His body flexed.

He wanted that woman. More than just in his bed.

She was unique, intriguing him, different by years and miles from Camille. Victoria Mason was intelligent, challenging, and full of capped passion, as savage in her loving as she was in hunting her bounties. And the tightly checked desire made her all the more alluring, for the explosive hunger her experienced tonight was only the beginning of what lay disguised and dormant beneath her cool demeanor.

And he couldn't wait for the next time.

And there *would* be one.

But as he sank into the softness of his big empty bed, wishing she was with him, he knew that he'd pay for making her aware of herself. Of how much she meant to him. A year ago, he'd sworn off women and giving his heart away so easily ought to be warning enough, but he couldn't dredge up the old wounds to barricade behind. He should. Because she could detach herself too easily. He'd witnessed it, in her eyes. Victoria wasn't staying. And he was damned if he knew how to change her mind.

June 1872

Sometimes, it hides in a place deep inside me, quiet, dormant as a tulip in winter. I forget it's even there, yet when I lay awake at night still, I feel it, swelling over me, drowning me. It's a hunger, a sudden unquenchable thirst, always coupled with pain. A horrible agony so cavernous it digs and digs, gnawing on my mind like maggots combing dead flesh for nurishment. I don't believe I will ever be free of it. Not in this lifetime. But perhaps in this newborn time.

Freedom. No one can touch me. No one ever could. Not even her.

I know what I am. A mother's nightmare.

And I revel in the freshness of a new beginning.

Chris rapped on the door. When no response came, he tried the knob. It opened freely and he let it go, a sense of dread filling him as the door swung open. The room was empty. He didn't have to step inside to see if anything else would contradict him. It was too small.

And she was gone.

Something inside him broke loose, floating in his gut. He didn't know what to think, nor where to look for her. She could *look* like anyone. Immediately he went to the front desk. The clerk glanced up, then straightened, moving to the counter.

"Where's Clara Murphy?"

"Misses Fotheringham dismissed her this morning."

"Why?" The clerk shrugged, glancing away and Chris leaned closer. "Why," came with deadly intent.

"The missus said she heard—" he cleared his throat and lowered his voice "—noises from her room, and a man's voice."

Inwardly Chris groaned. Did Fotheringham see her true face, he wondered.

"Old sour-puss said she'd dirtied her hotel's good name." The clerk smirked. "Miss Clara said if it got dirty it was 'cause she ain't got to cleanin' it yet."

Sarcasm, how like her.

"Where did she go?"

"Can't say. 'Cause I don't know!" he added quickly when the marshal looked as if he'd choke him. "She was gone at sun up."

Chris left the hotel, striding down the walk, searching every face, his dark gaze trying to rip away the real from fake. People moved out of his path, and he slowed his step, forcing the scowl from his face. He didn't need folks to be afraid of him.

Yanking his hat from his head, he slapped it against his thigh, then repositioned it. *Where are you? Why didn't you come to me?* He knew the answer instantly.

She doesn't need you. She doesn't need anybody.

The sweet sex between them last night didn't mean she was his woman. It only meant that she felt like one, looked like one—tasted like one.

Victoria was dependent on no one—least of all him.

That gnawed at him, for he needed to see her, to assure himself that last night wasn't a dream. But was she angry? Did she despise him for teasing her, for taking liberties?

He needed to know.

And as he scanned the street, verring off toward Duckett's and hoping to catch her at her usual breakfast, he had the distinct feeling it was a useless trip, that if she wanted, he'd never see her again. And he swore, if he had to line up every member of this damn town and make them strip to their drawers, he'd find her.

Noble Beecham liked a good passel of mystery as much as the next man, but the little lady was one he couldn't figure. At the dawn of his shift, he'd seen her, as Clara, and now, she looked every bit a young man, and Noble squinted as she crossed the street, trying to imagine what she looked like under all that shit. Dang, but he hoped she wasn't really a man with tits, as tall as she was.

Nah.

Marshal wouldn't be sniffing after her if she wasn't anything but a real hot-fire woman. Yet, as she stood on the walk, chatting quite amiably with Red Velvet Knight, Noble couldn't help but notice her mannerisms, scuffling her boots, shoving her hands deep into her pockets. She's good at it, he'd give her that, he thought, as she tipped her hat to Vel and broke into a ` run across to the livery. Noble watched her long legs eat up the dust, wishing he could see the face God gave her, then he turned away from the window. With a bored sigh, he dropped into his chair just as a knock jiggled the door.

Tiredly, he hollered, "Get in. I ain't no door man!" and the door popped open.

" 'Tis a fion howd-ya do!"

"Miss Abigale!" He leapt to his feet, his ruddy cheeks flushing with embarrassment. "This is a surprise."

"Hah!" she said not unkindly, bustling inside. "I thought we were friends enough that you'd tell me when he'd mended his broken heart." He took the basket from her, his pleased smile hidden beneath his heavy moustache.

"Who?" he teased, setting the basket on the desk. "The marshal?" Noble stole a peak beneath the linen napkin and got his hand slapped for the crime.

"That's for them."

"Well, them isn't a *them,* Miss Abigale."

He leaned closer, his gaze slipping over her full bosom and rounded hips with undisguised admiration. "They're like cats squaring off to fight all the time." That wasn't a lie, and though Noble swore not to reveal her secret, even what he knew to Chris, he figured those two would either love one another wildly or kill each other.

Her sweet cherub face fell at the news. "What did he do?"

"What makes you think it was him?"

"A woman would not be so stupid as to ruin her chances with a fine catch like my Christopher."

She looked all proper and righteous, he thought with a grin. "Says you."

"Aye, says me." She batted his hand away from the basket again.

"You gonna slap me if I reach for you, Miss Abigale?" he murmured silkily and her face flamed.

"Depends on what your hands wrap around, Mister Beecham."

The clatter of hooves and a shout from beyond the walls

couldn't drag his gaze from hers. "Then I 'spect you'd beat me to a tar." His implication was clear and she gasped, her skin darkening even further. Then with the determination of a man who knew what he wanted, Noble tipped her chin, yet just as he was sinking into Abigale's sweet kiss, the door banged open. The couple jerked apart and Noble decided that arrest was fair punishment for the interruption until the marshal stormed in, heading immediately to the storage room beyond his desk. He grabbed a sack and a saddle bag off a peg, jamming supplies inside.

A worried frown creasing her face. Abigale looked at Noble, then nudged him. The mountain man moved to the entrance, bracing his shoulder on the frame. He whipped out his Arkansas Toothpick and cleaned his nails. "Gonna tell me where all you're headed?"

Chris bit back a sharp retort and shoved dried beef, two cans, and a few trail essentials into a muslin sack. Dammit, he hated that she put him in this position and knew sticking to the truth was his best bet.

"Jake stole a horse."

"Jezz! You sure?"

Chris flung a glare over his shoulder, then continued gathering supplies and bullets, before dropping his single holster for a double.

"Hell. I'da never thought ss-he'd do somethin' like that. Dang, Chris, he's got to have a good reason." Noble thanked God Chris was too piss-fire angry to notice his slip.

"He flung a coin at Clancey and took off." With her backpack, with everything she owned and Chris had a feeling, one that drove through him like a stake, that she wasn't coming back. Either him or her bounty had her running.

"Well then, he rented the mount."

"Hardly." Chris brushed past him. "It was Caesar."

Noble cursed rudely. Abigale gasped. And Chris wrenched around to stare at her.

"I brought you and your woman-friend some lunch," she explained in a rush, his anger leaving her at a loss.

"Abigale," he said, crossing to her. "I told you—"

"I ken, I ken, but just call me hopeful and don't let me good cookin' go to waste." She wrapped some chicken and biscuits in a cloth and pushed it into his sack. "Least you won't be going hungry."

He recognized the fear in her voice, her expression, and he paused long enough to give her a reassuring hug. "I'll be back."

"You best be, Christopher, and in one piece!" she called, but he was already gone. " 'Cause I want to meet her," she murmured sadly, staring at the ruined meal.

"It ain't your fault, darlin', 'bout him and Miss Camille," Noble said softly. "A man makes his own decisions, then lives with 'em."

Abigale lifted her gaze, offering him a weary smile. "I suppose," she sighed, then poked in the basket, taking inventory. "Hungry?" She met his warm, probing gaze.

"Sure. That is . . ." He leaned closer, fixing to take up where they left off. "If'n all yer gonna offer me is cold chicken?"

Abigale harrumphed, then promptly shoved a chicken leg in his puckered mouth. Kiss that, she thought with girlish delight.

Chapter Fourteen

Hooves pounded the earth, kicking up rocks and sod and Chris scarcely acknowledged the dust coating his mouth, the sweat and grime clinging to his skin. His fingers were itching to wring her pretty little neck too much to bother. To satisfy the murderous urge, he gripped the reins tighter, spurred the horse faster. She was far ahead, only because of Caesar. Damn the horse for letting her mount him when he normally chewed into anyone who tried. He wasn't so furious that she'd stolen his horse, but that she left without saying good-bye.

And he feared, he'd driven her off.

Damn.

He pushed the beast over a low rise and reined up, scanning the terrain. The slow sinking sun blinded him and he squinted. Half the day and well into the evening lost to chasing that woman. God knows she left a strong enough trail. Digging in his heels, he pushed the horse toward the next rise, heading toward the railroad a few miles in the valley beyond. The horse's lungs bellowed as it labored up the incline, rocks rolling down the hillside as powerful hooves searched for purchase. He was going to kill the animal if he didn't slow down, he thought regretfully, and as man and beast broke over the mountaintop, Chris walked the gelding to cool him, then slid from his back.

Loosening his canteen, he sipped, then offered water to the horse. Re-securing the container, he stared over the saddle at the landscape and spotted Caesar grazing under the shade of a gnarled tree at the edge of the cliff.

He twisted and turned, searching for Victoria.

He was alone on the mountaintop.

Quickly, he approached Caesar, pulling the gelding under the shade and noticing his pet wasn't hobbled, the leads dragging the ground. Did she leave him here hoping he'd return on his own? The black beast would, but did that mean she was already on the train? The whistle howled, echoing off the valley walls and he moved to the edge. Steam rolled from the engine housing. A few travelers mingled, miners mostly, the station more for depositing supplies than hauling settlers to this part of the territory. Chris moved closer and saw her—or rather, her boots. Head down toward the valley, her elbows braced, she held binoculars to her eyes. At least they looked like binoculars, yet smaller. But one thing was for sure—she wasn't masquerading as Jake. Did that mean she was ready to take her bounty out with a bullet or take the felon back alive? Suddenly, she scrambled back, climbing to her feet and when she turned, she stopped at the sight of him.

Victoria tried to ignore the betrayed look in his eyes, moving quickly around him toward the horse, shoving the binoculars in her backpack and lifting her leg to mount.

"No." He clamped his arm around her waist, yanking her back.

She twisted. "Let me go, Chris." She twisted. "This isn't your business."

He tightened his grip, cutting off her air, telling her everything about her was his business. She stomped on his instep. He grunted, gripping her more securely and Victoria went limp, sliding down his body and ramming her elbow into his stomach. He folded with a rush of air, and she cupped the back of his knee and yanked. Chris hit the ground with a bone jarring thud. But Victoria came with him, splaying across him and driving him flat to the ground. He didn't release her and she covered his hand, digging her thumb into the apex of his and his forefinger. Pain shot up his arm, numbing it as she twisted his wrist, peeling bone and muscle back unnaturally.

"Damn it, Victoria!" He shifted to accommodate the strain.

"Give up, Chris!" She released him, rolling off and scrambling across the ground. "I have to get down there!"

The train was leaving and taking Ivy League on it. He was stalking. She could tell by the smug look in his eyes. He already had his prey selected and cultivated for the kill!

Chris grabbed her ankle, dragging her back.

She kicked out, frantic. "Butt-out!"

He lurched, throwing himself on top of her. "Not until you tell me why you're out here!"

"I'm a bounty hunter," she snarled, spitting grass and dirt. "I'm hunting."

She clawed the ground, trying to find anchor so she could throw him off. But he was heavy, pressing her into the soft earth.

She fought like a cornered mountain cat, clawing, elbowing him, and Chris caught her wrists, slamming her hands to the ground, his body driving her into the dirt. His knees were braced against the back of her legs. Seconds ticked by. Her back rose and fell with angry breaths, her body stiff beneath his.

"You going to beat the hell out of me again if I let you up?" He inhaled hard, trying to find his wind. Jesus, she was strong!

"No," she muttered into the dirt.

"Swear?"

"Chickenshit."

He smirked, his voice a low murmur near her ear. "Come on, Tori."

"Don't call me that!" she hissed, renewing her struggle.

Chris frowned. She might be seething with anger, but that was hurt he heard in her voice. He was sure of it.

"Why not? It suits you."

God, did he have to be so sweet? "I'm not going to get into this with you now!"

Frowning, he slid off her enough to look at her, still pinning her legs. Her forehead was pressed to the ground, her hair shielding her face. "Look at me."

She turned her head, tossing hair from her view and glaring at him.

"Why did you leave?"

"Not because of you."

Liar, he thought. It's in your eyes. "Who are you hunting?"

"A killer."

"As the marshal, I have the right to know who."

Time travel or not, he was right. "Algenon Becket."

Chris's brows rose sharply, objection in every feature. "You're wrong."

Her lips tightened into a flat line. Of course, he wouldn't believe her. She'd done nothing but prove herself a nut case since they met. The train whistle cried like a mourning mother, and Victoria risked scrapes and cuts and abruptly curled up on her knees, bucked, then brought her arm out and up to break his hold, inadvertently cuffing him on the chin. In his dazed moment, she grabbed her fallen hat, drawing the gun tucked inside and took off running. She could hear him behind her and pushed herself harder, skidding down the hillside. Earth crumbled beneath her feet and she reached out to brace herself and kept going. The train chugged and with a sudden burst of adrenaline, she lurched, only to be caught about the waist and slammed into the mountainside. Her gun flew from her grip as she choked for air, grappling wildly for freedom, slamming her fists into his solid flesh. "Hit all you want, woman." Chris suffered the painful blows, drawing on strength to hold her and not crush her.

"I'm not fighting you."

"Damn you!" She twisted frantically. "You don't know

what you've done!'' She reached for the land like a hurt child reaches for its mother and Chris drew her back. "Please. I need to get on the train. He'll hurt them,'' she sobbed, hating it, hating him. "He'll kill them!''

"Tori, Tori, shhh,'' he said, and although she'd run out of energy, she still struggled, even as the train moved around the narrow bend, leaving only smoke and fumes. "You're wrong, I'm telling you. Becket's not a criminal.''

She whipped around and glared at him, her voice low and ugly. And not even the unshed tears softened the bite. *"You don't know what the hell you're talking about!"*

His jaw tightened and he released her abruptly, and she wrenched away as if his touch fouled her clothes, then stood, searching and finding her gun before marching up the hill, scooping up her hat without breaking stride and dumping it on her head. Chris followed, watching her shove the weapon into a leather pocket fashioned at the back of her jeans, then dust the dirt from her thighs and bottom. And beyond the enticing shape of her hips in jeans without all the masculine enhancement, he recognized the dejected droop of her shoulders.

"He's going to purchase liquor, like he does every couple weeks. Like he has for the past four months.''

Victoria dropped to the ground where she stood, unable to go on. Four months. Four hours head start was *four* months. God, he could have killed hundreds by now. He's been around long enough, made enough trips that whoever he was stalking was comfortable. Oh, God. How was she going to find him now? How could she get ahead of him with such limited resources and a marshal who obstructed her every move? Christ, I'd kill for a helicopter right now, she thought, yanking off her hat and running her fingers through her hair. It cascaded over her shoulders and she searched the knotted mass for the broken rubber band.

"He'll be back in the morning. I swear it.''

Her gaze flew to his. He was standing a few feet before her. "How many lives are you willing to forfeit for that sureity, Marshal?''

A chill rode over his spine at her tone. It was dead, dried up with emotion. What had done this to her? Who made her turn inward and cut the world out? She pulled something from her hair, tossed it, then jammed her hat back on before drawing her knees up and bracing her forearms there. When he stepped toward her, her hand flew to her back and the gun appeared, pointed at his face.

"We've been down this road before, Tori."

"Don't call me that."

He squatted in front of her. "Why?"

She sighed, replacing the gun before he got too interested in the design. "It makes me feel like you care."

His brows rose in surprise. "I do."

She stared off to the side, at the setting sun. "Right."

He knelt on one knee, yanking at blades of grass. Caesar nickered softly.

"You don't believe me?"

"I did. Last night." She met his gaze. "But the morning has a tendency to bring on a hard case of reality."

He knew he didn't want to hear this, but asked, "And that is?"

It feels too good in your arms, so good when you call me Tori, but it's not fair to either of us, she wanted to say, but instead said, "As much fun as that was, we can't start anything." She'd had all night to weigh her options and her own came up short. "It isn't worth the trouble." She stood, searching the ground for wood.

"I'm a grown man, Victoria. I can judge for myself." His words were clipped with irritation as he rose and followed her.

"I'm not sticking around long enough for it to matter."

To hear her say it struck him in the chest and he stopped short. "Did I do it, last night? Did I drive you away?"

Victoria moaned, dropping the wood in a pile. "No," came in a whisper. "I like you, Chris—" her gaze slid over his broad shoulders, his lean muscular form with obvious regret "—A lot. But I have to take him back."

He didn't think the saloon owner was guilty of anything

except over-charging, but kept that to himself. She wasn't going to listen. "You can return, afterward."

"No." She swallowed thickly, staring at the kindling. "Never."

She cut him out in those words and it sent fury rising like a storm inside him.

"Nothing matters but the hunt, huh? Only the cash for a felon."

She looked at him blandly, refusing to rise to his baiting. It was too dark to head back and she wasn't up to sparing with him until dawn. "I don't get paid the bounty, Marshal. The court gets it."

He scoffed. "Since when?"

"Well, where I come from, that's how it goes." She went to her satchel, blocking his view as she flipped the catch and opened it, quietly unzipping the backpack front pocket and digging past her Bic for some matches. "I work for a bondsman, Fat Jack Palau. He puts up the bond. I chase them down when they flee."

"And Becket is supposed to have fled? When?"

She returned to the wood stack, concentrating on lighting the blaze. "The day before you *falsely* arrested me."

"Impossible," he said from across the fire. "I saw him the evening before and nearly every day prior."

Victoria clamped her lips shut, fanning the flames and tossing on more wood. Damn. She should have said she'd been hunting him for months before, for revealing the circumstances was out of the question. "Not according to my paperwork," she muttered, hoping her slip would slide by.

"Why don't we just wait until he gets back, on the morning train to confront him."

"No!" she barked, then glanced at him, her tone loosing its edge. "No. I'm not speaking with him, looking like this." She gestured to her face. "Not ever. Got that?" Her gaze bored into his, a silent battle neither would acknowledge. "And for the record, *Marshal,* I've never brought a defendent in that wasn't breathing."

She made his job sound like a dirty word and the secrets she still held from him, set his temper flying. "Christ, what pushes you to do this?"

"Murderers running free isn't reason enough?"

He scooted closer and she tensed. He tried to ignore how much the defensive move hurt him and concentrated on her. "Sure it is, but besides that you've got the wrong felon, I've never known anyone to go to such extremes."

His tone prodded, but she wasn't going to relive that for anyone.

"Look, Chris." She plucked off her hat and tossed it aside. "I told you. I do the get-ups to keep a low profile, if I want to live until the next case." Her tone turned bitter. "It's what's kept me alive for the past five years." And alone. God, I've been at this too long, she thought dismally. A Marine M.P., a U. S. Marshal for a couple years, then bounty hunting, and it all lead her here, to this time. She glanced at him. To this man? Or the one on the train?

"You sound sick of it." His gaze followed as she stood.

Her feet shifted, her gaze on her fingers, then with a jerk of her head, she tossed her head back and stared at the horizon. "I am." Her hair shielded her face.

"Then why go on?"

She sighed wearily, her deep voice tinny, fragile. "Because the killers don't sleep, Chris."

And neither did she, he thought, rising and following her to the horses. She looked drained, physically spent, and Chris wondered how much of it was their brawl in the dirt or their encounter last night. Something's happening to her, he thought, ashamed that he'd pushed her. But God, she was one sexy female. She just didn't believe it. He wanted to crush whoever made her feel so unattractive, wanted to protect her from the haunts he witnessed constantly in her eyes. But she wouldn't let him in, shoving back when he got too close and they moved around each other in tight silence, avoiding the slightest contact. As he loosened the muslin sack and saddle bags, she was right behind him, removing the saddles and positioning them near the fire, intentionally on opposite ends, Chris noticed—like he noticed everything else.

Like how she never opened her pack when he was close enough to see inside, nor allow him a long enough look at her strange small gun. Or those little binoculars. He cast her a glance as he gathered enough wood to keep them warm through the night. She was rubbing down the black, the fire light making her hair look lighter, yet the shadows and the darker hair surrounding her face gave her the definite appearance of a lion in wait. For a fight. He rubbed his bruised chin, the rest of him still aching from her blows and he didn't want to give her the opportunity to test those claws on his hide any too soon. Pulling a cloth from his saddle bag, he rubbed down the gelding.

She was humming, her hand smoothing over Caesar in a slow luxurious caress. It made him itch to feel those hands on him again. "Why did you take off the . . . get up?"

"It was hot as hell." A pause and then, "And Jake Farrell died today."

He was confused and a crooked smile tugged at her lush lips.

"I ripped his face off."

Chris chuckled softly, shaking his head and the crackling tension eased a little. She scratched Caesar behind the ears and the big horse snorted his delight.

"Betrayer," Chris muttered and Caesar hung his head sadly.

"Look, he's sorry." Victoria never saw a horse pout, but swore he was. "Me too, Chris." He met her gaze and her tone cajoled. "I sort of talked him into playing hooky."

"Forget it. If Caesar didn't want to run with you, no one could have climbed on that ornery piece of horse hide." The last he said close to Caesar's ear.

"See. Can't hang around me, boy," she said, grabbing the bridal and staring into the horses big black eyes. "I'll just get you grounded without oats."

Chris paused in reaching for the muslin sack. "Grounded?"

"Punished," she explained, then kissed the horse's black nose.

"Hungry?" He peered into the sack.

"Starving," she said without looking up.

She and Caesar seemed to be having a private conversation. "Abigale left us a lunch."

"How sweet of her."

Hiding a smile at the tightness in her voice, he settled to the ground, pulling a wrapped bundle out of a sack. "I needed a dip in the river, last night." He glanced up, her smile catching him in the chest. Then her gaze dropped boldly to the bulge in his jeans. He groaned, reaction swift and painful.

"Good 'cause I lost my oh-so-glamourous job."

"I know. I'm sorry."

"Saying that a lot lately, aren't you, Marshal?"

He gazed up at her, seeing her with all the facets he'd discovered. "You humble me sometimes, Victoria."

"That'll be the day."

"Around you, half the time I feel—"

"Condescending? Touchy? Bruised? What?"

"—inconsequential."

Her expression went somber, her ghost of a smile robbing him of air. "Not a chance, Chris." Her voice was husky with emotion when she said, "A dunk in a cold river, huh?" If that wasn't great for her ego, she was asking too much. "That bad?"

"It still is," he muttered under his breath, then said, "Abigale understood the dunking immediately and wanted to meet the cause of . . . my discomfort."

Abigale couldn't be his wife. "Your housekeeper?"

"If that's all she was," he said, enjoying the jealousy in her eyes. She wasn't as unaffected as she claimed. Good. Neither was he. "I don't think I could live without her." He handed her a portion of the chicken and biscuits. "Or her incredible cooking and sunny smile. Or her thirty years of nagging me to wash behind my ears."

"That's 'cause boys never wash there." She reached, grabbed his ear and checked, then smiled with approval. He grinned, making her insides dance.

" 'Course then there's her matchmaking . . ."

"Excuse me?" she said, hating the snap to her words.

He sank his teeth into a chicken leg, making her wait, adoring her eagerness, even though the telling would cost him his pride. She was worth it, he decided then and there.

"Chris!"

"Camille McCracken is my friend's sister. I called on her, we fell in love," his gaze faultered and his tone wore a touch of confusion "—or at least I thought I had. I was supposed to marry her next month."

Her breath caught. Next month? "And you're not, I take it?"

He finished chewing before he spoke, gathering courage and leaving his wounds out of the words. "She couldn't stomach the thought of marrying an Indian."

Her features sharpened. "The little prejudiced bitch!"

His brows shot up. "Victoria Mason!"

"But that's so backward!" Like this century, like the women in the store, she recalled. "Jeez, what would they do if they found out I'm . . . let's see," she stared thoughtfully at the night sky. "English, Costa Rican, Scottish," she met his gaze, "And Blackfoot."

"Blackfoot, hum?" He shivered dramatically. "Now I know where you get that mean streak."

"I'm not mean."

Her lower lip thrust out so adorably he wanted to kiss her. Boy, did he want to kiss her. "I have the bruises to prove it, darlin'." He made a show of coughing and rubbing his solar plexus.

"That's self-defense." Her gold eyes flashed devilishly. "Did I hurt you?"

"Hell, yes."

"Then you shouldn't have tried to stop me." Smug, edged with warning.

"You shouldn't have stolen my horse."

"Borrowed."

"All right, all right, I give." He threw his hands up in defeat, the chicken leg sailing back over his shoulder somewhere into the dark. He blinked at his empty hand, then her and she laughed, a throaty sound that stole through him like a stream of warmed honey.

She offered him some of her dinner and he took it, sinking down on his elbow, the motion bringing him closer to her. She met and held his dark gaze, pushing a piece of meat into her mouth and Chris swallowed, his senses so alive with her he thought he'd roar with frustration. His gaze slipped over her face, the smoothness of her complexion, the golden color of it making him ache to strip the heavy shirt from her body and taste every supple inch. She inhaled softly, her attention on tearing tiny pieces from the biscuit, his on the opening of her shirt, the swell of breast hinting she wore nothing beneath the cloth. He swallowed, clenching his fingers to keep from touching her.

Then she looked up, her gold and black gaze searching his face before she leaned forward, tenderly cupping his jaw and covering his mouth with hers. He moaned, sinking his fingers into the cloud of hair as her lips rolled smoothly over his. Her mouth was like dark magic, stirring him to ungodly heights, her lips tugging at his, her tongue outlining the shape, sweeping his teeth before pushing inside. Her kiss grew wilder, and for the first time in his life, he felt helpless and wonderfully tortured. She was like desert sand, shifting and changing with the wind and elusive to the touch. He wanted to capture her—he wanted—a chance to love her.

Was this all he'd ever have of her? A few kisses?

Victoria drew back slowly, her breathing erratic, her thumb brushing over his lips. "I love your kisses," she whispered, her voice rich and sultry.

"Kissed much?" he managed with his blood pounding like sledge hammer.

The corner of her moist lips tugged. "Enough."

"That sweet mouth of yours drive them crazy, too?"

She flushed. "Not one."

"Not even him?"

Her features went blank, like a slate wiped clean and she leaned back. "No."

Chris sat up, part of him telling him not to spoil it and let the subject drop, yet the man who wanted her with him, the man who ached to get beyond this shield she held between them, couldn't.

"How did he die, your husband?"

She looked as if he'd shot her, pain streaking across her lovely face. Then, it was hidden, subdued. Carefully, she set the half-eaten biscuit on the cloth and dusted her fingertips, her words falling away like the dry crumbs. "He and my daughter were in a McDonald's. It's a restaurant," she clarified, her tone oddly detached. "Some crazy, drugged-up fiend with a rifle sprayed the place with bullets. Kevin and Trisha were the first to get it." Victoria swallowed, her vision blurring. "Trisha didn't know her Daddy was stealing her from me. See, Kevin didn't like my job. It disgusted him that to get the defendant, I'd hang out with the jerks he was trying to put behind bars. He'd insist I bathe and change before coming near him. After a while, it got so bad that he refused to touch me." Pain and humiliation wove through her words and Chris longed to comfort her. "He got this look every time I came back. Suspicious. Like *I* was one of the criminals."

That hurt her the most, Chris realized, to have her honor questioned.

"When he asked for a divorce, I didn't argue. But I wanted my daughter." Her voice hardened. "We fought over her, and when I was out on assignment, he stole her from her nanny."

Her hands shook as she spoke and she clasped them tightly. "It took me two days to find them. When she saw me through the restaurant windows, she reached out to me, but Kevin held her back. It was mean and he knew it. She couldn't understand what he was doing to her," she moaned dispiritedly. "Then the junkie opened fire before I realized what was happening. I didn't have a gun." A single tear spilled, rolling softly down her cheek, and she looked at him, her lip trembling. "If he hadn't taken her—if I hadn't left my gun at home . . . if I'd thought—oh Jesus," she choked. "The bullets ripped right through her little body, tearing holes in my child like she was made of paper. But damn the bastard," she ground angrily. "She didn't die instantly—" she thumped her chest "—but in my arms, asking to go home in her sweet little voice. Oh God—" She swallowed and swallowed again, pressing down her grief, and Chris reached for her. She batted away his hands and started to rise, but he grabbed her, pulling her into his arms. She struggled briefly, then buried her face in his chest, sobbing helplessly. "Do you know what that's like? To see your baby reaching for you, begging for your help and you can do nothing! Nothing!" Her fingers dug into his arms. "Damn you. *Oh damn you!*" she howled like a beaten animal. "I could have gone a hundred years without remembering that!"

"I'm sorry, shhh, I'm sorry," he soothed, leaning back against the saddle and cradling her in his arms. She wrapped her body around him, her face buried in the curve of his shoulder, her legs entwined with his. And Victoria cried, her heart ripping from her chest and squeezing the last of her blood. She cried for Kevin, and the love they once shared, for the special little girl they made. Her shoulders jerked, her arms clung and she sobbed out the pain of losing Cole, the anger of his foolishness and hers for asking him to help her. Then she cried for herself, pitiful lonely tears, and he held her, letting her cling to his neck, letting her pound his chest with her frustration and he sheltered her like something precious and fragile, absorbing her pain, washing it away with the smooth stroke of his hands up her spine. And years of smothered torment tore through her soul, shredding her guard.

Her anguish clawed at his composure and Chris tightened his arms around her, a lump swelling in his throat. She was bleeding, and he cursed himself for opening the wound.

And he prayed she'd forgive him.

Again.

Chapter Fifteen

Chris squeezed his eyes shut and pressed his lips to the top of her head.

He'd never held a woman like this before, not as if he were her only lifeline. He wouldn't let her go until she wanted it, he promised. Time went on uncharted before her sobs faded into deep shuddering breaths.

God.

He'd wanted her to need to him, but not like this, not at this price. The heaviness of night fell quietly, punctuated by an occasional shifting hoof, a chirping cricket, and she was so still he thought sleep had taken away her pain.

He looked down at her, pushing back her lush mass of hair. Her dark lashes swept up and the sadness in her eyes tore him in half. "God, Tori." He smeared her tears away with his thumb. "I didn't mean to make you hurt like that."

"It's okay, Tonto," came in a quiet rasp and Victoria swallowed. "Not your fault. I'll live." But it will never be the same, she thought, gazing into his eyes. She'd done her worst to him and he was still here. No one stuck around beyond the initial greeting. Most men were either repulsed or intimidated by her. Except him, she thought, slipping her arm from around his neck and sifting her fingers in his soft black hair. She added pressure, drawing him closer, and Chris went willingly, her mouth warm and supple against his. Desire flared, heating her kiss, her sleek body shifting subtly along his own, sending a message he'd longed to receive. He trembled with need, a grinding that scraped roughly through his body and he savored the freedom he found in it for several moments, then reluctantly drew back. She reached for him again.

"Not like this," he whispered heavily against her lips. "As much as I want you, I can't help thinking I'd be taking advantage." He couldn't believe he was saying this.

"I'm a grown woman, Chris. I can judge for myself," she threw back at him, her fingers sliding down the hard plains of his chest, her palm flattening over his stomach.

His skin flexed at her touch and a knowing look flared in her eyes. She had an indecent amount of power over him, he thought, but a quick coupling in the woods wasn't what she needed right now. She was tired, confused, and when he took her to his bed, he wanted her to come to him without ghosts.

"Tori, please don't," he groaned when her hand traveled lower. "I'm not that strong."

"Me either."

It was more statement than response. A confession. Rock hard on the outside kept her demons locked away. She hunted bounty for the daughter she couldn't save. She hunted escaped killers so they couldn't kill another woman's baby. But when would she be satisfied? She was so caught up in it now—how long before it drove her into a nothingness of pure vengeance? And when she vanishes from your life, like she's promised, a voice asked, then what will you do?

Come apart, came an unbridled response and it scared him. He liked her, sure, but her grip on his heart made him feel as if he was losing all control. Camille taught him that.

He started to disengage himself and she gripped him, a strange panic seizing her. "No, please. I'll behave. Just hold me." She clung, trembling, her wide eyes searching his face.

"It's been so long since anyone's wanted to." Her plea sapped away any thought of leaving and he unbuckled his holster, drawing it away before he settled comfortably back against the saddle. She wiggled immediately into his arms like a burrowing kitten, throwing her long leg over his and pillowing her head at the bend of his shoulder.

"Thanks, Chris."

Her breasts pressed warmly to his side with unmistakable clarity and the image of her, naked and panting, slipped into his mind like a taunting beast. How could her husband not want her? Sleek and strong and independent, she had to be the sexiest woman in the territory. And Chris tried to concentrate on anything but the natural fit of their bodies and what it would feel like to have those long legs locked around his waist as he drove into her.

Hell.

It was going to be an unholy night if he kept thinking like that.

Yet he was in the arms of sleep when her voice whispered to him. "Chris?"

"Humm?"

"Camille was a fool."

His lips curved. "So was Kevin."

He woke alone. Really alone. Every trace of Victoria was gone—Except Caesar. He wasn't all that surprised. Last night drained him like cheap whiskey in the hand of a drunk. But his Cheyenne father would kick his rear if he knew a woman had gotten away from him while he slept like a careless baby. He was definitely getting soft. And it stung his pride, setting him on edge as he climbed to his feet and went searching for his hat. He heard the howl of the train whistle. Moving to the edge of the ravine, he punched out the dents in his crushed hat and watched the iron horse roll to a stop, brakes screeching, and he wondered if she was down there, ready to take Becket away. He'd have to stop her, he knew, giving the Stetson a four-finger pinch as he adjusted it on his head. There wasn't any evidence against the saloon keeper and no matter what he felt for Victoria, which was nothing short of absolute confusion, he had his job to do.

He waited until the last passenger left, the last crate was off-loaded and when he saw Becket climb onto his wagon and head toward the narrow road, Chris turned back to the camp site, stowing his gear and kicking over the smoldering embers. He bent for his saddle, hesitating when he recognized the depression of her body left in the grass. Damn, why did she have to leave like that? Things needed straightening out between them after last night. Or did she even care? Hurt washed over him and he re-examined his chivalrous act of restraint. No. He'd regret it if they'd made love under the stars and he'd have likely woken to a spitting, clawing female ready to blow a few holes in select parts of his anatomy. Yet he couldn't banish the feeling there was a part of Victoria nothing could reach. Not with kisses, not with compassion. Not with him. Hell.

She was driving him mad. No doubt about it, he thought, just as his gaze caught on something shiny. Dropping the saddle, he plucked a square of gold from the edge of the dead camp fire. It was paper, he realized instantly. Straightening, Chris tipped his hat back, frowning as he unfolded the wedge. Matches. *She used them to light the fire last night.* He'd never seen them like this, made of paper, and easily he tore one off, striking it against the rough strip fashioned on the edge. It flared with a hiss and he watched it burn before tossing it aside. He examined the worn package, shaped like a book with writing inside.

Tad's Lounge. Highway 17. Jacksonville. With a series of numbers printed beneath.

Jacksonville where?

He turned it over. The outside was gold, lettered with the establishment's name, and Chris scratched the cover. It couldn't be leaf. It would cost a fortune. Why anyone would would go to such an extravagance on matches was beyond him. And all secured with a thin metal crimp. Ingeniously convenient, he thought, making a mental note to ask Victoria about it before shoving the packet into his back pocket and hefting the pile of leather and wood.

He dropped the saddle on Caesar's back. "What do you make of her, boy?"

The black shook his head, his bridle jingling. "Yeah, me too. How long you figure it'll take me to recognize her this time?"

Chris didn't doubt she'd assumed an identity, probably before she left him this morning. Damn, he thought angrily, he was tired of wading through her disguises and on his way back to Silver Rose, he'd figure a way to get her out of them.

Permanently.

"Jake was going to miss the train, that's why he took off," Clara said, handing the leads of the gelding over to Clancey. "I met the marshal outside of town." She bowed her head and spoke to her feet, shyly. "Jake gave him Caesar and Marshal Swift asked if I'd bring that one back."

Clancey nodded, commenting on how much he'd miss that *youngun* and she dipped a little curtsy for show, picked up her satchel and left the barn.

Victoria moved swiftly down the street, ignoring the whispers and looks she received. Evidently, Miss Fotheringham spread gossip faster than frosting. Yet her step slowed as she remembered why she got fired. A man in her room. In this century, it was such a slutty thing to do. And she'd do it again in a heartbeat. I'm a shameless tart, she thought. But the man kisses like a master—a lost art, in her opinion. And Camille Mc-whoever was a stupid woman.

What does that make you?

Lonely.

The single word pierced like a bullet.

Don't think about it. Your life isn't here. Chris is a nice guy.

He's the best thing to happen to you in five years, a voice needled. *Maybe more.*

I know, I know, she thought, closing her eyes briefly and nearly missing a step. In that tiny place in her mind where she allowed herself to dream again, she was glad, too incredibly pleased that Abigale was his housekeeper, that he'd left her room aching as bad as she, that when she'd wanted to make love with him, he was man enough, honorable enough, to deny himself and simply hold her through the night. Jesus, what she wouldn't give to be able to stay and love that man the way he deserves.

But Victoria didn't think she had enough of it left in her. Kevin, Trisha, Cole, her parents, losing them robbed her of feeling anything but anguish.

You let death rule your life. Let it go.

I'm trying. I am.

But she couldn't think about herself, not until Becket was back in her time and in the hands of the FBI. But the waste of human tissue was always surrounded by people. She could never get close enough to take him without suspicion. Except yesterday. This bizarre adventure would have been over within a couple hours, if Chris hadn't stopped her. Though she could just hit the dirtbag with a tazer and take him to the dry waterfall over the back of a horse, now she had to get past Chris and would be forced to tell him where she was taking the saloon owner. Somehow, Victoria didn't think the unvarnished truth would go over real well with the marshal right now. Especially after she'd split before dawn.

But Ivy League was wanted in her century. And Victoria knew it wouldn't be long before he was in this one, too. The only way to get around this was to prove the town saloon keeper guilty. It plagued her that Chris and Becket might actually be friends. Were they close enough that Chris might question Becket and alert him?

Her last thought turned her stomach.

No, not Chris. If anything, he believed who she was, if not why she was here, and that scrap of confidence and respect kept her from going to him right now and demanding his word on secrecy. I trust him.

Then tell him the truth, all of it.

Yeah, right. The laws of physics and the timeline of history were probably already ripped to shreds with her being here. Let's not chance a total cataclysmic meltdown. The sooner she and Ivy League were gone, the better.

Climbing the steep back stairs, she pushed the matter aside and rapped on the door. The slow scuffle of feet came before it jerked open.

Red Velvet Knight sagged against the frame. "Hell, honey, don't you know we do our work at night. It's still dawn."

"My apologies, Miss Knight," Victoria said softly and stepped inside the lair of the viper.

Vel closed the door, eyeing her from head to foot, her gaze lingering on the scar marking her face from cheekbone to chin. Poor dear.

"I thought I'd get a head start, begin the washing, perhaps?"

Vel yawned, patting her mouth, a smoldering cigarette caught between two fingers. Victoria itched for a drag.

"I'll show you 'round, to your room first." Vel pushed away from the door, moving back down the hall. "Sorry, but it's up here with us."

Victoria knew Vel was being sympathetic to her reputation. "You'll hear the rumor by this evening, Miss Knight." She drew a breath, acting out her role of shy, plump Clara Murphy. "I was fired from the Excelsior Hotel for having a man in my room," she said in a rush, then stopped short when Velvet paused and cocked a surprised look over her shoulder.

"Well, hell. Ain't that a hoot?" Hope for the little mousy thing yet, Vel thought, continuing down the hall.

Victoria passed several closed doors, the rustle of sheets and moans of hung-over men coming through the thin wood. This ought to be an experience, she thought, suddenly excited about having some entertainment while she staked out Becket.

Vel paused at a room long enough to take a key, then headed back the way they'd come. At the first room by the exit, she unlocked the door and flung it open, stepping back and allowing her to pass. "Ain't much, but—"

"It's wonderful," Victoria said and nothing like the cheap porno movie style decor she expected. It was certainly better than she'd had since she arrived and ten times finer than the flea bag motels she'd been climbing in and out of in the past years. Even the walls were papered. A tall dresser, and what she'd learned was a mirrored commode, with pitcher and basin, graced one wall with a window toward the street. Excellent, she thought, right over his office. A lush green carpet covered the floor, flecked with black and looking cozy enough to sink her toes in. A pair of high-back chairs upholstered in black brocade and strategically placed near a barren hearth invited relaxation, and on the far right wall, papered with green stripes on white, were two night stands flanking a large iron bed. Though the green satin comforter and ruffled everything was a bit much, it spoke of quick sex and raw passion and bouncing springs.

"Get's yah all hot and bothered just looking at it, don't it?"

Victoria blinked, looking bashfully at the floor to hide the fact that the mask didn't blush. She cleared her throat. "It's very," she lowered her voice to a whisper, "sexy."

"It's the tamest room in the joint, Clara, believe me," Vel said on a secretive laugh and Victoria looked up. She was propping up the door jam, her voluptuous body draped in rich gray silks and satins, with an ample supply of bosom exposed. But there was something about this woman, a refinement beyond her brash talk, a fresh and comforting feeling surrounding Velvet Knight that Victoria tried to focus on and failed. Whatever it is, it attracts the men like flies.

Victoria gave a heavy sigh and tucked her satchel under the bed, then faced Velvet. "Point me toward the dirt, Miss Knight. I shall make it sorry it ever arrived."

Grinning hugely, Vel tossed the gal the room key, then nodded to the hall. "Come on, honey," she said, rolling around the jam. "If it's dirt you want, we got plenty."

Victoria trailed the madame, watching the sultry rock of her hips and wishing she'd half the sex appeal of this happy harlot as Velvet laid out her schedule, her duties, stressing that she must have the rooms prepared before six in the evening. Work hours, Victoria thought, though the bar opened at three. The customers had to be gone by eight A.M., and as she spoke, Vel moved back down and forth across and down the hall, rapping on each door, a warning since it was nearly that time.

The laundry was on the ground floor in the back, and Victoria stared wide eyed at stoves, tubs, and iron kettles so huge that Schwartznegger would have a problem moving them. Oh God. What did I get myself into? Lines, barren of wash, were stretched across the room, then again outside at the rear of the saloon. And there was a small bath house, tucked below the back stairs, and the fresh green wood told her it was new. And supplying the hot water was her job.

"The men have to bathe before they kin touch the girls," Vel drawled and Victoria speculated on how clean the water could ever be when a dozen miners and cowboys washed in it. In some small part of her, she had to give Ivy League credit. He'd upgraded this cat house. But, then, cleanliness and absolute perfection were his obsessions.

"You accept the position, then?" Vel asked quietly, unsure after witnessing the streak of panic on that homely face. Housekeeping for a cat house was a hell of a task, and they usually had two more girls to divide the chores.

"Seems a bit foolish, but yes," she answered, then muttered, "God, do I miss modern plumbing," as she unbuttoned her cuffs, staring at the overflowing baskets.

Rolling back her sleeves, she plucked a heavy apron from a hook and tied it around her padded middle, then headed for the massive pile of soiled sheets.

"Go back to bed, Miss Knight." She waved her off. "I'll wake you at a decent hour, if you like?"

Vel smiled at her back. "Thanks, honey."

When Victoria knew she was alone, she dropped down onto the pile of fabric with soft plop. She was tired, last night draining her energy. But as she glanced around the room, deciding the best course of action, she knew she had nothing else to do but work and wait.

Wait for Ivy League to return. If he didn't, she'd be out of here in a heartbeat. Marshal or no marshal.

Chapter Sixteen

"Quit that!" Chris hissed when Caesar nudged him again. He knew what the beast wanted—Victoria and her sugary treats and soft caresses. So do I, he thought and suppressed the urge to hunt her down, to find out what face she wore this time and ask why she ran from him. He'd stopped her from going after Becket, and he considered for a moment that she might have dismissed her personal rule of taking bounty in alive and gone after the saloon keeper. But he'd seen the man earlier, fit and pleased, unloading his liquor purchases with the energy of a man half his age.

She was still here. A woman like Victoria didn't fight that hard to get her bounty, then decide to leave. And if he reconciled with one part of her, it was that with her mind set on a course, nothing he could do would change it. They would never see eye to eye on the saloon keeper. But before he'd allow her to take the man out of the city, she'd have to show him proof.

He wanted to see her, unable to relinquish the memory of her kisses, her tears that felt like blood stains on his heart, or the incredible sensations simply holding her created in him.

Yet instead, he kept his attention to the street ahead and the man beside him, relaying a report.

"Duke and Buddy been shootin' at each other again."

Chris cursed softly. Doc MacLaren had taken buckshot out of those two so often she charged them by the pellet, hoping to deter their flagrant use of the other as a target. How they got any mining done was a miracle, when both imagined the other was trying to steal their claims.

"How did you handle it?"

"Made them give me their bullets."

Chris arched a brow in Noble's direction, and the big man shrugged.

"I figure if they've got only one bullet each, they'll save it for a snake or an attack. 'Tween the two of them they couldn't hit a bull at ten paces, anyhow."

Chris nodded his approval.

" 'Sides, I didn't want them in the jail." The marshal cast him a side glance. "Hell, Chris, they ain't taken a bath goin' on two years."

Chris smiled at Noble's sour face. "Fragrant, were they?"

"You could pickle eggs under their arm pits, I swear. And if it don't rain soon—"

"Spare me," he interrupted, putting up his hand. "Don't let them into town if they don't bathe. You can do it yourself, if the stench bothers you so much."

"Dang," Noble muttered, flipping his Arkansas toothpick in and out of its handle sheath. While Noble cursed his superior for not making bathing a law, Chris's gaze swept the streets. He waved to deputies perched in look out posts and walking the streets in slow purposeful rounds through quiet avenues. The main bulk of the city fanned out to residential area, most of the homes owned by either financial or mining businessmen or shop proprietors. As they strolled, the area became less dense, signifying the coming of ranches and small farms, then miles beyond, rising to mountains and the tent city of miners off in the distance as well as even a teepee or two.

Most folks didn't come to this area to stake out a new,

permanent life unless they could provide the area with a service. Silver Rose City offered two banks, five dry goods and general merchandise stores, separate men's and woman's clothing shops, a claims office, a laundry, a milliner, a seamstress, a livery, a tanner, a dairy, three hotels, a half dozen saloons, and five restaurants, ranging from the home-style, hearty fare of Duckett's, to the elegant service and cuisine of Etienne's.

Personally, Chris thought, he preferred Abigale's talents and hoped she wasn't mad at him for skipping breakfast. It wasn't like she didn't have enough stomachs to fill with his ranch hands.

A man called to him, and Chris stilled, frowning as Reid MacLaren barreled down the street astride his Palamino. He skidded to a halt before Chris and touched the brim of his hat.

"Well, this certainly makes it easy. We have the thief."

"We?"

Reid grinned. "Jenna does."

Chris didn't ask if he left his wife with a cornered thief; he knew better. "She have him nailed to the wall, or what?"

Reid scoffed pleasantly, his smile still there. "No, but you have to see this." He inclined his head, and Chris swung up onto Caesar's back. Noble mimicked his moves and together they headed to the MacLaren residence, a large two-story brown stone house set on the curve of the tree-lined road. People milled outside and as Reid raced into the house, Chris and Noble dispersed the crowd before heading in. They went directly to Jenna's offices off to the left.

Reid flung sliding doors back and Chris stared, stunned.

"I told you you had to see this."

The thief, a slim gaunt man in his late twenties, sat on the floor, his feet and hands tied, but it was his face that was the cause of excitement.

"Isn't that the loveliest shade of indigo blue?" Jenna commented with an elegant wave of her hand. She was perched on the edge of a stool, feet tucked beneath simple skirts and a knife in her hand. She toyed with it, as Chris had seen her do once before, the gleaming blade rolling over her fingers like oil sliding on her skin. She was as good as Noble.

"Jenna, love, I think the marshal would like an explanation."

She glanced at her husband, then the marshal. As if startled, she leapt off the stool. "Oh yes, of course." The thief cringed, gripping the blue stained cloth and glaring at her. "Well, we thought to set a trap. I was becoming quite peeved, you know. It hardly mattered where I kept the narcotics—he found them." She flicked a hand at the thief. "With a spring, a couple of decoy bottles filled with nothing but water and a bit of indigo—" She moved to the cabinet, demonstrating to Chris how she set the uncapped bottle of indigo so that it would spring forward the instant the door opened. "We caught him down the street a bit." She glanced back over her shoulder at her husband and smiled. "Reid did. He was not hard to spot."

Chris smiled, shaking his head. Even if the thief got clean away, the indigo marked him for his crime. "Ingenious, Jenna."

"Oh, I didn't think of it," she was quick to say. "Your man Jake did."

"What!" Chris barked.

"You mean skinny with glasses Jake?" Noble asked, as he dragged the thief to his feet and clapped on hand cuffs and leg irons before cutting away the ropes.

"Yes. Don't you recall his comments about the destruction of the hotel?" The lawmen nodded. "Well, from all indications, he was the culprit." She gestured with the knife to the shackled man. "I received an excellent description from a young lad there, then let it be known I'd received replacement drugs for those stolen. As bait, you see."

To the occupants of the room, he was calm and patient, but inside Chris was fuming. Victoria! Interfering with the law again. He ought to lock her up. Then Chris glanced at Reid, expecting him to be upset, or even a little annoyed, yet he simply folded his long arms and leaned back against the wall, watching his wife. Pride glowed in his eyes and envy stabbed Chris. His temper faded enough to allow reason to flood in. A blue bomb—how like her.

"But of course, I couldn't remain inside, nor could anyone else or the bloke—ah, the gentleman—would not attempt a theft, as Jake pointed out. He suggested a booby trap." Her russet brows drew down slightly. "Odd name that." Her expression cleared. "Regardless, it worked."

"That was dangerous, Jenna."

"And I feel properly scolded," she murmured to the floor, then flashed a wickedly pleased smile at her husband. "But I would never have attempted something so daring without Reid here."

"Of course you wouldn't, my love," Reid said dryly and she crossed the room to him, stretching up on tiptoes to kiss his cheek. When he did no more than give her a half-lidded glance, she tugged on his long braid and he straightened, slinging his arm around her shoulder and tucking her close to his side.

Noble shook his head softly, prodding the prisoner. "Jake, huh?"

"Yes, and thank him for me when you see him, Christopher." She left Reid's comfort to see them to the door.

"I'd like to do more than thank him," he muttered under his breath as he strode out.

"Christopher," she warned softly and the marshal paused on the front steps. "Jake could have remained silent and uninvolved. He'd nothing to gain by offering a solution."

"He wouldn't even take money, Chris," Reid put in. "Honest concerned people are a rarity."

But it didn't do much for the man who had his job undermined by that woman, Chris thought, again. "Jake's gone, Jenna." Disappointment briefly marred her lovely face. "I'm sorry, but he left last night on the train."

Noble frowned at his boss, glancing down the street toward the activity of the city, then back to the marshal. A small smile curved beneath his bushy moustache and he nudged the prisoner toward the jail, his horse trailing.

Chris strode alongside, as silent and brooding as the black animal behind him. Noble glanced between the master and his faithful beast, their childish sulking getting so Noble couldn't keep his opinion to himself another moment.

"Pride's a mighty thing, marshal."

Chris felt a lecture coming on with that tone. The prisoner's shackled footsteps marked each step.

"And you got a hell of a brave soul in that gal."

"She's headstrong and—" His head jerked up, his gaze flying to Noble's. "You know?"

Noble grinned, his hairy face hiding most of it. "Yeah. I'll keep the secret." He crossed his heart to seal it.

"Does she know you know?"

Noble reared back, scowling. "Don't talk much to her, do yah?"

"Of course we talk." But she keeps everything to herself.

" 'Spect that's what you did all night out on the mountain with her, too." Sarcastic, amused, and a muscle in Chris's jaw flexed.

"That's none of your business."

"Maybe it ain't." He shrugged. "But that don't mean I cain't like her spunk."

"She does nothing but interfere."

"Dang it all, Chris! Can't you see what kind of a woman you've got there." Noble moved closer, lowering his voice. "She's smart, hell, she's brilliant! And strong, got more courage and grit than any *man* in this town, present company excluded 'acourse. And if what Seth said was true 'bout savin' Lucky, she's got a heart as big as the territory."

"If she does, it's buried under a ton of rock." Most of it.

At the jail, Noble pushed the prisoner ahead, pausing on the threshold to look Chris dead in the eye. "You just ain't lookin' in the right places, son."

Chris scowled, and as Noble escorted the prisoner into a cell, he explained what he'd witnessed in the store last week.

Chris slammed the cell door, his grip on the bars tight, not seeing the thief staring at him oddly, but the woman doing everything in her power to keep attention from herself. Why would she defend him when they hardly knew each other then?

A heavy ache settled harder in his chest. She was leaving, so what did it matter? Then he remembered his dream, the path the cougar cleared and his harsh features relaxed slightly.

"Where is she?"

"You ain't gonna like it."

Chris pushed away from the cell door and faced the deputy. "I don't like much that woman's been doing, so what's the difference?"

Noble smiled to himself as he hung the ring of keys on a peg. "She's at the Pearl." He glanced over his shoulder. "Or least ways, Clara is."

Chris's eyes flared, then narrowed, his jaw so tightly clenched it threatened to snap. "Doing what?" came through gritted teeth.

Noble felt it from across the wide office. Barely checked rage and fear. It wasn't like Chris to show his temper, his Cheyenne blood usually giving him a control that Noble envied. It'd do him good to let off some of that steam. "Go see for yourself." Ought to be like two lions squarin' off, Noble thought.

Noble dropped into his desk chair and pulled out a sheet of paper, inking a pen and beginning the report. Chris stared at his deputy, then swiftly crossed the office to the door.

"What does she look like, Chris, really?"

Chris paused, his hand on the frame as he stared out into the street. "A wild beauty," he said in a rough whisper. His fingers flexed on the wood. "Spectacular." Untamed. In more than her physical appearance, she possessed an untouchable quality. As if she knew valuable secrets no one could ever imagine. And she kept them tightly gripped in her iron will. Expect last night, he thought. Last night she broke like a fragile glass in his arms and he would never forget, that for one moment, she needed him.

She was breathtaking, slim and yellow haired and my blade slid into her soft flesh as if she were made of butter. I felt her shock, in her body pressed to mine, then saw it in the contours of her perfect face. She thought I loved her. They all thought I loved them. But I could never. Not the ones who deserved to die. I'm helping the children. Why can't they see that?

It doesn't matter.

I'm like a dream, imaginary. No trail. No tracks.

Only a body, her own blood painting color to her pale lifeless lips.

It makes me hard to think about it.

Perhaps I'll get Dee to take care of that.

Victoria balanced the tray on her hip and rapped softly on the door, then waited for a response. She gripped the tray tighter, willing herself to calm down. She'd been working at the saloon for three days, avoiding any confrontation with him. Now, it was unavoidable.

Though she admitted that Chris had been right about the liquor purchase, Victoria knew that wasn't all he'd done. He was just to happy about being back—too smug. And she'd spent last night tucked in bed, combing over the tattered files she'd brought with her, hoping to find a clue, a scribbled note from a detective that would lead her to his true motivation. Who was he killing when he killed all those women? Aside from the method and that the bodies were found arranged the same, there wasn't much to connect them. The victims were from different working classes, had different jobs, backgrounds, and spread across the country like a scattering of pebbles. No connection, except—his voice spilled beneath the bottom of the door like an oil slick and no matter how cultured and smooth it was, it still gave her the creeps. She took a breath, dismissing her mental review and concentrating on the present. She pushed the latch. He didn't look up as she entered and crossed the room, but the instant she got close, he closed the book and casually slid it into the desk drawer. She pretended not to notice, pouring coffee, adding the correct amount of cream and sugar.

She lifted the cup and stared into the eyes of a serial killer.

His blue gaze moved over her face, his distaste in her scars only briefly visible in the twist of his perfect lips.

He took the cup, leaning back in the chair to sample the coffee.

"You're Clara."

And you killed Cole, she thought, responding with a soft, "Yes sir," as she placed the meal carefully on his desk, laying out the silver service with infinite care. He was a perfectionist, and recognition in that would endear her to him—sort of. She needed him to get comfortable around her, to dismiss her as a threat and into the woodwork. A droan.

"Who cut you?"

Her gaze flashed to his and she frantically searched her brain for a reason, a reason he couldn't investigate. Blaming Indians was out of the question, even if she could name an attack, which she couldn't. "My papa," she blurted when too many seconds passed.

He arched a brow, so sharp it was like a bend of metal. "Why?"

"I was rather pretty as a young girl," she said, hoping her diction sounded authentic.

"I imagine you were." She didn't like the way he was looking at her. It made her feel violated.

"I 'spect he thought if I wasn't presentable, he wouldn't have to worry over some man stealing me and my dowery from him." Good, she thought, plausible.

"Smart fellow."

Her gaze clashed with his and narrowed. How could he condone such a thing? Then she remembered who she was talking to. God, he was slick. "You think it's all right that he ruined me?"

The cup came slowly away from his lips and he leaned forward, frowning softly.

"I meant that perhaps he loved you so much he wanted you to stay with him forever," he said with a sincerity that made her cringe. He set the cup aside. "Some people don't even get that from their parents."

She stared at him. He was warped. "You're right, sir. But I'd have preferred to hear the words instead of feeling them mark my skin." God. She didn't want to talk with him, especially about a total fabrication. He was too sharp for a slip up.

"Perfection isn't always in the physical," he said softly, gently capturing her hand. Every muscle in her body clenched, her stomach rolling with anxiousness. His hands were ice cold. Even in the 80 degree heat, even after cupping the hot coffee, he was as cold as a corpse, and all she could think of was the innocent lives he'd extinguished with those manicured hands. Cole's life.

"I wish every one thought so." She drew back slowly, itching to run. Itching to see if he bled blood or ice water.

"Me too, dear."

What was Mister perfect-looks, perfect-background worried about? He was perfection. Was he offering a fraction of himself to a drab, plump wallflower? And for what? Penance? He released her fingers and Victoria retreated a step as he left the chair and walked with a slight limp to the window. An imperfection. He wore no jacket, his crisply pressed sleeves turned back, vest open, and she noticed two scratches on his forearm. They looked too much like fingernails to be ignored.

"Have you completed your duties for the day?"

He certainly had the verbage down pat. "Yes sir. Except seeing to Miss Velvet."

He nodded, gazing out the window. Carriages rolled down the darkened street, lanterns swaying like ship lights in the fog. "She insists you were sent from God. How you can manage the workload is beyond me."

I'll just bet, she thought. You never so much as wiped your ass without help.

"You have my permission to hire another servant to help," he told her quietly.

"Oh, thank you," she said, forcing gushing gratitude into her voice. She wanted to puke on his snake skin boots.

He waved negligently. "You may go."

She turned to leave, but his voice, steely and low, stopped

her. "Get some new clothes, Miss Murphy. My girls dress to perfection." He twisted ever so slightly, a shock of dark hair falling like a wave over one eye. He could have made millions in her century on his looks alone. "I will pay the bill."

"I'm not one of the girls, *sir.*" She put just a touch of defiance in her tone, and he smirked, as if letting her prostitute herself for him were the last thing he would consider.

"I realize that," he said with ample condescension. "Nevertheless, we have a standard to maintain."

Ah yes, perfection in pimping, too. How dignified, she thought, and nodded, slipping from the room with her back straight and head high like the proper spinster she was. Victoria didn't see him smile, nor did she see his gaze drop to her feet.

Beyond the closed door Victoria paused, taking a breath and running her fingers over her artificial scars. Damn. Silver Rose had too few citizens and even fewer visitors, and while the unappealing scars would have garnered no more than a pitying glance in her over-populated century, here they made her stand out like a Nordstrom window display.

Noticable. And now to the one man she didn't want to notice her.

This was not good, she thought, cursing her carelessness as she slipped beyond the private doors and crossed to a door left of the bar. In the small kitchen, she bypassed the cook hovering over a vat of stew and filled a small ceramic tea pot, Vel's own, full of hot water, spooned in tea, then discreetly checked her watch. She had just enough time to get this to Velvet before the girls started *working.* For the past days she made herself scarce around now; something about seeing a man who paid for sex turned her stomach. It was accepted practice, she knew, even advertised, and although she'd never hold their "jobs" against the women, the twentieth century female couldn't bear to see them degrade themselves. No woman *chose* to be a prostitute.

Hefting the tray, she moved quickly across the saloon and up the staircase, a fistful of skirt in her hand. She headed to the center of the hall and rapped on the door. It didn't take her but a day to understand Vel's comments about her room being the tamest in the bunch. Each had a motif, seductive and extravagant and enticing fantasies to run wild. Only Velvet had two adjoining rooms, a small sitting area and a lush bedroom decorated like a Sultan's harem. And when Vel's voice beckoned her from inside, Victoria pushed open the door.

On a mound of silken pillows, surrounded by carefully draped sheers of pink and red and yellow, was Red Velvet Knight, half reclined in half naked glory, her head bent close to a man who was whispering something in her ear.

And the man, Victoria realized with a stab of unspeakable pain, was Chris.

Chapter Seventeen

As Victoria crossed the threshold, Chris looked up sharply, his eyes flaring as they met hers. A split second later his features stretched tight, a guilty flush creeping into his handsome face.

And Victoria froze on the spot. She felt betrayed. For an entire heartbeat, she was stricken, her feet glued to the floor, a hard tearing sensation ripping through her body, her heart.

This hurts.

Oh, Jesus. It hurts.

She struggled for composure, suppressing the rushing agony fighting to the surface, years of practice clicking into motion as she crossed to the low brass table and set the tray carefully in the center. Bent, she poured tea, added sugar, then straightened, looking at Vel. "Is there anything else I can do for you, Miss Knight?"

Vel glanced between the two, her forehead wrinkling a touch. "No honey," she said carefully. "It was sweet of you to bother."

Victoria turned her gaze to Chris. "Something I can get you, marshal?" *Like a punch in the nose?*

"I've got all I came for, thanks." His low intimate tone twisted through Victoria like a snake, strangling her.

"Ain't polite to tease a gal," Velvet said on a laugh, giving him a playful nudge.

Victoria swallowed, the thickness in her throat like sandpaper. She liked Velvet; they'd become friends. But to see Chris pressed close to her, admiring her lush plump curves, acting so damn *familiar* with the half naked harlot shredded her heart into tiny pieces. She could feel each one break and fall away to dust.

She had to get out of here.

"If you'll excuse me, then. I've clothes to purchase."

"What yer wearing looks fine," Vel said with a glance over her Navy skirt and crisp high necked white blouse.

In perfect spinster-proper diction she said, "Apparently, Mister Becket insists his girls have a standard, and I attire myself below it."

Chris's expression sharpened as Vel conceded. "He is a bit finicky about that."

"What kind of clothes?" Chris gritted, eyeing Victoria.

She looked at him blandly. "I don't see where it's any of your business, Marshal."

He stood abruptly, fists clenched. "I'm making it mine."

"You should know by now not to push your nose into everyone's affairs, Marshal Swift." His dark eyes narrowed. "You could get it *cut off.*" Dismissing his anger, she addressed Vel, who was staring oddly at Chris. Let's see him explain that, she thought, her smugness only amplifying her hurt. "If you'll excuse me. I'll leave you to your privacy."

She spun on her heels and strode out the door, pulling it closed before hurrying down the hall.

The jolt of the slamming door made Chris flinch, and he cursed softly, pushing his fingers through his hair. The soft sheen of tears and her wounded expression, masked or not, was enough to cut him in half. He knew how bad this looked, but she had to understand. She had to. Christ . . . she wouldn't.

"Marshal?" Vel called softly, reaching for her tea cup. "What's going on?"

"Nothing." Hollow, regretful, as he advanced to the door.

"Like hell."

He paused and she met his gaze over the rim of china.

"Energy like that only a fool would miss." She sipped and inwardly, Chris groaned. Though he'd never destroy Victoria's plans, he hoped Vel was the only person who noticed their attraction.

"Clara isn't all that she seems, Vel."

The madame scoffed. "Tell me somethin' I don't know."

He frowned questioningly.

"That girl is different. Strange, but . . . heck, I don't know." She shook her head, rueful. "I just get the feeling she's ain't really what we're all seein'."

Chris almost laughed. Almost. But the memory of her sorrow visible even behind brown-green eyes, kept a smile from his face. "Thanks, Vel." He scooped his hat off a side table. "Let me know if you hear or see something."

"Shoot." She snapped her fingers. "Had you in my clutches for a whole hour and failed."

He paused, cocking a glance over his shoulder. "Sorry, Vel." He positioned his hat on his head. "But you're just not wild enough for me." She busted with laughter as he slipped out of the room, nearly running down the hall and ascending the back stairs in record time. He scanned the area, then swung around the end of the steps and into the men's bathing room beneath the stairs.

The sole occupant of the huge tub glanced up, his wash rag slowing as it moved across his chest. His gaze dropped to the star on Chris's chest.

"The maid?"

The man inclined his head to the rear and Chris backed out and strode further down the alley to the laundry at the back of the saloon. He slapped his hands on the frame, his gaze searching. The large room was barren but for steaming kettles of water and low tubs filled with washing. Did she abandon her job?

He started to push away from the frame when he saw her through the corner window, in the yard, pumping water steadily into a bucket, setting it aside and picking up another to fill. She was causing mayhem to the pump, jamming it down faster and faster and Chris smiled, wide and utterly pleased.

She was jealous.

Fire breathing, heart wrenching jealous!

He wanted to shout. Instead, he crept up behind her.

"Go away," she said without looking up, then hefted the buckets and turned, moving swiftly back to the wash room.

He followed. "Victoria."

She stopped and he nearly slammed into her, water splashing her skirts. "I beg your pardon? You must have the wrong woman. I'm Clara Murphy." She continued inside, setting a bucket down before emptying one into a kettle on the stove.

"I thought you were going to buy clothes."

She stilled for a moment. "I am, in the morning." She emptied the second bucket, then headed out back to repeat the process. "The shops are closed for the night."

Chris dogged her heels.

She pumped water, wishing he'd leave her to her misery. "Don't you have a job to do, Marshal?"

"I'm doing it."

Her gaze flew to his. "Patronizing a whorehouse in the job description?" Bitter, condescending, stinging across his skin with the bite of a whip. "How fortunate for you."

"I wasn't a customer, Tori."

His tone was sincere, making her uneasy, and she pulled the bucket away before the water flow ceased, splashing on his boots. She faced him, her next words sticking in her throat and sounding like a croak. "I don't care."

He grinned. "Yes, you do."

She shrugged. "Suit yourself." She moved past him, retracing her steps inside, pouring water, stirring wash. She dipped a pitcher into a hot kettle and walked swiftly to the men's bath, rapping once before entering. "Warm enough, pal?"

"Yes, ma'am." The cowboy tipped his hat back, his gaze shooting to the maid, the marshal and back as she set the pitcher on a low table beside the tub.

She took up a sponge. "Would you like me to scrub your back?"

"You're not scrubbing anyone!" Chris bellowed, stepping inside.

She cast him a quick superior glance, then swiped across the man's skin. Chris immediately caught her wrist. Eyes locked, jealousy now in his, fresh pain in hers.

"It's all right, ma'am. I kin manage," the man interjected, removing his hat and shielding what lay beneath the suds.

"This is my job, Marshal."

He knew what she was saying. She was here to take in a bounty and nothing more. And he was damn tired of hearing it and refused to believe she couldn't see they had something good and strong. If she'd just quit fighting him.

"Ladies don't wash strange men."

"No lady here, pal." She twisted her wrist, freeing his grip with surprising ease. "In case you haven't noticed." She stared at him for moment, watching his brows draw tighter, his eyes sketch her face before she turned away and dunked her fingers in the pitcher, testing the temperature. As the naked man in the tub nodded, she rinsed his hair and back, then set the pitcher aside to lay a stack of towels beside him. "Lila is in room four, waiting for you," she said in a hot whisper that infuriated Chris.

The man nodded dumbly and she turned to leave, forcing Chris to back out of the narrow doorway. She returned to the laundry and her duties, rolling up her sleeves well past her elbows and digging them into piles of wet sheets. She scrubbed and sopped and wrung them out yard by yard, and muscles, incredibly defined muscles, jumped and flexed with every motion. And as he watched her from the doorway, apprehension slithered through him.

Was he mistaken? Could she shut off her heart like she shut off the water pump? He stepped inside and got hit in the shoulder with a cake of soap.

Guess not.

"Don't come in here!"

He did, pulling the door closed, darkening the room. The lamp light cast a yellow glow off the walls, steam clouding her image.

"I swear I'll kill you if you come near me." Each word was punctuated with a vengeful twist of the wet sheet, and she wished it was his throat.

"I didn't mean to hurt you."

"Sleep with whoever or whatever you want, Marshal." Her voice wavered. "I don't give a crap." She snapped the sheet out, flinging water in his face. "So don't try to make this out to be anything that it's not." She turned her back on him to pin the sheet on a line and hoped he didn't notice her trembling.

"Is that what I'm doing?" He swiped his sleeve across his wet forehead as he advanced, his presence like a stalking panther, heightening her senses, unnerving her.

"Yes or you'd be gone." She jammed the wood clothespins, side-stepping away from him.

"I wasn't a customer."

Her gaze slid to his, his betrayal in her eyes. "I know what I saw. Guilt." She ducked under the sheet and went back to wringing another.

He followed. "That's 'cause you weren't expected," he confessed, following. "And you ought to know better than to believe what you see."

"There incognito, were you?" The last came in a grunt as she twisted the water out of the fabric.

"No." His voice lowered. "For information."

She stilled, titling her head slightly to look at him. "On whom?"

"Just general. I can't be everywhere, and Vel has the ear of this town."

She glanced pointedly at the bulge in his trousers. "So to speak."

His lips quirked. "Believe me?"

"Not really."

His jaw tightened, his eyes flashing with irritation. "Great mother, you are the most hard-headed, stubborn female in this territory!" He leaned down in her face, blocking the light, smothering her escape. "And you think if you don't face that you're jealous, *totally—womanly*—jealous at seeing me in Velvet's room, you wouldn't be hurting like you are!"

"How wise of you to clear that up for me," she muttered dryly. "I'll have to remember that for the future." She pushed him aside like he was a curtain and moved to the stove, ladling hot water into a bucket, then turning to the tub. She poured it over soaking sheets, stirred, then scrubbed against a wash board.

Go away, she thought. *Please. I need this hurt to keep me from wanting you.*

Chris yanked off his hat and raked his fingers through his hair. Properly dismissed, he thought, hating how she hid her feelings inside her disguises, and he was damn tired of *her* running this relationship into the ground. He advanced toward her and she looked up just as he caught her shoulders, pushing her away from the wash tub and up against the nearest wall. He needed help trapping this woman. And she fought him all the way there.

"I ought to make you a soprano." She tried digging her knee into his groin, but her wet skirts and his booted foot holding them down, prevented it.

"I ought to make love to you until you can't stand it anymore."

White heat shot through her at the thought of it. "Think you're that good, huh?"

His lips quirked. "That's what you need."

Arrogant pig. "A good screw, oh that's rich. Christ, next you'll be trying to rescue me from hidden danger, then riding off into the sunset."

"My Cheyenne instinct was to kidnap you and hold you

until that sharp mind of yours saw reason and *facts.*" He gave her a considering look. "And if it will get you out of that hideous mask, I just might."

"I'll fight you."

He flashed her a smile. "Yeah, I know."

Acceptance, a voice whispered. Why did it have to be him? Why now? "We can't finish this."

"Because you won't let it get started."

Started? Was he serious? She was hip deep in her feelings for him. "Someone has to keep a level head."

He pressed his long body full against her, mashing her to the wall. "But do you want to?" came on a husky murmur and she turned her face away. He forced her to look at him, hating the clammy feel of her fake skin beneath his fingers and gazed into her eyes, trying to reach beyond his profession and suspicion. His options were slim. Either arrest her, take away the barriers—

Or expose her heart. And his.

"Ignore me, I won't go away. Deny what we feel, it'll still be there in the morning." His voice lowered, almost threatening. "And if you run, I'll follow you."

"You can't," she cried softly, weak from his words, weak from wanting him so badly.

"I will. You *are* staying. You are," he added more firmly when she looked to protest. "If I have to help you find proof, you're not getting away from me. I can't let you, Tori. You're already in my soul."

She blinked, momentarily stunned by the heat in his eyes, the depth of his certainty. This wasn't a man who spoke like that often. "You just want—"

His mouth made a harsh slash across hers, cutting off the remark he knew would be rude as hell. She did that to put him off, but it wasn't working, and he increased his assault, his lips wildly molding and shaping hers, his tongue scoring her teeth and pushing inside. She fought him, her fists pushing and pounding at his chest, her body twisting maddeningly against him. Great spirits, what was he going to do with this woman! How could he reach her heart if she constantly pushed him away, despite her feelings? She was like a wild colt fighting the bit and his blood boiled, and he pressed his body harder to hers, hip to hip, letting her feel what she did to him. And where.

Then he caught her wrists, pulling her arms around his waist.

She pounded him there, except she kissed him back, opening her mouth wide, devouring him, her rage, her hurt and betrayal unleashing wildly in her soul-stripping kiss. She gripped his waist, fingertips digging, then drove her hands up his chest to catch his jaw between her palms, imprisoning him.

And the kiss became hers—liquid fire and untamed passion. Hungry. Wet. Possessive.

Chris's knees wobbled. His heart thrashed in his chest. When she gave back it unmaned him. "Admit it," he growled against her mouth. "You were jealous."

"Yes," she hissed. "Yes, yes!" Her fingers slid deeply into his hair, gripping handfuls. "How was I supposed to feel? I haven't seen you in three days, and I find you with Vel!"

"I thought you didn't want me to find you?"

"I didn't, but—"

He grinned, hugely.

"Oh, don't look so smug." With a narrowed look, she released him roughly.

"Please allow me this small moment of glory. You've emasculated me enough since we met."

"If you can't stand the heat, Marshal," she warned.

He shifted against her, his body contouring to hers with intimate clarity. "It's the heat I want, Tori. *Your heat.*" He brushed his lips across her mouth, then reached between them and unbuttoned her blouse.

"Chris!" came in a sharp whisper and she tried to stop him, but he found where skin and mask met and sank his lips there. Her legs softened, her head dropped back, and she moaned richly as he drew a wet tonguing path down to the bindings and corset.

"You taste incredible." His whispers cooled her heated flesh.

"Good, Tori, I want to feel *you.*" He palmed her bound breast. "It's not fair."

"Don't do this to me. Please. Not now, maybe later we can meet and—" She couldn't believe what she was saying, but the look on his face, joyously pleased and hopeful destroyed her will power. With this man, she had only just so much to fight with.

The sound of voices startled them apart and as Chris turned away and grabbed his hat, Victoria managed to rebutton her blouse before the door sprung open.

Ivy League frowned into the steamy room, and Victoria felt her heart sink to her knees and she prayed the hanging sheets shielded their recent closeness. What was *he* doing in here?

"Thanks for the information, Miss Murphy," Chris said striding toward the door as if he was on his way out anyway. He stopped short when he saw Becket, acting startled.

"Marshal Swift?" the saloon keeper said, frowning softly.

"Miss Murphy was a witness to a crime, or rather the clues leading to the criminal. At the Excelsior," he said easily, continuing to the door.

Becket nodded. "I hope she was of some help."

Chris paused at the threshold. "Between her and a drifter named Jake, we caught him."

Victoria's lip twitched and she bowed her head to hide it.

"Really? But wasn't that three days ago?"

Chris agreed, inclining his head toward Victoria. "I needed her account before I could file a report. I heard Miss Murphy had left the hotel and only recently learned that she works here now." Chris glanced back, calling to her.

Victoria looked up, cloudy water dripping off a sheet. He was turned so Becket couldn't see his expression and his dark gaze swept her like a rough caress, a vivid reminder, before he tugged at the brim of his hat. "Be seeing you 'round, ma'am." He winked, then faced Becket and shook his hand before striding past.

"You wanted something, sir?" She hoped her immediate

dismissal of Chris's presence squashed any suspicion that Ivy League might have.

He glanced around the laundry, his distaste souring in his expression. "About the new clothes."

"Yes sir?" she said patient, bland.

"Disregard it." Her expression didn't shift a fraction. "No one of value sees you during the day, and I've decided your attire is not worth my expense."

She tilted her head regally, making it clear she was not offended, poor ugly creature that she was. "As you wish, sir."

He left before her last word was out.

So, no new clothes. Good. Victoria would rather walk barefoot through broken glass than wear something he provided. She went back to work, wondering if he was hard up for money, then she remembered a conversation with Vel.

He wanted to sell the Pearl to her.

Was Ivy League leaving for fresher prey?

Chapter Eighteen

It was the book, Victoria thought, chewing the inside of her lip. Something valuable had to be in the book she caught Ivy League writing in the other day. And she needed to get a look at it, maybe even take pictures and tried to remember if she'd tossed her micro camera in her pack, the cheap disposable job she used to catch license plate numbers that she never failed to forget. Back in her century, she mused, letting her thoughts wander.

"Well, you're a bundle of laughs tonight," a voice called and Victoria looked up, startled for a instant as to where she was, her mind trapped in her time, in painful memories. She blinked, looking around the room at the women lounging on piles of large pillows, their bodies draped in lace and silks and seduction.

Victoria offered an apologetic smile. "Daydreaming, I guess." She shrugged, taking a sip from the cup clutched in her hands. She made a face. "God, this is awful," she said to the coffee and stood, crossing the room and pitching the contents out the window. A man howled, cursing her and Victoria looked sheepish. "Oops."

The room erupted in feminine laughter, and Victoria joined in, releasing a days worth of tension in the husky sound. The girls were like a secret sorority, and she'd been invited in, accepted, even though she wasn't a *working* girl. This nightly rap session was a ritual. They revealed secrets and spoke of their customer's ineptness or finesse, and sometimes mentioned their brutality.

To Victoria, it was a lesson in being totally female. They were the experts and Victoria studied them carefully, remembering what it was like to have few worries and no pain—to simply be wild and play. Be a woman.

"I had a live one tonight," a slim blonde said, leaving her cushions and walking over to the low table. She plucked a chocolate from a tray and popped it in her mouth. "That boy thought he'd come to my bed wearing spurs and his hat! Woulda tore my spread all to hell." She licked her fingertips, then added with a smile, " 'Cept he was so fast, he was done before he had me on it."

Giggles floated, then another girl spoke up, her voice child-like and breathy.

"Mine all treat me like I'll break." Disappointment laced her voice.

"You look like you would," Victoria said. She couldn't be more than sixteen and looked like twelve.

"Wish they'd treat me like that. Hell, I got the hard riders," Vel put in, stretching languidly. "And if I can walk tomorrow, I'll be lucky."

"But what did they leave you," one asked and Victoria turned her gaze to the plump redhead.

"Leave you, Vel?"

"Not what yer thinkin' girl," Velvet said, grinning. "I got one that slips into my room and leaves me stuff."

"Stuff? Come on Vel," Victoria said, honestly curious. "Out with it."

Vel twisted away and reached under her pillow, coming back with a delicate silver bracelet.

Everyone leaned close, in awe over the fine curling filigree flickering with marcasite.

"Who was it?"

Vel shrugged. "I've tried to find out, but none of my regulars will admit to it."

"It's beautiful."

Vel tossed it to her and Victoria caught it. "It's yours, honey."

"No, I couldn't. I didn't—"

"Earn it?"

Victoria looked at her feet.

"Don't worry, hon, neither did I, but if those fools want to waste their money, who am I too argue?"

Laughter spilled again, agreeing and comments heightened the noise, but Victoria went still, her ears tuned. She hushed the group.

"Shhhh!" she stressed again and they went silent. Victoria frowned. "Did you hear that?"

"All I hear is my bed callin' me—"

Victoria slashed the air, then her eyes suddenly widened. She tossed the bracelet to Vel and strode swiftly to the door, walking down the hall, then running. She rapped on a door, heard a grunt, then something hitting the floor.

The girls were behind her now and she glanced at the faces to see who was missing.

"Lila, you all right?"

Nothing. She tried the knob and found it locked, then heard the unmistakable sound of a slap. Hiking her skirts, she kicked at the door. It sprang on the first shot, banging against the wall. A man held Lila by the hair, his arm drawn back.

"Don't even think about," Victoria warned and he sneered, bringing his arm down.

Victoria lunged instinctively, ducking between Lila and his blow, blocking it with her forearm. Then she drove her fist into his stomach. The wind left his lungs and he folded. She grabbed his head and brought her knee up to connect with his nose. It fractured with a horrible crunching sound. Blood splattered, and when he tried to grab for her, she clapped her hands sharply against his ears. He howled, dropping to his knees and Victoria grabbed Lila, pulling her from the room and thrusting her at the others.

She whirled on the man struggling to his feet, keeping her gaze on his as she inched up her skirt to remove the knife strapped to her calf. She adjusted her grip and his bleary gaze moved from her face to the blade.

He swiped his sleeve beneath his bleeding nose, his small eyes boring into her.

"I know what you're thinking. A woman—I can take her. But am I worth going to prison for?"

He snickered as if that would be the last outcome he'd consider, swaying on his feet. He took a step, and she flipped the knife hilt up, gripping the blade point.

"Think again, pal." Her eyes narrowed. "Because if I go, you come with me."

He grinned, showing bloody teeth an instant before he lunged. She threw, the blade sinking into his shoulder. He screamed, staggering and just as quickly she advanced, her hand closing over the handle and using it to force him back against the wall.

"You're never going to strike a woman again. Are you?"

He panted, wide eyes shifting from the hand wrapped around the blade handle to her face. "You bitch." He grabbed her arm. "I'm gonna—"

She twisted the knife in his flesh ever so slightly and he whimpered, his touch loosening. "An inch downward and it's your heart, buster."

"You're crazy," he sneered, sweat beading on his face. "She's just a damn whore."

"She's a human being!" Victoria hissed. "Which is more than I can say for you. Remember *little* man," she said with a sweep down his body. "There's always going to be someone stronger and quicker than you. And next time you try beating a woman, she just might kill you." With her last words she yanked the blade out. He shrieked like a wounded animal and behind her, the girls gasped like a choir.

Victoria backed away as he covered his wound.

"Get out." She motioned to the door.

He moved, clutching his wound, side stepping, stumbling once. "The marshal'll hear of this."

"Good, you do that."

The ladies gave him an escort down the hall and out the door. And over the rail, if she had to guess, but she was trembling too hard, the rush of adrenaline singing through her body. She looked at her knife. It scared her, how easily she drove it into his shoulder. Am I like him? Like Ivy League?

No, her conscience battled. *You don't prey on the weak. You didn't take his life. You didn't stalk him until he was so terrified he couldn't fight back.*

Releasing a slow breath, she methodically cleaned his blood off her apron and put it away.

Vel hadn't moved, her arm supporting Lila, but she was looking at her strangely. "You're something else, Clara."

"Exactly what, I'm still trying to figure out," Victoria smirked, helping Lila to her bed. The other girls rushed back, hovering at the doorway as Victoria and Vel cleaned Lila's wounds and gave her a powder for the pain. The murmurs died suddenly, and Victoria felt the hackles rise on her neck as she twisted to see why.

Ivy League stood in the doorway, his gaze swiftly taking in the broken crockery, Lila's face, and Victoria. Dee clung to his arm like a frightened child. He dismissed the girls to their rooms.

"Thank you." His expression deepened slightly. "We seem fortunate to have you in our town, Miss Murphy."

There was a cryptic inflection in his tone that made her wary.

Victoria shrugged, looking bashful. "A girl alone learns things, sir." She turned her attention to Lila's swelling face and didn't take a decent breath until she knew he was gone.

"You all right, honey?" Vel said, reaching out to cover her hand. "You're trembling."

She met her gaze. "I don't like him." A weak statement considering what she really felt.

"Me either."

Victoria arched a brow.

"I mean, he's a good fella and treats us all real nice—" she cast a glance at the door, frowning. "—but I can't put my finger on it."

Victoria appreciated the sixth sense of the madame, but weighed her options and deciding it was best not to confide in anyone. The less they knew, the safer they were. But a little insight wouldn't hurt.

"What makes you say that?" Victoria asked, sinking down onto the bed and applying a compress to Lila's swollen jaw.

Vel shrugged, trying to put words to her feelings. "It's like he thinks we're all fools, beneath him, but doesn't come right out and show it. Granted, I'm no prize, but I know where I am in the way of things." Victoria noticed that when Vel was thoughtful, she lost her accent. "But he sees this," her gesture encompassed the saloon, "as a game. Not a business where you'd count damages, needed repairs." She shook her head, trying to understand what Victoria already knew. "He's meticulous, wants everything prefect and *clean.* Can't tolerate the slightest wrinkle in his routine. But he's good to us, like getting Dee to the doctor the other day 'cause her cramps were so bad she couldn't move—or work."

At the mention of cramps, Victoria's abdomen clenched. Her period would come in a few days and she had nothing to help her through it. For that matter, she didn't know what women did in this century. Whatever it was, it wasn't hygienically safe nor as simple as a tampon. She'd have to deal with that when it came, she decided, her mind dull with fatigue even as she tried to figure a way into that office without Ivy League around.

"He's done something, hasn't he?"

Victoria's gaze flew to Vel's. "He's . . . just be careful, okay?"

"Want some help?"

"No! Absolutely not," she hissed, gripping Vel's arm. "Don't do anything for me." When Vel simply stared, Victoria shook her. "Swear to me you won't get involved! And no matter what you see, don't cross him."

Vel searched her gaze, the panic and warning clear enough for a hick like herself. "I swear, honey." She patted her hand and Victoria relaxed. "Now you go on to bed," Vel said, watching the girl's brows furrow tightly. "You been up longer than the rest of us."

"I've grown accustomed to little sleep lately," she said, but handed over the compress and left the room anyway. She moved sluggishly down the hall, fishing in her pocket for the key and inserting it in the lock. She paused in opening the door, the sensation of being watched sending a chill over her arms. She didn't look up, suddenly aware of the man at the far end of the hall near the saloon's inner staircase. She stepped inside, closing the door.

Sagging against the wood, she clamped her eyes shut and prayed he'd leave, prayed she didn't screw this up and get herself or anyone else killed. Tiredly, she stripped off her clothes, leaving the padding in place and as she leaned over the commode and made to remove the mask, she stilled, deciding she was just too tired to go through the meticulous ritual and slipped into the bed, drawing the satin coverlet over her shoulders. She was asleep in seconds.

And a few hours later, close to dawn, she didn't hear the door open, nor the figure moving into her room. But suddenly, with heart-stopping clarity, she was awake and keenly aware that she was not alone. She heard breathing, smelled a scent, bay rum, then felt the cloying presence of a body hovering over her. She fought to keep still, to maintain even sleep-like breathing. Terror like she'd never experience raced along her bloodstream. She could feel his gaze, and for an instant wondered if it was Chris. Had Becket called him in? No, it was too close to morning. And to suppress her fear she turned her mind to the practical. What could he see? Her wig was still securely in place she assured herself, her few hours of sleep so hard she hadn't moved. But if he touched her face?

She moaned, shifting sleepily and he jerked back suddenly.

But he didn't leave, standing in the center of her room. Then she felt him fade before she heard the creak of the door closing.

She opened her eyes a fraction, a still closed look should he still be near, and when she realized he was gone, she slipped from the bed and very quietly vomited into the basin.

Chapter Nineteen

Victoria dipped the pitcher into the steaming kettle of water.

"Do you ever get a day off?"

She flinched, letting out a yelp and dropping the pitcher into the water.

Immediately, she spun on her heels.

"Don't sneak up on me like that!" she hissed, giving him a shove.

Chris smiled. "I never could before."

"What do you want?"

His brows rose at her sharp tone and she sighed, brushing damp tendrils off her forehead and offering him a small smile. "I'm sorry. I'm just a little edgy today."

"It's a wonder, going around stabbing everybody."

"One man, *one man,*" she reminded, holding up a finger in case he couldn't count. "And you don't think he deserved it?"

"I wasn't there."

"Take a look at Lila and you'll see why the son of a—" She clamped her lips shut and turned away, fishing in the pot for the pitcher with a stick. She was working herself ragged. Her lower back throbbed, her breast ached and her temper and nerves were unusually short. And she didn't want to take it out on Chris. She hadn't slept well last night, the image of Ivy League hanging over her bed preventing anything but nightmares and horror to intrude on her dreams.

"What's the matter?" Chris asked, softly, frowning his worry.

"Nothing." She set the pitcher aside and with both hands grasped her lower spine, arching her back. Her shoulders drooped. "Christ, I'm so tired I can't think straight."

There was a shiver in her voice he hadn't heard before, defeated.

"I just want this to be over with."

Pulling her beyond the hanging sheets and into privacy, Chris took her in his arms, holding her. It was exactly what she needed, wanted. Then his hands slipped to the base of her corset, strong fingers rubbing the small of her back in tiny soothing circles and she moaned quietly, laying her head on his shoulder and sinking deeply into his strong embrace.

"How did you know?"

His lips curved against the top of her head. "Life."

"Hmm?" She snuggled her arms around his waist, holding him with a desperation he couldn't understand.

"I'm Cheyenne, raised with the tribe. It's very close knit and *crowded*. There's little a young warrior doesn't learn when it comes to . . . nature. All things are within a circle of living, growing, dying. The cycle of a woman is a natural, necessary event."

"Well, I wish it would leave me out of the loop."

He chuckled softly, the sound rumbling against her ear pressed to his chest. "Besides, I saw my father do this for my mother."

"And here I thought you wanted me to think you were sage and wise, oh great mystic warrior."

"With you around?" Another chuckle, self-depreciating.

"Oh, Chris, that feels so good," she moaned as his fingers worked deeper, harder, and the pain left in slow increments.

But it would be back, she knew. Ever since her Norplant insert, her period always announced itself for days before it started.

He looked down, tipping her head back. He brushed his lips over hers. "Take the day off. Come home with me. Rest."

Home. His home Oh, God, *that* was tempting.

She started to push away, but he held her. "You're exhausted."

"I can't." She couldn't tell him what she was planning. He'd throw her in jail for sure.

"You promised me some time, alone."

Alone, without the mask, he was saying. Right now, she wanted it so badly she could taste it. She wanted to forget about Becket, forget duty and hide in his arms. But it was impossible to even entertain the idea. "I know, but I'm training the new help." It wasn't a lie. And to confirm it, the sound of footsteps and sloshing water came to them.

Chris released her reluctantly, observing her as she took the pail from the woman. She's fighting her body, her weariness. And him. He could feel the tension in her, see her hands shaking as she poured water into the kettle, then reached for another. The woman, older than Victoria by ten years, her expression offering no nonsense and no humor, spared him a mild glance. And from his perspective, she didn't need any training.

Chris couldn't think of one woman who didn't know how to wash clothes. Even his mother, pampered life that she'd been privilege to, knew that.

She was avoiding him, lying. And it hurt. Dammit, it hurt. When was she going to trust him? Then he thought of the telegrams he'd sent all over the country and he decided he wasn't doing himself any favors by remaining silent. But something kept an invisible line between them, something intangible and lost in his strange dream. But whatever kept her heart at bay, Chris didn't think she'd ever cross it enough to confide in him.

Victoria set the bucket down and turned to Chris, only to catch a glimpse of his broad back before he disappeared out the door.

Miserably, she dropped down on a stool.

You just keep screwing it up over and over, she railed at herself.

But what was more important? Chris's bruised feelings or a killer running loose? And how long before you're so tired that Ivy League takes you out of the loop?

Velvet Knight lounged against the edge of the bar, watching the crowd, her gaze straying to a miner who'd been giving her the eye all night. Her boss was making his rounds, shaking hands, smiling that strange smile. She thought back to Clara and the way she was around him, tense, wary, and her gaze scanned the room, knowing she wouldn't find the girl, but checking just the same. She was such a lonely quiet flower, Vel thought, seeing a bit of herself, years ago. But Clara wasn't what she seemed, beating the stuffing out of that man the other night told her that. And Vel hadn't lived this life, this long, not to pick out a Pinkerton or a government agent when she saw one, female or not. It impressed her, her conclusions, and the woman. And it made her feel she was right about her boss. He was trouble beneath a layer of class, and her eyes strayed to the bulk of a man making his way across the room.

"Ain't Miss Abigale gonna be in a fit?" she said when Noble Beecham stopped beside her, signaling the bartender for a beer.

His bushy brows rose up into his receding hair line. "Dang, nothing passes you."

"Not when there's a handsome man on the loose."

He flushed a bit, catching the bottle the bartender slid to him.

"Want a tussle, Noble?"

He continued to stare at the bottle. "I would," he said almost shyly. "But I can't shake the feelin' I'd be betrayin' her."

"Would you?"

"I guess that's why I'm here, to find out."

Vel shifted closer, her soft smile bittersweet. Noble was the best kind of man, a heart bigger than his chest and strong enough to admit he could still be confused about some things. Vel tipped his head until her looked at her, then leaned close, putting all her experience in a kiss as soft as her name and as sweet as her scent.

And Noble felt the pang of desire flare lightly, even as her mouth moved over his with practiced art. Then he leaned back, staring into her eyes.

"Who were you thinking about just then?" He opened his mouth, stuttering a bit. "Now don't lie, 'cause I kin tell, and I won't be hurt, Noble. I won't." Her voice lowered. "You're just a hard cock with money in his pocket to me." It was a lie, bald-faced and vulgar. But she knew his answer before he said it.

"Her. That I wished it was her."

And she wasn't going to let him ruin a good thing because of something they had years ago.

"Then go to her."

He took up the beer, prepared to drain it, but she stopped him.

"Not drunk." She took the bottle, nudging him away and he kissed her cheek and left. She watched him, sipping the liquor, her heart saying good-bye before turning her attention to the crowd. Without reason, her gaze lifted to the staircase, to the second floor and the rail usually populated with her girls enticing men to come up. A figure moved back beyond the edge of the wall, casting no more than a shadow, blending into the darkness of the unlit hall. With the beer in her hand, she pushed away from the bar for a better look. Her eyes flared. Clara. And the girl retreated down the hall with unusual haste. Vel's gaze moved to Becket, her heart picking up pace. She didn't know what Clara was planning, but Vel had her suspicions, and Becket would kill Clara if he found her near his offices. No one entered those rooms without permission. He even made everyone who did wipe their feet before entering his private domain. She watched him, smiling vaguely at the miners and cowboys, stroking their hair, teasing them, and she was right behind him, a table away. She glanced back at the doors and wondered if she was in there. *Don't do anything for me,* Clara had warned her. *No matter what you see.* Clara's desperation was overpowering. Be careful, girl, she thought. Extra careful.

Victoria jimmied the desk lock and opened the drawer. Carefully, she lifted out the book, laying it on the desk, careful not to disturb anything else. She opened it, pushing it beneath the light of a small lamp and skimming the pages.

Jesus Christ.

Life seeped from her body like the love denied from me, dismissed and discarded. She withered beautifully, her last breath shuddering erotically against my mouth. I drank it, like a rich Bordeaux.

Oh Jesus. Her skin crawled up her arms as she read one passage, then another. The Wichita murder. The Bloomington murder. He was so self-righteous in his reasoning, his method, the details incredible and she didn't waste time, pulling the microcamera from her skirt pocket and snapping pictures. The only sound in the room was the shoosh of the two-inch oblong casing sliding inside itself to forward the next shot. A breeze from the open window ruffled the curtain and she paused, glancing back over her shoulder, seeking eyes in the shadows of the alley.

She turned her attention back to the book and read a little, wishing she had more time, wishing she had a photographic memory.

We wanted the touch, the feel. Deserving the motherly concern. Without it, we grow restless.

We? she thought as her camera snapped softly, with no more sound than her quick breathing. Page after page she recorded on film, her eyes barely registering what she saw in his fluid beautiful script.

Then she heard voices and froze, her gaze dropping to the base of the door, the small area between floor and wood. Shadows shifted, casting uneven fractures of light beneath. Her heart locked in her throat.

Ivy League.

Vel spoke to a cowboy, telling him she'd give him something better to handle than that hand of cards, when out of the corner of her eye she caught Becket moving to his offices, saying good night to his customers like a king dismissing his servants. She kissed the cowboy on the head and tried to head him off.

"Algenon," she called softly and he stopped, turning slightly, his hand on the knob.

"Velvet." He nodded cordially, a shock of brown hair sinking over one eye. Damn, but he was handsome, she thought. "About that offer, to buy the Pearl?"

He stared at her blandly, waiting.

"Well, I can't get the money up unless I get a bigger slice of my earnings."

His brow lifted, his look cynical, belittling. "You want *me* to pay you so you can purchase *my* saloon?"

"How else am I going to do it? You have the upper hand here. And most of our earnings."

"Work harder."

She tried not to glance at the door. "Then you have to stop restricting us."

"In what way?"

"The skins, the bathing."

His expression hardened. "Never." And he turned to the door.

"All right," she conceded quickly, grabbing his arm. He looked down at her touch and she immediately let go. "I've got about three thousand saved."

"The deal was five."

She groaned. "It took me years to get that. I got to send some to my kid and—"

"You have a child?"

She blinked, stunned at turn of conversation, the inflection in his voice. "Well, yes. I had to give her up, because I couldn't take care of her . . ." Her brows knitted deeper. His expression changed from casual interest to a predatory stare and he folded his hands on the cane top, gazing down at her for a moment before he spoke.

"Couldn't or wouldn't?"

"Couldn't, not in a place like this. Ain't fair to a kid—"

Immediately, his face darkened, a brief mask of fury so horrible she was speechless. He grasped the door knob, and in one motion shoved open the door and pulled her inside.

"Algenon?" Terror raced up her spine. He scanned the room and so did she. There was nothing amiss. "What's the matter?"

"Be quiet." They came softly, the words, with a patience that soothed and frightened her in one breath.

He looked down at her, his smile gradual and not the least bit comforting. Vel trembled. "I have to get back."

His grip flexed. "No. Not anymore."

"Are you firing me?"

"Of course not, my dear." His hand, still gripping the cane, came up to caress the edge of her jaw, the line of her throat, seductive promise lighting his blue eyes and spreading into his expression. Vel relaxed a little. He just wanted to bed her, that's all.

Releasing his hold on her elbow, he slid his arm around her waist, pulling her against him, cradling her like a lover. He brushed his lips over her eyes, sealing them shut and she could feel his hardness pressing against her. Then he snapped his wrist, the motion sending the cane across the room and Vel's eyes flashed open. He smiled, thin and hungry, his mouth close to hers, and she barely caught a glimpse of light bending off a rapier-like blade before she felt it pierce her rib cage and impale her heart.

Victoria dunked her hands in hot water, pulling out the soggy sheet and wringing it. Her heart beat violently in her chest and she struggled to calm it, twisting the fabric. She'd made it out the window in record time, running here and lighting a lamp, making herself look busy.

Her gaze flicked to the open door, then to where her satchel was hidden beneath an overturned tub. She'd taken precautions, recognizing that after finding him in her room, he'd entered with a key. Later, she thought, pinning the wet sheet to a line, she'd hide it in a more convenient place, but for now, she wasn't letting it out of her sight. She wanted to read over her files again, compare the notes with what she'd glimpsed in that journal. Her skin shifted and a sound drew her around the edge of the sheet. She frowned, withdrew her gun from her pocket and moved to the door. The alley was black as pitch, the dim lights from neighboring buildings drawing shadows in the darkness. Nothing moved, and she kept the gun hidden in the folds of her skirt, her gaze scanning. Light bloomed, a wedge bouncing off the next building. Ivy League's office. Just a quickly as it was on, it went out.

This is too risky, she thought, releasing her breath, then concealing her gun in her pocket and retrieving her backpack. Quietly she made her way up the open back stair case, thanking anyone who'd listen that her room was just inside the door. She didn't breathe relief until she was firmly intrenched in her bed, her pack beneath a pillow, her hand looped tightly around the strap. Even as tired as she was, the remainder of the night crawled by with an eerie slowness before she drifted into sleep.

And when she did, she dreamed of Chris.

Chapter Twenty

The door rattled.

Victoria bolted awake, blinking at her surroundings, her mind as slow to focus as her eyes. She struggled to sit up, her abdomen cramping miserably and she rotated her neck, then flung the covers back and her legs over the side of the bed. That was the worst night's sleep in reported history, she thought, smirking at the pun. Her entire body hurt, her head throbbed and she dashed the contacts with solution, then popped them into her eyes. Blinking, she looked at the barricaded door as the summons came again, more urgent. I'm late starting work, she thought. Leaving the bed, she tossed the covers over her back pack and glanced at her watch. It was nearly nine. Nothing in this place stirred before noon.

Checking her appearance for ripples in the mask, she pressed a crimp in place, then dragged a robe over her body, removed the chair tilted and tucked under the knob before opening the door.

"You seen Vel?" Dee asked, her dark eyes wide. Victoria's gaze slid past her to the two women hovering close. Lila's face bore ugly purple bruises from her abuser and Priss, the baby, as Victoria came to think of her, looked like she'd rather be sleeping off lasts night's activities than standing in the hall.

"Not since yesterday, in the saloon. Why?" Victoria didn't want to hear this, she knew it.

"Her bed ain't been slept in, by anyone."

Victoria swallowed, glancing back to be certain nothing incriminating was lying around before ushering the girls inside. "Who saw her last?"

"I saw her talking with the deputy marshal, but he ain't seen her neither," came from Priss, breathy and soft.

So, Victoria thought, they've checked. "Is Mister Becket around?"

Dee frowned. "Yeah, still sleepin'."

"Did you share his bed?"

Dee adjusted her dressing gown, the motion almost proud. "I did."

Victoria's gaze lowered briefly to the stains marring Dee's garments, white on the black silk, like dried sea water. "When?"

She looked as offended as a whore could get. "Why you got to be so nosy?"

"Just answer the question, Dee." Her hard stare warned her to shuck the act and spill it.

" 'Bout one in the mornin'."

Don't panic, Victoria warned herself. If he was with Dee at one, and I left the office near ten-thirty, that's only a couple of hours. *Long enough to kill and discard the body,* her professional mind countered and the thought made her stomach twist in knots.

"Sadie said Mister Becket took her into his office."

Victoria grasped the iron bed frame, her knuckles white. "When?"

"Don't know, didn't ask."

Victoria jerked around. "Then ask her!"

Dee spun on her heels and left, returning in a moment and looking extremely put out. "She cain't say, after eleven, maybe later. She was more interested in her customer, than Vel's chat with—''

Victoria looked up. "Chat?"

Dee put her hands on her hips, giving her bountiful head of dark hair an arrogant toss. "No, I don't know what it was about, but Vel sometimes goes to see her kid, from a distance, mind you. It's just that she tells us when she goes, is all."

"Why didn't you say so in the first place! Christ, Dee!"

Dee huffed out of the room in a flurry of lacy ruffles and slapping heeled shoes. Victoria relaxed a little. Maybe Vel had asked his permission? "Perhaps that's where she is then? How long does she usually stay away?"

"Just overnight," Lila interjected shyly.

Okay, Victoria thought calmly. She'll be back tomorrow. All Victoria had to do was check out the livery, see if she boarded the stage or rented a horse and wagon.

"Well, we can't do anything til tomorrow."

"I wasn't worried," Priss said, dropping into the chair, yawning. "I think Dee's upset 'cause he didn't take her."

"Excuse me?" Victoria wrenched around, confused, her thoughts already on finding Vel.

"He didn't fuck her, Clara," she said bluntly. "She was horny as a mare in heat and he just held her. And she wouldn't come out an' say it, but I think he cried."

Victoria frowned. Becket? Cry? Hardly. But she waited for Priss to elaborate.

"She was wet, where he'd laid his head on her chest."

The water stains on Dee's clothes, Victoria thought, alarms singing in her head, yet she shrugged casually, casting it off as nothing and urging the girls back to bed.

Closing the door, Victoria stripped off her robe and dressed quickly, searching for her new boots, tossing back covers and fallen pillows. Nothing mattered now, except finding answers. She was caught up enough in her chores to warrant a day off without suspicion and as she buttoned her blouse up to her throat, her gaze lit on the files protruding from beneath the coverlet.

She stilled, recalling the scraps of information Cole had uncovered for her, the coroner's reports she'd conned out of an old friend, her notes from investigating officers who were anxious enough to add her to their list of hunters. But nothing pointed to what she'd uncovered today; What would make a man like Algenon Becket III, a wealthy, arrogant cold blooded killer, cry in the arms of a whore?

And where, God help her, was Red Velvet Knight?

Noble Beecham, rubbed his forehead and nodded to the stage manager.

"You're the second person to ask about her. What's happened, Mister Beecham?"

"I'm not clue, Cal," he said with a friendly grip of the man's shoulder. "But it don't look good."

Noble bid him good day, then reined around, heading back to the office, pausing to speak with each deputy and warning them to be on the look out. Dang, Vel, honey, where are you? He scanned the street, his pace slowing for pedestrians and wagons and driving his impatience clean out his throat. By the time he halted his horse before the office, he was ready to smash something. Stomping the red clay from his boots, he stepped inside.

Chris looked up as he strapped on his double holster, recognizing defeat in his friend's eyes. "Anything?"

"No, but someone else is looking, too."

Chris knew it was Victoria. And though he hadn't seen her since yesterday afternoon in the laundry, he was certain she was aware of Vel's disappearance. "You questioned the girls?"

"They were still asleep," he said, moving to the stove and pouring himself a cup of coffee. "Dang if it don't make me madder than a stuck pig, though, them going on as if Vel didn't matter."

"Doesn't matter," Chris corrected. And Noble's features tightened, the cup poised at his lips.

"Yeah," he conceded, ashamed that he'd given up already.

"I'll be at the Pearl."

Noble glanced at the clock. "They're still sleepin'."

"Too bad," Chris tossed over his shoulder as he left. He headed to the Pearl, his long strides determined and angry. Townfolk moved out of his way, not that he'd notice, his mind busy going over the facts. Victoria could tell him what was going on. There wasn't a thing that got past that woman and he didn't go in the front door, and instead, headed into the alley toward the laundry. Poking his head inside, he found only her helper, busy washing. She glanced up, frowned indignantly.

"Clara?"

The woman shrugged. "Ain't seen her."

"Since?"

"Early this mornin'. She's gone," she added quickly when her half answers tried his patience. Chris turned back toward the saloon, deciding not to use the side stair case and headed out of the alley. He paused at the outer door leading to Becket's office, something indistinct catching his attention. He moved closer and bent, his fingertips skimming over deep scuff marks in the wood threshold and stoop, thin lines, jagged. Like marks from a chair. Or heeled slippers, he thought. But neither Becket, nor Victoria wore them and those were the only two who'd be out in the alley. His gaze crawled along the ground, searching. No dig marks in the dirt, and he back tracked, finding boot prints, yet they were nearly obliterated by splashes of water and likely the maid's shoes. Then he discovered hoof prints, deeper than they should be and Chris squatted, tipping his hat back. Three shallow, one deep. Two riders, he thought, one horse. A chill skipped up his spine and he lifted his gaze to the horizon, a narrow strip between the buildings. Colorado never looked so huge as it did at this moment.

Tori, sweetheart, what have you gotten yourself into this time?

Straightening, he left the alley and mounted the front steps to the Pearl Handled Saloon, shoving through the winged doors and scanning the sparse crowd for Victoria. She was nowhere in sight and he clamped a vice on his anxiousness and strode to the offices.

He rapped once, stated his name and when the door opened, he pushed his way inside.

"Marshal, how good to see you."

"Where's Velvet?"

Becket's smooth brow drew down slightly. "I'm not certain. She did say something about her child." Smugness laced his tone, an odd smile faintly curving his lips and suddenly Chris was seeing this man a bit differently.

"Child? Vel?"

"Yes, it was a surprise to me, but I understand she visits her. I suspect that's where she is." Becket looked so thoughtful he seemed scholarly. "Though I wished she'd warned me. Bad for business and all."

"When did she leave?" Chris moved around the room, glancing out the window facing the alley.

"Sometime yesterday evening."

There were no stages out last night, Chris thought. Maybe she went by train? "I want to question the others." He refrained from reaching out and fingering the edge of the scared sill. The cuts in the wood were recent.

"Be my guest." He waved toward the upper floor. "But at this hour, I can't guarantee their moods."

Chris twisted a look back over his shoulder, eyeing him suspiciously. "You don't care, do you?"

"Velvet is a grown woman, Marshal, and I can't force her to stay here. She's an asset to the Pearl and knows she'll have a job when she comes back."

"And Miss Murphy. Where is she?"

He shrugged. "She asked for the day off and I granted it. The girl works hard."

Harder than you think, Chris thought, crossing the room. He brushed too close to the desk, knocking a ledger to the floor. Excusing himself, he bent to retrieve it, frowning at the carpet. A small area was brighter than the rest and with his head bowed,

Chris's gaze discreetly swept the floor to the back door leading to the alley, bolted shut.

"Marshal?"

Chris straightened, handing over the ledger and without a backwards glance, left. Outside the door, he paused, that chill intensifying and he looked up the staircase to the line of doors disappearing down the hall. She's searching too, he thought. He hoped. For if she wasn't, Chris didn't know what to do. He mounted the steps, heading straight to her room and a horrible sick feeling rolled in his stomach at the sight of the barren wardrobe and dresser. Further investigation confirmed his suspicions. Not only was Vel missing, but so was Victoria.

An hour later, Chris thought he'd retch from the fear racing through his bloodstream. Becket *had* spoken to Vel last night. He was the last person to see her alive after Noble. And the marks outside his private door and the freshly cleaned carpet heightened his suspicions. He didn't want to believe what Victoria had told him all along. He didn't want her to be right—not this time. Not when he couldn't find her. He checked every shop, spoke to every passing citizen. No one had seen either woman. Re-entering his office, he found Noble talking with Jenna MacLaren.

"I received this from the physician, in Black Hawk." She immediately handed Chris a telegram.

Need help. Cannot establish cause of death. Victim bled internally. No visible wound found. Circumstances extreme.

Chris's heart skated up to his throat. "Wire him for details."

"I have. We should have a reply in a couple of hours." She frowned up at him. "You look upset. Can I help?"

"No, thank you, but let me know the minute you get a reply." She promised, gave him a reassuring pat, then left. Chris turned to Noble, praying he had some news. He didn't and his optimism plummeted.

"Clara's vanished, too. Becket said she had the day off."

Noble's features went taut. "But you don't think that's it."

"Hell no, she took everything she owned with her!" His voice strained and Noble didn't think he'd ever seen Chris so high-strung.

"I would have thought she'd come to you."

"Me too." Chris yanked off his hat, flinging it on his desk. He dug the heels of his palms into his eyes. "Put a man on Becket, warn them to be as discreet as possible. Rotate them every couple of hours."

Noble arched a brow, but wasn't going to question his boss. He never liked the dandified saloon keeper, anyhow. "Maybe she ain't out an' around lookin' like Clara."

Chris lowered his arms, his expression almost sheepish. Then he frowned. "No. I don't think she'd drop the disguise, not for anything. It's too risky." Secrecy was her foremost concern. From him and everyone else.

"Describe her. So I know what to look for."

Chris's expression changed, softened, a half smile curving his lips. "Tall, shapely, very muscular, but not that you'd notice right off. Dark gold hair streaked a half dozen colors, about to here," he measured just past his own shoulder. "And she has eyes like a mountain lion."

Noble straightened.

"What?" Chris snapped when the color drained from Noble's face.

"One of Clancey's boys rented a horse to a tall woman this morning. Said she was in a all-fire hurry to be gone."

"Did he say where?"

"The train." He rushed to add, "But I already sent a telegram," when Chris was nearly out the door.

He paused on the threshold. "But for Vel, not Victoria."

He was gone and Noble sagged against the edge of the desk, raking his hair with beefy fingers.

"Did I hear you talkin' about that long-legged woman?"

Noble wrenched around to glare at the deputy coming out of the back cells. And at his superior's hard look, Seth sputtered, "It's just that I saw her, talking to Lucky."

Noble bolted for the door, but Chris was already gone, Caesar's hard ride kicking up a rolling cloud of red dust. Then he caught sight of Lucky sitting on the steps of the hotel two blocks down, throwing pebbles in the street and about to get booted off by the proprietress's broom. Noble walked closer, casually, aware that his size somehow scared the little fella. He didn't know how much help the boy'd be, muddled as he was, but he was the last person to see Chris's woman alive. But when his shadow passed over the boy, Lucky looked up, wide-eyed and though Noble called softly, swearing he wouldn't hurt him, the child bolted, disappearing into crowd of shoppers. And like the jaws of a snake, the throngs of people swallowed him whole.

Chris sawed back on the reins, his gaze drifting over the terrain, the setting sun making him squint. He'd come here, to where he'd first found her asleep in the forest, as a last hope. But nothing indicated that she or anyone else had been here and his frustration mounted. Though he could trace where she'd been early this morning, he was no closer to finding her. And he had a feeling she'd intentionally covered her tracks.

He stared down at his fist, the reins wrapped around his gloved hand. His fingers worked the leather impatiently and he felt a sting in the back of his throat.

Come to me, Tori. I'll help you. I swear I won't push you for your secrets. Just come to me.

He remembered the vision he had days before they met— the haze of a figure coming through a cloud of wet mist, water splashing, coupled with a steady whirling sound, like the whine of a Spaniard's bolo, chopping the air. And voices, hollow, tinny. But as the figure became clearer, human, it bent, growing sleeker, taking the shape of a mountain cat and moving gracefully across the ground. Human eyes had looked at him, a human soul.

His Cheyenne rearing believed the vision was an omen, a warning or a prediction. Victoria's identity was locked in the mist, beyond his reach, beyond his comprehension, yet he'd spent too many years in the white world to believe she was a spirit in human form. But the vision had come true, he reasoned, and longing and fear speared through him as he remembered the end, the figure tumbling back into the mist, returning her to her world. Forever.

Not yet, he prayed to the darkening heaven. We haven't had the chance. Please give it, he begged the Great Spirits. And if she wants to go, I'll let her. But keep her alive.

He didn't know what he expected, the sound of a bird or a crack of thunder maybe, but only silence answered him. Achingly empty and lonely.

"Come on, boy," Chris murmured, directing the horse out of the forest. He dreaded going back without her. At least out here, he didn't have to face that he might never see her again. His heart clenched at the thought and he glanced back once more, a strange sensation splitting through him. Somewhere in that forest were her secrets and shadows, he thought, then considered the ridiculousness of the idea.

Just the same he scanned the wooded glen once more before facing ahead and spurring Caesar to a hard gallop. He would tear this territory apart, he decided. If he had to call in every friend and favor to do it.

Chapter Twenty-One

Two days.

He hadn't laid eyes on her in two days and Victoria's disappearance was swiftly encroaching on the third. Time scraped by like a limping soldier, dragging Chris painfully with it. Propping his elbows on his desk, he cradled his aching head in his hands, fingers sunk into his hair. He'd spent so many hours in the saddle his rear hurt, and he couldn't recall the last time anything besides coffee passed his lips.

And Chris thought he was very slowly going mad.

Every resource he'd tapped panned out to nothing. Lucky was his last card and he knew the boy would appear only when it suited him. Yet he was the last person to see Victoria alive.

Jesus. Don't think like that.

She's not a careless, stupid woman, he reasoned again, raking his fingers through his hair, dragging bits of bramble and spilling crumbs of dirt on his shoulders. She's trained, almost deadly.

And she's lied to you.

He ignored the voice in his head, his anger boiling at the thought of her clever deception, he snatched up a telegram, re-

reading it as if it hid a sliver of hope that was quickly slipping away.

More lies.

A numbness settled in the region of his heart, straining the blood flow, and the paper crackled as his fist closed slowly, tightly, around it. Chris jammed it into his shirt pocket. He needed answers and so often he couldn't count, he wished to God she'd walk through that door so he could shake them out of her. Thrusting out of his chair, he crossed the office to refill his cup. His hand trembled slightly as he poured and he set the tin pot down with a thump. *Damn you, Tori. Don't scare me like this.*

The door flung open and Chris whipped around as Noble stepped inside. He took one look at Chris and his expression fell. He looked like a train about to wreck.

"Go home, son."

Chris dashed back a gulp of coffee. "No." He speared his fingers through his hair again, then mashed a hand over his face. "I can't." Pain streaked across his features every time he allowed his imagination to run. Was she dead? Had she been attacked by animals? His Indian brothers? Becket hadn't moved from the saloon, so Chris was fairly certain he hadn't gone after her, but why didn't she come in? Why didn't she ask him for help?

Trust, a voice snarled back at him, dashing salt in a fresh wound. He set the cup aside and scooped his hat off the peg as he moved to the door. "I'm going out."

"You been riding the hills all day, Chris, think about Caesar. He ain't covered that much earth in two years.

"I have to try again." *I'm dying in here,* he thought. Her absence hurt, like a repeating blow to his middle. And every passing minute made him feel more helpless. And angry. At her for not coming to him, for not telling him everything so he could help her. And for making him suffer like this. "Once more, then I'll be at home."

"Go, go." He waved. "Drive Abigale clean up her broomstick."

"That a telegraph?" Chris asked, nodding to the yellow paper in his hand. Noble blinked, as if just realizing he had it, then handed it to the marshal. "I 'spect you're the only one who can read that."

Chris unfolded the paper, barking a short laugh. It was written phonetically in Cheyenne, the same manner they'd passed messages during the war.

Found nothing. STOP *V.M. does not exist.* STOP *Palau either.* STOP *Still have markers to call in.* STOP *Can be there in two days if you need me.* STOP

H. McCracken.

It was the fourth telegram, a representation of favors he demanded be repaid, in the war department, the Pinkerton agency and from several people he even liked, for information, answers. But the evidence was stacking against her, quickly.

Noble observed his expression and hated to say it. "She's gone, Chris." The marshal's head jerked up, his blood shot eyes narrowing. "You got to see past your heart, son. She's fooled us before, giving us different names, usin' those disguises. Maybe she's the one who—"

Chris was in his face before he finished speaking, clamping his hands on Noble's shirt front and yanking. "Never," he growled. "Not in a century will you get me to believe there's anything but honor and courage in that woman. Never."

He's in love with her, Noble realized suddenly. A painful bittersweet love. For Noble had a strong feeling Victoria and Chris were never meant to be together. And the events of the past days were proving it.

"All right, Marshal. I've trusted you this far."

Chris blinked, his gaze lowering to his hands gripping his friend's shirt. Suddenly, he released him and stepped back.

"God, Noble, I'm sorry."

The deputy-marshal clamped a hand on his shoulder, giving him a friendly shake, accepting the apology. "Answer the telegram, Chris, and go get some rest. I'll send any word to the house.''

Chris nodded, resolute, turning toward the door.

''And a bath wouldn't hurt, either,'' Noble tossed.

Chris glanced down at his dust-covered green shirt and black pants, his lips curving in a tight smile as he looked back at the mountain man. ''You got a thing about bathing, huh?''

''You would too, if you got a whiff of yourself.''

Chris smiled for the first time in days, donned his hat and left. But the break in his mood didn't last, and after he sent another telegram, he mounted Caesar and rode the rounds, checking in with deputies. A solemn head shake answered his inquiries and his spirits plummeted. With each negative report, he kept remembering all the times she'd warned him not to nose in her business, not to get close to her, to want her, to think of her presence in anything but the temporary. He refused to believe she'd leave without at least saying good-bye, but the alternative sliced him to the bone. She's alive, he assured himself.

Reining around and heading out of town, Chris lolled in the saddle, his body aching with fatigue. His mind floundered from one possibility to another, the outcome scaring him. Rubbing his stinging eyes, Chris knew he couldn't function like this, couldn't help her if she finally reappeared, and he headed down into the valley toward his home.

His dry voice chanted a Cheyenne prayer to the mountains, the tone haunted and pleading. And in the words, a broken piece of his heart drifted on the wind.

Chris paced to the window, then back to his desk, dropping into the chair and thumbing through his accounts. The numbers jumbled, his eyesight strained with the pain throbbing in his head. He slammed the book closed and prayed for sunrise, for light enough to search. A bath and food only restored his energy, the driving need to be doing something to find her, to find Vel. But the night made it impossible. He'd already attempted it with torches, yet the terrain was too rough. Even Caesar balked. His stomach knotted with a sickening fear, the kind that made him want to vomit, made him dizzy, and he pushed away from the desk and stood, crossing to the sidebar. He plucked the stopper of a crystal decanter and poured two fingers of brandy into a glass, then drained it without stopping, letting the heat of the refined liquor calm him. It wasn't enough, and he repeated the measure.

"That will not help, m'lord," came softly, and Chris wrenched around to see Randel move into the room, collecting up remnants of his dinner, newspapers, returning the chaos of his study back to the butler's originally tidy preference.

It made Chris angry. "Leave it." He tipped the full glass to his lips, swallowing half.

Randel stilled for an instant, then decided to ignore him and straightened his desk.

"Dammit, Randel!" Chris hurled the glass into the fireplace, the crystal shattering into a spray of transparent stars.

Randel's gaze shifted to his master, to the broken glass and liquor staining the polished wood, then back to the man. His lordship stood on the far side of the room, his fists clenched bloodless, body rigid, the air around him charged enough to ignite water. His dark hair looked as if he'd run his fingers through it one too many times, and his eyes were narrowed to mere slits, seething with rage and a blaze he'd never seen before in the man. Randel thought it best to leave before the room erupted in flames.

But as he made to depart, Abigale rushed in, freezing on the threshold. She looked between the mess and the men. "Christopher!" She said it in her most scolding manner, looking indignant and put out, hoping to defuse what lay behind that vicious stare.

Without a word, Christopher crossed the room, brushing past her, his footsteps shaking the walls, and Abigale and Randel remained motionless as he pounded up the staircase. The crashing bedroom door rang through the house, and Randel exchanged a cautious look with the housekeeper. She let out a breath, her gaze shifting up the short staircase. She prayed for him, for his wounded heart, and the woman who left him to suffer while it broke.

Christopher twisted on the sheets, punched the pillow, jammed it under his cheek, then finally gave up and flopped onto his back. His hands laced beneath his head, he stared at the ceiling, his body singing with an unnamed energy. He hated waiting. His father always said it was his white blood, his impatience, his temper, and he'd tried all his life to master both. Well, you failed miserably today, he thought. Yet the longer he waited, helpless to produce a clue or Victoria, the brighter, more vivid everything about her came into his memory. Her scent seemed to permeate the air he breathed, his imagination conjuring the dark feline look in her eyes when the desire she always fought finally took her, and she turned it on him, as if exacting payment for making her feel it, making her want him. Come-apart wild, he thought, swallowing back a sudden thickness in his throat. He loved that she was tall and strong, fearless, a warrior woman, as much as he adored her vulnerability, the incredible softening in her eyes when he kissed her, and the way she wrapped herself around him like a long, hungry mountain cat. He wanted her in his arms, so bad they ached, and that he might never feel her against him again, left him hollow and terrified.

"Marshal? You 'wake?"

Chris bolted upright at the soft voice, swearing it was her, praying it was. Yet he reached for his gun, closing his hand over the stock and squinting into the darkness of his bedroom. Then it came again, the call. And his heart sank and rose so hard he thought he'd choke. He tossed back the sheets and swung his legs over the side of the bedding.

"Lucky?" He couldn't see and leaned out to light the lamp. The hissing match illuminated the boy's face and Christopher crushed the urge to drag him inside and shake information out of him. He kept his movements slow as to not startle the boy.

"You naked!"

Chris touched flame to wick and covered it with glass. "I know."

He was at the window, his elbows braced causally on the sill, his chin cupped in his palm. "You sleep naked lots?"

"Yes. Indians do."

"That right," came sagely. "You spirit warrior."

Chris's gaze sharpened on him, briefly, before he inclined his head. Lucky ignored the balcony door to his right and like a frightened squirrel scrambled over the sill and into his room. He was a filthy mess as usual, his hair dusty, his feet bare. And he scampered over to him, crouching on the floor. It broke Chris's heart to see him like this, like a dog begging for crumbs of attention.

"Come up here, Luck," he said, his voice sad, and Lucky straightened, glancing out the window, then to the door. He grabbed Chris's pants off the back of a nearby chair, shoving them at him.

"Put pants on, we go."

"Where?" Chris stood and immediately pushed his legs into his pants, fastening them quickly, then reaching for his shirt.

"We go now, please." He looked at the door as if it hid some claw footed creature. "Please."

Sweat broke out on Chris's brow. Lucky hadn't spoken this much to him or anyone since he'd known him. He and better than twenty men had searched for Vel and Victoria. And Lucky was the last person to see her. Had he found her? Was she hurt and sent this wild child to bring him? As Chris donned socks and pulled on his boots, Lucky walked around the room, avoiding the door. He picked up a book flipping the pages as if his interest was no more than it would fan a breeze before putting it down, his attention instantly directed on something else.

"Where shall we go, son?"

Lucky stilled. "Not you son. Nobody's son." Lucky was staring out the open window at the slope of the valley, the shadows of trees. The moon offered an angelic profile of the lost boy.

Chris came to him, resting his hand on his shoulder with a gentle weight. "No man would be here if they weren't somebody's son. Would you like to be mine?" He'd do anything for this child, anything to know he felt loved, just once in his short life.

"Maybe." He shrugged, then started to climb over the sill.

Chris caught his arm, gesturing behind him. "We can use the door."

Lucky shook his head wildly, his eyes blooming. "Miss Abigale make me wash!"

Chris had to smile and grabbed his holster off the chair.

"Don't need that," Lucky said as he slipped over the sill and onto the balcony. "Already dead."

Chapter Twenty-Two

The smell hit him first.

The stench of death reeked through the still night air as he approached, the lantern held high. Please don't be Victoria, he thought wildly, his heart thrashing up to his throat.

Behind him, Lucky hovered on the edge of lantern light, Seth and one of Chris's ranch hands, Joquin, beside him as Chris ducked into the mouth of the abandoned mine. Pebbles crunched beneath his boots, echoing off the shallow walls. The odor was heavier, thicker, and Chris stilled when light spread across her body.

Everything in him drained to his feet. He staggered.

She looked beautiful, was his first thought. Angelic.

And Chris dropped to his knees, relief sweeping him in crushing waves. The lantern rattled as he set it on the ground. He hated himself for feeling this way; Velvet was his friend. She didn't deserve to die like this. But during the entire trek up here, Lucky wouldn't talk, wouldn't say who it was, only a woman. And all Chris could think of was Victoria. Now, he felt delivered and it took him a moment to compose himself, to regain his objective and consider the threat this meant. Death was a natural part of life, but this was murder.

Her spirit will walk the earth, he thought fleetingly. Yet aside from the empty look in her eyes, the pallor of her skin, she appeared alive, as if staring at something incredible lovely.

He didn't touch her, his gaze taking in the details. Flies skittered about her body, her green eyes now opaque black. The stench wasn't body fluids but decay. In fact, faintly, beneath the layer of rotting flesh, he smelled perfume, an abundance of it. She was dressed to perfection, her jewelry carefully placed, her hair curled and combed. Even her face held the blush of powders and paint. And she was wearing the gown, the only item the girls at the Pearl could swear was missing from her room. A snow white gown, he thought briefly, his gaze traveling over the position of the body, upright as if in a chair, her hands folded on her lap, legs together and angled to the side. There were shoes on her feet.

A painting. Still and poised and very dead.

There were no blood stains, yet her feet were black from blood pooling there, and he swallowed back bile rising in his throat as he inched closer, shifting her enough to see her back. Nothing.

How the hell did she die then?

Picking up the lantern, he let it hover over the ground, seeking foot prints, discards, anything to lead him to her killer. The area was swiped clean, all tracks brushed away.

He straightened, leaning out with the lantern to examine her face. Then he noticed her lips, crusty and black, with the tiniest thickness in one spot. Perhaps death had done something to her mouth, the size or shape, he thought. He needed to speak with Doc MacLaren about that. Suddenly he remembered Jenna's telegram. *Bled internally. Circumstances extreme.* A dark icy ripple moved up his spine. More than one, a voice taunted and he left the mine and straightened outside, facing Lucky.

"I right?"

He set the lantern down. "I'm sorry, yes."

Tears welled in the boys eyes, his lip trembling, and he pushed away from Seth and walked up to the marshal. He stared up at him, little tears moving down his dirty cheeks, his body stiff, and Chris's heart ripped. He shouldn't have to see horror like this. Reaching out, Chris stroked his matted hair and Lucky slammed against him, his thin arms wrapping around Chris's waist. He clung, shaking violently with silent sobs. And as Chris hefted the boy in his arms, holding him tightly, rubbing his bony back, his gaze drifted to his house, the light blooming like the eyes of a skeleton in a sea of black.

This was very close to his land. Close to the town. And Victoria was right. A murderer lived in Silver Rose City. And she was out there, hunting, alone.

At two in the morning, his house was a buzz of activity, at least three deputies milling about. Noble stood off to one side, staring out the window, grieving. Lucky had complained about having to wash, yet Abigale, sleepy-eyed and determined, had hustled the boy off to the bathing room.

"Lucky!" Chris barked when the boy dug his feet in, refusing in a high-pitched whine. Chris's patience snapped. "Do as Abigale says and don't even think about running away." This child needed discipline, now, or he'd end up dead, Chris knew, then gentled his tone. "Is that clear, son?" Lucky's lower lip quivered, but he settled, his little body softening against his fight and Chris crossed to him, kneeling to look him in the eye. "I don't want anything to happen to you." Lucky shivered and Chris rubbed the boy's slim arms. "Give me your word you won't run away."

Lucky glanced at the house, at Abigale, then back to Chris. He thrust out his hand. "My word, sir," he said in a very adult voice.

Chris clasped his hand, then drew him into his arms. "It'll be all right, partner," he murmured into his dirty neck. "I'll fix this."

"The tall lady?" he whispered as if sharing a secret and

Chris closed his eyes briefly, terror and anger racing along his blood stream, hope bleeding through his heart.

"I'll find her. I promise."

Lucky jerked back and smiled as if the marshal's word was gospel, then calmly followed Abigale. Chris raked his hands through his hair before he straightened and faced Noble. His friend was propped against the foyer wall, his big hands making a mutilated mess of his hat. The deputies murmured something to him as they left the house, but Noble only nodded a response.

"Ain't fair," he murmured more to the floor than to Chris. "If we'da trust that gal first off—" His throat worked and Noble didn't think he could take a breath, then did. "Dang, Chris."

"I'm sorry." What else could he say? He felt responsible somehow, and the need to right this injustice clawed through him.

"I want to see her."

"No. You don't."

Noble's gaze jerked to the marshal's. "It ain't like I never seen a dead body."

The mine was boarded up until morning, when Doc could take a look at her. Chris remembered the odd smell, the careful position of the body, the folds of her gown, even the placement of her fingers. "Not like this, Noble." God, nothing he'd witnessed during the war compared to that. "This is going to set the town into panic and I need you to send those telegrams, discreetly, and keep this quiet." His hand on Noble's shoulder, he ushered him out the door and onto the porch. "At least until I find Victoria."

Chris stared bleakly at the darkness that held her from him, almost dreading sunrise and what it might bring him.

"This bastard ain't gonna hurt her," Noble assured softly, recognizing the worry in Chris's eyes. "She's too smart." Chris nodded, but didn't share Noble's confidence. Vel was dead, a ritual death, and what if Becket was wise to Victoria? Wise to Clara and her spying? Chris didn't think anything would stop this kind of killer, not even the expertise of Victoria Mason.

Closing the door after Noble, Chris strode into his study, needing quiet, seeking a sliver of peace in the madness that was his mind. It didn't come, the calmness his father, his people, taught him, eluding his grasp and the anxiety he'd tamped down before others seeped beneath his skin. And he gave into it, pacing wildly, grabbing up a crystal decanter and draining half of it. He paused only to slam the glass container onto the side board, then turned away, glaring at the room, at the faceless terror. He couldn't think straight, couldn't breathe right, his gut wrenching in hard ropey fists. His mind kept seeing the decorated corpse in the mine, yet no matter how hard he told himself it was Velvet, the face he imagined was Victoria's. And his first instinct was to go to town, tear Becket from his bed and beat the crap out of him. But that wouldn't help Victoria, even if he had evidence, even if she was here. But he had nothing. *Nothing.*

And the emptiness of his arms, his heart, drove unspeakable agony through his blood, choking him and Chris gasped for needed breath, dropping to the floor on his knees. His fists flexed on his thighs as he fought for control, fought to keep from tearing his house apart, from lashing out at his friends. His father schooled him to never take his anger into battle, for to forget those he left behind, those who would mourn his loss, made him forget why he raided, why he'd done his fighting behind enemy lines during the war.

Fear made him sharp.

Anger made him careless.

And loving Tori, he thought, just made him hurt.

Chapter Twenty-Three

The light of dawn glowed into the modest study from the windows, but Chris didn't notice the incredible beauty unfolding in his valley. He focused on the matches he'd found days earlier, turning them over in his fingers as he paced before the hearth, his steps short and agitated. For a moment, in the darkness of the hell surrounding his heart, he thought this bit of paper and sulfur might be all he'd have left of her. Then with a foul curse, he flung the folded gold paper across the room and dropped into the settee, staring at the small morning blaze.

With stinging clarity, her fight to board the train came to him, her unbending insistence that his stopping her had let a killer roam free.

Something biting and nasty crawled along his spine. Guilt or regret, he didn't know, but she'd no evidence to substantiate her claim and wouldn't reveal how she knew anything about Becket. Even his own suspicions lacked much evidence. Yet Velvet Knight was dead, and Chris couldn't think of a damn thing Vel could have done to deserve such a gruesome death. I'm clinging to threads, he thought, his hope that since Victoria was seen around town *after* Vel disappeared she might be alive. And as soon as it was clear enough to ride, he'd try again. And again.

"M'lord?"

Chris twisted around, looking over the back of the settee. Randel stood in the doorway, his dark suit flawlessly pressed, his shirt collar so stiff it looked as if it would cut his wind pipe. "For pity's sake, Randel, go back to bed, the hands aren't even up yet."

"Yes, sir. You have a guest, sir."

Chris glanced out the window, frowning. A deputy? "At this hour?"

"Well, sir. They haven't exactly come calling."

"Randel," came impatiently as he rose from the sofa.

"I believe there's a very dirty woman, sir, asleep on your porch."

Chris's features pulled taut and he rounded the sofa's edge, sprinting to the front door. He flung it open, the early dawn offering only a shadow of the figure curled in the corner near the railing. But he knew who it was.

Without light to see her or the husky sound of her voice, he knew.

"Tori," came on a whispered, relieved, thirsting.

Swallowing hard and crossing the porch, he crouched, resisting the desperate urge to smother her with kisses and reached out. His hand shook, and he clenched his fist once, then gently shook her. She roused with a fight and he caught her wrists, hushing her. Victoria blinked up at him and Chris stared into dark gold eyes filled with misery.

She tried desperately not to cry.

"I didn't know where else to go?" A tired scrape, and his gaze slipped over her face, coated and smeared with red dust. Dark circles of fatigue ringed her eyes, her clothes were torn and stained, her hair tangled, wild.

"Jesus, Tori." He pulled her upright; her hands were like ice. "Where have you been?"

He would never forgive her was her first thought. Never.

And she swallowed dryly before she spoke. "I've looked every-where for her. I waited for the stage coach, asked around, even went to the train station. Lucky said something about caves and mountains. I've combed every inch, Chris—" Her eyes glossed with tears. "But I can't find her. It's my job and I can't."

"Shhhh," he hushed, gathering her in his arms and she shivered. "It's all right." He slid his arm beneath her knees and scooped her off the porch.

"I can walk," she sniffled, squirming to be let down.

Chris squeezed her, hard, cutting off her breath and she gazed into dark eyes. "Don't," he growled, warning in his tone, in his piercing stare. "Just . . . don't. I've had about as much of your stubborn *single-minded* independence that I can take." Each syllable came clipped and dry, his handsome face lined with strain. And before she could say anything he cut her off with, "Randel, the bag," and the butler retrieved the case, following his master inside. Without a word, Chris went imme-diately to his study, and though his heavy footfalls reeked of anger he laid her gently on the settee. He moved away quickly, turning his back on her and staring at the floor.

And Victoria's gaze moved over him, his rigid spine, his fists clenching and clenching and she thought, any second he'd swipe the lamp from the table beside him.

"Leave us," came in a low hiss and the butler set her satchel on the floor and pulled the doors closed.

The air crackled with nerve-tingling silence. And with a grimace, she swung her legs off the sofa, one hand gripping the arm.

"Look at me, Chris."

He didn't. He couldn't. His desire to hold her and shake her waged a battle inside him. And he thought if he touched her now, he might hurt her.

"Please."

It was the tone of her voice, the smoky-deep sound that brought him slowly around. And her heart slammed against the wall of her ribs. His face was tight, etched with emotion, with a pain she couldn't name. Blood shot eyes stared at her.

"You vanished without a trace," he rasped, tormented, wounded. She stood and limped to him and his gaze dropped to her pants, the tears, the cuts in her boots, before climbing to her face. God, to finally look at her like this again . . .

Victoria reached up, brushing a lock of black hair from his creased forehead. Her fingers trembled, and she swallowed, her throat dry with apprehension. He'd suffered. It was written in the tightness of his mouth, the smudges beneath his eyes.

"You really worried?"

His hard expression broke, and he hauled her up against him, burying his face in the curve of her throat. He chanted her name, and she clung fiercely, arms around his neck, holding tight, holding him. *Don't let me go,* she prayed. *I need you.*

Chris's fingers sank into her hair, urging her to look at him and when those feline gold eyes met his, he saw guilt and exhaustion and pain.

"I made her promise not to interfere, but—" his mouth stopped her.

Chris couldn't help it, he needed to kiss her, to feel the warmth of body against his and her lips beneath his own, to assure himself she was here, alive and in his arms. And he devoured her mouth like a man starved, laving the sweetness of her lips with his tongue. She shuddered, answering him with untamed hunger, digging her fingers into his shoulders, arching into the hard contours of his body.

Victoria couldn't get enough of him. She'd missed him like breathing, needed him so badly in the mountains when it was cold and lonely and her desperation reminded her of how forgotten she was. She wanted this man, wanted him forever and a lifetime and she couldn't have him. She knew it. It spoke to her over and over while she was in the hills digging in the dirt, searching through abandoned mines and caves and wishing she was with him, safe and warm and feeling adored—like this. But with the solid feel of him against her, the softness of his worn jeans beneath her palms as she smoothed her hand over his buttocks, urging him to give her more, Victoria felt as if she'd finally come home.

Chris rained kisses over her face, *her face.* The disguise was gone, all of it. And his hands wouldn't be still, running roughly over the roundness of her hips, up her back. Nothing obstructed his touch but a thin chambray shirt beneath a short leather vest. And he wanted that gone.

"God, I missed you," he breathed softly. Now that she was here, he wasn't letting her go. "I've been going crazy, woman. Why didn't you come to me?"

"There wasn't time." She took his mouth again. "And I couldn't trust anyone to get a message to you," she said between kisses, capturing his jaw in her palms. Her touch inflamed him, his mouth savage and hot, taking and taking, long and deep and probing and she whimpered at the power of it, felt it sweep her body and destroy her worries for a moment, a small moment.

"Don't ever *ever* do that to me again." He shook her, anger lingering.

"I won't, I swear, but I'm scared, Chris." She met his gaze. "She's dead. I can feel it."

"I know."

Her eyes flared and she stilled.

"I found her. Lucky found her—"

She dropped her forehead to his chest, a deep shuddering breath quivering through her body before she slowly pushed out of his arms. "How's Lucky?"

"Scared. Hurting. Worried about the *tall lady.*"

She sat hard on the sofa, drained. "Oh God." Her hand trembled as she covered her mouth, willing tears to remain submerged. *I'm sorry, Vel.*

Chris eased down beside her, enfolding her hand in his. "It wasn't pretty."

She cleared her throat, a few false starts before she spoke. "She was sitting upright in white, her clothing and jewelry arranged," Victoria said in a strange tone, rote, and the hackles rose on his neck. "Her hair combed, hands folded, legs together, ankles to the side. She even had shoes on." She lifted her gaze to his, a jerk of her head tossing her hair from her eyes and she saw horror and amazement in his handsome expression. "She looked meticulously perfect, and there wasn't a drop of blood around. Except on her lips."

Chris's gaze narrowed, his heart racing. "How do you know all this, Tori?"

His words came so carefully, so measured, she frowned, her gaze sketching his features. "You think I did it?" she whispered, stunned.

"No! Jesus, no!"

"Well that's what it sounds like!"

"It sounds like a lawman with a murder on his hands and you're the only one with answers. Answers you shouldn't have. What am I supposed to believe?"

In me, she thought, scrubbing her hands over her face. But knew she hadn't given him reason enough. Lowering her hands, she gazed at the fireplace, watching flames eat the wood. "He's killed eleven women like this, all over the country." In my time, she thought, in my world. "He murdered my best friend, Cole. Algenon Becket thinks he's on some mission of mercy or something." She waved tiredly. "Hell. I don't know anymore."

"Christ almighty, Tori, when are you going to tell me the truth?" She looked to the side, her gold eyes bright. "Victoria Mason doesn't exist, nor your boss. There is no warrant for Becket." God, he didn't want to get into this, not so soon. He just found her again. But he needed answers now. "A bounty hunter doesn't hunt without good reason."

"He's murdered twelve—no, thirteen!"

"Says you."

"And my *efforts* to apprehend aren't proof enough?"

"Not anymore."

Victoria dropped her gaze to her hands on her lap. If she told him, she had to reveal her time travel. "I knew this was a bad idea." With a weary sigh, she stood and headed toward the door.

"Coming to me?" That stung and he caught her hand, pulling her around to look at him. "Damn it, woman! Talk to me."

"I can't tell you what you want to know. It's . . . inflexible."
She pulled her hand free. "And that's all there is to it."

He pushed off the settee and blocked her path. "I thought
you trusted me?"

"I do," she cried, her shoulders sagging. "But this isn't
about trust. It's about revealing things you're never supposed
to know."

He shook his head as if to clear it. "You're not making any
sense."

She laughed shortly, a bitter broken sound. "I know. Isn't
that a kick? If I were you I'd lock me in a padded cell and
forget I existed." Her voice sounded tinny, near hysterical,
even to her own ears.

"I *need* more," he said softly, a little pleading.

I'm going to drive this man nuts, she thought, her head
pounding with pain and fatigue. She couldn't expect him to
trust her word when she wasn't being honest. But the truth was
dangerous.

How much more than giving the law your findings, Mason?
You always have before.

"Let me think about it," she said, then moved passed him,
but Chris didn't have the time for evasions and at the threshold,
he blocked her again.

"Why was there no wound?"

Her time was up, she realized, staring at his handsome face.
"There is, it's just very small. He uses a stiletto, an Italian
blade—"

"I know what it is," he snapped and black eyes warred with
gold and his anger gaining power. He wanted all of it and the
matches told him that beyond the murders, she was still holding
out.

"His blade is over nine inches long."

"Then where's the blood?" Impatient, sharp.

"He thrusts it under the ribs, straight up into the heart. He
keeps it there, sort of dragging out the thrill he gets, I suppose,
until the heart stops beating and the blood flow ceases. The
bleeding is internal."

Circumstances extreme. Bled internally. He's killed before.

"What?" She searched his face. "What do you know?" she demanded.

His expression went instantly cynical. "Is this a trade?"

"Damn it, Chris."

"Christopher! Stop badgering the poor dear. Can't you see she's exhausted?" Abigale crossed to her, curling her arm around Victoria's waist, urging her toward the stairs. "Come lassie, we'll get you a nice bath and some breakfast and a soft bed."

That sounded too much like a slice of heaven. "No." Victoria pulled free, turning away, refusing to look at Chris. "Thank you, but no." Abigale's look pleaded, but Victoria ignored it. "I can't stay here." She wanted him so badly, wanted to share her burdens with him, be free of the sorrow and ugliness and forget she didn't belong here, in his century, in his life. She wanted to pretend at being happy for a little while, but she wasn't staying long enough to make it real. A universe separated them, and it wasn't fair—to her or to Chris.

She scooped up her satchel, heading for the door. Head down, she donned her dusty stained hat. "I can't." There was a fracture in her voice. Chris felt it down to his heels as she reached for the knob.

"Tori, darlin'—"

She wrenched around, her gaze honing in on his like the lash of a whip. "Don't you *darling* me, Christopher Swift." The loss of her dreams sharpened her tone. "If you didn't butt your nose in my business, we'd be gone by now and maybe Vel—" Her voice caught, unexpected tears filling her eyes. It hit her all over again. "Oh Jesus." She glanced away, fighting her sorrow. "She's dead, and it's my fault." She rubbed the space between her eyes. If only she'd figured it out sooner. She could have warned Vel not to tell him about her child.

"And just where do you think you're going?"

She lowered her hand, hating his Papa Bear tone. "Back to work."

Chris would bind and gag her before he'd allow her to leave

his house. "You can't." He took a step. "Jesus, Tori, if what you say is true—"

"It *is.*"

"—then you're next."

Her composure was back, a steely glint in her eyes. "It's a risk I'm willing to take." She turned the knob.

"Well, I'm not!" He crossed the foyer, closing his fingers around her wrist and pulling her away from the door. He slammed it. "I'm the law here, Victoria Mason. And this is my problem now."

She twisted free, giving him glare for glare. "Because I had him in my sights and you stopped me!"

"You didn't have cause! You still don't. It's your word against his and it will never hold up in a courtroom!"

It and the film will hold up in mine, she thought, seething. "He did it. You already have something that clues you in, I saw it in your eyes."

I'll keep my own secrets too, he thought maliciously. "Show me hard evidence, Victoria, because all I have now is you, obstructing justice. And if you set so much as a toe off this property, I'll lock you in a cell until it's over. I've let you run wild in my town—"

"Your town—?"

"Yes, *mine,*" he growled, baring down on her so hard she stumbled back against the sealed door. "Don't push me, woman. You've put me through the worst nightmare imaginable, and I'm not about to relive it!"

A brief spark jumped in her chest, snuffed out by his chauvinism, and she shoved at his chest, forcing him to step back. "Don't tell me what to do, Christopher Swift. I'm a big girl. I work alone. You've fought me the whole nine yards, yet I still came here for your help. But *nooo,* now that the ball's in your court you need to play boss. Well, let me tell you, *Marshal—*" she advanced, poking his chest "—that I'm-the-man-and-I'll-take-over-now-honey, condescension ain't gonna cut it here!"

Suddenly, Chris caught her hand and ducked, tossing her

over his shoulder, knocking the air from her lungs and carrying her back into his study. He kicked the doors shut, then unceremoniously dumped her on the floor. She glared up at him, swiping her hair from her view, yet every time she tried to stand, he pushed her back down.

"Give up," he growled. "I win."

She spun on her rear, her long leg clipping his ankle. He landed on his rear so hard his teeth clicked.

"I call it a draw," she snapped as he pushed onto his haunches. Slowly, he tilted his head back, retribution fuming in his eyes, and he lunged, covering her body with his, mashing her to the floor. She fought him. And he clutched her head in his hands and kissed her, hard. She gripped handfuls of his hair. And he kept kissing her, deeply, thoroughly, filling her mouth with his tongue and moving with heavy torturous strokes. And she responded wildly, driving desire harder down his body and he caught the back of her knee and pulled up, spreading her thighs and wedging himself between them. She made a tight hungry sound in the back of her throat and he drank it.

"You're staying here," he said against her mouth. He liked that she was gasping for breath, her skin flushed. He liked it a lot. "You're going to bathe and rest and if I have to see to the task *myself,* you are not leaving my house. You're in danger, Victoria Mason. Because once word gets out, mousy Clara will be under immediate suspicion because she stabbed a customer and disappeared the same time Vel did."

Victoria hadn't considered Clara would be another convenient murder suspect to make Becket feel comfortable or make him nervous that he'd been found out.

"He'll know, if he's as clever as you say. He'll know." He watched her face, her lovely expressive face as she weighed and discarded point for point. "It didn't take Noble long," he reminded.

"That's easy. I'll just change disguises—"

"And I'll burn everything you own," he promised darkly. "I swear it."

She believed him. He was determined enough to tie her up

and leave her in the barn. She couldn't let that happen; the micro film was her only evidence.

"Chris." Cajoling, soft, and he steeled himself against the throaty sound.

"Am I not the law here?"

Her lips worked to hold back a response.

"Am I?"

"Yes," came gritted through clenched teeth and Chris knew he'd get her this way. Bounty hunter or not, she knew the law and honored it.

"This law says you're interfering with a murder investigation, you're in danger, and it's my duty to protect."

A brow arched. "Flexing those masculine muscles, huh?"

"No. The articles of the constitution."

She made a frustrated sound. "You can't do this without me."

"I wasn't planning on it."

She blinked. "You'll tell me everything you find?"

His brow knitted. "I recognize expertise when I see it, Tori. Of course."

She smiled, the sweetest, most delicious grin he'd ever seen on her. And he felt it dance down the pit of his stomach.

"Besides." He shrugged. "You'll just beat it out of me, anyway."

"Nah." She patted his cheek. "You're too pretty to smash." Her body softened beneath him, shifted as she cupped the back of his head, drawing him closer.

But he held back. "Partners?"

She knew what he was asking. "You can't ask how I got my information, Chris." Her gaze moved swiftly over his features as if memorizing them. And the look scared him.

"One of these days you'll really trust me, Tori," he said, then sank into her mouth, a hot slide of tongues and lips and liquid warmth and Chris groaned, moving against her, loving that she wrapped sleekly around him. Victoria knew she had everything she wanted in her arms and savored the moment, the fraction of happiness and pleasure. It had been so long since she'd felt this good. *Then take it,* a voice cried inside her heart. *He's giving, so take it.*

"Christopher," Abigale demanded from beyond the door, rapping impatiently. "If you do not convince that woman to eat and rest, I swear by the blood of my ancestors I will never forgive you!"

Chris broke their kiss, inhaling through locked teeth, the only sign of his tempered desire. "Abigale likes you." He pressed kisses to her temples, her cheeks. "That blood of the ancestor's thing doesn't get used unless she means business."

"And what do *you* mean, Chris?"

His gaze sketched her face, so lovely and dirty and for a fleeting moment, he saw fear, unshuttered, without the steel of her composure, but soft and vulnerable. I mean to keep you, he thought. I mean to love you until you can't stand it and then I mean to love you more. But she wasn't ready to hear that. She wasn't ready for anything he had in mind.

But Victoria saw it in his face, in his incredibly dark eyes, and her heart thundered up to her throat, threatening with a cry, her fingers mapping the creases of his face and for a moment, she let herself dream and float. Go ahead, love me, she thought. Love me so much while I'm here, it will last a lifetime when I leave.

"God, Tori, when you look at me like that, all I can think about is—"

"Christopher!" came this time filled with warning. " 'Tis improper behavior I'm seein', laddie."

"Jeez, I hope not," Chris murmured with a glance down. "She'll box my ears or something."

Victoria laughed, rising up as he sat back. They stared for a moment and she felt as if she were the most beautiful creature in the world.

Ridiculous.

"Coming, Miss Abigale," Victoria answered, trapped in his gaze as he stood and held out his hand. She accepted the help, her body screaming with bruises and when she straightened in front of him, she leaned into his embrace.

"Kissing a deal out of me was *not* fair."

He gave her a rascally smile. "You said you like my kisses."

Her hand smoothed down his hips to his thigh, bringing tension and pleasure with it. "That's not all I like." She nuzzled his throat, her fingers boldly shaping the bulge in his trousers and Chris froze, his lungs half full, his body reacting with embarrassing quickness.

And she felt it. "Hmm? That why they call you Swift Arrow?"

He choked, casting her a lazy half-lidded stare and Victoria grinned up at him, then moved around him, her hand lingering on his body before she slipped away to open the doors. Chris didn't move a muscle. He couldn't. He was going to snap in half if he did.

"Ought to be ashamed of yourself, Christopher," Abigale hissed, glaring at her employer's back.

"Shameless, wasn't he?" Victoria said, and behind her Chris's shoulders shook softly.

"Imagine the man verbally bludgeoning you like that. Laird kens I've taught him better," she tisked, urging her up the short staircase and into a guest room. Chris was there, on the threshold and for the second time that day a woman shoved him back. Abigale sniffed the air. Chris grinned. And she took great satisfaction in closing the door in his face.

Abigale turned and Victoria folded on the spot, clutching her stomach.

Chapter Twenty-Four

Quickly, Abigale knelt beside her.

"Lass?" She stroked her mussed hair off her face, feeling her forehead.

"It's my period. My monthly," she added when the woman frowned.

"Have you dousing strips?"

Good God, what the hell was that? "No."

"Well, you just wait right here."

"Um . . . ma'am?"

"Call me Abigale, lass."

Those were the kindest eyes in the universe, she thought, like Grandma. "Do you think you could find some cotton, string and a few strips of cloth? Scissors, too."

"I believe I can," she said, frowning a little. "You get out of those clothes."

She left her alone and Victoria struggled to stand. God, I just love being a girl, she thought cynically, scarcely noticing the room. It was going to break inside her, she could feel the bloating pressure and was grateful that it had waited until now to start. Thank God it only lasted a couple days.

Abigale returned in a few moments, a small basket on her arm and Victoria was still sitting on the edge of a chair, trying to work off her books. Her feet were swollen, most of the area she covered too rocky to risk the mare's legs. Which was wise, since she'd fallen off that mountain twice and every bone in her body felt nicked.

"I've got a bath running for you." She set the basket aside as Victoria looked up.

"Running? As in running water?"

Abigale beamed. "The only home in the territory," she explained as she busied herself with helping the girl off with her clothes. "Pumps into the house, into a fancy room Christopher built. There be a stove for heating water. My back is thankful for that, you ken. Buckets are heavy." She tisked at the blisters and bruises coloring her body as she helped her into a robe. " 'Tis mine, lovey," she smiled as the garment circled the girl nearly twice around.

Grabbing the basket, she crooked her finger and Victoria kicked her satchel into the corner, then padded to the door, Abigale peeking out, obviously scoping the area for any male intruders, then waving her down the hall and into another room. It was cute, large, understandably old fashioned, slightly masculine; dark green rugs lay on the wood floor, with polished brass and wood fixtures and green curtains. Water simmered on a small black stove and while Abigale worked a pump, spilling more into the claw footed tub, Victoria examined the drain pipe disappearing into the floor, recalling that the blacksmith had made Chris a decent length of pipe. For this? Stacks of towels, wrapped cakes of soap and assorted bottles and jars filled a tall open armoire, and a chair of sorts rested in the corner, a huge brass canister fixed directly above it on the wall. And a chain.

"There you go, lovey," Abigale said after emptying the huge kettle of water. She swished, testing the temperature, then refilled the kettle from the pump and replaced it on the stove. "Give a call if you need me." Victoria dragged her attention from the canister to the older woman. "Your necessaries are in there." She gestured to the basket on a low table she'd moved close and smiled, a rosey I'm-glad-you're-here smile before she left. It made her feel welcome, and Victoria recalled how Abigale bossed Chris like a mother. And what about that English butler, she wondered, then dismissed her curiosity and immediately walked over to a chair and lifted the seat, sighing with absolute relief and joy. A toilet. She peered into the hammered brass bowl, then up at the canister. A flushing toilet! Crude but . . . oh, this was silly—getting excited over a toilet. Closing the lid, she moved to the tub, her steps measured and careful, and slowly peeled off the robe. She ached all over. And smelled like something undefinable. God, how could Chris even want to kiss her when she reeked like this? But he did, she thought, smiling, glad he'd done his best to bully her into staying. The last thing she wanted right now was to glue on a disguise and live in the saloon without Vel, she admitted, gingerly stepping into the tub. Her feet sizzled as the water seeped into the cuts and blisters, and she sank into the hot water with a low moan. The scrap on her side stung mercilessly, a reminder.

"Thank you, God, for not letting me fall into that mine," she said, then dunked herself fully, working dirt and grime from her hair.

Sliding up the back of the cool porcelain, she laid her head against the rim. Stream rose in slow curls from the surface and she hunted for the energy to wash, the heat soothing her cramps to a dull throb and making her sleepy. Lazily she reached for the soap, lathering and scrubbing until she was squeaky clean. Her hair was another matter, since the water was too dirty to make this a success, but Abigale who could only have been lingering outside the door to know Victoria needed her, bustled in to rinse Victoria's hair. Then as if sensing her need for a long soak, Abigale freshened the bath water, draining half and refilling the tub.

A few minutes later, with her clean hair wrapped in a towel, Victoria hung over the side of the tub, making tampons. This is a hoot, she thought. It was easy; heavy cotton wadding halved with string, dampened, then rolled tightly in a short strip of cloth. When it dried, it would be stiffer, serviceable, but now, she had enough to last the next days. God, I'm sharp, she commended herself, then collected the *necessities* into the basket. She didn't see Abigale peek in nor watch her make one, and slowly stood in the tub, taking up the pitcher and sluicing warm water over her body.

Popping the drain cork, she left the tub, preparing herself for the inevitable, then donned the oversized robe and discarded the head towel seconds before Abigale rapped.

Victoria responded and Abigale poked her head around the door. "Oh, you look a sight better."

"I feel better," Victoria said, eternally grateful. "Thank you."

Abigale swung the door open and gestured. "Come, lovey, I've a tray of food and a warm bed for you."

Victoria smiled through a yawn and relinquished herself to Abigale's care. She hadn't been treated like this since she was a kid, home sick from school and she decided that after the past weeks, she deserved at least to sleep in a decent bed, without a mask, without the worry of Becket hovering over her while she caught a few Zs.

That was one reason she didn't want to go back to the saloon. She had a feeling Becket was wise to her and she'd no intention of getting a blade in her ribs just to be stubborn. Chris was right, she admitted, following the chubby housekeeper down the hall. *Clara* would be suspect, perfect should he be accused, and she needed to let the memory of the mousy girl fade.

Deep in her own thoughts, she didn't realize she was in a room until Abigale threw open a large window.

Victoria glanced around, checking first for her satchel, then noticed the decor. The colors were softer than what little she'd seen of the house, paler greens, mauve instead of the deep maroon in Chris's study and in the foyer, more cream than anything.

"It's so . . . feminine," she said with honest surprise.

Abigale glanced over her shoulder as she untied curtain bows. "Christopher let me do up this one." She went to the next window, releasing the bow. "I told him the house was too masculine, no lass would want to come visit."

"Like Camille?"

Abigale spun around, her face flushing red. "You know of her?"

Victoria nodded. "And I know he's half Cheyenne, too."

" 'Tis not a bother for you?" Abigale ventured softly.

"No, Abigale," Victoria said, tiredly dropping on the bed. "And I have to warn you," she was thinking of this woman's *proper* sensibilities as she spoke. "I'm not like most women. Sometimes it doesn't make me very happy, but I just can't help it. I've worked with men too long not to have a few, no, *several* sharp edges. This," she gestured to the delicate room, "is something I've rarely experienced in the past five years."

Except for my daughter, she thought, absently accepting the brush and dragging it through her hair. Trisha had everything little girls wanted—Barbies, tiny purses and fake make-up, fancy dresses, hats and patent leather shoes. And for a moment, Victoria was caught, in the day she had to pack it all up and give it to the shelters. She'd cried over every piece before putting it into the boxes.

"Miss Victoria?"

Victoria looked up, blinking back tears. Abigale's expression was sympathetic, as she drew back the bed covers, gesturing for her to climb in.

"I dinna be the one who matters," she said and Victoria allowed the older woman to tuck her in. She seemed to want to so badly. "And as to being girlish," she said, easily cluing into the young woman's misery. "Have you looked in a mirror lately?" Taking the brush, she set a breakfast tray on the side of the bed, handing her a biscuit and encouraging her to eat.

"I try not to," Victoria said around the food, then excused herself. Abigale waved, taking residence in a chair and smiling as the woman cleaned her plate in moments.

"Thank you," Victoria said, a little embarrassed. "That was the best meal I've had in ages."

"You don't look like you've had many of them." Abigale took away the tray and Victoria stripped off the robe, sliding deeper beneath the sheets and quilt.

"Good, 'cause as you can see I eat like a horse."

Abigale smiled happily to herself, gathering up soiled clothes as the young woman who'd driven her Christopher to distraction in the past days, drifted into sleep. She was a lovely creature, vibrant and strong, but blunt and Abigale recalled the couple's argument, this lass meeting Christopher bite for bite. Aye, wild they were together, and she loved the sappy look on the lad's face when he convinced, or rather forced, her to stay. She'd never seen the boy so lad-de-da over a woman, but understood why. This one was different, ingenious like her Christopher, a match for his quiet strength. *'Tis 'bout time,* she thought, and watched her for a moment before closing the door.

Out of the corner of her eye, she caught him lingering in the darkness of the hall, but she ignored him, adjusting the bundle and heading below stairs, smiling richly.

Christopher refused to leave his ranch, and it amazed him how afraid he was that if he did, he might return and find her gone again. He worked the horses in the yard instead, refraining from attacking his latest project, yet when Doc Jenna arrived, he *had* to leave to take the physician to Vel's tomb. Jenna was justifiably horrified. But she confirmed what Chris already suspected. Victoria was right, again, deadly correct—a small wound under Vel's rib cage, her badly discolored skin making it difficult to recognize.

Jenna looked up from her examination, dusting her hands on her split buckskin skirt. "This," she gestured to the corpse, "is very similar in detail to that telegram I received from Black Hawk."

"Why didn't you tell me you'd heard back before now?"

She gave him an impatient look. "I tried to see you, but it seems you were rather intent on finding a mysterious woman, that you didn't answer my summons."

"Summons, was it, Lady Jenna?" he said, bowing deeply.

She made a face, utterly lacking in her usual refinement. "I confirmed the details twice." She pulled the crimped telegram from inside her short jacket, offering it. "For I must admit, I thought there something incorrect in the translation." Chris scanned the paper. "It's too exact to be ignored, Christopher, except that the victim was younger." Jenna looked back at Velvet, her eyes sad. "Why would anyone go to such lengths *after* killing her?"

"I wish I knew," Chris muttered, stuffing the missive in his back pocket before bending to wrap the tarp over Vel. With a *travois,* he and her assistant brought the body down and the dark haired man cradled Vel in his massive arms like an infant, then gently laid her in the wagon.

Jenna agreed with Chris's request for discretion and as her assistant rode away, Jenna swung up onto her horse.

"When do we meet the woman of your heart?" she asked in Cheyenne and Chris's gaze jerked to hers, narrowing sharply. "Or are you going to keep her locked away?"

His expression softened. "For as long as I can."

Jenna frowned slightly before a smile spread across her face. "Taking captives. My, my, how very Cheyenne."

"If you ever met her, you'd know why. She's stubborn." His smile was light. "Even worse than you."

"I like her already."

Chris's expression grew serious. "She's in danger, Jenna. That kind of danger," he said, nodding to the retreating wagon and her lovely face drained of color.

"She knows who did that?"

God, she was quick, he thought, folding his arms over his chest. "Go home to your husband, Jenna, you're becoming a pest again."

A cheeky smile lit her face as she reined around, riding through his valley like the wind. Reid must have his hands full and loving it, he thought, then jerked his gaze to the house. Suddenly, he needed to see Victoria, touch her.

Chris pushed open the door, glad he'd oiled the hinge and simply watched her sleep. The sun streamed through the window, casting a ripple on the carpet, the breeze moving the curtains like Hindu slaves fanning their princess. His chest constricted as he stared at her lovely face, somber in sleep and he wondered what spirits sought to smile on him, giving him the chance to know her. He wouldn't think about her leaving, like she'd claimed. He couldn't. It just plain hurt too much. Giving into temptation, he walked until he was beside her. The sheets were twisted around her, sculpting her lush form in pristine white, telling him she was naked and reminding his body how glorious that bare skin tasted, felt beneath his touch, how complete he felt holding her in his arms, warm and sleek.

And if Abigale wasn't constantly hovering over her, he'd crawl into bed with her right now.

"Christopher!" came in whisper.

He dragged his gaze from her to Abigale, a stack of clean clothes in her arms.

" 'Tis improper, yer being in here."

His lips tugged and he returned his gaze to Victoria, then bent, dropping a soft kiss to her lips. He obeyed his housekeeper, but only to avoid waking her and kissing more than her mouth.

He paused on the threshold, glancing at the clothes. Victoria's. "I need you to go to town, Abby."

Her eyes lit up with the prospect. "I've just the thing in mind."

Chris moved past her. "Me, too."

"Aye, I ken. And you won't be doin' it," she called after him, "not under this roof, Christopher Swift."

Chris chuckled softly, a sinister telling sound that made

Abigale harumph with indignation. And she had a right to be worried, Chris thought, continuing down the stairs. Victoria was within his reach, without disguise or her mission to distract her, and Chris would use every advantage to unlock her secrets and keep her.

Chapter Twenty-Five

Victoria sat cross-ways in the leather wing back chair, her legs slung over the arm, watching the flames curl around the logs in the fireplace. Better than TV, she thought, sipping from the mug of hot chocolate Abigale had made for her before going off to bed.

The Scotswoman was like a fairy godmother, turning up just when she needed her, with water so she could take the last couple of Tylenol she had in her pack or a lap blanket to cover her bare legs. Highly improper, her wearing only panties, a man's shirt and white ankle socks to cushion her tender feet, but since "the men folk were abed," Abigale conceded to her scandalous attire, a funny smile on her face as she patted Victoria's shoulder, then trotted off to bed.

Victoria shifted in the chair, listening to the comforting creeks of the house, her skin rejoicing in the lack of disguise, yet her mind wouldn't shut down.

Reality check. She was living in 1872.

Prostitution was legal, hanging was legal and there were only a few prisons across the territory. And a train was the fastest mode of transportation. Gone were all things familiar, the conveniences and advantages. Not that she missed much beyond air conditioning and fast food. Whoever said this was a harsh and rough time didn't live in a twentieth century city with street gangs, drive-by shootings, child molesters and serial murderers. She rubbed her forehead, trying to adhere to her earlier promise—not to think about her job or Becket. At least for one day.

Shifting in the chair, she finished off the chocolate and set the cup on the carpet, flexing her calves and examining the bruise blackening her knee.

"How did you get that?"

Victoria flinched, then twisted a look around the edge of the chair. Even in the dark she could feel him, smell him, and wet her lips as Chris moved into the glow of the fire. The air caught on her lungs. Barefoot, he wore a dark silk robe, loosely sashed at his waist. And from the clean lines of the fabric, that's all he wore.

Her heart picked up pace. "I fell in a mine shaft."

His eyes flared, snapping from her gorgeous legs to her face. "Jesus, Tori. You could have been killed."

"I know." Repentant, ashamed.

"How did you get out?"

"Dah." She rolled her eyes. "I climbed."

He smirked and crossed the parlor to the side board. Uncorking a bottle, he splashed a draught of brandy into a snifter, then twisted toward her, an offer in his raised brow.

"Yeah. Maybe that'll put me back to sleep."

He filled her glass, collected them in one hand and Victoria couldn't take her eyes off him as he crossed to her, his step graceful, soundless. As he offered the drink, she reached, her gaze slipping to the gaping robe, his hairless chest carved like a granite. Her fingers itched to touch him and she pulled the snifter close, murmuring something close to thank you. She didn't know. She felt suddenly vulnerable and defenseless, in his house, his living room, drinking his liquor—with his eyes gazing at her as if he could see into her soul.

She took a gulp of brandy, grimacing at the burn of aged

liquor and his lips curved mysteriously as he settled into the matching chair a foot away.

She was actually nervous. The notion stunned him and Chris decided this was good, very good, and as he took a sip of brandy, he studied her over the rim. A bath and sleeping away the entire day had amazing results. She looked like a just-picked orchid, sensual, exotic, and he missed her, missed the opportunity to simply look at her without a disguise and decided right then, that a man's shirt and socks on this woman were as enticing as silks and lace. He wouldn't have thought this common attire would stir his blood, but then, Victoria stirred his blood dressed like a man.

"Will you quit staring?"

"No."

She flicked her hair back, but it spilled like a golden-brown waterfall over her shoulder, the darker shade framing her face like a velvet halo. Half woman, half feline predator, he thought.

"At least you're honest."

"Unlike you."

She arched a brow, taking a sip. "Are we in for a sparing match, Christopher?"

She sharpened her claws on his name. "Depends on you."

"We had a deal."

"Ah yes." he rested his head in the oxblood leather, giving her a half-lidded stare. "Don't ask where you got your information."

"Yes," came carefully. She had a feeling she was kicking at a dammed up river and didn't want the rush that would follow. He looked too confident just now.

"You really expect me to just accept what you say, if you say anything, which hasn't been much."

"I have my reasons."

"That's before these came." He dug in his robe pocket and withdrew a stack of papers, offering and she leaned out, her shirt sagging open, giving him a lush view of her breasts. His throat worked. His body tensed and he nearly choked on a healthy sip of brandy as she swung her legs around and positioned her back to the fire, using the light to read.

Her eyes skimmed the page, glossing wet in the firelight. "Oh, God," she breathed. "Oh God!" She read one after the other. Three murders—three and all the same. He'd started again.

"You knew this and didn't tell me?"

"I had to confirm it, first."

She threw the papers at him. "How much more proof do you need, Chris?"

"Tell me what you know, Victoria," came in a dark command.

Her hand shook as she drained half the brandy. Swiping the back of her wrist across her lips, she met his gaze. There was no way around this. She had to do as she promised and give him information, and she searched her mind for the first logical piece.

"Do you know what a psychological profile is?"

Scowling impatiently, he shook his head.

"In my line of work," she chose her words carefully, not ready to reveal her time travel. "It outlines a suspect's past, how he'd react in a given situation, confrontation, casual greeting— Stuff like that. It's a pattern of what motivates a person to commit a certain crime."

"Such as?"

"If a woman is raped, for a while after she'd be terrified of men. If a store was robbed, the owner would be overly cautious and the next time he's threatened, he'd likely be quicker to draw a gun and shoot before calling for help." He conceded with a regal nod. "A drug addict, while paranoid—"

He cocked a crooked glance. "Para-what?"

"Suspicious of everything and everyone," she explained. "He'd risk more and more for the drugs, feeling fearless. The drug does that, adds to the motivation. Need drugs. Get drugs." Her hand tick-tocked as she spoke. "Need more drugs. Might get caught, still need drugs, rob or even kill for cash for drugs." She cupped the snifter in both hands. "It just gets worse.

But killers, certain types, are different. The pattern is deeply ingrained in their past. And in Becket's case, it's his mother.''

"You really expect me to believe his mother caused him to kill?''

"Come on Chris, imagine.'' She swung her legs off the arm and sat up, leaning forward a touch. "Just dismiss what you've believed and play along.''

Chris agreed, reluctantly, and she left the chair, pacing before the fire as she spoke. "Algenon Becket is the only son of a very wealthy man, from a prominent, charitable family. His parents are jet-set—ah, they travel extensively,'' she corrected, waving off a list, "attend tons of parties, charity auctions, real social butterflies.''

She stalled, gaging his confusion. Blank as a sheet of paper. Handsome, but blank—a tough audience.

"His father paid little attention to him, his mother none at all.'' She stopped and jerked her head, tossing hair from her view. "I mean none. Zip. She never held him or nursed him as a baby, never touched him, no pats on the head, no good night kisses or stories. She wasn't there to chase away the monsters when he cried at night.''

"You're certain of this.'' He knew that before asking.

"Sure. Got it from his nanny.''

He arched a brow, cynical and curious.

She flashed him a feline smile and paced again, her luscious legs scissoring across the small space. "For attention, he's now the perfect son, in appearance, his women, excels in school and athletics. He has all the girls chasing him because he's handsome and rich, but still momma doesn't see him.''

Chris tried desperately to listen, but the sight of prancing naked legs was driving blood to his groin. He wanted to be between them, feel them around his hips.

"Sit down, Victoria.'' He said tightly, pained.

She stilled, frowning, then followed his gaze to her legs. Her gaze snapped back to his and she folded her arms over her middle. The shirt hiked and Chris groaned. "Pay attention. There *will* be a quiz.''

He was trying, dammit.

"Becket starts getting into trouble. Daddy gets him out of it. And suddenly he's the center of his parents attention again. Trouble with the law and," she snapped her fingers, "here comes Dad, paying off judges or victims or whatever, to keep his name and his reputation perfect. But—" she held up a finger, stopping the interruption he'd no intention of making "—still, no mother. The crimes get bigger, with a higher sentence. And Daddy finally washes his hands of him. Becket's an adult with his own money and he gets himself out of the scrapes. And that's the last we hear of him. Now he's careful, crafty," she said in a sinister tone, crossing the few feet and dropping lazily into her chair. "Now he doesn't want anyone to know what he's done, no more attention. He prefers sitting back to watch the authorities scramble for an answer. The satisfaction comes from within himself."

"How did you figure this out?"

Mounds of paperwork and a slightly deviant mind, she thought. "It took a while to find a common thread but, Cole, my best friend, gave me the information."

"The man who died?"

"The only man Becket murdered," she clarified. "He was a private investigator. When I got a defendant to hunt, he gathered all the information. In this case, he talked to servants, old nannies, everyone who'd come in contact with Becket. Even teachers, athletic coaches."

"Why?"

"So I could get inside the perp's head. I need to know what they'll do next."

"Have you ever been wrong?"

"No," she said without missing a beat.

That didn't surprise him. Nor her lack of arrogance over her expertise.

Her eyes shifted back and forth as if searching. "Where was I?"

"Becket likes watching the law hunt for him."

"Oh yeah." She sank deeper into the chair, slinging one

tanned thigh over the arm. Chris ground his teeth, forcing his attention from the revealing folds of fabric. "He believes he's above the law. Becket's never seen the inside of a prison, but he's in one," she tapped her temple with a forefinger. "In here. It's like a cage, torturing him mentally, and the only relief from his private hell in his murders. It soothes him, a justification for the pain. And he thinks he's doing the world a favor. Righting a wrong he imagines was done, not only to him, but to others. But he also gets his jollies in actually killing and decorating the corpse."

"Why Velvet? He was going to sell her the Pearl."

"I know, but the night she disappeared he was talking to her outside his office."

His brows shot up. "You saw them?"

Victoria bit her lower lip, glancing briefly away. "I was inside the office."

"Jesus!"

"I didn't take anything." Except pictures. "And I'm a bounty hunter, Chris. No rules apply."

"Goddammit, Victoria," he said, thrusting out of the chair. "I ought to lock you up!"

"Yes, you should. No wait," came laced with sarcasm. "You should lock Clara up. She did the snooping."

"What did you find?" he gritted through clenched teeth, his fists braced on the mantle, head lowered between outstretched arms.

"A journal. He's written it all down, every detail, the murders he committed before. But I think that Vel told him she was going to see her child, the one she gave up and that set him off."

He snapped a look over his shoulder. "He saw it as a personal rejection."

Her lips curved—at least he was trying to understand. "Vel's circumstances didn't matter. Remember, his brain waves aren't smooth." He scowled and she reworded her thoughts. "He's got that constant torment going on his head, of feeling inadequate in his struggle to be perfect. Her innocent confession must have been the nudge that pushed him over the edge. Hell, he may have had another victim selected.''

He faced her, arms loose at his side. "You make it sound like a grocery list."

"His kills aren't random, Chris. That tiny infraction, in his mind, is his mother rejecting him all over again. What's really scary is that it could be as common as seeing a mother refuse her child candy before supper. Just depends on his mood."

"Good God, this whole town could be in danger." Finally Chris understood her desperation at the train, and he had to live with the guilt that if he hadn't stopped her, Vel might be alive.

"Not necessarily." Victoria stood and he watched her every move as she crossed to him. "You can't blame yourself, Chris."

It was eerie, that she knew his thoughts. "I do."

She gripped his arms, silk slipping beneath her fingers as she gazed into worried dark eyes. "He's sick, but he knows right from wrong." And that made him sane enough to stand trial. "When he's got a candidate, he cultivates them until they're comfortable around him. No fear, no resistance. He's a nice guy." A tapered brow rose sharply. "Even you liked him."

That suddenly made Chris feel like an idiot. "He kills to save the children from the life he suffered?"

Her lush lips twisted in a smirk. "Yeah, if you call being worth ten million dollars at the age of eighteen suffering."

"Now that's total fabrication."

She lowered her arms and flopped back into the chair, legs outstretched. And Chris's gaze traveled upward from the socks, across tanned marble skin, to the tail of the shirt at the top of her thighs. He clasped his hand in front of him. The woman had no idea of what she was doing to him, let alone his mind.

"He came to town wounded, didn't he?"

Only her gold eyes shifted and Chris nodded.

"I tracked the blood trail. It was in the woods when we first met."

Chris scowled, waiting.

"Cole shot him after Becket shoved a blade in his chest. Becket was out on bail, but he kidnapped the daughter of the cop—ah, sheriff—who discovered the connection between the murders. Doc MacLaren had to have examined him."

"She did, Tori. I was there. Jenna informs me of every gunshot wound. He said he was ambushed."

He's keeping details too, she realized. "Plausible. But how did he pay? For that matter, how did he have cash to get into a poker game and win the Pearl?"

"He sold a cigarette case."

"Gold with his initials on it?"

Chris's features tightened. "Yes."

"It didn't strike you odd that a man with gold to sell, arrived without a horse or money?"

"Neither did you."

Careful girlfriend, a voice warned. You're getting into rough territory here. "Yeah, right."

"Care to explain?"

"No," she said to her lap.

His jaw tightened. "Even about those masks and the colored glass you can put over your eyes . . . or the knapsack you protect like the U.S. Mint?"

Her shoulders tensed. "No." She flicked at a loose thread in her shirt, hating her deception, aching to blurt it all out. And what? Watch him run for the hills? If he doesn't lock you up now, that will make him throw away the key.

Chris moved quietly away from the fire, dipping into his robe pocket. He stopped before her and she looked up. God, he looked so . . . wounded. But when she opened her mouth to speak, he grasped her wrist and slapped something into her palm.

"Let me know when you can spare the whole truth."

He left her alone and Victoria didn't need to look at her hand. She could feel the shape of the matches she'd lost.

Damn.

* * *

Abigale wiped her hands on her apron, eyeing Christopher as she put away the dishes. He sat at the kitchen table, eating his supper without tasting it, she knew, his eyes focused on some forgotten spot out the window. Since she'd found him at Miss Victoria's bedside, he'd done nothing but move restlessly through the house or stare for long moments out at the mountains. He gripped his fork so tightly that his knuckles whitened and every once in a while she saw a terrible fear in his handsome face. She'd never seen him like this, glaring toward the hall, the stairs, to where Miss Victoria lay sleeping, for the second day in row, the poor dear. He wanted to wake her, Abigale could tell, but didn't, and right now he appeared as if a roar crested inside him, and doing his best to keep it from passing his tightly clamped lips. Truly, she didn't want to be near when he exploded, but . . .

"She's the one, isn't she?"

Chris looked up from his plate, the fork poised at his lips. His eyes narrowed, in that way that told her he didn't want to talk and Abigale remembered when Camille jilted him, and how often she'd seen it, directed at her. But this was different.

"The one—" she swallowed, "who sent you to bathin' in the river."

His features yanked taut and he set the fork down slowly. He swiped his lips with his napkin. "Yes." He tossed the linen over his plate, then pushed it away.

Abigale came forward to take it. And Chris noticed her hands shook.

"Abby?"

She met his gaze. "I don't think God intended for you to always live alone, Christopher."

It was the wrong thing to say. His expression withered and the chair scraped back as he stood abruptly.

"My happiness is not your problem, Abigale."

"Yes, it is."

His brows shot up.

"Your mother and father charged me to take care of you."

"That was England. I was a child, alone in a foreign country then. In case you hadn't noticed, I'm all grown up. This is my home."

"Why did you build this house here, Christopher?"

He blinked, taken back. "Land was cheap."

Slowly she shook her head, her sad features softening to a smile. "You had more opportunities to settle before, in England, on the Reservation with your father, and the Saint's know closer to civilization."

"Are you saying that Victoria had something to do with my settling here?"

He was giving her *that* look, the hard unpenetrable stare that got him sent to bed without his supper when he was a child.

"Don't be glarin' at me, Christopher." She pushed him back and took the plate over to the dry sink. "Or there'll be no desert."

"Don't want any. Finish your thought, Abigale."

She tensed, but plunged on. "Remember what you said when you found this place and the feelings that brought you here."

Chris was silent, his mind rolling back, his heart accelerating. He didn't recall telling Abigale about that.

He was waiting for something, expanding the ranch, the house, inventing things he'd never had the notion or desire to tackle before. God, he'd spent hours fashioning pipes and pumps, thinking of small tasks made more convenient. And then there was the dream that had come true. Cougar who walks like a woman.

"Christopher?"

His gaze slid to hers. "I remember."

"She's different. Like you."

He folded his arms over his chest.

She wrung her hands. "I've already seen her make things, like you."

His brows rose into his forehead. "What things?"

"I can't say, but—"

He lowered his arms. ''Great mother in heaven! Is there a woman around who won't keep secrets from me!'' He stormed from the kitchen and into his study, slamming the door.

'' 'Twas only too private,'' she peeped, then sighed dispiritedly and went back to doing dishes.

Chapter Twenty-Six

It wasn't hard to avoid Chris, physically, for his house and ranch were large, and where he went, she . . . well, she stayed in the bedroom. But mentally? That was another matter all together and confusion was the state of the day.

And she admitted to herself that she was a coward, a sensation she detested.

Except her only slightly objective logic insisted that nothing but irrevocable damage would result if she explained how she'd arrived in his town, yet her heart screamed she couldn't go on dealing in half-truths and had nothing to lose.

Except him.

Her breath caught at the thought, her chest aching like the clench of a thick fist.

Deep inside, she had her answer the first time she tasted his incredibly warm mouth, felt the undeniable heat of his skin. And she knew it the instant he carried her off his porch, dirty and tired and needing him so desperately.

Then let him see your toys and take your shots like a big girl.

Apprehension slithered through her.

But I'll be like the alien from another planet.

And it will be the last barrier you have, a voice needled. Then what?

"How the hell should I know," she hissed, shifting her position on the floor from push up to sit up. Flexing a kink out of her shoulders, she tucked her feet under the low long dresser before the window and pumped a quick thirty.

Even as she forced out twenty more sit ups, sweat trickling down her spine, she knew what would happen.

She'd admit she'd fallen in love with him.

No. I haven't.

She swung around onto her stomach and arched her back, grabbing her ankles and stretching. I haven't. Really.

"Holy—!"

Her foot slipped from her grasp, thunking to the floor and she glanced to the side. One look in his eyes and she knew she was lying to herself.

Chris felt her stare drain him of energy, draw him in and sink into their golden softness.

And she looked away before he could understand what he saw.

"Don't knock much do you?" She recaptured her foot.

"Sorry." Not the least bit apologetic. "The door was ajar."

"How convenient for a Peeping Tom like yourself." Like when he was in her hotel room, watching her and Chris winced when he heard her back pop.

"You're going to hurt yourself."

"Nah, feels good actually," she grunted, before releasing her feet and pushing back to sit. She spread her legs wide, arms up and tipped to the side.

Chris swallowed.

Her position was . . . intoxicating.

"Why are you doing this?"

"To keep my girlish figure," she muttered dryly, coming upright, "and outrun a bounty."

He ignored her last comment. She wouldn't be doing that for a while. Yet, even as last night's conversation sang through his head, her complete and absolute logic of the crimes and theory and raising more questions, he knew she wouldn't offer answers until she wanted. And he dismissed their problems and concentrated on the bare legs aching to be touched.

"You look spectacular already."

Victoria allowed herself a private smile. Honest enough, after the way he was salivating over her last night.

"And what, may I ask, are you wearing?"

Victoria stilled, met his gaze, then tipped to the other side, touching her fingers to her toes. Truth or mild lies, she thought. "Cut off jeans."

"I meant—" he waved at her chest.

"A tee shirt." A tank really, plain white, but she wasn't wearing a bra and sweat made the material cling to her. She stole a covert glance at him and saw the effect. "And if you get any harder, you'll split those pants wide open."

His features yanked tight, then a slow smile stretched his lips. "Keep doing that and we'll see who loses their britches."

She paused briefly, smiling and looking him over. "Oooh, threats, I like it."

She leaned forward, arms outstretched as if to beckon him and slowly lowered her torso until her arms rested on the floor. The last time he'd seen anyone that limber was a Chinese acrobat in San Francisco. And he thought for the hundredth time what an extraordinary creature she was, even though she thought the opposite. And he loved that about her, this take it or leave it woman, with her tough talk and frightening independence.

"Did you come here to throw me out?"

"You're not going anywhere," he said as he crossed the room, sinking to his knees between her legs.

"That so?" Her hands lowered to his biceps, her expression half confused, half wanting.

He couldn't take his eyes off her mouth and brushed his thumb over the lush seam. "Uh-ah." He wrapped his arms around her waist, pulling her close, pulling her onto his lap.

"Bossy injun, aren't you?"

He grinned. "Yup."

"Well, Tonto, I don't like being bossed around." Her legs closed around his hips, bringing her femininity flush against his groin, and her body reacted, hips pushing and Chris groaned. His hands slid to cup her buttocks and fit her more closely.

"I want you, Tori."

Her heart did a quick slam against her ribs. She'd known that, of course. And she wanted him so badly she ached constantly, even when he wasn't around. But it was the way he said it, a promise of forever in his tone. He didn't mean it—he couldn't. He knew she had to leave eventually.

But what if you can't leave, a voice asked, so reasonable, so calm when her heart was racing up to her throat. His fingers flexed on her bottom and she wet her lips.

A tight sound worked in his throat.

"Right now?"

The corner of his mouth quirked. "Abigale would cut out my heart with one of her knives."

"Christopher Waythorne Swift!"

Victoria's gaze shifted, her cheeks pinkening, but Chris didn't take his eyes off her, didn't move.

"She's arrived to see the deed done," Victoria whispered.

"Leave us, Abby." Hurry. Before he did split his trousers. "And close the door."

"I will not!"

"Abigale." His voice came softly, yet rang with command. The woman reluctantly backed out, obeying.

"We've sent her moral fiber in a twist, you know that." Her fingers sifted the dark curls covering his nape. It was so deliciously soft.

"She'll get used to it."

There it was again, Victoria thought, the forever tone.

His hands smoothed over her hips, warming the skin of her thighs. Back and forth, back and forth, heightening her senses. His touch felt like butter sliding on her skin.

"I love your legs," he murmured.

"I gathered that."

"I want to taste them," he rasped, ducking to nuzzle her throat instead. A breathy sound escaped her, her arms tightening about his neck and she dropped her head back. "I want to be inside you, Tori."

She whimpered, plowing her fingers into his hair and tilting his head. Her mouth covered his, her head shifting back and forth as her lips savaged his, her tongue driving deeply inside and Chris's heart pounded, rushing blood to every cell in his body. Breathing came labored and harsh. Bodies pushed, seeking release. He scooped her breasts into his palms and she went wild, laving at his mouth, arching to the pressure. His thumbs circled her tight nipples.

"Chris, Chris," she whispered. Between her thighs grew damp and slick.

"I remember what you taste like, Tori. I remember what these," he stroked her nipple slowly, "feel like in my mouth, against my tongue."

"Oh God, Chris, don't say anymore. I—we . . . can't."

The hot press of his mouth drowned out her protests and she enjoyed the power of it, then pulled back, her skin flushed, her breathing labored.

She gave herself up to feeling. "I want to, really." He smiled, so sexy and inviting that the hot throbbing inside her increased. "But I—" She lowered her gaze.

Where was all that boldness? She was shy and embarrassed and then he remembered. Her cycle.

"Do you hurt?" He brushed her hair, damp and curling, from her forehead. The gesture was tender, his expression sympathetic and her heart bloomed with something undefinable. That his concern was for her, not himself, spoke volumes about this man.

"I'm fine—oh, God, that feels good," she moaned as his fingers dug into her spine, massaging away the stiffness. She buried her face in the curve of his throat.

"I have lots of ways to make you feel good," he promised, keeping up the motion and she cocked a one-eyed look at him.

A tiny mischievous smile painted her lips. She couldn't wait to find out—and try a few on him. "Sure of yourself, huh?"

He sent her a half-lidded stare. "Yup."

She was suddenly scared. Scared of what she was letting herself in for—sheer heart stabbing pain. She had to leave this man, to never see his handsome face, enjoy his touch again. It would kill her.

But that could be days, maybe even weeks, she thought hopefully. God. Where had her drive gone? Becket needed catching and soon, and now he was wanted in two centuries. And if they didn't watch him, others would die, but Chris's strong fingers were working over her skin, easing tension and pain and Victoria dismissed her just-cause to *her* need and slid her mouth over his, tasting him, loving him.

She had the opportunity to be loved and feel love. Here, in his century. And for now, without anything to keep her from experiencing what she'd missed in her marriage, she wanted everything she could get. Recklessness ripped through her. Could she pack a lifetime of loving in a fistful of days?

Yes.

Was she so desperate to grab it that she'd risk hurting him when she knew she couldn't stay?

Yes.

Would he let her go when it was over, when Becket was in handcuffs and on his way through the fall?

He had to.

Or would he try to follow?

That could never happen. Never.

She straightened on his lap, gazing into his eyes.

She had to tell him. It was only fair that he knew the stakes before he made the bet.

"I have to go."

His eyes widened. "Now?"

"Yes." She scooted off his lap. "I need to run."

"From me?" Hurt and anger marked his voice.

Still on her knees, she cupped his jaw, her thumb rasping over his lips. "No. Not anymore."

His eyes softened.

"But I need a little time, to think this out." God, how was she going to tell him she was from the twentieth century! It would blow him away.

His pulse galloped and he realized he'd finally get his answers. As he climbed painfully to his feet and pulled her off the floor, he suppressed the ungodly urge to push the matter.

"I'll be here."

"I know." I don't deserve him, she thought, turning away and shoving her feet into her boots. She knelt to tie the laces.

"You mean you're actually going to run, for exercise?"

"Yeah, it clears my head."

"Like that!" He pointed to her bare legs.

She spared him a mild glance, then stood. "Got a problem with it?"

"Yes, dammit! A lady doesn't expose herself—"

She stiffened "I'm not a lady. And if you're expecting one, forget it. It ain't gonna happen."

He saw the self-depreciation in her features and crossed to her, slinging an arm around her waist and jerking her against him. "You try to hard to be ferocious." She gazed into his eyes, her hair half covering her face. He brushed it back, watching his moves. "And, as to being a lady . . . you are, darlin'. A lady has strength and courage and—" he smiled into her eyes "—excessive amounts of stubborness, I've realized."

Victoria beamed, settling her arms around him. "Thanks, Chris." She needed to hear that. God, how she needed to.

"Go ahead, wild one. Run half naked, if you like. My relatives do."

"So do you," she said, then cast him a sly glance. "Going to strip down to your breechcloth and join me?"

He frowned. "I thought you wanted to be alone."

She didn't, not anymore. She'd spent the past five years that way and realized it made her more than just lonely. "Not if I can get to look at the cute behind wrapped in deer skin."

He blinked, then grinned.

" 'Course, you'll be eating my dust."

He arched a brow. "That a bet, woman?"

"Cheyenne warrior afraid of soft white woman?" she grunted and he chuckled mysteriously.

"Tori, darlin', you obviously don't know much about my people." His brows wiggled. "We're all gamblers."

Excitement coarsed through her and she backed out of his embrace.

"A wager, eh? What are the stakes?"

He gave her the sexiest look imaginable and her knees melted. "Promising, but unfair."

"All right, then . . ." He was thoughtful, glancing around the bedroom for a clue. His gaze snapped to hers. "I win, you wear that." He nodded to the dresses draped over a chair.

She agreed. Easy enough, she thought, she'd been dying to wear one anyway. "And if I win?"

"Name it," he said, folding his arms over his chest.

"You show me your inventions."

His brows shot up. "That's it?"

"Seems fair to me." She bent, snatching her shirt off the floor, and Chris groaned at the sweet curves of her buttocks peaking out from beneath the cropped pants.

Fair? With her dressed like that! She was lucky he didn't toss her on the bed and ravish her right now.

She straightened, realizing she ought to wear a bra to run and that Chris was still standing close, a pained look on his face and a bulge in his trousers.

She couldn't resist teasing him.

"Well, go get half naked."

"We haven't sealed the bargain."

She dropped the shirt and came to him, gliding up against his body, fitting herself to his hard contours as her muscled arms snaked around his neck, her mouth hot and liquid on his. And Chris's knees wobbled and he staggered for balance, crushing her to him, pouring his heart into the kiss. Abruptly he released her and she stumbled back, blinking, touching her lips.

"Whoa." Her breath rushed in her lungs. It boggled the mind, the way they ignited.

"Yeah." He struggled for air, raking his hand through his hair. Alone. On the mountain, with her. In short pants! Who was he fooling? "Five minutes," he managed, then left, and Victoria rubbed her hand over her face, her body pulsing and briefly, she closed her eyes, waiting for it to turn down to a low simmer. Then she searched her backpack for a bra, unaware that he'd turned back and caught a glimpse of the satchel's contents and the scrap of lacy fabric dangling from her fingers. He moved away without a word.

Patience. Yes. He could stand a few more hours, couldn't he?

He met up with her at the back of the house near the paddock. All work had ceased as his ranch hands gawked at her long tanned legs.

Chris barked at them to turn around and Victoria laughed as he dragged her behind the barn and out of sight.

"Never again," he growled down at her.

He looked absolutely beside himself, she thought happily. A man's jealousy was something she'd never experienced before. Ain't bad either, she decided, letting her eyes feast on his bare chest and upper thighs. His moccasins were actually leggings, attaching somehow beneath the flap of his breech cloth, yet while the garments covered his calves, knees, and most of his thighs, generous portions of corded muscle and naked hip was exposed.

And she wanted to pull one of those raw hide strings and see what would happen.

"I hope they know better and keep this quiet," he griped, slinging a quiver of arrows over his shoulder.

"Yes. Let's not let my sins get out."

His gaze flew to hers and found hers dancing with mischief. "You don't care?"

"Only for your sake."

"I'm the black sheep of this town." He dropped the strap of a hide-covered bladder over one shoulder and beneath his arm. "Hardly matters."

"You have to live here, not me."

His eyes flared, like an unexpected wound, and Victoria didn't want to see it, didn't want to think about what might happen later. Now was important. Grabbing happiness and running with it. She hoped he was game.

"Where's the finish line?"

He nodded to the mountaintop, still searching her face, and she looked up at the imposing land. She'd never make it, but wasn't about to let him know.

"To that clearing, near the rocks."

She met his gaze. "Ready to lose?" She knotted the shirt she'd thrown over her tank top at her waist.

His sadness faded, blending into a smile. "I'm going to win, Tori. Again."

"You just want to see if I can walk in a dress without padding."

Slowly he shook his head. "I want you in it, so I can take it off."

"You're just too damn sure of yourself, Swift Arrow." She snaked her hands around his trim waist, pressing his lower back and drawing him willingly against her. Then her free hand dipped beneath the soft flap of doe hide and cupped the bare skin of his buttocks. Air hissed through his teeth.

"What are you doing?"

She smiled, stroking tight smooth flesh in maddening circles. "Evening the odds."

He was growing hard and she knew it.

"Ready—"

"Tori," he warned as she moved away.

"Set—"

"Victoria!"

"Go."

She took off and Chris groaned, his hand brushing across his arousal. The little witch. It was no use trying to hide it, yet he wanted to see her in that blue dress so damn bad that he grabbed his bow and lurched after her, his long legs tearing across the terrain. He had one advantage. This was his land and he knew every inch like a father knows his child.

"I give," she gasped, bent over, her hand braced on her thighs as she struggled for air. Her quads and calves burned and quivered from exertion. Her clothes were soaked, her feet screaming for a rest and Victoria managed to lift her head. He was still running, the show off. And worse, he didn't make a sound.

Dragging off her shirt and wiping the sweat streaming over her body, Victoria watched him. He looked like a deer in flight, darting around trees, leaping gulleys, and she imagined his hair longer and laced with feathers. He was born in a teepee, grew up in a southern Cheyenne camp, traveling where the food moved. A plainsmen. His people lived for the moment, the season, not wasting anything and never waiting for the future to come to them. It startled her down to her bones every time she thought about where she was.

And she didn't have to turn her head to see the untouched glory around her. She felt it, smelled it, tasted it on her lips with each hard breath. It made her remember where she came from, the little chicken ranch in California that scarcely survived year after year until a worn out kerosine heater torched her family's home.

And it made her want to stay and start again.

Shaking her head, she dropped down onto a bolder and tried to whistle. She couldn't catch her breath and shouted.

"Hey, He-who-won-this-one. Stop!"

Chris slowed to a halt and turned, swiping the back of his hand across his upper lip. He headed back down. "Cougar-

Who-Walks is conceding defeat?'' he said with a quick lift of his brow.

She enjoyed the rolling gait of his hips before she said, "Don't be smug. I'll get my wind in a moment." Empty threats, she thought.

He dropped to the ground at her feet, bracing his forearms on his knees.

"I can't wait to see you in a dress, a real dress."

"You wanted to so bad, you bought some?"

He smiled, lighting a fire in her heart. "Abigale picked them out," he managed, drawing the strap to his quiver and water bladder off over his head. He offered her the bladder and her brows wrinkled as she loosened the hide strings securing the opening. It was amazing that this thing still held a drop and she tipped her head back and let it trickle into her mouth.

She swished and turned her head to spit, catching his smile, then drinking more. She handed it back and he repeated the measure before tying it off.

She gazed down at him. He looked so comfortable here, in tune with the wild nature. Sunlight dappled across the dead brush and leaves, glowing off the vibrant green of the trees and scrubs offering them a cooling canopy. But it was the way he was looking at her, his emotions in every feature of his handsome face. She wanted to capture the image and freeze it in her memory.

Now or never, girlfriend.

Her eyes stung and she moved off the rock and knelt before him. Please don't hate me, she prayed. Don't push me away.

Chris watched her throat work, her eyes sheen and knew what was coming. And it terrified her. He couldn't think of a damn thing to ease her suffering.

"If it hurts you this much—"

"No." She dashed at a single tear, annoyed with her weakness. "No. I just don't want to spoil this." She gestured between them. "And it will."

"Trust me, it won't."

She scoffed. "It's bizarre, Chris. Hell. It's totally out there!" She waved above her head.

He caught her hands and felt her trembling. "Then I have something to tell you first," he said and she nodded mutely, much like a prisoner awaiting sentence. "I knew you were coming here."

Chapter Twenty-Seven

"This is not funny, Chris."

Her lips scarcely moved, he noticed, and her jaw was set against him.

"I don't mean it to be, but I knew."

"Hell. I didn't, so how could you?"

He loved the mutinous fold of her arms across her middle. It pushed her breasts up out of the *tee* shirt rather enticingly. He shook himself, reminding to be serious. She'd beat him up if he teased her now.

"I had a dream."

She scoffed, the reaction he expected.

"Dreams are doorways of the soul and the future, Tori."

Doorways. Why did he use that word? she wondered and searched his features carefully for the lie. He was Cheyenne, raised with the Sun Dance and vision quests and she respected that, and in the New Age of the twentieth century, people, herself included, drew on the ancient ways to find balance in their lives. Didn't she meditate to release stress? Hell. It was safer than valium.

"Okay, so tell me." Nothing was going to beat her story

and she relaxed back against the rocks, stretching her legs out beside him.

He eyed her suspiciously. She didn't look the least bit responsive.

"In the dream I saw fog, a heavy mist and heard the rush of water, like a fall."

Her eyes widened and she shifted, her arms unfolding and her palms flattening on the ground. Oh Jesus. He went on, describing his vision, the human figure emerging out of the mist and turning into a mountain lion, a cougar, a hunter. *Cougar Who Walks.* Yet, it was the whirling sound, like a bolo, that Victoria could only explain away as helicopter blades knifing the air, the chopper that circled over her head just before she stepped into the fall. How could he have known? Her blood skated through her veins with a strange unnameable excitement.

"Wait, wait," she interrupted when he got to the part about the cougar clawing him. "You think *I'm* this animal?"

"Yes." Unquestionable.

"Bull."

His lips twitched with a smile. "You *have* fought me, Tori, every step of the way," he patiently pointed out. "And you've also appeared in a form other than the delectable sight I see now."

True, but delectable? She glanced down at herself—sweaty, grimy, with unshaved legs. Hell, if he liked it, who was she to argue? "You have strange tastes, Chris, but go on."

"The lion protected me." His brows knitted and he struggled to mesh feelings and vision into words. "It was as if the beast was bringing me back into the fold of the town, carving a path."

"I didn't do anything. Except give you a royal pain in the—"

"Clara did," he interrupted smoothly, grinning proud. "Defended me in the general store. Noble saw it."

Noble has a big mouth, she thought. "Okay, I'll give you that. And they deserved it, you know."

"I'm sure you played judge and jury quite well." Steam

rose around her and his lips stretched into a teasing smile. "The cougar," he continued before she socked him "—was within the mist again, this time gentler, no longer the hunter and then changed into human form."

He paused, his expression clouding, the sadness in his eyes felt like a blunt smack through her chest. "You're stalling," she warned.

"It—*you* tumbled back into the mist, vanishing."

She wet her lips and swallowed. "I see." She exhaled slowly, not liking what this dream meant, could mean, but Christ, it was just too coincidental. "You believe this, don't you?"

"Yes. Of course." Again, doubtless. As if there were no other reasoning in existence.

"And the cougar was alone?"

He nodded.

"And it—"

"You—"

"Okay, *I* returned alone?"

Sadly, he repeated the gesture.

"If that's so, then your dream is wrong, 'cause I'm not leaving without Becket."

She was determined to go, and that she'd leave him so willingly tore him in half just to consider it. And when he spoke again his voice came softly, a flicker of hurt and wonder in his tone.

"And where will you take him, Tori?"

Their eyes locked.

"Through time. To my century."

His expression didn't shift a fraction, patient for an explanation.

And she suddenly felt one brick short of a full load. But now that she'd said it, she had to convince him.

"You were right about the mist, the water, the sounds." She plucked nervously at pebbles and twigs, watching her moves. "I followed Becket's blood trail into a waterfall. There's a corridor behind it and it opened . . ." her gaze flew to his, "into this century."

His features yanked tight.

"Yeah, I know. Told you it was—" she made a circular motion beside her head "—out there."

"That night, in the forest when we first met? You'd only recently come through this fall?"

"Yeah." Her gaze slid over his bare chest, the deerskin enhancing his physique, and she remembered that night. "Believe me when I say you were the *last person* I expected."

He liked the way she said that. A lot. And splashes of moments played in his mind—Victoria beating the stuffing out of three drunks, as Vic Mason in his jail, arrogant, defiant, and then panicked.

"When did you realize you were not where you imagined?"

"In your jail."

Great Mother of Earth, he thought, trying to understand what it was like to find herself in another century, another world. "You didn't intentionally come here then?"

Her tapered brows flicked up. "Walk through time? Hell no. Oh, don't look so hurt." She nudged him playfully. "I followed a serial killer and didn't care where he headed, just that I had his scent and went for it."

Scent. How like her.

"Yet there's no fall in that area." Skeptical again, edged.

"On this side. On mine, it's there and a stream. With a few hundred marshals and FBI combing the area." He opened his mouth and she added, "Federal Bureau of Investigation."

His look approved, then fell into confusion. "But that was weeks ago."

"Time doesn't move there, when it moves here. I went back to check."

His dark eyes flared, panic seizing him. "You've traveled back—?"

"—Forward," she interrupted, leaning close. "I'm from the future, Chris. And get this in while it's hot. I'm a bounty hunter in the twentieth century. *Nineteen ninety-seven.*" If he was going to turn away, she wanted it done now. "I was a U.S. Marine, then a Federal Marshal, and when I couldn't bend the rules to get the perp who killed my daughter, I went to bounty hunting. I did what it took to get them.''

The disguises, the personas, the coldness. ''Even losing all you know and love?''

''They're all dead except—wait! Whoa.'' She shook her head, her hand up, then peered crookedly. ''You believe me?''

''There's far too much about you that cannot be explained, Tori. And you will begin now.''

He folded his arms over his chest, looking less like the Cheyenne warrior and more like an impatient child waiting to be amused with a wild fairy tale.

''I—I—can't believe you're taking this so—easily.'' She eyed him up and down. ''What's the catch?''

''I am wondering why you didn't tell me before.''

''Are you serious?'' she shrieked, her voice echoing in the dense forest. ''Oh, excuse me, Marshal, while you've got that gun at my back and about to lock me up for a crime I *didn't* commit, I'm a time traveler. Just in case you needed reason enough to throw away the key.'' He was scowling as if that was the last thing he would have done. And they both knew it was a lie. ''You weren't very accepting, Chris, even after you knew I was a woman.'' A flicker of old hurt stirred in her eyes, and he regretted causing it.

''It's hard to admit a woman is more capable.'' Sullen, apologetic.

''Make you feel better to know I have a hundred twenty-five years of other marshals, sheriffs and rangers experience to draw from and not just a talented hunter with legs you lust after?''

He blinked, not sure how to answer. And she laughed softly, like smoke laced Bordeaux, scooting closer.

''Plead the fifth, Chris.'' She patted his knee, then stood. ''Besides,'' she took a few steps to stretch her muscles. ''I still don't think it's such a hot idea you knowing any of this.''

''And why not?''

Propped against a tree, she gazed at him, her arms folded. ''Think about it,'' she said, brushing her hair off her cheek.

Her hand trembled and Chris studied her dirt smudged face. "Is my being here screwing up your life? Will you die because I'm here?" Her voice wavered, belying her casual stance. "Will I? What events have changed just because I talked to *just one* person, not to mention what harm's been already done to Vel and the others. And what about my interference in your investigations?"

He could hear the guilt in her tone, see it in her eyes. "I would have searched for the wrong person. Raif would be dead and Sean might never have found peace, Tori. God, Lucky is alive because of you. Raif and Lila, too."

She shook her head. "Raif was probably supposed to die."

"I don't believe that and neither do you. It's our job to preserve law and life."

Our job. It made them sound like . . . more than partners. "But Velvet—"

"Vel's dead because of Becket." He rose and went to her, gripping her upper arms, forcing her to see she couldn't carry a killer's guilt. "*He* killed her. And God knows how many others if you hadn't followed him—" His words ceased abruptly, his gaze searching hers. "Does he know he was followed?"

She shook her head, her heart racing so hard she couldn't think straight. "But he had a four-hour head start and in your time, it's been four months."

Chris's expression fell away to sadness. "No wonder so many have died."

"He has to be stopped."

"My men are watching him." His tone clipped off each word. "He hasn't moved from the saloon since Vel vanished. He was asking about Clara to some of the locals, though."

Suspicious still, she thought. "He's slick, Chris. He moved Vel's body without anyone seeing him. And he had to have gone right past me to do it."

His jaw tightened. "I have him covered."

"I know," she said without doubt, her palms rubbing his biceps. "I trust you."

He let out a long breath. "Finally," he said to the heavens, then drew her into his arms. His look was serious, his gaze sweeping over her face. He brushed a smudge of dirt from her chin with his thumb, let the calloused pad slide over her lips. Her tongue grazed the tip and he inhaled, a short gasp. "I'm very happy you found that cave, Tori. Very glad. And as to *screwing up* my life—" He shook his head at the odd phrase. "It wasn't much of one until you arrived."

She made that sound, one he'd heard too often, a scoff of disbelief, as if she couldn't matter in the grand pattern of life, and he realized she never recognized the measure her worth beyond the next bounty. He'd change that.

Then she said something that astounded him. The pure admittance he never expected.

"I never realized what a pitiful life I chose," she said, taking the blame. "Until—"

"What?" His gaze searched. He'd never seen her so uneasy.

"—you showed me how low I'd sunk."

"Do not credit me with that." Chris responded sharply, angrily.

She shook her head, hoping he'd understand. "You reminded me, with all the finesse of a bully, that there were other things in life besides hunting bounty."

His expression was knowing. "Ahh, in the hotel."

"Guess it wasn't memorable enough for you, huh?" Her tone dripped with sarcasm.

He tightened his arms and ducked to whisper in her ear, "I fall asleep every night with the image of you finding rapture beneath my questing fingers." A little moan escaped her and her hands flexed on his arms. "You were so wild and hungry for me—"

"Stop."

"—wet and panting—"

"Chris."

"And the scent of you makes me ache to taste—"

"Okay, okay, enough." She rested her forehead on his chest, tucked beneath his chin and his low chuckle rumbled softly.

"Come, Cougar-Who-Walks-Like-A-Woman, tell me of your world."

"I don't think you should—"

"Ah!" He touched her lips with a fingertip. "Do not think for a moment that I'm letting you off this mountain without details."

She considered him for a moment, then realized it would do little good to hide anything now. "On what?" Stupid question.

He looked thoughtful. "You are convinced this ... portal will not allow entry?" He was thinking about after she took Becket back.

"It was unstable. I mean ... when I came back after checking, it was harder." She shrugged. "I can't imagine it being flexible. It was pure chance that I could get back."

"Why?"

"Chemical make up in the body or something, I suppose. I'm no physicist, but Becket and I must have what's necessary."

"You're so sure?"

"Yeah, or this place would be full of twentieth century Federal agents. They aren't stupid and if anything, thorough. They'd try to come through." She looked at him intently. "He'll stand trial here, too, Chris."

"He may die here."

She wasn't going to get into a debate with him now. "Next question."

His gaze caressed her face and he leaned close to whisper, "It's been driving me mad."

Even sweaty, he smelled good. "Hmm?"

"What in God's name are you wearing under that shirt?"

She grinned. "A bra. Brassiere. A garment to support a woman's breasts," she said, deadpan.

His fingertip trailed the edge of the tee shirt, hooking the fabric and she let him peek inside.

"Fascinating." His breath warmed her skin and Victoria throbbed for his touch.

"I'll show you, if you're a good boy."

His glance was sly and hot. "What constitutes good?"

''If I have to explain, you aren't working hard enough.''

He grinned, urging her back against a tree. Thigh met thigh, chest met breast and molded, yielded. He swooped down to cover her mouth with his. He licked the outline of her mouth, scored her teeth, then pressed his intention with his tongue between her lips and his groin against the sweet divide between her muscled thighs. She gripped his waist and rocked against him.

''Oh good, very good,'' she gasped and met his kiss again, sinking slowly to the ground and taking him with her.

Dry leaves crackled beneath them as they met the ground, her long limbs curling around his, and Chris felt hot desire singing through her, making her shiver. Her lips toyed lusciously with his ear lobe and he closed his eyes to the tantalizing sensations, experiencing them as he never had before.

His broad hands molded familiarly over her hips and buttocks, teasing the curve of flesh revealed beneath the frayed edge of denim.

Her lips rasped across his collarbone, tasting the salt of his flesh.

Somewhere a bird chirped.

A breeze rustles leaves to swirl around them.

Victoria decided she could do this forever.

''I was scared, Chris.''

He cocked a look at her, surprised.

''Telling you my secret.'' He frowned softly. ''I thought you'd be, you know—disgusted or something?''

He shifted to his side, cupping the gentle curve of her jaw in his hand. His thumb brushed her cheek. ''I adore you, woman, when are you going to realize that?''

Something akin to pain flared in her dark gold eyes and she wet her lips nervously. ''Maybe when you kiss me again?''

His smile was slow and rascally before his mouth covered hers, a slick roll of warm lips as he pushed her onto her back, his body cloaking her from the sunlight.

She felt the hardness of him cradled snugly against her and Victoria's body rocketed with a desperate heat so primitive and hungry she would have stripped right then and had her way with him. It felt as if she'd waited a lifetime to be naked and loved by this man. But the irony of being a fertile woman wouldn't allow that and the restraint tore at her, his low moans when she found a satisfying spot on his body making her greedy to hear more.

And more.

She spread her thighs and wrestled him to his back, kissing a grinding path down his throat, over his hairless chest. His Adam's apple bobbed.

Straddling his thighs, she hovered, running her tongue around the flat coin of his nipple.

Air snagged in his throat. "I think we'd better head back."

"Yeah, right." She shimmied lower, her tongue dipping into the indentation in his stomach. "I'm off and running. Can't you tell?"

"Tori," he groaned when her hand combed down over his arousal. He gripped the muscled thighs hugging his and she straightened.

Eyes locked and held.

And he wondered about that devilish smile aching to get out.

Then he knew.

Victoria plucked at the raw hide strings, loosening them.

"Tori?" His throat worked violently, his fingers pressing deep into her flesh.

Without a trace of reservation, she slid her hand beneath the tanned hide, enveloping him. "Ohhh, Christopher," she said, long and breathless.

Instinctively, he arched into her gentle pressure.

"Tori, I thought—ah, *Jesus.*" He trembled beneath her stroking and she caught his silent question.

"Shhh. There's a lot more to making love than just you moving inside me."

Chris thought he'd come apart with the image she offered.

"You taught me that." His need for her blazed in his dark

eyes and Victoria wanted to ignite it, wanted to hear him moan, wanted him to writhe beneath her touch as she had for him.

She slid down his body, taking the doe skin breechcloth.

"Tori, no." He reached for her.

She brushed his hands away. "Yes." And she didn't give him any choice.

She lowered her head and Chris's eyes widened further, then snapped shut as her mouth touched him. He fell back, boneless, surrendering himself. Sweat broke out on his brow, his beautiful muscles rippling with strained power. And moments later, his howl of rapture echoed through the valley, stirring the birds.

Victoria smoothed the deep blue dress at her waist. It was hell getting into all this crap. A chemise, layers of petticoats that made her feel like a million, stockings with dainty little flower garters and small shoes that felt like slippers. Everything laid out was the epitome of femininity, lacy, threaded with ribbons.

But she wasn't about to wear the bustle. The tons of fabric made her waist look tiny, but her rear, huge. Style or not, she couldn't harness herself into a wire cage for the sake of fashion. Not that she ever followed it, anyway.

What she did like was feeling sexy, alluring. And that was new.

Now if she could only walk without tripping over the hem. What was it about a floor-length gown that made a girl feel elegant and positively graceful? Of course, the effect was spoiled when she picked up her backpack and headed out of the room. She flew down the stairs and crossed the foyer into Chris's study. He was standing near the fireplace, sipping coffee, his hair still damp from his bath and Victoria smiled when she remembered Abigale and the verbal lashing she'd given them both. His for being in the woods so long that it gave her a scare, and Victoria for walking about bare-assed, as Abigale put it. Bare legged was a crime of etiquette.

Victoria knew that, of course, but she found she liked shocking the kindly old woman about as much as she enjoyed seeing Christopher climax in her arms. God, I'm a tart, she thought. She'd never done that before with any man, never felt such an overpowering need to give him pleasure. But then, no man ever made her feel so comfortable with herself—nor wanted her just the way she was.

She cleared her throat and he turned, his features stretching tight. Slowly, he set his coffee cup on the mantle, almost missing the edge.

She felt his gaze caress her from slippers to plunging neckline and her skin flushed with quick heat.

"Incredible." Chris whispered in awe.

"For Christ sake, Chris. It's only a dress."

He crossed to her, taking the pack and dropping it where she stood, then ushering her back out the door. A mirror hung on the wall and he positioned her before it.

She gazed at the reflection that didn't look a thing like her. Not like the woman who hunted bounty, ate fast food and lived in her car.

"Oh my."

"Yes." He slid his arms around her waist, drawing her softly back against him and the soft crush of crinoline luring his imagination.

"She's beautiful," he said to her reflection and she reached up, cupping his jaw, watching as he touched his lips to her bared throat.

Briefly, she closed her eyes, unfamiliar feelings racing through her. And she admitted the woman in the mirror had changed. The dress made her feel sexy and elegant, but she looked . . . as if she were born to wear it. And she tried to see what Chris saw.

It was a simple classic design of the period, yet made of rich watered silk. Her hair was twisted up on her crown, secured with pearl-tipped pins that Abigale had produced. Tiny curls framed her temples and nape and a pair of pearl-drop earrings dangled from her lobes. Chris caught one in his teeth, briefly, then kissed her throat. Her body sprang to life the instant she saw him but now his teasing was making her throb.

"You're making me crazy."

"You catch on fast."

His dark head nestled against the curve of her bare shoulder and throat, he dropped sweet intoxicating kisses along the line to the edge of the gown hugging her upper arm.

"I love your shoulders, so smooth and flawless."

"I thought you loved my legs." She laughed uneasily.

He looked up, meeting her gaze in the silver glass. "I do." He grinned. "But now I'm the only one who'll enjoy seeing them."

"Ohh, possessive, aren't you?" came with the arch of her dark brow. "I never would have thought."

"You're my woman, Victoria. Make no mistake."

There it was again, that forever tone.

She didn't want to ignore it. She wanted to wrap it around her like a warm blanket.

"I can't wait to take it off you."

A little moan colored the space between them, and he knew she wanted him, too.

"You take my breath away, Tori," he whispered in the shell of her ear. "You always have."

One hand vanished from her waist to reappear before her vision, a necklace dangling from his fingertips.

She frowned into the glass. "I don't want gifts, Christopher."

"Then don't keep it." Though he wanted her to, he wasn't going to argue. She'd just remind him she was leaving, that what they had, they time they could spend together was only temporary.

He refused to believe that.

He swept the necklace around her throat, securing the clasp and vanity pushed her closer to the glass. It was delicate, silver clasping a lovely blue stone.

"It was my mother's."

"I can't." She reached for the clasp, facing him. He caught her hands, bringing them to his lips.

"Humor me." His smile was sad. "For a little while."

She nodded, watching his tongue snake over her fingers before he pressed her palm to his lips.

"Chris," came on a breathless whisper and his eyes flared.

She gasped for needed breath, her hand resting possessively on his hip. Suddenly, she needed his kiss, needed to feel his strength. He saw it, and their arms swept around each other, locking tight as lips clashed and crushed away fears and worry to the onslaught of desire. Watered silk felt like liquid against his palms as he shaped her back, discovering the absence of corset and stays, then lowering to find no bustle. He loved it. She was absolute defiance in her manner, even though every man in this town was going to be panting after her.

"We'll have none of that."

They broke apart like startled adolescents.

Chris swiped his knuckle across his mouth and begged for air.

"And you, Miss Victoria," Abigale huffed, playing the mother hen. "Dinna our little chat mean anything to ye?"

"You mean about restraint?"

Abigale nodded, her hands on her ample hips.

Victoria glanced at Chris. "Nope." She shrugged. "Sorry."

Abigale resisted a smile. She was going to keep these two apart until they couldn't take it. Then she'd see them wed proper.

"And Christopher—"

He put up a hand. "When is dinner?"

"About an hour," she said, frowning.

"Knock first." Chris grabbed Victoria's hand and drew her quickly into the study and closed the doors.

"She's looking out for your virtue."

"I don't have any."

"God, I'm glad," he said with feeling, then kicked at the pack.

She lifted it and handed it to him, gesturing toward the fireplace and the small settee. Her skirts rustled as she moved and Chris watched as she settled onto the sofa with casual grace.

"Aren't you going to open it?" she said when he kept staring at her.

He blinked, then looked down at the knap-sack. "How?"

She unzipped it and he bent closer, examining everything in the workmanship of the cheap pack with great care. My inventor, she thought, and could hardly wait to see his projects. Abigale said they were all in his bedroom, and he never let anyone touch them or see them until they worked.

He opened the pack like a child on Christmas. His hand trembled a bit as he drew out her tazer.

"Careful." She took it and pressed the button. The blue white crackle charged across the polars. "It subdues a perp. Sends a few thousand volts of electricity through their body."

"That would kill them!"

"No, it just stuns them for a few hours." Her delicate brows wrinkled. "If you know about electricity, how come you don't have lights, currents, wires?"

"I haven't quite figured out how to harness it for any length."

"You have?"

His tone was patient. "Electric batteries have been around since the 1700's." This was news to her. "I've seen it ring a bell and make light without heat." He touched the tazer button and made a face, setting it aside. "I've even heard of experiments on a carriage without horses."

"Automobiles."

His gaze flashed up. "So they do it?"

"Yeah. It's become more dangerous, though, because there are so many of them."

He nodded and she knew he wouldn't understand the impact and sat back, propped her elbow on the edge of the settee and cupped her chin in her palm.

He poked and examined and she answered his questions and knew he wanted to take everything apart.

But when he pulled out a baggie, she snatched it from his hand.

His grin was crooked. He'd seen the sheen of fabric and lace and he leaned over and kissed her thickly on the mouth, then took back the prize.

"Secrets again?" He shook the pouch.

"Just try and open it."

It took him only seconds, mostly because he studied the plastic more than the contents, before pulling out the bundle and spreading it on his lap. He frowned, twisting and stretching the fabric.

And Victoria's embarrassment, of which she couldn't understand the source, ebbed. She took one white lacy panty and held it up correctly. "Panties, a thong," she clarified, then stood and held it up against her hips.

"But there's nothing there, Victoria."

She loved the edge in his voice.

"That's the point."

"Ahh, to entice a man." His grin was wolfish.

"*Very* good, Marshal, next lesson." She bent to stuff the panties back into the bag.

He settled back into the settee, his gaze flicking over her, halting briefly on the lovely swell of her breasts against the neckline of her gown and he remembered the wonderful contrast of skin in that particular area. Alabaster white against golden tan. But how?

"Ahh, Tori?" She glanced up. "You don't actually wear those, in the sun, without covering."

He looked flustered.

"I mean, you're tanned except—" his shoulders moved restlessly, "well, except *there*."

God it was cute. The gentleman warring with his curiosity. And a bit of jealousy. Though bikinis and why people wanted a tan would be another discussion, she said, "I laid out in Cole's back yard, Chris. In private."

He was only mildly pacified.

"There was a privacy wall."

He nodded and she heard his breath escape in a soft rush. She patted his cheek, amused by his sour look. Moving around the furniture, she helped herself to the coffee service on his desk, letting him investigate as he pleased, answering questions as she strolled around the room. The decor was dark, maroon and hunter green and she noted the elaborate family crest in a frame, the sword, a Union saber, she assumed, on the wall, all in sharp contrast to the coup stick adorned with old dry feathers. There were other things that spoke of how little she knew of him. Like the pieces of jade from China, or the African blowgun on the mantle.

"Tori?"

She turned and looked down at the thread mic head sets cradled gently in his hands. Her face stretched with a smile and she set the cup aside.

Flipping one on and tuning the freque, she said, "Take this and go to the other side of the room." He did and she moved to the opposite end. He watched as she put it on her head and adjusted the mic. He copied her. She motioned for him to turn his back.

"Hi, good lookin'."

"*Jesus!*" He whipped around and she was yanking off the headset, rubbing her ear.

"You don't have to do anything more than whisper. I can hear you breathe."

They tried it again, and Chris marveled at the invention.

"You've used these?"

"I was wearing it the night he killed Cole."

It was a moment of thought before the impact of that ripped through him. "But you can hear everything, Tori. Did you?"

"I heard him die, Chris."

"Oh God, darlin' I'm sorry."

"It's okay."

He felt her tears, even if he couldn't see them.

And he sought to lighten her mood.

"Could I talk to you while you were in another room with these?" The thought of it amazed him.

"Yes," she said carefully. "The distance isn't that good and the batteries are probably running low."

Battery power, he knew what that was.

"Why? What did you have in mind?"

He couldn't even see her lips move, but he could hear her as if she were in his arms.

"I want to make love to you."

"Ooo, mic sex."

He blinked. Her wide smile told him an in-depth explanation would follow later. He could hardly wait.

"I want you, too. So bad I can still taste you."

He groaned, his body clenching like a fist.

Her expression softened like a cat before a bowl of cream. "I don't think I've ever stopped, from the moment I saw you in the woods."

"I wanted to kiss you then."

Her gaze slid up and down his body encased in dark trousers and a crisp white shirt and she inhaled, the exhale a slow shudder that drove desire down his spine.

"I wish you would now."

But he didn't move, eyes locked across the room.

"I want to explore every part of you, Chris."

He gulped and her words crawled through his blood like the scrape of a hot poker, the memory of her boldness on the mountainside rising to life with unmatched clarity.

"The feel of your skin, the wonderful rich color. It makes my palms itch. Do you know what it's like for a woman like me, to feel that again?"

He didn't know how he did it, but he shook his head.

"It's heaven, Chris." Throaty and thick with honesty.

Victoria leaned against the window frame, watching his physical reaction to her words and reveling in it. His black trousers grew tight across his hips. And she felt her body warming and pulsing with seduction at her own words.

Her breathing increased, and he heard it.

"I'm going to make love to you, Tori. Soon. All night. I'm not going to leave your side, and when we want each other, we'll take."

Her body tingled and moistened as he went on, sculpting

image upon image of how he wanted to love her. They could go anywhere. Fulfill any fantasy.

And Victoria, weak for him, would let him.

"Wild sex isn't your need," he told her in a husky whisper. "Wild loving is."

Love. Oh God. She did love him. Not because he was the sexiest man alive, but that he wanted her just as she was, wanted to make her happy, that he respected her as an equal and wanted her to stay. He didn't have to say it. In fact, he hadn't in a while, but Victoria wasn't so caught up not to know that's what he needed.

Christopher Swift was a marrying, kids and home kind of man. Solid strong, dependable, generous, compassionate and passionate. And she didn't have an eternity to spend with him.

They stared across the room, suddenly silent, but the message was clear and Chris's heart leapt with hope. I love you, Tori, he thought and wished she was ready to hear the words. I love you madly.

A hard rap sounded and they both jolted, tearing off the mics. He crossed to her, handing the equipment over and she stuffed it into the backpack before he answered the call.

"Dinner is ready."

Abigale glanced between the two. Miss Victoria still looked the essence of grace and loveliness, but Christopher, well, his skin was red, his hands shoved deep in his pockets. And he looked like a child caught in the midst of mischief. She huffed and spun away.

"Hungry?" he said to Victoria, offering his hand.

She slid into his arms like a sleek schooner on a wave and kissed him deeply. "Always," she whispered and Chris smiled, seeking another kiss, but she moved quickly away.

Resolved to the crowding in his trousers, he followed her, his gaze lowering to the wonderful sway of her hips. He caught her arm, whispering in her ear. "What are you wearing under all those petticoats?" Wondering if it was one of those thong things.

"Nothing, except garters and stockings."

Briefly, he closed his eyes, seeking patience and finding only the picture she created.

"Gonna drive you nuts, ain't it?" She patted his cheek, merciless to his discomfort.

"And you, my luscious time traveler," he whispered close to her ear. "Will suffer for it."

Chapter Twenty-Eight

Victoria watched anticipation wreath his tanned face, his smile so boyish that a wealth of love grew inside her as he waited for Abigale to return with dessert.

If he didn't have such elegant manners, she imagined he'd delight in banging his utensils against the table.

Abigale swept into the long dining room carrying an absolutely decadent confection of cherries and glazed chocolate cake on a pedestal plate.

She set it next to Chris, slapping his hand when he swept his finger across an edge of dripping icing.

"Mind your manners, Christopher."

Laughter swept around the table, masculine laughter, and Victoria glanced at the men lining the table. They all looked mildly amused.

"Didn't know you have a sweet tooth, Chris," she said as Abigale slid a plate in front of him.

"Hell, he's got ten of 'em." This came from Caleb Peabody, a long drink of water with a soft voice and a shyness that was endearing. And even as she looked at him, he dropped his gaze and a flush crept into his cheeks.

"Tell me you don't eat like that every night."

"It's a curse, I swear," he said with false honesty, then Chris plunged his fork into the gooey cake and shoved a portion into his mouth.

Abigale stood by, awaiting comment. Chris closed his eyes and moaned, chewing slowly, savoring every flavor exploding in his mouth.

"Magnificent again, Abby." He rose enough to peck a kiss to her cheek, then ignored everyone to the feast of sugar and cherries.

"I have never seen a man eat so much sugar and not become fat." Joquin patted his own round stomach. "It truly is not fair."

"I agree." She passed a slice to Lucky who sat to her right, constantly gazing up at her with undisguised adoration. "I'd have to run twenty miles to work that off."

"Want bite?" Lucky said, offering some.

"Do you want a bite," she corrected and he repeated the sentence slowly, then smiled. "Yes," she said with feeling and tasted from his fork. She hummed her praise and the little boy grinned, so bright and happy, and the room full of people followed. "Go on," she whispered, urging him. "Kids are supposed to have cake."

"And I'm not?" Chris looked insulted and she smiled.

"Within reason. He'll burn it off. With exercise," she clarified.

"So will I." He winked at her and her cheeks flooded with color. A soft chuckle from the ranch hands made it even worse.

Abigale whacked Chris on the shoulder as she passed and Randel, even Randel, the stoic butler who never spoke, fought a grin. Victoria schooled her features into a polite smile, then promptly kicked him under the table. The jolt brought another burst of laughter and Chris chuckled, leaning back in the chair and sipping coffee.

"I likes Miss Toria." Lucky spoke to no one imparticular, chomping into his food without looking up.

"Do you?" Chris said, his gaze shifting between the warm motherly look on Tori's face to the boy.

"She beat up the marshal."

"Lucky, how could you say such a thing!" Abigale spouted.

Victoria looked at Chris and shrugged.

"Seen it."

"I saw it," Victoria corrected automatically. "Saw what?"

"On the mountain."

Her eyes flared and she didn't dare glance at Chris. Please don't let it be today.

"Looking at the train."

Victoria gagged with relief.

"Beat you up, din' she, Marshal?" This Lucky directed at Chris.

All eyes turned to him.

"I wouldn't say that exactly," Victoria began.

"Yes, she did."

"Christopher!"

He glanced left at Abigale, where she was serving Garrett, his iron man.

"It's true. Whipped the stuffing right out of me."

Victoria nudged him under the table.

He was oblivious. "Those feet are deadly."

She glared at him now. "I'm pretty good with a knife, too. Care to have me *demonstrate?*"

His gaze flew to hers, his features tightening at the fury in her eyes. His expression clouded briefly, then he sighed heavily, mashing his hand over his face. She ignored him, sipping wine and talking with Lucky. But the conversation in the dining room had suddenly ceased.

He left his chair and went down on one knee beside her. He gazed into gold eyes sparkling with hurt. She hadn't wanted anyone here to know that side of her. She was dressed with elegance and carried herself so and it was as if she'd sought to smother the expert hunter for a little while.

And he just ruined it.

"I'm sorry."

"You say that to me a lot, Christopher."

"And will you keep forgiving me?"

She held her response back, then sighed, her smile light. "Oh get up, for crying out loud."

"Forgiven?"

"Of course. God, you're hopeless, you know that?"

Hopelessly in love with you, he thought as he straightened, the back of his knuckles grazing her cheek before he bent and kissed her full on the mouth, her hand coming up to lightly touch his jaw.

A soft whistle came from one of the ranch hands.

"Now, Christopher," Abigale said. "There's a child present."

Lucky beamed at the couple.

"You two are the kissin'est pair I ever did see." Peabody laughed.

Chris stepped back and cleared his throat before sliding into his chair. He ate the cake without tasting it.

And Victoria was proud of the way she sloughed the whole matter off and started the conversation in a different direction—especially with her ears ringing. Christ. It wasn't bad enough that all through the meal he was undressing her with those dark eyes, now her mouth throbbed for more.

"What's an Iron Man," she asked Garrett.

He set his fork down and wiped his lips with a napkin, slow deliberation in his moves. He was a gunfighter once, Chris had said. It wasn't hard to imagine. He had long hair flowing over his shoulders, a droopy moustache and a patch over one eye. She didn't want to know how he'd lost it, but beneath the patch, the scar slanted from forehead to cheekbone. But one thing was for sure. He was drop dead gorgeous, scar or not.

"Iron man brands the livestock, ma'am."

"Call me Victoria, please."

His one penetrating blue eye flashed to Chris, and he nodded. "Miss Victoria."

She wasn't going to argue. With these men, that's as casual

as it got. "I know about chicken ranches, but zilch about cattle or sheep, so please go on."

"Chicken?"

She glanced at Chris. "I was born on a chicken ranch. Smelly business—"

His gaze combed her, a wondering smile ghosting his lips. There was a lot he didn't know about her, Chris realized. And he intended to spend years finding it all out.

"—though I can't imagine branding a chicken."

"I do believe it would fry it, ma'am," came from Randel as he cleared dishes. Victoria blinked at him, then smiled. She hadn't heard him speak before and decided she like his droll delivery.

"These three—" Garrett gestured to Peabody, Joquin, and the ever silent, Batista, a Navajo Indian "—Round 'em up, and I brand 'em." He shrugged as if that's all there was to it. "Mostly, I do it on the range. 'Cept the horses."

Victoria poured a glass of milk and handed it to Lucky, motioning him to wipe his mouth. He did, then drank, leaving a white moustache behind. With loving care, she blotted it away.

"Who catches the horses?"

Joquin raised his hand. "They like me," he said with a bashful shrug.

"Caesar loves Victoria," Chris told them with great relish.

"What!" came from around the table.

"She's ridden him."

"Oh, Miss Victoria, that be dangerous!" Abigale whispered.

"That ornery pile of horseflesh," Garrett sneered, looking mean and nasty.

"I got scars from that beast," Peabody added, rubbing his shoulder.

"You be careful, senorita, he will turn on you."

"Oh, chill out." They frowned, the room silent. "Relax," she said. "He's a boy. He like girls."

Batista's smile lit up his scarred face.

"Me too," Chris whispered.

"Really?" She peered at him. "I hadn't noticed."

"Coffee on the porch," Abigale announced and everyone rose, filing out of the house, the fine meal making their moves slow.

"Abigale, that was wonderful. Can I help you with the dishes?"

"Certainly not!" She shooed the girl, practically pushing her and Christopher out.

"Me go, too?" Lucky said, tugging on her skirt.

She smiled down at him. " 'Can I go, too?' " she corrected and he repeated obediently. "Sure, a few minutes, but then it's bedtime."

He nodded and Chris was amazed at the change in the boy. Scrubbed clean and wearing fresh clothes, he didn't look at all like the ragamuffin everyone remembered. He obeyed Victoria without question, his eyes bright with adoration as he gazed up at her, and Chris felt that stirring again. The same that he'd had while caring for Sable's nephew, Little Hawk. He wanted children. After Camille, he'd simply dismissed the prospect from his mind, but now he wanted babies—with Victoria.

"Why are you looking at me like that?" she said as Lucky scampered ahead of them out the door.

"You're so wonderfully patient with him."

"I try." Her expression went bleak with quick pain. "My daughter was like Lucky. Handicapped. Special. Impatience only frustrates them. It's hard enough to survive and learn when you don't have the advantages of a sharp mind. And an adult harping on their inadequacies only makes them turn inward."

Chris caught her chin, tipping her face up and brushing a soothing kiss to her lips, and it swept away the painful memories. He was so good at that, she thought, stepping onto the porch as Lucky wiggled into a wicker chair. He gazed at the cowboys with undisguised awe and her sadness cleared into a smile. Was this orphaned boy her second chance, she wondered fleetingly, then left Chris to sit on the edge of the porch rail.

As Chris settled into a fan-shaped wicker chair, Joquin adjusted a guitar on his lap, strumming idly. Abigale and Randel appeared, serving coffee, but it was Randel who offered her a cup.

"Cream, no sugar, miss," he said as she accepted it.

"Thanks for remembering, Randel."

Chris eyed Randel from the back, then watched him leave. Victoria met his gaze and shrugged, sipped.

Joquin tried to play a tune, which was difficult since he was missing three fingers on one hand and two on the other. And though she didn't recognize the melody, she sensed what he was trying to achieve.

"Hold the fret down for two more bars, then change," she said.

All eyes turned to her.

"You can play, senorita?"

Great. Confession time. "A little, yes."

He offered her the guitar.

She shook her head.

"Come on, Tori. Joquin has been entertaining us for months."

"And I am certain they are weary of my poor talent, senorita. Please."

Victoria met Chris's gaze, and he saw her apprehension. She likely wouldn't know any common tunes, and he was suddenly uncomfortable for her. And as she handed Chris her coffee cup and took the guitar, he could tell her mind was racing for a solution.

"Do you know Clementine?" Peabody asked.

"Sorry, no." She strummed, tuning the guitar with deliberate practiced moves.

"Lived on a ranch, can play the guitar, what else am I going to discover about you?"

Only her gaze shifted. Maybe how much I love you, she thought, then said, "I can carry a decent tune, too."

A pleased rumble erupted from the group. Lucky clapped. Chris straightened, grinning hugely, and Victoria glanced around at all the faces. A command performance. All men. Any girl would be loving this attention—except her.

It had been an extremely long time since she'd sung, even for herself. She always made a point of never revealing too much of her personal nature to anyone. She was supposed to hang back, be a wallflower.

They were all staring at her. Waiting. Christ. What the hell was she supposed to play that wouldn't leave a ripple in history? Then she considered that since there weren't any recording studios, or CDs for that matter, she was pretty much on the safe side.

But what would please them? Something slow and somber, she decided right then. Cowboyish.

Her fingers brushed over the strings, the intro like a soft hand pushing each man back into his seat. Chris propped his booted feet on the low table and stretched himself out. Victoria liked the way he looked, anticipating, long and sleek like a dozing panther.

And although she sang a twenty year-old James Taylor ballad for the odd ball crew of strays Chris employed when no one else would, she couldn't keep her gaze from lingering on him.

"There is a young cowboy. He lives on the range. His horse and his cattle, they're his only companions . . ."

Her voice, sultry like her, sank into his skin like the rays of the sun and he felt his smile widen.

"He works in the saddle and he sleeps in the canyons, just waiting for summer, his pastures to change . . ."

She didn't notice Abigale or Randel emerge from the house, nor two other ranch hands, astride horses, ride up slowly and stop to listen.

"And as the moon rises, he sits by the fire, justa thinkin' 'bout women and glasses of beer . . ."

Sappy smiles ringed the collection of weathered faces. Even Garrett rocked to the sweet poignant rhythm. And Chris realized that without paint and masks, without spirit gum and padding or the bounty of a lifetime to chase, Victoria was blossoming before his eyes. In only a few hours, Chris saw the transformation. It wasn't just the dress or the styled hair but she was allowing herself to feel again, sinking herself into life and the living, instead of always being on the outside, waiting for the criminal. Though nothing was going to stop Chris from keeping this woman, the ready acceptance Abigale, Randel, Lucky, and the ranch hands offered her, was another stitch in the patchwork of their relationship. Each day tightened the threads, and he wanted her to know she was needed by more than just him, that regardless of what her century offered, his offered her more.

It would be difficult to complete with the advances she'd mentioned, yet as Chris absorbed the vivid current of her voice, he didn't doubt for a moment Victoria Mason was meant to be with him. If only he could convince her.

"He says, Good night all you moonlight laaa-dees, Rock-a-bye sweet baby James . . ."

Victoria struggled with the lyrics, and if Chris wasn't looking at her like one of Abigale's desserts she might not embarrass herself—or him. However, when the last cord melted into the night, she wondered at the silence and her lack of talent. For they simply stared.

"Holy cow, Miss Victoria, that was somethin' else!" Whistles, hoots and soft applause scattered around her like diamonds before a princess. A lump swelled in her throat and Victoria didn't think she'd ever been appreciated more than in this moment. She ducked her head, acknowledging, and Lucky yawned hugely. Victoria thought to send him gently into sleep. She stared at the little boy, her strumming making his lids heavy, yet when she sang again it was for Chris alone.

"The secret of life is enjoying the passage of time . . ." Even as the lyrics tumbled off her lips, she realized she was speaking in a way nothing else could; of how simple love could be. That no one knew how they got to this time and place, but they should enjoy it while they had the chance.

Her honeyed voice, smooth and husky-deep, wrapped around Chris with the heaviness of a sated lover's embrace. He listened with his heart. For Tori was speaking with hers. Her emotions shaped her lovely face, her eyes glistening. A little pleading.

He knew she was afraid, like her ballad said, and that she was only here for a while.

God.

It hit him how confused and torn she must feel, not knowing whether or not she belonged. She did. The Great Spirits brought her to him.

Then she finished her song, wiped discreetly at a lone tear and smiled at the soft applause.

Lucky was sound sleep, and she handed the guitar to Joquin, then made to carry him into his room. Chris stopped her, lifting the boy in his arms and together they headed inside to put him to bed.

A collective sigh colored the warm night.

"I believe the Double Arrow will finally have a mistress."

Abigale and Randel exchanged a glance, then smiled.

In the tiny bedroom, Chris laid Lucky on the bed and Victoria busily removed his shoes and socks, loosened his clothing, then tucked him beneath the light coverlet. She couldn't help it and sat down beside him. Chris stood close, his hand on her shoulder, gently rubbing as she brushed hair from Lucky's forehead.

"He needs this cut," she said absently.

"Maybe you should try? Every time Abigale gets near him with a pair of shears, he runs for the hills."

She laughed, light and short. "I'll bet."

"I can't get over the change in him, after one day."

"I must look like his mother," she said, covering Chris's hand with hers. "He has no reason to trust me or obey me like he does."

"Maybe he senses you won't lose patience with him."

She twisted a look up at him, her eyes wet with unshed tears. He frowned questioningly, stroking the line of her jaw.

"I miss Trisha so much sometimes." She left the bed and went into his arms and Chris closed his eyes, offering her his strength. God, for this woman to cry was like a knife through his chest.

"I'm usually a lot stronger than this," she whispered, clinging to him.

"I know."

"I don't know what's wrong with me."

He smiled against her hair. He knew. "It's been a long day, darlin'. And a lot has happened."

She tilted her head back, gazing into his eyes. "I'll say." A devilish smile toyed with her lips and a flush crept up from his neck.

He groaned, scattering kisses over her face. "If you keep reminding me of that I'll go mad right here." She inhaled deeply, her body pressing warmly against his and Chris slid his hands lower and cupped her buttocks through the heavy fabric.

"Do you know what you've done to me, knowing all evening that you're bare beneath this."

"Yeah, I have, and so has everyone else."

Her hand slipped between them, feeling him swell for her. "God, I want you."

He choked on his own breath, drawing her out of Lucky's room and pulling her into an alcove near the stairs. He kissed her as he pressed her to the wall, letting her feel how hard and throbbing he was. She felt her skirts tug upward, his warm hand on her thigh, smoothing up the back and enfolding her curves. And their kiss grew hungrier, seeping with checked desire. A whimper caught in her throat, their breathing rushing as his fingers inched closer to her heat. Her body begged, his kiss fueled and distantly they heard someone clearing their throat.

Chris cursed, removing his hands and blocking a view of her body before he spun around. Randel back-stepped, yet the butler stared blandly at his employer, his gaze direct and sparing Victoria any embarrassment.

"I beg your pardon, m'lord, a message from town. Those brothers—"

"Duke and Buddy?"

"They seemed to have found bullets and Mister Beecham requests his lordship's assistance."

"Dammit." He looked at Victoria and found her staring at him strangely. "I guess I'll see you in the morning."

She nodded and Chris kissed her briefly before moving past Randel. The butler immediately followed.

"Randel?"

He turned fully to address her. "Miss?"

"Why do you call him my lord?"

"It is his station, miss."

Her hands on her hips, she was suddenly fresh out of patience. And he knew it.

"Mister Christopher Swift is a peer of the realm, Miss.

"You mean he's titled?" she squeaked. "English titled?"

Anger and amazement filled her expression and Randel, feeling he'd misstepped where he shouldn't, sought the smoothest route.

"His lordship is the only son and grandson of the House of Claybourne."

"I thought his father was a Cheyenne Chief?"

"Quiet so, but his mother is Lady Katherine Waythorne, sole heir to the title."

"Why isn't he in England doing what lords do?" She waved, having no idea what that entailed.

"He relinquished the title, Miss, when he was younger. A bad falling out. His denouncement was the scandal of the century."

"Oh, really?" she said as if she understood. She didn't.

"It did have one advantage though."

"You mean besides you?"

His lips curved gently. "His title gave him the opportunity to purchase land. Indians are not permitted the luxury."

"Buying their own land would be a contradiction. Heaven forbid the government look foolish, huh?"

Again, his lips moved in a smile. "Quite, Miss."

She heard the door shut and knew Chris was gone. And even though a part of her wanted to be included, she wasn't ready to face anyone without her disguises yet. She headed toward her room, but Randel's cultured voice stopped her.

"May I bring you some chocolate and milk to help you sleep?"

He really was awfully considerate. "No, thanks. I think I'll wrestle out of this dress and hit the rack. Go to bed," she said when he frowned his confusion.

Randel nodded, thinking his lordship was doing a fine job of wrestling her out of it before he came upon them.

Chapter Twenty-Nine

Noble smothered a grin at the sour look on Chris's face as he slid from the saddle.

"I've ridden through this entire town, Beecham, and I don't see anything so damn important you had to call me away—"

"From Miss Mason?" Noble finished with the arch of a bushy brow.

Chris's gaze narrowed, then suddenly softened. He raked his fingers through his hair and looked sheepish. "Yeah. I guess that's it."

Noble inclined his head toward the office behind him, yet was staring thoughtfully at his boss. "Already locked up Buddy and his idiot of a brother." The man's got it bad, he thought.

"Any wounds?"

Noble shook his head, a little smile eeking out from beneath his thick moustache. "Made 'em go back to back, count off and fire."

"A duel?"

"Neither of 'em had the guts to pull the trigger. Knew they wouldn't."

Chris smirked, tossed the reins over Caesar's head and started down the street. Noble fell in step beside him.

Caesar followed obediently.

"You're going in?"

"I need to."

"You know I never liked that prissy ass citified—"

"I get the point, now why?"

Noble shrugged. "He's too smooth. An' when he showed up here claiming to be ambushed, I didn't believe it." Chris cast a side glance. "How'd he get all that money to play in high-stakes poker if he was ambushed?"

Chris stopped short. "He pawned the cigarette case."

"To pay the doc, and maybe a few dollars more," Noble reminded. "But he sure as hell didn't get enough for it to play against Sean Galloway and Alex Trevor with a little hunk of gold."

The two richest men in the territory—Alex flaunted it, Sean disguised it. Gates, the former owner of the Pearl was in that game, too. And all he had was his saloon to bet, for at the time, it was run down and making little money.

How had Becket come by so much money, Chris wondered as he continued walking. He was a time traveler and Victoria had shown him currency of her time. Becket would have been branded a counterfeiter if he'd showed so much as a coin. Had he killed and robbed some drifter? Chris tried to remember if Becket had disappeared for any length of time before he was in the middle of that poker game and stealing Gates blind. He couldn't and knew Velvet would have known. Sadness crept into his mood, the dark and nearly empty street enhancing it. Only a few cowboys milled about, reading hand bills for a big picnic. Yet a nervousness tightened the air, and he didn't doubt that burying Velvet lent to the unease. Victoria had wanted to attend the funeral, but he wouldn't let her. A *new* face would stir trouble right now. She hadn't fought him long, and it made him wary. She'd already said good-bye to Vel, she'd told him. But the burial sent rumors flying, whispers of terror, though the ritual of Vel's death, the revolting set of her body in the cave, were still sketchy. Chris prayed for a few more days before everything erupted.

Leaving Noble to watch the street, Chris crossed the threshold of the Pearl and the noise suddenly softened. God, he hated that. It made him feel unwelcome, not that he ever spent much time in here, anyway. He didn't realize he was scowling until the murmurs came to him and he schooled his features, strolling across the room to Sean.

The rancher looked up. He's aged ten years since Kelly died, Chris thought, studying his face.

"I never did thank you, Chris."

Chris arched a brow.

"For ending it, for finding out what happened."

"I didn't, Jake did." Chris remembered what an ass he'd been about the whole thing and wished he could tell Sean that Jake was really Victoria.

"If you ever see him, thank him." Sean kicked out a chair for Chris and he sat, noticing that Sean wasn't drinking liquor, but milk. A huge glass of the stuff.

The bartender himself came over to take his order, but Chris waved him off before he crossed the room. The man frowned, then shrugged and went back to his duties.

"You been in here much?"

"Nearly every night. The house feels so big and empty now." Sean stared at his glass, then drained half of it to coat the knot in his throat. He wondered if he'd ever feel good again.

"Still want to kill Raif?"

Sean's gaze shot to Chris's, malevolence in his stare. "Yes. I do. I'll never stop wanting it, either. Raif's foolishness killed my wife. Not something I can forgive."

Chris fished in his pocket for a sack and papers. "Not something you *choose* to forgive."

Sean rolled his shoulders and sat forward, bracing his arms on the table. "Why are you in here, Chris?" Only Chris's gaze shifted from the smoke he was rolling. "In five years, I've never seen you set foot inside except to bust up a fight."

If it was that obvious to him, was it to Becket or anyone else enough to talk? Was this a mistake of the worst kind, he wondered as he licked the paper, then slid the cigarette between his lips and struck a match to the tip.

"I needed a break."

"From her?"

Chris gaze shot to Sean's, his green eyes laughing for the first time in weeks. "I heard you've got a treasure hidden in your valley, Marshal."

Chris exhaled smoke in a rush. "From whom?"

Sean spread his arms and shrugged. "You've got a lot of hands working for you and people talk."

"And they say?"

Sean sipped his milk, swiping the back of his wrist across his mouth and enjoying Chris's squirming. "I heard she's tall, pretty, bold as brass—" He grinned when Chris's fists clenched "—and turning you inside out."

Chris's gaze thinned.

Sean's lips curved. "Rumors are right, huh?"

He took a long pull, blowing a couple smoke rings before saying, "Don't believe all that you hear."

Sean leaned close, his voice low. "I also heard about Velvet. The story floating is that she was on her way to the train, attacked, robbed and left for dead."

"But you think otherwise."

Sean grit his teeth, itching to throttle his friend. "D'you forget I live out that way? I might be mourning Kelly," her name caught in his throat, "but I can tell you're trying to keep a lid on trouble. Real trouble."

Besides Hunter McCracken and Noble, Sean was one of his closest friends. Chris nodded, not trusting himself to say more.

Sean leaned back in the chair. "Let me know when you need help."

Chris's look showed appreciation, and Sean's curiosity niggled. He kept a discreet eye on his friend, wondering who he suspected.

Chris glanced around, searching for Becket and finding him

just leaving his office, all smiles and handshakes as he crossed the room. Chris checked the time. Ten thirty exactly, as Victoria had said. Becket passed before the large mirror slung over the bar and discreetly checked his appearance, smoothed his lapels, adjusted his string tie before moving on to the next customer. But his gaze strayed to the mirror again and again, the silver glass offering a full view of the saloon. He caught Chris's gaze and nodded cordially, then immediately turned his attention to Dee as she sidled up to him. Dee didn't touch, wetting her lips suggestively, yet when he shot her a lethal glance, she retreated to the bar, fawning too obviously over a young cowboy. Even as she teased the man mercilessly, her gaze slipped to Becket more than once during her seduction.

Chris shifted in his chair, blowing the tip of his cigarette and keeping Becket in his sights. The man ordered liquor in clear precise tones and drank it as if staged to be a majestic moment, then made his way toward Chris, bracing every other step on the polished oak cane.

"Marshal?"

Chris dragged on the smoke. "I see business isn't hampered."

"By Vel's passing? No."

Passing. A mild word for what you did to her, Chris thought, coming slowly to his feet. "You didn't waste time clearing her room, though." Dee resided there now, proclaiming herself the new madame.

"Did you expect me to make a shrine to a whore?" Becket snorted, but a sinister heat glazed his eyes.

"If that's all she meant to you."

Becket's color blanched a little, but his features remained impassive. "I adored her, but she was just an employee."

"You're saying you valued her as an asset." Becket nodded confirmation. "Then why didn't you offer her an escort?"

"She refused one."

"You protect your interests," his gaze shifted meaningfully to his girls "—but not her." A flaw, Chris thought, in his demeanor. "A perfect gentleman would insist." Chris saw his features sharpen a fraction, almost predatory, like Victoria's did when she was on the hunt. He'd struck a nerve. Good.

"Have you ever tried to insist anything with Vel?"

Smooth answer.

"And besides, Vel carried a gun."

Chris casually folded his arms, sounding thoughtful, almost seeking advice. "You think she wounded her killer, maybe?"

He shrugged negligently, then adjusted his coat sleeve. "I couldn't say, since I wasn't there."

Chris caught sight of the scratches on his wrist, healed and only a shiny stripe on the skin. "I was."

Becket met his gaze, a frosty blue empty of emotion.

"I found her."

Becket braced his palms on the top of the cane. "Really?" Mildly interested, his gaze shifting to inspect his crowd, his serfs.

And what Victoria was trying to point out to him—but he was too pig-headed and righteous to see—was there. Becket was evil. Beneath the well-honed surface of perfection lay a calculating madness that reached beyond unfeeling. Make me your target, Chris thought viciously. Not a mother. Not a woman just trying to raise her child the best she can. Choose someone worthy of a fair fight.

"Takes someone twisted to prey on a helpless woman, don't you think?"

He spared him a glance, his lips pulling in a flawless smile. "Unless perhaps, they deserved it."

"Punishment?"

Up went one brow and he seemed to be looking down his nose at Chris.

"Hmm," Chris murmured, remembering all Victoria had told him and couldn't resist one last goad at the monster within. "Then who's being punished, the victim or the murderer?"

Maybe it was his moving gaze, too random, or the flexing of his fingers on the cane. Chris couldn't point and say there it was, yet he felt it. An evil so thick with suppressed rage, it made his skin crawl up his back.

And he realized with undeniable clarity that he needed Victoria to decipher it, to find its direction.

It was time, he thought, to bring her back to town.

Chris trudged up the steps, careful not to wake anyone, but disappointed at not finding Victoria below stairs, maybe wearing the shirt he found so enticing.

He wanted to see her in those tiny scraps she called panties. Hell, he thought, he just wanted to see her.

But it was past midnight, and even though the recklessness of his actions tonight still lingered, leaving him agitated, he resigned himself to wait until morning. Crossing into his bedroom, he unbuckled his holster, hooking it on the back of a chair. Moonlight spilled from the wide-open window, lighting the room enough to see and he dropped into a chair to remove his boots and socks, wiggling his toes before rising to strip off his clothes and wash away the odors of the saloon. The wind picked up, rustling the drapes.

A soft crackle caught his attention as he wiped his thighs dry, and he frowned in the dark.

It came again with the breeze and he lit a lamp, glancing at his bed, then walked over to the four posted monstrosity. There on a mound of pillows was Victoria's head mic. And a note that said two words. *Wake me.*

Wrapping the towel around his hips, he smiled and picked it up, tugging the paper free before pushing the on switch and adjusting the contraption over his ears.

He heard even breathing. Lord. It was like she was pressed against him.

"Tori," he whispered.

He heard a moan, low and sultry, then the rustle of sheets. "Tori?"

"Hi." He could feel the smile in her voice, imagined her lazily stretching on the bed. Was she naked? His heart thudded at the thought.

"What time is it?"

"After midnight."

"Have fun?"

"No. I missed you."

"Did you?"

"Yeah." He dropped onto the bed. "I talked to Becket."

A hesitation and then, "Tell me later."

His brows rose. That was not the reaction he expected. Or did she sense trouble brewing?

"What did you do while I was gone?" He flattened out on the bed, crossing his ankles and folding his arms beneath his head.

"Took a bath. I smell real good."

She drew out the words and he closed his eyes. "I can only imagine."

"What are you doing?"

"Laying on the bed."

"Tired?"

"No," he answered honestly. "Restless."

Again, he could feel her smile.

"Guess what?"

There was along pause. He could heard her draw air and imagined her chest swelling with each slow breath. "What?" he finally said.

"I want you."

He swallowed.

"Is this . . ." his brows knitted, "mic sex?"

"You could say that." Her tone turned devilish. "Know what else?"

"I cannot begin to imagine the workings of your mind."

"Oh, but you will . . ." Her voice was hypnotic, a throaty whisper in his head, filling his mind with torrid images of slick bodies and liquid passion. She described what she wanted to do to him—with him—and Chris's entire body clenched with quick heat. His groin hardened painfully. Sweat broke out on his brow. It wasn't what she said, but Christ, how she said it.

"Tori, stop," he hissed.

"Liked that?"

"I'd like you here," he said, licking his lips.

"Open your eyes, Chris."

He did.

She stood at the foot of his bed, a white robe frothing about her curves as she pulled off the headset, shaking out her hair. He came off the mattress in a rush, tossing the set to the floor and reaching for her. He dragged her over the footboard and into his arms.

He kissed her, an explosion of warm lips and tongue, crushing her mouth, devouring her as if she were the rich desserts he craved, and she tore into him like a thief into the night. She pulled the towel from his hips as he yanked frantically at the sash at her waist, aching for the taste and feel of her skin and when he bared her, she couldn't wait and climbed onto his lap, straddling his hips.

Skin meshed and rubbed and brushed, moans of pleasure and satisfaction pricked the air and Chris stripped the robe from her body, scrubbing his hands up her spine, over her shoulders, down her arms.

There was no patience between them, weeks of wanting and waiting climbing to a boiling eruption. He chanted her name against her lips, enfolded her lush breasts, feeling lace and smelling the heat of his woman.

Her low surrendering moan speared him like a lance.

Her nipples tightened, pushing against the fabric, against his palm, her sensitive body screaming to be assaulted and ravished and adored. And he did, dragging his mouth down her throat, her shoulder, a slickening of fire and moisture to her breast.

Anticipation inflamed her, her thighs tightening as he found her nipple through the lace, teasing her as he laved it with his tongue.

"Am I being good?" he said, his breath cooling the burgeoning tip.

"Oh, God, yes."

His finger traced the edge of the lace surrounding the plump swells before he unhooked it and drew the fabric down. Her nipple spilled into the open heat of his mouth and with a dark groan, Victoria threw her head back. He sucked, drawing her tighter and deeper between his lips, his hand richly fondling the mate before sampling the nectar of her bosom.

A humming blasted through her body, wrapping around her waist and diving between her thighs. Her head felt light, her thoughts foggy. Nothing in her life felt this sensual, this erotic— this natural. She could stay forever in his arms, she knew and combed her fingers through his hair, shaped his face, his shoulders, his strong muscular arms as he fumbled with the clasp and stripped the bra from her body. Impatiently, his hands swept roughly over her warm skin, cupping her buttocks, fingers feeling the slim thread of fabric dividing her firm cheeks as he ground her to his arousal, letting her know there would be no time wasted, no time left for sweet talk and teasing.

And her answering pushes, the heat of her sex, made him thicken, blood throbbing to hot, tight pleasure points of need. She smiled into his eyes, nipping his mouth with dripping kisses as her slim fingers wrapped around his erection.

''Sweet Jesus,'' he breathed and dumped her onto the mattress, driving himself against the bead of her desire and she welcomed him, arching for more, impatient for him to be smooth and solid inside her. But Chris was not satisfied with the frustration of restraint. He wanted her in agony and he lay thick lush kisses to her breasts, her tight ribs, licking a steamy wet line down the indentation of her stomach, his thumbs catching the white lace panties. His wicked gaze told her he loved the scrap of nothing. The white triangle teased him mercilessly with what lay beneath and he ground his mouth into the curve of her hip as he drew the tantalizing fabric down, down over her softness.

Then his mouth took her, and she cried out, straining for his touch, straining to move her legs imprisoned by his weight and spread herself wider, for more, more, but he wouldn't let her, dipping his tongue deeper, luxuriously deep, loving the sheen of sweat on her body, her hands fisting in the sheets, his name on her lips.

And Victoria thought time ceased to exist and the earth opened up to swallow her whole. Her body was alive as never before, his tongue and mouth swamping her with sensation after glorious sensation until she couldn't stand it and begged him to come to her.

"Oh God, Chris, please. Please!"

But he refused, taking her essence and torturing her into madness. Yet when Chris felt her sculptured body quake on the brink of rapture, he shifted, tearing the panties free of her legs and covering her with his weight. She opened for him, reached for him, covering his mouth with hers, clawing at his shoulders, plowing fingers into his hair.

He filled her in one long driving thrust, a savage kiss smothering their cries of utter satisfaction. Then he retreated and plunged, over and over, heightening desire with every long, rampant stroke, the slick glove of her grabbing him back, deeper, quicker, hotter. Her strong arms and legs enfolded him, captured him, fusing solid to soft, heart to heart. He rose up to look at her face, braced as their bodies met and parted in erotic cadence.

She stroked his chest, whispered how much she wanted this, how right it felt and how she knew it would be wild and untamed. Her husky words owned a power, hungry and exotic, turning his blood molten and stripping him of control. He pounded into her, driving her across the bed, swallowing her moans with hot, dark kisses.

Their bodies possessed a motion of their own, pulsing and pushing, fed on sweeping caresses and the power of their loving. She thrust herself against him, against the point of his possession and passion, seeking, seeking. Her gasps quickened. Her heart thundered.

A whimper of need caught in her throat.

"Join me," he whispered into her mouth and she did. Like a crack in a dam, desire unleashed, and they fused as if to stop the break, yet urged it on and on and on. Sweat slickened bodies arched tightly, grinding, the shattering deluge of pleasure and liquid desire rushing through them like quicksilver, spilling, spilling. Rapid bursts of everlasting fire cast moans and whispers into the darkness, gray moonlight bathing over them, the bed a lake of wrinkles and tangled limbs, love born on a bond they knew would never be broken.

Chris took pleasure in her mouth, savouring her flavor. Her breath rushed along his cheek.

"Tori, Tori, oh God—"

"I know, I know," she whispered near his ear, stroking his damp hair, his slick back. She gripped him snugly, almost protectively from the sounds of the night, of reality, squeezing her eyes shut and hoping he didn't notice her trembling, hoping morning would never come and take this dream away.

He pressed his lips to the bend of her shoulder, the touch incredibly tender after all the wildness they shared. And she sighed back into the down bedding.

Chris struggled to lift his head and look at her.

She smiled, the gentlest smile he'd ever seen on her face and brushed the curling black tendrils from his forehead. She watched her movements and he tilted his head and kissed her palm.

Something hard and sweet caught in her chest at the sight of him, his eyes closed, savoring the taste of her as if she were something precious.

She loved this man. With her heart and now her body and she never wanted to leave his embrace.

"Chris."

He met her gaze, his tongue tracing a vein in her wrist. She sank her fingers into his hair and drew him to her mouth, bursting to tell him her heart and knowing she'd shatter his. For they could never be—never. And it would destroy them, she knew it. Yet she poured her feelings into her kiss, the heat and madness of passion sated, now simmering into him from her soft loving kiss. And Chris felt it, felt it fill him and take him places he never imagined.

The back of his eyes stung, his mind painfully aware of their uncertain future. Yet he kissed and held her as close as he could, his heart chanting to hers.

Stay with me, love, stay. No one will love you more than I. No one.

Not in this century, nor yours.

Chapter Thirty

"I should go back to my room," she whispered against the crook of his neck.

"No," came almost panicked, his hold tightening.

He didn't want her to leave him, ever, and not so soon after loving her. It felt incredibly comfortable and natural to have this woman lying beside him, her leg entwined with his, her head on his shoulder. Her fingers skimmed the center of his chest.

"You came through the balcony door, didn't you?"

Her lashes swept up. "Sneaky, huh?"

His smile agreed. "You were right about those panties." He inclined his head to where they hung, somehow hooked on his holster. "They served a very definite purpose."

"I could tell." She shifted, half over him, her breasts warm against his chest and he toyed with her nipple, watching her gold eyes flare and darken.

"Trying to start something, Marshal?"

"Yes."

"Hell of an appetite, Mister."

"You give it to me." His hand rode the curve of her spine,

pushing the twisted sheet down so he could fondle her buttocks. Her head dipped and her tongue snaked out to circle his nipple. His inhaled breath hissed through his teeth. "God, I never thought that would feel so good."

"Me either. You have such a beautiful body, Chris." As she spoke her hands skimmed his muscles, her eyes inspecting and approving and his lips quirked. She'd no notion of how exotic she looked, her muscular body tanned except for her breasts and the treasure between her thighs. Her hair was a wild tangled mass, her skin flushed.

And when she half sat and leaned out to pull the coverlet over them, he rose up and stopped her.

"I'm cold."

"I'll warm you, love," he said in a dark voice, and she smiled as he pulled her against him, his chest to her back. They knelt, tucked close, the heat of his skin warming the coolness of hers. Her buttocks nestled to his groin, Chris made her be still, his hands gliding softly over her body from knees to breasts, palms skimming her nipples, cupping the firm lush globes, rubbing. Her head dropped back onto his shoulder, tilting to him, one hand coming up to cradle his jaw and she kissed him, a slow drugging kiss. He toyed with her nipples over and over and she gasped into his mouth, surging back against his hardness warming between them.

"Tori, don't," he hissed when her hand slid between to touch him.

She disobeyed. "Why?"

He could feel her smile against his lips. "Because just your touch brings me to the edge of—"

"Yes?"

Her fingertip slid mercilessly over the moist tip of him and he choked. "Madness."

"How nice."

"Tori."

"You're so warm, Chris. I can't help it. I love touching you, feeling you grow harder in my palm." She licked the line of his lips before adding, "and getting wet."

He groaned, catching her jaw as he filled her mouth with his tongue. She dueled and suckled, retreated and teased. And the smoldering desire turned to white hot passion, his hands gliding more forcefully over her body with every stroke of her firm hand. Then his fingers found her, slick and fire hot and she whimpered against his lips, covering his hand, pushing, urging him, and their kiss broke for a moment as she rose and pressed his erection between her thighs. She rocked wetly along his length, taunting him.

"Tori, oh God, Tori," he rasped. She grasped the footboard, leaning out and he surged inside her, thick and stone hard.

Then she clamped her legs tightly closed.

And Chris thought he'd explode then and there.

He hovered, his body curved to hers, her breasts in his palms and she drew away and slammed back.

"Slow, darlin'," he said into her ear. "I'll hurt you."

"No, never."

His hands drove down, between her thighs, fingers stroking wildly, feeling himself join and part from her. Wood creaked. Breaths panted. Their pace quickened and she gripped the wood frame, surging and slamming back into him, crying out her need, demanding he join her *now,* and he grasped her hips and plunged, her tight velvet sheath pulling and flexing, dragging his climax to the limit of sanity. It felt like an eternity before the spiraling feel of liquid heat and feminine power slowed, drifted into a humming that would live in his veins.

His arms circled her and they collapsed on a heap of down and quilts, sweating and breathing fast, bodies joined.

"You're going to kill me, woman."

Sluggishly, she twisted to look at him. "Oh, I haven't even begun."

Slowly he lifted his head, a slight frown wrinkling his brow. Then his features softened into a smile. "We'll see who begs for mercy."

She patted his cheek. "That's the idea."

* * *

He awoke and found himself alone and it scared him. He shouldn't feel this way, but he immediately swung his legs over the side of the bed and lit the lamp, glancing around. Her robe was missing but she left the delectable little panties hooked on his holster, like a trophy of the night. He smiled, pushed his legs into his pants and went looking, without boots, without thought, as if he could hear her breathe. Making love had forged more than bodies, and he knew she was in the barn and with the realization his panic ceased, abrupt and dismissed. Then he saw her and the sight knocked him breathless. The lantern hung on a nail, high and to her right, casting shadows and light across her freshly brushed hair, the fluttering dressing gown sashed loosely at her waist. Yet even through the haze of fabric, the yellow glow outlined her body in perfect clarity down to her bare feet. She looked like a wind spirit come to tame the wild black beast stomping in his stall. But his enchanting image faded when he realized she stood before Caesar's stall, an uncorked bottle of beer in one hand and an apple in the other.

"Well, which is it. Now think hard, 'cause you don't know what I had to do to get you a beer, pal."

Caesar's big head nudged the beer and Tori sank her teeth into the apple as the horse lipped the bottle, caught it, then tipped his head back, draining it.

"Uh-ahhh!" she warned, grabbing the long necked bottle before Caesar could throw it. The horse belched and she rolled her eyes. "Pig."

Chris chuckled and she turned, biting the apple, slowing her chew. "Hi."

Caesar nudged her and she stumbled toward Chris. She glared at the black beast. "Mind your own business," she said, then faced him. He looked so damn sexy, leaning against the door-frame, arms folded over his bare chest. She liked that there wasn't a hair on it either, polished, gleaming with a touch of sweat.

She flung the bottle aside. "Want a role in the hay, Marshal?"

He smiled, a flash of white teeth. God love her, she was never subtle, he thought as she moved closer, the yards of white fabric scarcely touching her skin, teasing him, yet he had the intense feeling of being stalked. When she was within reach, he caught her close, gripping her wrist and stealing a bite of her apple.

Her gaze sketched his face, watching his wonderful mouth and a little gasp sharpened in her throat when his tongue snaked out to lick the juice dripping down her thumb. She really shouldn't be thinking what she was thinking. They'd made love countless times tonight, but Christ, he was just so damn intoxicating.

He took another bite. "I'm starving."

"Gee, wonder why?"

"Because you, my huntress, are insatiable."

She never was before. In fact, sex had been pitifully boring, and she attributed that to herself. She'd let herself forget what it meant to be female in the most basic ways, going from Corps to cop to hunter with no thought of what it had done to her. She'd closed herself off after Trisha's death and Chris brought her back. No one drew emotion from her like this man. And right now, just to look at him, and have him look back with loving promise and heat in his gaze, she flung any residual restraint away and leaned into him. Her thighs pressed his, her knee slipping between and his free hand immediately went to her waist, the touch light, elusive.

She gave him the fruit and let her juice moistened fingers map his naked chest before she bent and licked the flavor of apple and salt from his skin. His chewing slowed and Chris clutched her, closing his eyes as her tongue moved across his flesh.

"I love the color of your skin. It's like new bronze, so smooth." She licked his nipple and she heard his indrawn breath. "And what's so fascinating is—" her hand slithered to his waist band and she flipped a button "—that it goes all the way down."

Chris dropped the apple. It bounced and rolled and Caesar dipped his great head and snatched it up, devouring it as Victoria opened Chris's trousers, each tug of a button driving through him like a sledge hammer.

He cupped her face in his palms. "What are doing to me?"

"Making love to you, Chris. Haven't you learned yet?" She didn't wait for an answer. "I guess I'll have to show you some more."

"Here?"

"Yeah. Kinky, huh?"

Gripping him by the waist of his trouser, she backed stepped toward a stall filled with fresh hay. His heart steadily climbed, each beat slamming harder and harder in his chest. She was looking at him as if she couldn't wait, that it didn't matter that they had been rolling over his bedroom floor a couple of hours ago.

"We can make noise," she enticed. As if he needed coaxing.

"I'm not the one who's loud."

"Hah. I seem to recall a distinct begging when I found that spot at the back of your thigh."

Chris would have had the decency to blush if he hadn't enjoyed that so much. "Ahh, so we're back to that?" He backed her up against the slatted wall, pushing his thigh between hers. She clamped him.

"No mercy, Tonto." She opened another button, dipping her hand inside and with a deep groan he covered her mouth, plunging his tongue between her lips and she opened for him, her head tilting to take more, her fingers seeking his arousal. But Chris couldn't stand it, he was already on the edge. All it took from her was a touch; bold or subtle, it still had the same effect, like a rush of lava, searing him to the core. He caught her hands and she smiled, wrestling with him for a moment until he spread her arms, hooking her fingers over the edge of the separating wall.

"I want to touch you." And she reached.

"No," he said and replaced her hands, holding her until she understood he would not be denied this. She didn't pout prettily or make a face as most women might, but leaned her head back and threw a challenge with her gold eyes. Make me beg, they said and he opened her robe, spreading it wide.

His gaze ripped over her body, the tanned thighs vulnerably open for him. Then he met her gaze and arched into her long body, covering her hands. He kissed her and kept kissing her until he felt her barring down on his thigh. Warmth seeped through the rough fabric. He drew back slightly and when her lips sought him, he smiled. She licked the taste of him from her mouth and Chris's jaw flexed.

"Make noise for me, Tori," he growled and let his hands slide down her arms, then enfolded her breasts. But he didn't touch her nipples. He touched her everywhere except there and her body throbbed and warmed and the words were on the tip of her tongue. If only he would. Then his mouth came into play, and he moistened every inch of her skin, the contact of cool air drawing her nipples, the skin of her breasts tight and taut. And when the heat of him, the incredible natural heat of his skin hovered near, she thought yes, yes, now, but he didn't and sank to his knees.

She blinked and he braced her thighs apart. "Oh God, Chris, this isn't fair."

"After what you did to me?" he said, then his tongue slid up her slender column of muscle and skin. His kissed and tasted, moistened and laved around and around the dampening cleft of her womanhood. But never touching *there*. He could smell the musky scent of her, feel her exquisite muscles jump and flex with anticipation, but he wanted some power. He was a useless pile of quivering flesh when *she* touched him. His breath fanned the dark patch and her hips thrust invitingly, her body speaking what she refused. If only he could capture her heart as snugly.

His hands smoothed up the back of her legs, spreading over her buttocks, dipping and teasing close and she moaned and twisted and rocked into his touch. "Chris."

"Hmmm?" he murmured against the flesh of her thigh.

She looked him in the eye. "I know you're about to explode," she taunted in a husky voice that smoked through his blood.

"Oh?" His lips brushed her and she gasped. "I like seeing you squirm." His broad dark hands splayed her upper thighs, thumbs meeting over the throbbing bead of her sex. Thumbs dipped and spread and she thought the floor had fallen out. Then it did. He licked.

She screamed softly. He let loose a fiendish chuckle and touched her again. Her lush body shook with the force of her desire. She squeezed her eyes shut, fighting the rolling sensations, her breathing hot and heavy between her parted lips. She wet them and his name tumbled like a siren's lure.

"Christopher, now."

On one fluid movement, he stood, flipped open his trousers and pushed into her.

"Yes," she sighed on a soft laugh of supreme pleasure. "Oh yes, yes, damn you!"

Smiling devilishly, Chris hooked first one of her long sleek legs on his forearm, then the other, gripping the slats behind her and driving upward. She gasped for air. He was thick and solid and he withdrew and sank into her again. Quick. Demanding. She felt exquisite and frustrated, open and vulnerable. And she loved it. Loved that he knew without asking, loved the insistent push of his body into hers, her breasts tight to his chest, the hardness of wood at her back.

His kisses were thick and heavy and dark with passion.

It was raw and powerful and hard.

Wood jolted with every surge of his hips, her fingers flexing. Eyes locked and held. Caesar stomped and whinnied. The scent of hay and leather swirled around them.

Chris ravished her mouth, feeling woman-flesh grip him and suddenly she pressed her mouth harder. A tight feminine whimper clutched in her throat, pushed into his mouth. Chris plunged long and hard and they hung suspended for several moments, fused like bronze and gold, letting life and heart, melt and mix. Chris's legs felt like wax, his heart beat slamming up his throat.

Still kissing her, he released her legs, felt them slide around his waist as his arms enveloped her. He tipped his head to look at her. Her eyes were damp, her expression somber and unguarded.

"Tori, I lo—"

She pressed two fingers to his lips, stopping the words she knew would hurt them more than heal. Weakly, Chris sank down onto the mound of hay and held her. He loved her more than he ever imagined he could. If only she would take it.

Abigale huffed and set another dish on the tray braced on her hip, and Victoria looked up from her book, a book she wasn't really reading, and cast Chris a glance over the edge of the settee, then meaningfully eyed the housekeeper.

Chris leaned back in his desk chair. "Is there something wrong, Abby? You look upset."

Beyond Abigale, Victoria's eyes flared with warning, but Abigale glared murderously at Christopher.

He sank in his chair a bit. "You want to talk about it?"

"Nay, I dinna." She clacked another lunch dish on the tray, glanced sympathetically at Victoria, then snubbed Chris, marching from the study and muttering, "Raise a child to a man, and think you've done right . . ." Her voice faded off as she headed deeper into he house.

"She knows."

Chris shrugged. "We're adults, Tori. What we choose to do is not her concern."

"Come on, Chris. She's like your mom. I hate to think she's dogging you as if you seduced a whimpy, starry-eyed virgin. Especially when it was my doing."

"Was it?" he said, closing the ledgers.

Her lovely mouth curved in a sinful smile. "Who begged who for mercy last night."

"Me," he said without regret. "And I believe it was this morning—" He left his chair and rounded the desk. "—On a scratchy Indian blanket—'' He crossed to her, lowering onto the couch beside her, crushing her skirts. ''—by the river.''

''Yeah, it was. You howled like a coyote.''

He pressed his lips to her throat, inhaling the scent of cinnamon. ''Did I?''

''Uhh-huh,'' she managed, her heart thudding wildly. ''Had to dump you in the water to cool you off.''

''It didn't work.''

''God, I'm glad,'' she said and caught his jaw, covering his mouth with hers. He sank into her kiss, going willingly when she pulled him down on top of her, wishing for privacy and a wilderness of freedom to love her.

''Ochaiii!''

They jerked apart and wiggled up to look over the edge of the couch, but saw nothing beyond the doorway but Abby's skirts disappearing around the edge.

''I'll talk to her,'' Victoria said.

''No.''

''Yes.'' And to prove her point, she pushed him off her.

He caught her hand. ''Tori, let it be.''

''She's blaming you when it was our choice. I know what moral standards are in this century,'' she said, lowering her voice. Lovingly she stroked his hair from his face. ''Trust me on this. It's a girl thing.''

It touched him that she'd intervene. Abby did have a way of making his life miserable when she was mad. ''Five minutes,'' he conceded. ''I'll rig the carriage.''

She blinked and stood.

''We're going to town.''

Her brows rose. ''Gee, I sorta liked being your prisoner.''

He grinned, his dark gaze filled with promise. ''We won't stay long.''

''We're going to see him.'' She'd blocked Becket out of her mind for the past hours, wanting to stay in this warm cocoon of pleasure and love. It was a hard slap of reality she didn't want. And his next words set her temper flying.

''I provoked him. Last night.''

"What!" she hissed. "Jesus, Chris. You don't mess with this man. He's like a changeling. God, he could have stalked and killed you."

He stood, grabbed her closer and silenced her tirade with a deep and thorough kiss, then pushed her toward the door when she wanted to question him. "You can burn my ears off later."

She whirled on him, poking his chest and he thought she was extraordinary, even in her rage. "Don't pass me off like that again, Swift. And believe me, you're ears aren't the only thing I'm going to burn off."

She spun away and headed to the kitchen and Batista crossed the foyer, the mute Spaniard glancing at his boss, then his lady. Chris grinned, leaning against the door frame and shoving his fingers through his hair. The woman was fire, he thought, in bed and out.

Abigale was easy to pacify, especially after she discovered that Victoria was a widow and had once been a mother. That seemed to smooth things over, except when Abigale mentioned that she could conceive. It wasn't possible with the Norplant, but Victoria couldn't tell Abigale that. Hell, she hadn't told Chris. But the thought of having another child, Chris's child, was a wish she couldn't fulfill—not unless she stayed here much longer than she could. And yet a knotting pain scraped through her chest every time she thought of leaving him.

Standing on the porch, she inhaled deeply, banishing her sorrow into familiar recesses, but a pang shot up when Lucky called to her. She waved. He was astride his pony, riding alongside Garrett Nash for a day of rounding up strays. Victoria would never have imagined the ex-gunslinger to be so good with kids, especially Lucky. He was just like Chris.

"You look wonderful," he said from behind her, close to her ear.

"Thank you." She smoothed the chocolate brown dress at her waist. "But flattery ain't gonna work, Tonto."

"On what?" he said innocently, coming around her and

signaling Batista. In a jingle of hooves, harnesses and wood, the elegant open black carriage rolled in front of the house.

"Don't get cute."

Chris sighed. He might as well suffer this out, he thought, gesturing for her to precede him. "Well, you'll have plenty of time. It takes longer by wagon than horse."

"I'd prefer a horse."

"I know." He handed her into the buggy. "But I want to show you off."

Her gaze narrowed at the chauvinistic remark. "I'm not a prize, Chris."

"Oh, yes you are." He leaped in beside her, taking up the reins. "You're the find of the century."

She laughed as he snapped the reins. The carriage lurched. "Don't expect much. And I swear, if you leave me with those petty nit-wits you call ladies, I'll beat you to a pulp."

He arched a brow. "Never. I asked Jenna and Reid to join us, for lunch."

"The doc?"

"You'll like her. She's just as mean and stubborn as you are when she gets mad. Ask Reid."

"I'm not mean and I will. Now don't think to change the subject, Marshal." She shifted toward him, bracing her arm on the back of the seat and twirling the strap to a dainty satin bag. "What did you say to Becket? And don't leave out a word."

Chris gave her a side glance. She looked elegant and refined, her coloring complimented by the dress, her hair swept up in a soft twist. Tiny gold earrings decorated her lobes, ones he'd love to nibble on just now, and though he adored that she wore his mother's necklace, she looked ready to wrap that silken cord around his throat.

"All right, huntress," he said and she smirked. "Remember what you said about him selecting his victims . . ."

People came out of shops and saloons, stopped walking and stared as they rolled into town. Victoria felt self-conscious as hell and glanced at Chris. He flashed her one of those heart-stopping grins and she returned it, letting him play the gentleman and help her from the carriage. He purposely let his hands linger on her waist before escorting her into his office.

Noble was reading the paper, his feet propped on the desk, but as Victoria ducked inside, he looked up. Instantly, he shot out of the chair.

"Hello, Noble."

He peered, his gaze moving appreciatively over her.

"That you? Clara—I mean . . . Miss Mason?"

"Clean up pretty good for a bounty hunter, huh?"

"Dang. Well, just dang!" His gaze shifted briefly to Chris. "You was right, son, she's a wild beauty."

For the first time in ages, a blush stole into her cheeks. "Why, thank you, sir." She'd decided on the ride out of the valley that she'd do her best not to bring the markings of her century under scrutiny and embarrass Chris. Guess that means no cussing, she thought, crossing to the man and taking his offered hand. "Thanks for being so nice to me before, Noble." She brushed a kiss to his ruddy cheek. He'd no idea how much it meant to her.

Suddenly the doorway was filled with deputies, each elbowing the other to get inside.

"Christ, like stags sniffin' after a doe," Noble muttered and Victoria laughed. Noble flushed red. And Chris introduced her to his staff.

"Now I know why we ain't seen the boss," a short stocky man said.

"Where you from, ma'am?"

"Denver."

Seth eyed her for a moment. "I feel as if we've met before."

"It's possible."

Noble snickered and Victoria promptly took a step back. On his toe. She met his gaze and he was effectively silenced.

"You a teacher?"

"No," Chris said and she looked at him, anxious. "She's a bounty hunter."

They inhaled collectively and gawked at her, then glanced at their boss. His gaze on her, Chris smiled, nodded, then folded his arms over his chest.

"And one of the best."

Something warm tumbled in her stomach. "You didn't always think so."

"Had it pounded into me." He rubbed his chin.

There was a stunned moment of silence, his deputies slack-jawed and looking between the two before they practically bludgeoned her with questions. She answered as best she could, and over the top of Tomas's head, she met Chris's gaze. He wasn't ashamed of her job, and it touched her so deeply she thought she'd do something useless and stupid, like cry.

"Hell, 'scuse me, ma'am. Heck, I'd do a crime, if you'd come after me."

"Careful, Charlie, don't let looks deceive you." Among other things, Chris thought, seeing her as they did, statuesque, tall, vibrant, but a woman. He knew better. She was tough as nails or soft as a kitten when she chose to be. She was a lady—his. And damn tired of his men fawning over her, Chris ordered them back to their posts. Reluctantly, they shuffled out, tipping their hats and Victoria experienced the respect and gentle reserve they'd offered Jenna Thorton when she was among them.

She looked at Chris, then flew to him, wrapping her arms around his neck and kissing him soundly. Noble coughed, but Chris closed his arms around her, accepting the kiss for what it was, a thank you. He would never hide his love and respect for Victoria, no matter the cost.

"Dang, you two."

They pulled apart, smiling.

"Better marry that woman quick, Chris."

Victoria's expression instantly shattered.

Chris's didn't. "I think I will."

"We can't," she said, a wounded fracture in her voice. "And you know why."

His eyes darkened, probing hers as if he could see into her soul. "If you could, would you?"

Victoria searched his handsome face. Stunned, she whispered, "You're actually serious!"

He nodded and Noble slipped into the back room.

"But—"

"Forget everything else, Tori, and just answer."

Listen to your heart for once, his eyes pleaded, and the moment stretched. *For once, just listen.*

"Yes," came in a breathless burst. "If it were actually possible, I would in a heartbeat."

His expression brightened.

"But it won't happen."

He leaned close to her ear and whispered, "I bet that's what you thought about time travel, too."

Chapter Thirty-One

All through lunch with Reid and Jenna, Victoria felt a little numb. Chris wanted to marry her and made it sound like a challenge. She wondered why he'd even bothered to ask her when he knew it was not possible. Did he *like* feeling rotten about it? She didn't want to hurt him or get hurt, but that was wishful thinking. They'd become too involved in each other not to feel pain. As if he sensed her anguish, he covered her hand, fingers flexing reassuringly, and Victoria experienced instant comfort, the sting of regret leaving her mood.

She lifted her gaze to his. He sat lazily in his chair, one arm slung over the back. This is not reality, she knew. He makes it too easy to forget the future.

Reid said something in Cheyenne to Chris, yet only Chris's eyes shifted.

"What did you say?" Victoria asked.

"He was being rude," Jenna said, nudging him hard enough for Reid to wince.

"Forgive me, lass," Reid said, a lilting brogue in his deep voice.

Chris's gaze slid back to Victoria's. "He asked why we bothered to have lunch with them, since I'm dining on you."

Victoria's eyes widened and she peered at Reid. "Excuse me?"

Her biting look didn't effect him; he'd seen the like in his wife often enough. "It's only that the man hasna heard a word I've said in the past half hour." Reid shrugged his massive shoulders and Jenna muttered something about the finer points of horse breeding boring her to tears. "And that was not an exact translation." His gaze pinned Chris. "I said dining on your beauty."

Victoria choked. "Fit your husband for glasses, Jenna."

"But you are lovely." Jenna looked at Chris, blaming him for not making her her see the truth. He crossed his heart, swearing he was trying. "And such a relief from the droll ladies around here." Jenna eyed Victoria, a warning in the look. "They hardly accept a woman physician doctoring their husbands and sons, they'll positively drop their pantaloons when they discover a woman bounty hunter."

"Now that I'd like to see." Victoria felt an instant kinship to the red-haired woman, and they exchanged a smile.

Chris looked at Reid, then between the women. "You sound like you're cooking up something."

"I don't cook," Jenna and Victoria answered at once, then laughed.

Chris's expression said he didn't care, and beneath the table, Victoria slipped her hand to his thigh. His body tightened and she flashed him an innocent smile, then looked at Reid.

"So you going to tell me why you have a braid half way down your back and why you," she said to Jenna, "can both speak Cheyenne?"

Jenna wiped her mouth and pushed her plate aside. She glanced at her husband. "I was rescued by a dashing Cheyenne warrior from certain death."

Reid's eyes clouded with memory, with pain. "You almost did die, my dove," he said softly.

She patted his hand reassuringly, yet her attention was on

Victoria. "I was foolish and headstrong and got into a tad of trouble."

Victoria frowned. It didn't sound like a *tad*.

"It's a long story," she waved airily, "one I'll tell when we've a chance to be alone."

It bothers her husband to hear it, Victoria realized.

"But I was taken to a Cheyenne camp, nursed to health. That's where I met Chris and Reid."

"You?" she said to Reid.

"He was the adopted son of Christopher's father." Jenna smiled at her stunned look.

"The stronger son."

"Giant's usually are stronger," Chris quipped and Victoria recognized brotherly love in the light banter.

Reid smirked and cuddled his wife close. "This," he flicked his braid back over his shoulder, "is a wee reminder of my heritage, and a man who gave me a home and hope when I had none." Reid and Chris exchanged a look, filled with memory and boyhood friendship.

It comforted Victoria to know he had strong ties with his friends. He'll need them when she was gone. And who will you turn to, a voice prodded, making her frown.

"I'm sorry to end this," Jenna said dispiritedly, after checking the watch pinned to her dress, "but I've a patient in fifteen minutes."

Chris stood as they did, and Jenna reached out to take Victoria's hand. "I'm very happy to know you. Please come visit soon." She spared a brief look at Chris. "It isn't proper that he keeps you all to himself, you know."

Victoria felt a wealth of kindness from this young woman. Jenna was honest, with a wonderfully dry sense of humor which he let loose on men. That she was English nobility, Chris had told her, hardly mattered, yet that Jenna was also a doctor, in this century, in a mining town, was a feat worthy of Victoria's admiration. And she had a feeling her *tad* of trouble wasn't half as hard as gaining the respect of the people in this town.

Reid towered over them all and leaned down to press a kiss

to Victoria's cheek. "He needs you so," he whispered before stepping back and shaking Chris's hand. She stared as they left, hand in hand. Through the panes of glass she caught a glimpse of Ivy League and tensed, her eyes narrowing as he tipped his hat to Jenna and strode past.

He's out again, hunting.

"Tori?"

She looked up, schooling her features, then left her chair. "You have very interesting friends," Victoria said as Chris paid the bill and escorted her out of the tiny restaurant. "But having lunch with them isn't the only reason we're here, is it?"

"No, to shop."

She made a face. "Yuck."

His brows rose.

"I've lived with just the essentials so long that it annoys the hell out of me." She eyed him. "And don't avoid the question."

Chris slipped her arm through his as they walked. "I just want to see his reaction after last night."

"That's playing with fire."

"You said he likes watching the authorities search for clues. What would he do if nothing happened, nothing outward?" He stopped and brought her hand to his lips.

"I don't know." He brushed his mouth over her knuckles. "It might push him to commit another murder."

"He'll have plenty at the summer social." He inclined his head to the poster nailed to the wall behind him and she spared it a glance.

"A social?"

"Big picnic with lots of children and mothers."

"And victims." She swallowed tightly. His lips were so warm on her skin. "That's dangerous—for everyone."

"I know." He couldn't tell her that he wanted this over with—that he wanted Becket in jail and her free to stay with him. She'd just fight him harder. "But we need to watch him *work.*"

"What we need, Chris, is a hotel room."

His teeth clenched along with every muscle in his body. "Wouldn't the gossips love that."

"Who cares, I would."

Suddenly, he gathered her close and kissed her, quick and hard and through the haze of desire Victoria heard gasps of outrage and masculine chuckles. When he pulled back, he was smiling from ear to ear.

"What was that for?" Not that she didn't like it.

"Staking my claim."

Normally, she would have been incredibly offended. "Sorta like a wolf marking his territory?"

He flushed a little. "I want every man in this town to know you're off limits."

She straightened her shoulders. "I can handle myself."

"It's not you I'm worried about. It's what I'll do to them if they so much as touch you."

Her lips pursed.

"Am I smothering you?" he asked and a little fear crept into his voice.

"No. No," she added more firmly, her hand covering his heart. "Go ahead, smother away." It was so different from being treated like one of the guys, she thought, though she knew she'd brought that on herself.

He pressed a roll of bills in her hand. "Go have fun."

"This is blatantly pacifying, *dear.*" Her look said she needed to be included in anything to do with Becket. "And where will you be?"

"Acting natural." His gaze shifted to somewhere over her shoulder and she felt a chill dance up her spine.

"It's him." Doubtless, and it always amazed him, her keen senses.

"He likes what he sees."

"That makes me want to puke."

Chris smirked, steering her past the saloon and Becket standing in the doorway. "If last night did anything, we'll know it soon enough."

"You want me to bait him?"

His grip tightened over her hand on his arm. "Don't even consider it."

"I'm not fair haired." Like his victims. "But I could be a blonde by tomorrow."

"Jesus, Tori, don't do this to me." There was absolute terror in his voice, anguish in his features.

"Chris," she said calmingly. "We have to get him, any way we can. If setting him up to bite is the way . . ." Her words trailed off and he knew she was right.

"Luring him with you isn't what I had in mind."

"It's not like I want to. If we could get him away from spectators, I could zap him with my tazer and take him back."

"He's killed here too, Tori."

Her expression withered. "I know," came softly, guiltily, and he tipped his head close, lowering his voice.

"I don't know how, Tori, but he'll pay in both centuries."

At the corner he stopped, brushed a kiss to her cheek, then urged her toward the stores.

She balked. "I hate shopping."

"Consider it a new experience of this century."

"What am I supposed to buy?"

"A hat?"

She rolled her eyes. "Oh, get real." Then she crossed the street, noticing that more than just Becket watched them.

Chris left his office, pausing on the street to search out Victoria. He smiled when he saw her leaving a dress shop, her arms loaded with packages. Doesn't like to shop, huh? He stepped off the walk, heading toward her, but stopped short when she did. He followed her gaze.

At the grocers, a woman was trying to select apples while a tired, hot child hung on her skirts, trying to yank her toward the mercantile and the candy displayed in the window.

But it was Becket she was watching.

Chris approached slowly, his gaze shifting to Victoria as she tucked herself back near the store entrance, seeming to adjust her packages. She even dropped one for effect and a cowboy retrieved it.

Suddenly, she looked straight at him, and Chris recognized worry and fear. Discretely, she waved him back and he paused to roll a smoke, tugging his hat low over his brow.

Careful, love. Careful.

He was stalking. Victoria knew it as sure as she knew she loved Chris. Ivy League was hungry. Like a cat sniffing for scraps, he'd moved through town, taking everything and everyone in. She'd been one step behind him most of the afternoon. Covertly, she'd watched him, chatting, making small purchases, noting how he salivated over the mothers and their young children. It turned her stomach, and she resisted the urge to race out into the street and warn them.

Not yet. She'd kept close to the young mother and her child when she noticed Ivy League lingering near, yet couldn't remain without drawing his attention.

But she'd heard enough.

The child tugged at her skirts, pleading in a whine.

The woman swiped damp curls from her forehead and spoke absently. "Not now, Joey, later."

"But momma!" came long and drawn.

"Joesph Acuff! Mommy will not hold you until I'm done."

She ignored the whining and Victoria peered into a shop window, watching Ivy League's reflection in the glass. His hand tightened over the hilt of the cane, again and again. Then he approached the mother.

Every muscle in Victoria's spine tensed. He wouldn't do it here, would he?

He knelt before the child. "What's the matter, little fella? Why the tears?"

God, Victoria thought, how comforting his voice sounded.

"Momma's mean to me," the child pouted and the mother looked down, giving her son a displeased look.

"You're fine—oh, hello again."

Again? Victoria thought.

"Why is she mean?" Becket said, stroking back the boy's hair.

"I need candy."

Becket laughed lightly, amused.

"Oh you don't need anything, Joseph. You just ate lunch."

Becket's eyes narrowed like a viper about to strike as he rose to meet the woman's gaze. She smiled wanely, apologizing for her son and Algenon Becket grinned. The sight of it sent a chill over Victoria's skin and she wet her dry lips, glancing back over her shoulder to where Chris leaned against a post, watching.

Becket and the young woman moved down the walk, the child still tugging at his mother's skirts as Becket spoke to her, easing her embarrassment, flattering her with a familiarity that told Victoria he'd spent considerable time with this woman before.

Victoria moved with them, heard him offer to buy her and her child a lemonade.

"A generous offer but, no thank you, Mr. Becket."

"But you're both so warm and exhausted."

"We have to get home."

"Surely a glass of lemonade wouldn't delay you much." He reached to take her arm and she flinched back. Becket continued to smile, apologizing for his forwardness.

That seemed to put the woman at ease and she walked beside him, laughing at whatever he was saying.

Becket glanced around, his gaze lighting on something, and before he could suspect her, Victoria halted before a hat shop and tapped the window for the shop keeper's attention. She gestured to a hat in the display and the owner turned over the price tag. Victoria acted suitably impressed with the bargain and smiled her thanks. The owner backed away and Victoria watched Becket, her heart beating in her throat. Clouds moved, sunlight reflecting off the glass, blinding her. What she wouldn't give for her sunglasses right now, she thought and squinted. Maybe a hat wasn't such a bad idea.

When she could finally focus she realized that the woman, child and Becket were nowhere in sight. Her head snapped back and forth, eyes seeking and she swung around and looked helplessly at Chris.

Turning back, she gripped her packages and moved between the throngs of people. Then she spotted them. Her footsteps quick, her head down, Victoria caught the woman's words.

"Please do not speak that way to me, Mister Becket. I'm married and love my husband dearly." The woman pulled away and with a glare of vengeance, Becket reached for her.

Victoria plowed right into the man.

She gasped, clutching her packages before they could fall. "Oh, I am so sorry. How clumsy of me," she gushed, hoping the heat gave her face the flush of embarrassment.

The woman and her child skittered quickly away. Becket watched them go, then turned his attention to Victoria. His expression spoke of more than she wanted. He was pleased to see her, the glazed look he gave Misses Acuff turned suddenly and completely on her. He smiled thinly. Victoria pretended obliviousness and blinked innocently up at him. Slim bucket.

He introduced himself and she oohed and ahhed appropriately.

Chris nearly leaped off the walk when Becket clamped his hands on her to steady her. He could see her stiffen, yet her smile was plastered in place. Good girl. Becket offered to take her packages, but she refused, yet allowed him to walk her across the street. Becket did most of the talking from what Chris could tell and he moved toward them, his body coiling tighter and tighter with every step. This was a stupid idea. Just seeing her near Becket brought to the fold that Victoria was here for one reason. To take that man back.

"I haven't seen you in town before," Ivy League said.

Liar. "I've recently arrived."

"Aren't we fortunate then?"

Victoria made no comment, yet smiled artificially, bid him

good day and tried to step around him. He blocked her effort-lessly. Is this how you corner them? she wanted to ask.

"Did I see you with the marshal?"

"Yes." She moved around him and stepped into the street. He followed. "A fine lawman."

She slanted him a look. "The best." She adjusted her pack-ages while she waited for a pair of riders to move past.

"Are you certain I can't carry those for you?"

"No, thank you." Victoria wanted to scream at him, hit him, shoot him. God, he'd killed Velvet, stuck a knife in her heart, then dressed her up like a Kewpee-doll, yet he stood here, trying to make a pass at her! She hastened into the street. He was right beside her.

"You remind me of someone."

Alarms rang in her head. "Really?"

"A young woman, Clara Murphy."

Victoria felt the color drain from her face, but she forced her expression to remain wrapped in his every word.

"Perhaps it's just the height."

She shrugged.

"Or the walk."

Victoria kept her pace as even as before though her knees suddenly felt like pudding.

"Victoria."

She looked up and nearly slammed into Chris.

"Afternoon, Marshal." Becket nodded, glancing between the two.

Chris kissed her lightly, then took half her packages. "I see you've met my lady." The last he said with such possessiveness her ancestors would have known it.

And Victoria's jaw flexed, yet she fastened a bright smile on Becket.

His perfect brows rose, his blue gaze shifting between the couple, but there was a glint in his eyes. He seemed to shake himself, then said, "I've been meaning to ask, any progress on Velvet's death?"

Beside Chris, Victoria tensed. "No."

"Fascinating." A smugness weighed his tone.

And Victoria wanted to claw his face off.

"What about Clara Murphy? She seemed to have vanished about the same time." He leaned out on his cane. "About the same time you arrived, Miss."

"Perhaps. I don't know."

"A droll mousy woman. Scarred, plump, but efficient."

"Enough to kill Velvet, you're saying?"

He looked offended. "Hardly."

"Just what is it that you're implying, then, Becket?"

"That you haven't a clue to the killer."

Victoria could almost see him sanding his hands together and bit down on her tongue. Rage radiated from her and fearing it would alert Becket, Chris swept his arm around her waist. Her breath escaped in a soft puff.

"You're right, I don't. There were no tracks, no motive, no weapon. It looks like it'll be an unsolved case for some time." Chris tipped his hat. "Now if you'll excuse us, we have to be getting back."

"Will we see you at the picnic, Miss?"

Victoria glanced back over her shoulder and tried to look flattered. With the finesse of an Oscar-winning actress, she lowered her gaze briefly, then met his. "Of course." She looked into Chris's eyes, her own filled with innocent pleading that would put the best coquette to shame. "Won't we, Chris?"

He was glad his back was to Becket because his expression was a mask of confusion when he ought to be playing the jealous lover. "Sure, darlin', and we'll bring the boy, too."

Behind Chris's back, Victoria waved lightly. Out of the corner of her eye, she saw Ivy League's fingers flex over the cane hilt, over and over. Well, this was a selling point. Becket was hot for her.

In the office, Victoria propped her feet on Chris's desk and slumped in his chair, dragging on a cigarette he'd rolled for her. It tasted like cow pies. But she needed it, hell, she needed a drink after being so close to that maggot-laced fiend and having him look at her like she'd invite his touch. A shiver shrank her spine and she dragged on the smoke again, watching Chris's cute behind shift inside dark jeans as he paced before the carved desk. He was working himself into a fit.

"Come on, Chris. Lighten up. It was too good an opportunity, and you know it. He was going to hurt that woman."

"You don't know that," he snapped, but even his tone doubted.

"That wasn't the first time they'd met. I had to do something and couldn't reject him flat out."

He said nothing and paced some more.

"I didn't mean for it to happen."

"Well it did, and now we're stuck." He stopped and leaned across the desk, taking the smoke, dragging once, then handing it back. He strode to the stove and poured coffee. He didn't drink it and moved around the large open room. How could he let this happen?

"We can do this, Chris. And what safer way to lure him than with us? If we have his attention, he can't put it on anyone else."

She knew his methods too well, and Chris was fast picking up on the scenario that was Becket's twisted brain. "But it's you he wants now."

"Don't be so sure."

"I am, Tori. I'd recognize the look in any man. Obsession."

"Seen it in the mirror lately."

He scoffed, feeling helpless and loose. Victoria swung her feet off the desk and came to him, catching him about the waist and yanking him up against her. He went still as glass and she slid one hand slowly up his chest and cupped the back of his neck.

She drew him down to her mouth and he sank into her kiss with a harsh groan.

He thrived on her loving, anxiousness slowly draining from his body as she kissed him and kissed him. He filled his hands with her buttocks and and ground her hard against his throbbing groin. She made a pleased sound.

"Shhhh," she hushed when he opened his mouth. "Let it go for now. Just keep him under surveillance, but let it go." She stared at his chiseled lips, then whispered a kiss across them.

"I saw Abigale and Randel."

Something akin to hurt flickered in her eyes, but he couldn't decipher it. "Grocery day," he muttered.

"Doesn't that mean the house is empty?"

He sent her an arched look, scowling, then his features went taut. He grabbed her hand, scooping up the packages and leaving the office. They left town amid outraged stares and a cloud of Colorado dust. The small carriage never moved so fast.

Chris tossed the reins to Batista and dragged Victoria from the carriage, his long strides eating up the distance to his study.

Pulling her in, he kicked the door closed, then instantly covered her mouth with his. He'd done nothing but think of her, doing this with her. His tongue filled her, sweeping and hot as his hands raced roughly over her body. She tore at his shirt buttons, diving her hand beneath the fabric and molding his chest. He kissed her deeper, his palms curving over her bottom, squeezing, lifting her to fit against his arousal.

He was long and hard beneath the fabric, his rocking motion answered by her own.

"I can't wait." He pushed her up against the sealed door. "I'm sorry." He shoved up her skirts, his finger finding her slick and hot for him. "Jesus, you drive me crazy!"

Frantically she tore at his trousers, freeing him.

"Then don't."

In one thrust, he was inside her. Her legs wrapped his waist, her body rocking onto his. He withdrew and plunged with a hard thrust of his hips and she gasped, tearing open her bodice and letting him bend to suckle her breasts. She clutched his head and he pushed and pushed.

The hinges jolted, wood rattled and he pumped into her hot slick depths. Her fingers dug into his shoulders, her head thrown back. He chanted her name over and over and lifted his head.

"Look at me."

She did. He left her in a long smooth motion, then plunged, driving her up the door. She gasped, her eyes flared.

"No, look at me. I want to see it in your eyes," he rasped and thrust and thrust and she bucked, pushing back, their pace frantic and near violent.

Then her silken depths flexed and grabbed him, his lips in a tight line and he reached between them, stroking the core of her, slicking his fingers over the wetness of their joining. Victoria gripped handfuls of his thick dark hair, whimpering for his power, refusing to break his gaze, her hips tucking in short frantic pulses.

"Come for me, love, drench me," he whispered as he flicked his damp fingers over the bead of her sex. She arched and fused her womanhood to him. Her breath came in a ragged gasp, clipped and clipped, then a hot rush against his mouth. Her pleasure darkened her eyes, seeing it drove him over the edge and he stroked her, pushing his erection deeper and deeper, withdrawing once more then filling her hard.

He exploded, his gaze locked with hers, his climax smothering over him, surrounding him as he released himself into her body. She closed her eyes, her feminine muscles clamping, stealing all he had and draining him of energy.

He buried his face in the curve of her throat.

The sudden silence was sharp.

"Are you all right?"

She smiled, closing her eyes. "Of course."

Slowly he released her legs.

He ground into her once more before leaving her body. Victoria made a face and he smiled.

He withdrew a handkerchief from his back pocket and she tried to take it. He eluded her grasp and kissed her, pressing it between her legs. His strokes were as tantalizing as his loving. She hummed against his mouth, covering his hand riding the dying flames of their passion before he stepped back, smoothing her skirts down and righting his clothing.

He had trouble with the last button, his hands shaking. She helped him, smiling like a cat with whiskers full of cream. She pecked kisses to his chin, buttoning his shirt. His hand tightened on her waist, smoothing up to tuck her breasts back into her bodice.

"Tori?"

"Hmmm?" She kissed his chest as she closed each button.

"Would you leave me if you carried my child?"

She blinked, taken back. "No." She didn't want to discuss this now . . . "But it's not possible."

He scowled and was about ask when she took his hand and placed it at the curve of her elbow. His brows drew down as he felt something wobble beneath her skin.

"It's birth control."

He looked skeptical and a little disgusted.

"In my century, woman have control over their bodies and choose when they have children. Some use condoms, devices or pills. This is a Norplant, flexible tubes of a estro—a chemical released over time to prevent conception."

His eyes narrowed. "How much time?"

She wet her lips. "Five years."

His eyes widened. "How long have you had it?"

"Ever since Kevin and I were having problems."

He inspected her arm. That's why she always scratches there, he realized. Only his gaze shifted to hers. "Can you take it out?"

She tilted her head, frowning. "Yes. With minor surgery."

His gaze shifted from her to where his thumb grazed her skin. He couldn't even see it, but he felt it and though a thousand questions raced in his head, he dismissed them to one fact.

If a child wouldn't keep her, was his love strong enough?

Chapter Thirty-Two

There was such a marked sadness in his eyes that Victoria broke her eye contact, brushing loose hair from her face, but when she made to kiss him, he jerked back, releasing her arm.

His gaze moved between her arm and her face.

Her eyes thinned to mere slits. "We're you trying to get me pregnant so I'd stay?"

"No!" But the consideration had occurred to him, and a guilty flush crept up his neck.

"That's a cheap shot, Chris! Really low."

"Christ almighty, Tori. I didn't know about that birth *control.*"

She tipped her chin up. "It wasn't necessary for you to know."

He was fuming now, his eyes pinning her to the door as hard as his hips had.

"It's my body, Chris."

He stepped closer, his voice cutting with anger. "And mine was inside yours, spilling inside you. Did you think I'm so—" he struggled not to claim his love, not now, *"enamoured* with you that I didn't consider the consequences?"

It touched her somewhere deep inside that he had. "Well, you don't have to worry. There aren't any."

He clenched his fists, trying desperately to handle his temper. That she would exclude him so coldly from this information severed through him. "Is everything so cut and dry to you?"

Not with you, she thought. Never with you. "Look," she began tiredly. "This device," she tapped her arm, "has been in place so long I don't even think about it. It's like getting out of bed every morning. Not telling you wasn't deliberate and when I thought about it," her voice wavered, "it was pointless. I don't have to risk pregnancy to prove I . . . have strong feelings, Chris. I can't separate mind and body like a whore."

"I didn't mean it like that."

"Well, making love with you and making love for a child aren't the same, and if you can't figure it out, maybe you can just go find the Widow Bingham and get laid!"

He looked as if she'd struck him. How did she find out about her? Nobody knew except . . . Randel.

"I'll kill him," he growled.

"*She* told me."

He scowled. "That doesn't sound like Angela. And when did you see her?"

"This afternoon in the store. And she didn't have to say that you sleep with her on a *regular* basis, for Christ's sake." Men were so stupid sometimes. "She took one look at me and said, 'so you're the reason he hasn't been by.' She lives fifty miles away and no one but Randel knew who she was. It wasn't hard to figure out."

He fought a smile. "You're jealous."

Victoria couldn't decide whether to kiss him or knock his teeth in. "No, I'm hurt."

"Aw Tori," he moaned. "There isn't anything between us."

She made a disgusted sound that was totally artificial. "I could care less. But I thought we were being totally honest with each other?"

"Like you were with me?" He gestured to her arm.

"I'm protecting myself, Chris. And you."

He stared at her for a long moment and when he spoke, his voice rasped with hurt. "You're protecting your heart, too. No ties, so you can just walk away."

Tears bloomed in her eyes. No, no, her soul screamed, this is too soon. "It has to be that way."

He stiffened, his expression suddenly unreadable. "And I can't live like this anymore."

She inhaled a sharp breath. "I see."

A door slammed, Lucky calling for her, yet she didn't move even when the little boy pushed open the doors.

"Miss Toria?"

Chris continued to stare at her as she clasped the child's hand in her own. Lucky's gaze shifted between the adults, noticing her tears and ending on Chris with a scowl.

She bent and kissed his dust-covered head, smelling little-boy dirt and missing him already. She closed her eyes tightly and a tear spilled over her cheek. "How was your day, sweetie?" she whispered in a fractured voice. "Come tell me." She turned and the pair vanished in the recesses of his house.

And Chris watched her go.

Chris muttered a curse and totaled up the column of figures for the third time, trying to ignore the cheers coming from the paddock. He was used to hearing it when Joquin brought a horse to bridle. But his mood was foul already, distracting him from the accounts he'd neglected. Tiredly, he sank back into the leather chair, rubbing the bridge of his nose with thumb and forefinger and when he looked up his gaze fell on the earring he'd found on the floor earlier. He picked it up, his chest tightening as he remembered how she'd lost it only hours ago. And the fight that ensued. She was pulling away. He felt it when he'd sought her out and tried to talk with her. She made an excuse about getting Lucky cleaned up and closed him out of the bathing room.

His only peace since was Noble's arrival minutes later, bringing the news that Becket had been asking about Victoria. They both prayed he didn't find out she was a bounty hunter.

But seeing her with Becket on the street, the way she cultivated him into her palm proved again and again to Chris that she was willing to do anything to see justice done—Even at the cost of their love.

His fingers wrapped around the earring until it bit into his palm, her rejection like a sabre through his chest, turning hurt to fury. *Anything for the bounty, huh Tori?*

She'd knowingly pushed herself into a deadly situation to catch Becket off guard, yet somehow, Victoria's interruption of his kill, twisted his lust for blood, Misses Acuff's blood, into misshappen feelings for Victoria.

It was just a sick feeling Chris had, but Becket's undercurrent of suspicion and bizarre need to see the authorities struggle for a solution, was there for anyone to see. Anyone who knew would know what to look for. And all Becket needed was to catch her alone or hear her talk, and he'd be clued into her, her century. And she'd be dead in seconds. Trained bounty hunter or not, Chris refused to put her in jeopardy. He had two days to come up with a plan and convince her otherwise.

The cheering beyond the wall grew steadily louder, and he left his chair, moving to the window and pushing back the curtain.

His features sharpened and he immediately left the room, storming through the kitchen, past a startled Abigale and out into the yard.

Damn that woman!

With Victoria astride, the angry mare curled and bucked, yet she held on, her hat flying off, body arching, her arm up for balance.

He shouted her name as he ran toward the paddock, leaping the fence.

"Don't!" she commanded, catching sight of him out of the corner of her eye. "She's almost there!"

Then the horse rounded the ring, its hind legs slowing in the incessant backward thrust to knock her off.

Chris's heart lay lodged in his throat until the horse settled, and Victoria rode the line in a cantor, then a smooth-gated walk. He didn't breath until she slid from the saddle.

His hands whistled and applauded, but a wicked glance from Chris silenced them. Briefly, she glanced at Chris, frowning, jerking the horse into obeying her lead and walking around the corral. He listened to her soft crooning, watched her pet the beast, then reward her by letting the mare race her steam out around the paddock.

She clicked her tongue and the horse slowed, prancing over to her with that I'm-doing-this-because-I-want-to look. She stared into black eyes, holding her bridle, then nodded, letting go and the horse moved away. Proudly, she scooped up her hat and dusted it off as she crossed to him.

He practically leapt on her.

"What the hell do you think you were doing! Bronc busting is dangerous business."

"I know."

"What in God's name possessed you to do that?"

"It looked like fun."

He smoldered with suppressed rage.

"I was right. It was."

"You disobeyed me, Tori."

Her eyes narrowed. "You'd better check your hormones, *my lord.* I obey me and that's it."

"Not with my animals."

"Oh, for Christ's sake, what the hell was I supposed to do? Jump off when *you* wanted. I would have been trampled."

"Exactly. Dammit, Tori, what if you fell off?"

"I had no intention of falling." She glanced back over her shoulder and waved to Joquin. "It was two women fighting it out." She looked back at him. He wasn't mollified.

"Did Joquin tell you how he lost half his fingers."

"Yes." Bronc busting.

Her fists were on her hips, her breathing still labored. And Chris thought she looked beautiful, even covered with dust and sweat. "And this didn't deter you?"

"Obviously not."

All Chris could see was her flying off that horse and breaking her neck. "You are forbidden to ride a wild mustang."

Her icy look drove the air from his lungs, and he expected her to unleash that temper on him, but her expression suddenly melted, covered with blandness.

"They're your horses." She shrugged. "Fine." She brushed him aside. Ranch hands waved, congratulating her before she headed to the house. Lucky clapped wildly, scampering off the back porch and launching into her arms.

And the sight of the pair struck Chris with a mortal blow. How could she block out her emotions like a shuttered window?

"Did real good, Miss Toria."

"Thank you, sweetie."

Lucky leaned back in her arms, and Chris saw the boy frown, then brush at Victoria's cheeks, before she clutched the child tightly and carried him into the house.

It was a shower. Outside, near the back porch.

Except for the rustic look of it, it didn't appear any different than one she's used at summer camp when she was a kid. A tank sat perched on the roof, a pipe extending down into a frame. She'd inspected it earlier and knew that within the frame was a nozzle dotted with holes and a chain attached to a lever.

The stall was wood, the top and bottom two feet open to the world, the excess water draining through the slatted platform onto the ground. But Chris had constructed a wood walk toward the house and the bunk house so no one had to walk in the mud.

But the reason she was studying it now was that Chris was using it.

And she had a perfect view of his long body from her position on the balcony above. She watched him scrub, smoothing lather over his hairless chest and wishing they were her hands. her mind drifted back to this afternoon in the study, a smile ringing her face.

"Does it look like one from your century?"

She flinched, focusing. His arms propped on the edge of the stall, he stared up at her, wiping the water from his face. He looked good wet, she thought, then cleared her throat.

"Yes. What made you do it?"

"I grew up bathing in a river and never could get used to sitting in a tub of dirty water." He shivered dramatically and she couldn't help but smile. "The water is heated by the sun."

"I gathered that, but what happens in the winter?"

"I have to resort to a tub," he said plainly. "It's frozen over."

He snatched up a towel, drying himself. She watched the motion, aching to join him.

Don't say anything, she warned herself. Don't let him know how badly you hurt.

"Ever thought of making one in the house?"

He looked thoughtful, sanding his hair dry. "But the water—"

"A storage of water constantly heated, say with a larger stove." She didn't know exactly how to regulate hot and cold but he was smart enough to figure it out and could see the wheels in his brain turning. "Later, Einstien."

"Who?"

"A scientist, twentieth century."

His mouth quirked wryly. "This all must seem so primitive to you."

She let her gaze drift over the horizon, the sun setting in his beautiful valley. "It's a good kind of primitive."

Chris gazed up at her, enjoying the serene look on her lovely face as she admired his lands. He could feel her spirit drift into it, absorb it. She belonged here, damn it.

"Tori—"

Her gaze snapped to his. "No. Becket goes back and I'm taking him."

"You're utterly certain this . . . wall will not let you back in, back here?"

"I can't hope." Her lip trembled. "It hurts too much," she whispered.

She left the rail, and Chris gripped the stall ledge for long moments, then sighed heavily, dropping his head between outstretched arms. He swallowed the knot in his throat, then slammed his fist into the wood, shattering a slat.

And in her room, Victoria buried her face in the pillow, smothering her cries.

"Victoria, come into my study. I need to speak with you."

Victoria. He hadn't called her that in weeks and his demanding tone spoke volumes. Bossy Injun struck a nerve.

"I'm helping Abigale right now." She took another dish and rubbed it dry with the cloth.

He stopped, cocking a look over his shoulder. "That's her job. You aren't supposed to be working in my house."

"I have two hands and a brain, Christopher, and I've never been a freeloader in my life."

He turned fully. "Come here, Victoria."

"Go to hell, Chris."

Abigale gasped, but Victoria didn't spare her a glance.

"I'll see you when I'm done."

"It be all right, miss."

"No, it isn't. The marshal seems to have forgotten his manners. Or that I hate being ordered." She set the dish on the stack and advanced. "Or that if he didn't bark a command like I was one of his ... flunkies, and simply asked, I'd talk with him. It might be wise for him to remember *exactly* why I came here." Great, just dig the knife deeper, she thought. "And it's about time I got back to my job."

Chris exploded, hurt and uncertainty making his voice sound like the low growl of a bear. "Never. Do you hear me, woman? Never. If I have to cuff you to me, you're not going into town without me."

Her fists clenched in the folds of her skirt, her stare mutinous. "Is that a threat, Marshal?"

"No, Victoria," he said with deadly calm. "*That* is an order."

He turned on his heels and stormed to his study, the slamming door ringing through the house. Ranch hands who'd obviously heard the argument stood helplessly in the foyer, glancing between her and the closed door.

Victoria sighed, defeated and regretting her threats. It was just that she was so scared, about having to take Becket in, having to leave all these wonderful people, the comfort she found here. And she knew she had to. Duty came first.

But what about to yourself? a voice niggled. Where will you be when this is over?

Alone.

Totally, cruelly alone.

They were faking and not fooling anyone. Abigale and Randel kept sending them looks that clearly laid the blame at Chris's feet. His ranch hands glared at him through her serenades, for they were soft and sad, yet if he came near her, she made excuses—brisk, emotionless excuses. And he realized how quickly she turned back into the hunter, leaving her emotions tucked where he couldn't find them. But despite that he'd told her he couldn't live with this torment, he wasn't ready to give up. He had a feeling too many people gave up on Victoria before, brushing her feelings aside as if they were meaningless, herself included, and he'd no intention of joining the fold.

He loved her too much.

He stood in the entrance of the dining room, watching her. She and Lucky sat close together, hovering over a sheet of paper and the little boy's tongue stuck out and lined the route of his lips as he made his mark. She whispered secretly to him and he smiled proudly, in went the tongue and he tried again.

"Victoria?"

"Yes." She didn't look up, knew she'd collapse if she did. "Keep practicing," she urged Lucky. "Two more, then we're done for tonight."

"Look at me."

She didn't.

"Please."

She lifted her gaze.

"I'm sorry."

She nodded once, then turned her attention to the boy. Chris didn't think she'd accepted it.

"Very good!" she praised the child, then re-examined his work and gave him a kiss. Lucky stared up at her, then let his gaze slide to Chris. His little face wrinkled in a frown and he scooted back from the table and left, but not before he stopped beside Chris, motioning for him to bend down.

"Don't make her go away."

Chris's heart clenched at the worried plea. "I'm trying, son."

"But she sad at you."

"I know."

"You yell, why?"

"Cause I'm afraid."

Lucky's eyes grew round as coins. "You?"

Chris nodded, cast a quick glance at Victoria, who was looking over the papers, then back to the child. He squatted down to eye level and gripped the boy's shoulders. "See, I don't want her to leave either, but she might. And I'm not sure how to stop it."

He looked so scholarly thoughtful, Chris smiled. "Kiss her lots. She likes that."

"Think so?"

He nodded vigorously, then sent Chris a warning look. "But don't stick your pecker 'tween her legs and move it 'round."

"Jesus!" Chris gasped. "Where did you hear that?"

"Saw saloon girls. They don't like peckers much. Hurts 'em cause they's moanin' and screamin' and—"

When he started making too authentic sounds, Chris clamped a hand over Lucky's mouth. "I don't *ever* want you to discuss that with anyone," he said darkly. "Except me. Later. Much later. Like when you're about eighteen. Understand?"

Gagged, Lucky nodded.

"Go to bed, now."

Again the nod.

Chris removed his hand and Lucky launched into his arms. His soft whisper stole into Chris's heart.

"I happy here, Marshal."

Chris closed his eyes, giving the boy a squeeze. "I'm glad, Lucky, really glad."

Lucky wiggled out of his arms, raced back to the table to kiss Victoria, then ran out of the room. Seconds later, a door closed.

Except for the sound of conversation coming from the porch, the house was silent.

He tossed a stack of papers on the table and they scattered toward her. She didn't move, frozen with her gaze on Lucky's schoolwork.

Chris willed her to look up. Finally, she did.

"I love you, Tori."

She seemed to crumble before his eyes.

"Don't do this to me."

He strode close and pulled her from the chair. "I love you." She kept her head bowed and he tried to look under it. "I didn't mean to hurt you, but, Jesus, it tears me up when you remind me that this is all temporary to you."

She hadn't been thinking that way for a long time now. "I wish it wasn't."

"It doesn't have to be."

Her lips pressed to a flat line.

"Dead or alive, Becket goes back." His voice was flat, tired.

She nodded, the stone in her throat making it impossible to answer.

"Then maybe I'll just kill him."

She looked up at him, thick tears streaming down her cheeks. He felt each one as if they were drops of his own blood.

"All I have to do is confront him with my suspicions, let him make his move, and shoot him. If he were gone, you wouldn't have reason to leave."

"You won't. I know you, Chris. There's no justice in that."

He scoffed. "This isn't your century, Tori. And I'm the law here."

"I know what you're trying to do. Will you sacrifice your honor for me, Chris? Will you really break the law for your own selfish reasons?"

"When I have to fight a murderer for the right to your love, yes. But if you really don't want to make a life with me . . ." His expression was infinitely sad, his voice faultering. "I love you enough to let you go."

He backed away, dropping his hands. He left her without a sound and she sagged into a chair, cradling her head in her hands.

It wasn't fair.

"Don't make me choose."

It wasn't a decision she could make, not after all this time, all she'd done to get Becket. Her gaze strayed to the papers he'd tossed. Reports, scrawled by his deputies and a quick glance told her they'd monitored Becket's every move as well as she had.

Was this a useless fantasy? Believing she could do her job and love at the same time? This is what happened to her marriage, so caught in it she lost her husband's love and her daughter as well.

Are you willing to make the same mistake twice?

Be careful, her conscience warned. There is no second chance.

Chapter Thirty-Three

Chris gripped the railing and watched her ride out in the twilight of the night.

I love you enough to let you go.

And never thought he'd have to put his love to the test, yet he stood on his porch, watching her leave him. And her direction was unmistakable. The portal of time.

Fool!

You forced her to choose and now look. See what your need and pride has done?

But she loves me, I know she does. I see it in her eyes.

And if you are wrong?

Then I have gambled on her love and lost.

But they had no life together if he forced her to stay.

No life.

Victoria stared at the cave, swiping the damp hair from her forehead with the back of her hand. It was still there, still penetrable, wobbling like an invisible curtain of liquid rock. She didn't dare move closer, afraid it would steal her back when she was struggling under the burden of indecision. All night she'd tried to imagine herself going through, never seeing Chris or Lucky again, the ranch hands or Abigale and Randel. Never knowing Jenna as the friend she knew she could be. Victoria tried desperately for the realistic view that kept her alive and one step ahead of the perp for the past years, and in it she found clarity.

The price was too big.

Christopher.

And what waited for her on the other side?

A swift trial, an execution, and then nothing.

Justice would be served, and you will be forgotten and alone.

Stabbing pain made her wince and gulp back tears.

Just the thought of walking through this gorge of earth and its mysteries terrified her. She didn't belong there anymore.

And she didn't really have to come here to know that. From the first moment in Chris's arms she was lost, her heart opening for his gentle smiles and teasing and patient persistence. Her feelings couldn't be tucked neatly away with the pain anymore. Not for duty's sake. For the pain of the past was gone and the only hurt she felt was her own making.

She'd never had to choose. Falling in love with Chris took that away.

She was just too stubborn, and too used to fighting her emotions to recognize that her vengeance for Becket was just a barrier she grasped for the wrong reasons.

And she'd come here to say good-bye. To Trisha, Kevin, Cole and the ugliness she'd wallowed in and hid inside. Her gaze lifted to the night sky, then she sagged back against the thick muscled horse hovering like a protector. He nudged her impatiently.

"Yeah, I know." She patted his sleek neck. "Let's go home, Caesar."

Caesar nickered and stomped in agreement as she swung up onto his broad back. She stared once more at the short stout cavern and murmured a good-bye, then reined around. She didn't worry over injuring the horse in the darkness, for without so much as a guiding tap, the stead picked his way over the terrain lit by the silver moon.

She was going home.

And she prayed Chris would forgive her.

Victoria bedded down Caesar with sweet fresh hay and a handful of sugar cubes since she was out of beer, then headed to the back of the house. It was incredibly quiet and when she slipped inside, she went directly to Lucky's room.

She found the child curled on his side and tucked beneath soft coverlets. When she bent to brush a kiss to the top of his head, he reached out and took her hand, squeezing it before opening his eyes. His sleepy smile lit the darkness.

"Hi, sweetie."

"You stay, huh?"

He was too insightful for his age.

"Yes, honey, I'm staying." He leaned up and hugged her tightly.

"I knew you loved us," he whispered, patting her somberly, and she squeezed her eyes shut. How could she ever have thought of leaving them?

Then with the innocence of a child, he laid back and snuggled into his bed, content with her assurance.

Casting one last look at him, she softly closed the door and went to search out Chris. Her heart picked up its pace as she examined room after room on the first floor. Nothing and she frowned at the quiet when it was scarcely ten o'clock. A light shone from beneath Abigale's door as she tiptoed past and she assumed Chris was in his bedroom. She started toward it and paused, looked down at herself and grimaced at her dirty clothes. She veered into the bath room quietly, stripped and washed before sneaking to her room with only a towel around her.

Slipping on a robe, she belted it as she crossed to the balcony door, flinging them open. A cool gust of summer air hit her and she inhaled the scents of 1872 Colorado. No smog, no noise, just the incessant chirp of crickets and an occasional bray of cattle.

Home.

Turning to Chris's room and the wide open window, she took two steps and stilled. She could see the magnificent four poster bed for the lamp was lit beside the fairy tale creation. And it was empty. She moved closer, slipping around the edge of the balcony door and further inside.

Empty.

In a panic, she thought he'd gone to town or after her, but she knew no horses were missing from the barn.

Where the hell was he?

Past caring about making noise, she marched through the house, the robe opening and revealing bare muscled legs. She thumped down the stairs and Abigale's door opened, then Randel's, but she didn't see it. From either end of the lower hall Abigale and Randel exchanged a nod. Abigale clasped her hands in a hopeful gesture and Randel sent her calming look, shooing her back to bed. Both slipped into their rooms.

Victoria was frantic. The house was large and rambling but she couldn't find him. He'd vanished, and unless he'd taken his bow and set off to get in tune with nature, he had to be here. He was avoiding her, she realized freezing in the foyer. Hiding? Nah. Not Chris. But just the same she was scared.

She turned and caught her reflection in the hall mirror and scarcely recognized herself. Her skin was vibrant and flushed, her hair lighter around her forehead from the sun, but something was different—very different. And she moved closer. Quickly she struck a match to the candle on the narrow table pressed to the wall, the flame highlighting her with a ghostly image in the glass. She peered inspecting her face, her throat, even brushing open the robe a bit to see the curves of her breasts. Between them lay the necklace Chris had given her. She'd never taken it off.

And inside the recess of her logical, very analytical mind, she belonged with it. Her gaze flicked to her face, gaze for gaze meeting in the glass.

Her eyes were clear and gold. No longer haunted with sadness.

She smiled and they seem to glow with an inner fire. Is this what he sees?

Taking the candle sconce she moved through the house, still searching for him, whispering his name. Padding down the hall leading east, she frowned. It was a part of the house she hadn't investigated, assuming it simply led to an exit. She advanced slowly. Slivers of gray light passed through slats in a pair of tall doors, like silver bars on the floor, a wider wedge of light bouncing off the opposite wall from the half open doors.

It beckoned her, the rich scent of flowers filling her senses and she extinguished the candle, setting it on the floor as she approached.

She slipped passed and froze, her gaze quickly taking in the night faded colors of flowers and scrubs encased by high stone walls. A spreading tree grew like a giant in the far left corner. The soft trickle of water broke the silence. It was like another place, so set apart from the dusty ranch. Moonlight gleamed white off a small stone path and she stepped, cool slate beneath her feet.

She squinted, searching the perimeter.

Then she saw him. Tears immediately filled her eyes, his heartache reaching out to squeeze the breath from her lungs. *I did this.* He was sitting lengthwise on a stone bench, his back braced on the wall, one long leg over the edge, the other bent and bracing his arm. He stared down at something in his hands, looking desolate. The moonlight dipped and waved over his shiny dark hair, cast his bare chest in shadows and she could see that the top button of his trousers were open against his washboard stomach. It made her insides lurch.

And as if he sensed her presence, his head jerked up.

"Tori?" Stunned and wondering, the sight of her kept him rooted to the bench. He tossed the flower aside.

She wiped at her wet cheeks with the back of her hand, almost angrily and took a step, coming into the full glow of moonlight.

"I, ah, I—Oh God, Chris," a soft wail, needy, pleading and Chris felt as if someone just scooped a chunk out of his heart.

She took a hesitant step.

He slid half off the bench, one knee on the stone tablet, a bare foot sinking into the soft ground. But she stood there, looking like heaven and clutching the folds of her robe.

"I know you're angry with me—"

"No, I'm not."

"But—"

"I'm not. I should never have pressured you like that. It was selfish. I can't expect you to give up your entire world. I can't make you choose. I won't."

He thought he saw her nod and felt his chest bite like a mighty vise around his heart. So. She's come to end it now, he thought.

"I went to the . . . doorway."

"I know." He stepped away from the bench, then stilled, closing his fists in effort not to take her into his arms. "I thought you had left me."

Wildly, she shook her head, her hand out as if to touch him across the distance. He heard her breath catch in her throat as she tried to force out the words, words he knew would destroy him.

"Can you forgive me for hurting you?"

"Yes," came without pause and the hammering in his blood intensified. Hope surged unexpectedly and he swallowed, a gravelly lump jamming in his throat. "What are you saying?"

Her lips trembled, her voice scarcely a whisper. "I love you."

Chris thought he'd never breathe again. Then he did.

"I love you and I can't go back. I won't. I don't care if Becket pays here or there, and if you don't say something I'm going to—to—"

"Punch me?"

She shrugged uneasily. "It's a start."

"I love you," he said with every cell of emotion tangling inside him. "Come to me, so I can show you." The words were snapped off as she slammed against him, nearly knocking him off his feet. His arms instantly enveloped her, crushing her to his long length and they sank to their knees on the ground.

"I love you so much," she whispered into his ear and Chris felt the sky open and shower them with warmth. She plowed her fingers into his hair, making him look at her. "So much it hurts sometimes."

"I know." His throat worked. "Me too."

"I need you, Chris. I would die in my century and I'd rather live in yours, with you."

His hands slid over her spine, rough and seeking and she held his face in her hands, devouring his mouth until he couldn't stand it another moment.

"Oh Jesus, Tori," he gasped. With both hands he smoothed her hair from her face, searching her eyes. "What about Becket?"

Uncertainty skittered across her face. "You're the law here. He's your problem."

"But you've worked so hard, waited all this time."

"I won't risk taking him back, Chris." A determined glint flickered in her gold eyes. "I won't. I'll lose too much."

His tone turned desperate. "I don't want you to regret this."

"Never." She gripped his arms. "I was scared," she confessed softly. "Hell, I'm still scared. But not enough to risk going through the window for him. Not if it costs me you."

"Maybe we could—"

She covered his lips with her fingers. "It's too unstable. I could see it even in the dark. What if I were caught on the other side?"

"God wouldn't be that cruel." He opened his mouth, sipping at her fingertip.

Her voice was thready as his tongue rasped over her skin. "We'll think of something." In the dark he kissed her palm, her wrist, urging her arm around his neck. "I know I'm a bit slow on the uptake—" he opened her robe and the tight tips of her breast grazed his chest as she breathed. "But—" she swallowed "—what we have *here* is too priceless."

"You don't have to convince me." His hands skated up her body from her naked knees to her ribs.

"Lucky thing, huh?"

His thumbs brushed across the lush cushion of her breast, eliciting a ragged almost soundless gasp.

"You scared the life out of me."

Regret in her eyes. "I'm sorry."

"I'm still not over it."

"What can I do to help you see things my way?"

"You're a damned stubborn woman, Victoria." He tried to sound irritated and failed, coming more like a compliment.

"Well . . . yes."

"And so ferociously determined." His thumbs moved back and forth, avoiding her nipples and he glanced down to watch them pearl and bud for him. "With great legs."

"So you keep saying."

Slowly he dipped his head. "And lovely plump breasts."

"Oh God, Chris that feels so good," she groaned when he closed his lips around her nipple.

"And deliciously vocal," he said, taking the other in the same slow laving fashion.

"You like vocal?" She watched him taste her.

"Um-hmm." He had her in his mouth, then he opened wider, taking more of her.

"Oh, Chrriiss."

His lips curved as he dampened a trail to her mouth, holding her with the restraint of a man driven to madness and brushed the robe off her shoulders, dragging it from her arms and baring her in moonlight. Then he stood and peeled his pants down over his hips, loving that she watched every part of him revealed.

"God, you are so beautiful," she said, her hand gliding up the back of his thighs, finding sensitive spots and caressing him. He knelt close and let his gaze move over her, the silver light gliding off her breasts and thighs. He reached, closing his hands over them, darkness shutting out the light and moving in slow circles across her soft skin. Her head tilted back and she moaned with pleasure.

"I love you."

She looked into his dark eyes shadowed by the night. "I've always known that, I think."

"It scared you." A statement, even as his arm slipped around her waist to pull her flush to his naked body. The contact made her gasp. He was like a smoldering fire.

"I've never been loved like this, Chris."

"And you never will again."

Tears threatened as she smiled and felt the lines of his face, brushed at the shaggy locks of black hair at his temples. This man was everything to her. This man had given her all she'd missed and lost, tenderness, love, respect and a family to love again. And when his mouth covered hers she felt a tinge of uncertainty and sought to ease it.

"I'm not leaving, ever. I love you. I love Swift Arrow and the marshal and I'm *in* love with you."

Emotions strangled in his throat. "Oh God, Tori. I feel like I've been waiting all my life for this moment." He kissed her softly, whispering against the curve of her mouth, "And I want to savor it."

He kissed her softly, trembling, almost frightened the moment would shatter, then it grew stronger deeper and she gripped his shoulders, his kiss driving her back over his arm. With strength and tenderness born in love, he lowered her to the ground, the crush of sweet cool grass draping them in fragrance.

Chris reached beyond her and plucked a flower, dragging it over her cheek, the seam of her lips and she closed her eyes trustingly as he let the soft velvet petals tease her skin. He swirled it over her nipple and her lips parted in a soft sigh, across her tight stomach and her muscles flexed, then up her long thigh to the dark tuft glistening with moisture and she opened like the bloom, turning to him, touching him.

Her hands offered pleasure, smoothing lightly over his muscled chest, the bend of his hip, stroking him again from sleek
spine to corded thigh.

"I love touching you," she whispered. "To feel this kind
of power and know you are the gentlest man I've ever met."

Chris smiled and gathered her into his arms, adoring that
she wrapped him in her body, shielding him when he wanted
to shield her. Then she kissed him, a slow thick kiss, outlining
his lips with her tongue, stroking his teeth, then sinking into
his mouth with a possession he reveled in. Victoria was his,
in every way. He could feel it in her as if he shared her thoughts,
her breath, so infinitely warm and giving, felt it in her touch,
a gentle glide across his skin, all of his skin.

Gone, this night, was the frantic rush of desire, the heated
passion that rent them open with explosive power. In its place
was tenderness, patience and neverending love. He led, she
followed, in touch and taste of their bodies, saying more in
this moment than they could in words.

She loved him with her soul. She'd opened it countless times
to him, but this time she let him walk inside. And as he slid
over her, she opened for him again, her soft touch guiding his
warm hard flesh into the damp folds of her femininity.

He sank smoothly, deeply, and their sighs were of complete-
ness, her body closing around him and holding him when he
was most vulnerable. Chris gazed down at her, brushing her
hair from her cheek as her arms slipped around his waist. For
long moments they simply stared. A single tear formed at the
corner of her eye, hovering on the edge and he kissed the spot,
drinking it, drinking the essence of Victoria.

"We share the same heart, Cougar-Who-Walks-Like-A-
Woman," he whisper into her ear. "Do you feel us beat as
one?"

"Yes." And she did. His chest pressed snugly to her breasts,
their heartbeats pounded in perfect sync. "And I never want
to live without you."

He withdrew and her breath shuddered softly into the moisture of his mouth. His arousal was thicker, warmer inside her as he pushed into her tight sheath, his torso braced on his forearms, his hands spreading her dark golden hair over the ground. He left her and slid smoothly home. Eyes locked, he saw his loving in her eyes, heard it in the short breaths escaping her lips, felt it in her body grasping him back again and again. She chanted his name, in his native tongue, told him she loved him, would always love him, even when she walked the spirit road. And Chris loved her more, for understanding him, for taking the time to learn, for giving it to him when he needed it most.

Then she offered him more of her, digging her heels into the earth, her hips undulating up to greet his long smooth thrusts. His gaze never left her, hers sinking into the fathomless eyes where legends were made, where native son and white man blended and formed into honor and gentle understanding and all that was good. Victoria didn't think she could love him more, but each moment that passed, each time he filled her, she felt her heart expand and explore all there was of him.

She never wanted it to end. She wanted more.

"Wrap around me," he whispered as their pace quickened. "Ahh, yes," he breathed when she did. "I love it when you do that." His words teased her lips, her arms holding him snugly.

"Chris—" she gasped. "Oh, Chris."

"I can feel your pleasure," he growled darkly. "Every muscle wrenching with me, around me." She whimpered against his mouth, her kiss hungry and wet. "Yes, that's it, yes," he coaxed. "Let me feel you drench me."

He thrust long and solid and they fused like bronze and gold, separate in touch, together in heart. Time ceased for them, stretching the moment with unearthly pleasure as they pushed and shuddered against and into each other.

His body throbbed helplessly inside her and she sheltered him, accepting him, trembling in his embrace as swell after raging swell surrounded them in a mist of exquisite pleasure.

Midnight clouds shifted, spreading silver moonlight across them like a blanket of warmth, covering them. And within the fragrance and sounds of the darkness, they whispered forever love.

Chapter Thirty-Four

Before dawn, Chris proposed and she accepted.

Before dawn, he carried her through the house to his bed and made love to her again until she was breathless and exhausted and sleeping in his arms.

And, at dawn, they were discovered slumbering peacefully, wearing nothing but silly smiles in their dreams.

Abigale and Randel exchanged a look, then focused on the sleeping couple.

"Is this what you envisioned?"

"With the racket that was coming from here last night, aye."

Randel's lips twitched and he stared down at the tray in his hands. "I suppose I should prepare for two."

"Aye." She looked at him, enjoying the laughter in his eyes. "Aye, for two."

His gaze narrowed on her. "What have you in mind, Abigale?"

"To see them wed properly."

"Ahh, a compromising situation."

" 'Tis for the best, they'll see."

"We already do," came from the opposite side of the room.

The tray rattle in Randel's hands and Abigale looked bug-eyed at Chris.

Against his bare chest, Victoria stirred, her eyes still closed. "I love you," she whispered, the words loud in the still room.

Abigale smiled so hard tears came to her eyes.

Chris dropped a kiss to Victoria's forehead and told her he loved her. Randel cleared his throat, blushing down to his starched collar.

Victoria moaned dreamily, her hand sliding beneath the sheets and Chris flinched, then gently shook her awake.

Lazily, she opened her eyes and smiled. "Hey, Tonto."

"Good morning, love." He couldn't resist kissing her. "We have company."

She blinked, instantly alert.

He nodded to the doorway and she slowly turned her head. "Oh, shit." She sank beneath the covers, dragging it over her head. Chris chuckled softly and she punched him.

"This isn't funny, you rat."

"Nay, 'tis not." Abigale marched across the room, grabbing up Victoria's robe and holding it out. Chris nudged her and Victoria lowered the sheet, then took the robe, mumbling thanks and tossing him a why-didn't-you-wake-me-sooner look.

Abigale flicked a hand, and Randel came to her side. She tried desperately not to smile as she set the tray on Chris's lap with more force than necessary. Being horrified when she knew she had the couple cornered was much too much fun. Then she pulled a chair close and sat, hands folded, her expression grim. And, as if she wasn't about to converse with two naked people in her employer's bed, Randel the goat, slipped out.

"Abigale," Chris began and she waved her hand for silence.

"Abby," Victoria tried, but she received a deadly look that would put the best interrogator to shame.

"You can be wed by next Saturday, at the latest," she said. Victoria knew the woman was on a roll, listing all that had to be done. She glanced at Chris, but he wasn't paying attention to anything except the cleavage of her robe. She closed it to her throat and smiled.

"And an announcement in tomorrow's paper," Abby finished with a firm nod. "That will take care of the gossips, laird kens they'll have fun with this. I'll arrange for everything."

"Okay, sure," Victoria said, then bit into a slice of toast.

Both Chris and Abigale looked at her in shock.

She shrugged. "I'd just as soon do it today."

"Today?" Chris said, then cleared the squeak out of his throat and repeated himself.

She arched a brow, her lips twitching. "Getting cold feet already, Tonto?"

He smiled hugely, full of masculine pride. "Nothing I have gets cold around you, woman." He tipped her head back and kissed her leisurely.

Abigale was still trying to swallow her astonishment. That was far too easy. Then she shook herself and stood.

"Dinna be letting the wee laddie see you like this until the wedding and you two willna have the chance to be—" She waved at the vicinity of the bed and what lay beneath the covers. "Cavorting until then. Is that clear?" She sent Chris a penetrating glare that looked distinctly like his mother's. "If you're mother knew I let this happen, she'd have me heart on a platter."

"You didn't let anything happen, Abigale," he said as sternly as he could with Victoria's hand creeping up his thigh. "And send a telegram, for Hunter and Sable, and my parents. Tell them if they can't make it, the wedding goes on without them."

Abigale threw up her hands, totally confused, yet pleased. She marched past Randel, who was delivering a second coffee cup, and the butler hardly looked at either of them, but Victoria could see the trace of a smile. He left as quickly as he came.

"Chris?" He was nibbling at her throat, pushing the robe aside. "What about Becket?" She scooted lower for better access.

"I really don't want to invite him, sweetheart."

She smirked, reaching past him for another slice of toast. "Again, this is not funny."

He heard her crunch, felt a sprinkle of crumbs against his

cheek and he sighed, giving up on his seduction and taking the tray. She snatched a slice of bacon before he set it on the floor.

She ate, waiting for his response.

"We need his journal. We also need the murder weapon."

"He isn't likely to have it on him. You think it's in his office or his bedroom?"

Chris nodded. "He hasn't left there since Vel's death, until you showed up in town." His expression and tone told her he didn't like that one bit. "He'll attend the picnic. We'll have to wait until then to search."

"I'll do it," she said and he shook his head slowly. "A bounty hunter has rights you don't."

"He'll notice you and I have reasonable cause."

Her brow rose.

"He was the last person to see Velvet alive," he ticked off his fingers, "she was *in* his office the night she vanished, and there are scuff marks on the windowsill and threshold, the carpet is cleaner in one area." He frowned thoughtfully. "Probably dirty by now, though."

"You aren't going to inform him, are you?" It was a stupid question. If they did, he'd head for the wall of time, and they both knew it.

"We have to make him believe the investigation is the last thing on our minds."

He slung his arm around her waist and pulled her closer, shifting over her and she spread for him, opening her robe and letting him fill her in one smooth stroke.

"I don't think we'll have a problem, do you?"

"Oh God, Tori," he gasped as she drew her hips back and surged against him. "I can't think of anything else."

"Good, then you won't mind if I flirt with him."

He stilled, instantly tense.

"He has a royal *misguided* case of the hots for me, Chris. What better way to get close?"

"You're mine, Tori, and by tonight, everyone in this town will know it. How is that going to look?"

She stroked his hair from his brow, her fingertips erasing

the harsh lines of his face. "I won't have to say or do anything, Chris. He's already suspicious. And he doesn't go for single women. Married with children," she said, then smirked to herself. "It would be me and Lucky he'd focused on, regardless if he wanted to get me in bed."

Chris heaved a sigh, dropping his head to her shoulder. How he could even concentrate with the feel of her body pulsing around his erection, one he'd had since he'd woken with her lovely body draped around him, was beyond him. But he couldn't argue her point. She knew Becket better than he did.

"All right," he mumbled into the flesh of her throat, kissing her there, his hands slipping beneath the sheet to where their bodies joined. "I agree. But—" He stroked her slick feminine flesh with painstaking slowness. "—you will remain armed and promise not to invite trouble until the picnic?"

She was quiet, her breathing quick.

"Tori?"

His finger brushed the bead of her sex and she gasped, "Yes, yes! We do this together—" His fingers moved heavily, languidly. "—your way, your laws, your time."

His grinned, full of his power over her. Eyes closed, her lower lip was caught between her teeth, her body undulating to his every touch. "Our way, Tori."

He left her body and drove back with a hard thrust. "Our time."

She smiled up at him, her gold eyes dark with desire and love. "Yeah, ours."

They were seen around town, dining out, always touching each other and twice, scandalously kissing in public. During the day, Lucky was often with them, and most folks didn't recognized the orphaned child. Some commented that Lucky looked like Victoria, and she loved that, because Chris and she planned to adopt him. Lucky was thrilled at the prospect, calling her Momma as if to try the title on for size. Although each time she heard it was like a little arrow into her heart, she would never begrudge him, nor understand the resilience of children—especially when he asked for brothers, and soon, please. The townspeople gossiped, mostly about her, but Victoria was too happy to let their useless comments bother her—until they defamed Chris. Then, the ladies of Silver Rose got a stinging taste of her twentieth century tongue.

"That was marvelous," Jenna said, walking away from the red-faced group. "Now what exactly does, 'bust his chops for a pack of left-wing, narrow-minded yuppies' mean, Victoria?"

Victoria spared her a glance, then let her anger go. "Ask me later."

"You'll tell about—" Her forehead wrinkled briefly. "—A three fifty-seven magnum and where it belongs, then too?"

Victoria had to laugh. "Sure, girlfriend. Now I have a date."

Jenna sighed. "You two are becoming so predictable," she murmured sourly.

"Look who's talking." She nodded to somewhere beyond and Jenna glanced around until she saw her husband, then flung a hasty good-bye as she raced, in a very unladylike fashion, across the street. Reid looked different, Victoria thought, watching him swing Jenna off the ground. Less intimidating in jeans and a dark shirt. But no matter what the *ladies* (which was debatable in Victoria's opinion) of this town thought of the female doctor, her husband made them sigh with envy. Reid was a looker. Of course, she thought as she headed to the jail, not as fine as her fiance. She paused on the threshold of his office, the realization striking her square in the chest.

Married, in a few days.

And when he saw her, he pulled his boots off the desk and stood, his eyes locking with hers. "You look scared."

She shook her head, depositing a basket on Noble's desk, then crossing to Chris's and laying out their lunch. He caught her arm, stopping her and she met his gaze.

"I can't understand sometimes why I got so lucky to find you."

"Ahh, darlin'—" He slid his hand to her waist, squeezing

gently. "I'm the lucky one." His lips brushed lightly over hers, drinking in her sigh.

"Another debatable subject."

He frowned, confused.

"Never mind. Sit, eat." Chris had consumed half his lunch before coming up for air. "Christ, you can sure pack it away, Swift." Victoria sat on the edge of his desk, eating a sandwich. She offered him another. "You'd think you were active . . . all night."

He scowled, catching her meaning. "With watchdog Abigale around? I bearly get to kiss you good night."

It was frustrating and fun, and they both knew it.

He sank lower into his chair, propping his feet on the desk again, his gaze traveling over her loose hair, her new beige Stetson hanging against her back, the raw hide string caught at her throat, and then past her cream colored blouse to her skirt.

"Don't make faces—it's a compromise."

His gaze lingered on the split skirt of deer skin molding her hips and buttocks. "Shows too much of your figure."

It was cute, his possessiveness. And she had the perfect ammunition to defuse it. Leaning closer she said, "In my century, women wear skirts cut above the knee." She knew why. Gowns and even these things were hot as hell. "Or shorter."

He gave her his well-honed that's-indecent look, and she smiled. He didn't.

"Jenna talked you into this, didn't she?" The women had spent a considerable amount of time together, and though Chris hoped friends would make her feel more comfortable in his time, Jenna had a way of stirring trouble.

"I preferred jeans." Victoria wouldn't give up her friend, not even to Chris.

His gaze lifted to hers. "But?"

"I didn't want the local tongues slinging any more trash at you, because of me."

His expression sharpened. "Have they?"

"Yes." She held up a hand, warding off the spew of Cheyenne curses she could never understand. "But I can take care of it. My tongue gets a good sharpening."

"Bet you left them confused and not knowing if they'd been insulted or not," he said on a grin, coming to his feet and leaning out to take a bite of her sandwich. She waved at his meal, unfinished.

"Yours tastes better."

She leaned close, a hair's breath from his mouth. "*You* taste better."

A dull red crept up his neck, and he glanced around. No one was within earshot and she laughed lightly.

"God, I love shocking you." Her smile widened and she laid her hand on his chest, feeling his heart beat quicken. She let it drift lower.

"Don't. I can't take it, Tori. I swear." He looked her up and down, his breath hissing out through his clenched teeth. "You keep teasing me like that and our wedding night will be over too damn quick."

"That's okay." Her palm slid to fit over his hip and he caught it before she moved lower. "I've got a lifetime to frustrate you."

Chris searched her face her warm, gold eyes and he was unmaned by the emotions sinking through him like hot mulled wine. "I love you, Victoria Mason."

"I know," she whispered against his lips, cupping his jaw. "I know."

He kissed her heavily, then drew back, restraint in every line of his face.

"Jenna and you have fun?" He grabbed his sandwich, biting into it before he bit into her smooth throat.

"Fun?" She rolled her eyes. "I watched her take a bullet out of Buddy. A frequent customer, I'm told." She started to eat the sandwich, then tossed it aside. Chris apparently had no problem eating. "Now—" she folded her arms. "Why didn't you tell me you owned all this land," her wave encompassed the town, "and were a lawyer," she said with mock disgust. "A Harvard grad, no less."

"Jenna has a big mouth."

"Jenna thought I knew."

He groaned, slipping his arm around her waist and kissing his apology. "I'm sorry. I bought the land years ago, and it sat untouched until someone discovered silver. I sold off parts when anyone wanted it."

"And why did you walk away from your law career?

"I found I preferred stopping the trouble before it got to court. People stay alive that way."

She touched his jaw, wondering what in her life made her deserve such an incredible man. "I love you, Chris."

He felt unhinged whenever she said it and he tightened his hold on her, pressing her breasts firmly against his chest. And kissing her deeply.

"Jeez-zoo, Peabody was right. You two are the kissin'est pair."

They broke apart. "Hi Noble," she said still looking at Chris, then faced the mountainman. "Ah, Miss Abigale asked me to give you that." She nodded to the basket on his desk. He smiled brightly, then tried to hide it as he peeked inside the folds of linen.

"Dang that woman—!"

"What? Not what you expected?" She exchanged a glance with Chris, who appeared totally confused. "She said you'd understand."

"Oh, I do, all right." He lifted out a handful of chicken legs, fried chicken legs and dumped them on the linen. "She's mad at me."

Victoria saw no significance behind chicken and biscuits. "How would you know? You can't have seen her lately."

Noble's face flushed. "Shoot," he muttered, then snatched up a chuck of meat and bit into it. It melted in his mouth. If she were really, mad she'd have burned it or spiced it so hot he'd be running for the horse trough.

Chris folded his arms over his chest and tossed Noble's own words back in his lap. "You know, for a man who's had three wives, you don't know beans about women."

"Dang, I guess not." He looked at his boss. "I need the afternoon off, Chris."

The marshal nodded, trying not to laugh. Noble looked so out of sorts and confused just then. Bet he doesn't know what he did, either, he thought as his deputy marshal jammed his hat on his head and left, but not before filling his pockets with Abigale's chicken.

It wasn't just a church picnic, a *social,* whatever the hell that was. It was a no-holds-barred fair, with livestock auctions, cakes and pie sales, hardware and crafts on display, and even a target range to test out the newest Smith and Wesson. Sides of beef were spitted and turned by eager children and the smell was heavenly. Cowboys galore walked with their bow-legged strides and girls, dressed to the nines, were out to impress one into asking them to dance. The dancing is where Victoria was stretching it, trying desperately not to step on Chris's toes. He winced a few times and she apologized, but she was way *way* out of her element in this.

And it annoyed the hell out of her that he found it all extremely amusing.

"It's just that you're so damn good at everything else you do, I guess I imagined a dance would be easy."

"Tell that to your toes."

"They'll survive," he said, spinning her effortlessly across the wood dance floor. He felt her stiffen in his arms and turned her again to see the cause, yet he knew.

Becket stood on the outskirts of the spectators. Liquor wasn't served at the fair until the evening, and then only beer, but he seemed to be waiting for night and profit. Elegantly dressed in midnight blue, he was the only man wearing a full coat and tie. He didn't fit in, didn't even try, Chris thought. He seemed to enjoy hovering on the edge of life.

Possessively, Chris held her closer, knowing he didn't need to stake his claim, but doing it just the same.

Victoria eyed him, aware of the direction of his gaze. "You could kill with that look, Chris."

"His smugness makes me wish I could."

"Come on, chill out," she rubbed her hand up and down his back. "The auction's going to start and you have horses to sell." He mumbled something unintelligible. "I've never seen an auction, Chris." He looked at her, a little stunned. "Nor a fair, nor got up close and personal with a cow."

He smiled softly. "Just chickens?"

"And if you think cows stink wait until you smell chicken sh—"

"Victoria!"

She laughed and onlookers stared, watching them move through the crowd together, sampling pastries, trying on hats, Chris insisting she be measured for a decent pair of boots. Custom made boots, she thought, realizing the fortune they'd cost her in her time, and fiendishly enjoying the murmurs of outrage when he bought her a pistol and holster from the gunsmith.

"I know the rules," she said, then tucked it in their basket where Noble and Abigale sat, Noble trying desperately to make up with Abigale and tripping all over himself in the process. Abigale was lapping it up, the sly smile she sent Victoria speaking volumes.

Lucky raced up, his cheeks covered in white cream and she wiped his face, kissed it, then took his hand.

They reached the livestock pens just as one of Chris's horses was led in. The auctioneer began, and for the life of her, Victoria couldn't see who was bidding, yet the price kept rising.

"The army usual buys most of my stock, but these are—"

"Beautiful. God, they look like Caesar!" There were three, each a shade lighter toward brown, one was only black until the handler brought him into the light, then the reddish tint of his coat shone.

"They're his boys."

She cast him a side glance. "And you look like a proud grampa."

He chuckled, his forearms braced on the rail, watching her admire the horses, pointing out features to Lucky who was perched on the rail between them. Chris leaned around the boy and whispered, "Do you want him?"

She snapped a look at him, then shook her head. "No, you could get good money for him, Chris."

Chris waved the handler over.

"Chris, no," she whispered, pinching his forearm.

He caught her hand and spoke to the handler. The young man glanced at Victoria, grinned, then led the horse into the paddock. She rounded on Chris and he caught her shoulders, effectively silencing her.

"I'd sleep better knowing you were on the best mount I had, darlin'."

"No one has ever given me anything like that." Without words, Chris knew she hadn't received a gift of any kind in a long time, the necklace hinted at that, the horse only confirmed it. And the uncommon sheen in her gold eyes brought him to his knees.

"Thank you, oh, thank you," she whispered, and in front of the entire town she threw her arms around his neck and kissed him. He sank into her, forgetting the scandal they consistently caused and only feeling the heat of her body against his. Lucky giggled. Several people cleared their throats noisily and they pulled apart. Chris noticed the area was strangely silent. Victoria did, too, and together they scanned the crowd of mostly men. Grins popped through the sea of faces like bursting bubbles before a sudden cheer shook the wood and startled the horses.

"Your face is red," Lucky pointed out.

"Horrible, huh?" Victoria said and Lucky launched into her open arms.

"Well now," the auctioneer bellowed. *"You all* know the marshal expects to be paid in dollars for his horseflesh." Laughter erupted and Chris waved to Joquin, trusting him to get a fair price and followed Victoria toward the paddock so she could see her horse. They hadn't moved much beyond the crowd when she stopped. He bumped into her. He followed the direction of her gaze, then casually turned his attention to Lucky when the boy asked to visit a litter of puppies he'd seen.

Victoria kissed his cheek in agreement and Chris warned, "Don't go far," as the child took off running.

"You see him?"

Becket was on the far side of the grounds, but his presence unmistakable, his eyes on Victoria. "Yes," Chris ground out.

"We need the murder weapon or that journal," Victoria said for his ears alone, pausing to examine tack hung up for sale. "And he can't approach me if you're glued to my hip."

"Victoria," he warned, his expression worried.

She faced him, grabbed the edges of his black leather vest and pulled him beyond the edge of the holding pens. Then she pulled him down to meet her face.

"I love you."

He grinned, his breath catching.

"And now that I have you—"

"And my undivided attention—"

"You have to give me some rope."

"To hang yourself?"

She made an irritated sound. Then she kissed him, a thick, wet sexy kiss that drove the air from his lungs and the blood to his groin.

"Now that you can't hover," she said, sliding her hand down his body and cupping him warmly.

She had great hands, he thought, closing his eyes and peeling them from his body. "God save me from twentieth century women."

"Uh-ah, I'm one of a kind, buster."

He opened his eyes. "I love you so much."

"I know, but I'm *still* a bounty hunter and I have to socialize, give him an opening."

"If you reject him—"

"He'll try to kill me."

His fists clenched and he muttered something vile in Cheyenne. "This is dangerous."

"And our job."

He stared at her for a long moment, absorbing her vibrance like strong wine. He could never stop her from being who she was, not because they loved, but it didn't keep him from feeling helpless.

"Go partner." He inclined his head toward the crowd. "Go on."

She took a step away. He caught her arm, pulling her back for one last kiss, putting all his love into it.

"Keep me in your sights for as long as you can," she whispered before walking away.

The tremor in her voice told him she was scared.

Good.

Fear made you cautious.

It brought little comfort, for when he rode back to town to find the journal, she was on her own.

Chapter Thirty-Five

She could feel his eyes on her as if he were touching her and it made her flesh shift and creep along her bones.

Licking her lips for the hundredth time, Victoria refused to look in his direction, concentrating on the little boy rolling in the dirt with puppies lapping at his face as if he were made of chocolate. She smiled, kneeling, tickling him and he suddenly latched on to her neck and dragged her down into the confusion of doggie breath and red Colorado dust. People nearby laughed softly, some huffed at her *display* and she resisted the urge to read them the riot act about loving a special kid like Lucky. Instead, she enjoyed him, the feel of him in her arms making her chest tight with need. And she realized again how much she stood to lose.

Before, she was agonizingly alone and it suited her job best. The risks were to herself, and the waiting and pain left to no one. But now she had everything, everything she desired and dreamed about and Becket stood in the way.

Lucky cupped her face. "You fun, Miss Toria."

"You are fun," she corrected and he nodded and repeated. She kissed the top of his head, settling him close and letting the brown and white puppies race around him, nipping and barking. The Baretta in her skirt pocket dug into her thigh.

"I likes dem."

"I like *them*," she schooled and covertly glanced around for Chris. Up until fifteen minutes ago, she knew exactly where he was, but now he was gone. Immediately, she searched the crowd for Becket, her gaze casually skipping right past him to Noble and Abigale, who were dancing. She smiled at the couple, recognizing that Abigale was no longer making Noble suffer for not visiting her.

Rising to her feet, she dusted off her doe skin skirt and pulled Lucky to his feet. He pouted and she sent him a warning look. "We'll ask Chris if you can have one. *If,*" she stressed when his face immediately brightened, "if Mister O'Brian wants to give one up."

Lucky hopped from one foot to the other. "He does, I asked."

"I'll speak to him."

"Miss Toria." There was a whine to his voice, a higher pitch, and she struggled with patience considering her nerves were tight as wire and Lucky was playing right into Becket's hands. She didn't want anything to happen without Chris near. He was her backup, and it would be at least an hour before he'd return. The fair was beyond the edge of town, partially in the shade of the forest, and even if he raced back, which he wouldn't because it would draw attention, it would take him at least ten minutes.

Drawing Lucky away from the dogs, she approached a man shaving ice off a huge block, then scooping it into folded paper cups before pouring syrup over the top. She bought two, handing one to Lucky and thinking this kid was going to be on a sugar high for a week after cream cakes and penny candy.

Children called to him and he looked stunned, then wary, first glancing at her, then to the boys. His expression revealed his insecurity and the memories of how he'd been treated by this town.

"You don't have to go," she whispered, dropping her hand

on his shoulder with a gentle weight. He looked up, biting his lower lip.

"But can I?"

"Sure," she said and he gulped down the melting ice, crammed the sticky paper in her hand and took off.

Victoria watched, gaging whether they were going to make him look foolish or allow him into the game as a true player in the foot race. Some of the boys ribbed each other, snickering at Lucky. It set her teeth on edge. Lucky lined up with the rest and the reverend counted off "on your mark get set" and Victoria's stomach tightened as he dropped the white scarf.

Lucky didn't seem to know what happened, the other kids were running and she realized he'd expected the word go, or even a gun shot. But instantly he knew and ran. *Boy, could he run,* she thought, her heart leaping hard as he sprinted like a deer. And he was in the running now, keeping up with the others twice his size and she ran to the sidelines, to the finish line. Sweet beaded beneath her clothes.

Come on, baby, show them. Show them you can do it.

He saw her and smiled, and she felt the surge of power in him, the pride he'd lost over the isolated lonely years and he pushed ahead, air hissing through his teeth, his arms pumping like mad. Victoria ran to the finish line, oblivious to the cheers, oblivious to her own screams of encouragement and thinking, *I wish Chris could see this.*

Then he crossed the finish line first, straight into her arms, into her heart and she swung him around and round and laughed and told him she was so proud of him.

Deputies and Noble patted him on the back, passing him around like a prize, and Lucky beamed, smiling like she'd never seen him smile before and tears came to her eyes as the other children approached and congratulated him. She watched him skip along with his new friends and Victoria knew a profound and joyously sweet feeling of victory for more than just a race.

Someone offered her a handkerchief.

She looked up to see a deputy, Seth, standing close.

"He's like a wildfire."

"More like a stampede, don't you think?" Seth chuckled.

"I never knew he could run like that." She wiped her eyes, waving to Lucky.

"He had to run or get belted," Seth said.

Victoria stilled, slowly lifting her gaze.

Seth back stepped, intimidated by the rage in her eyes. "It's why we could never find him. He stole to eat, but never got caught. He runs like the dickens."

"He'll never have to steal again," she told him.

"I know, ma'am. The boss has been trying to get him to live with him since we first saw him, but it's you that kept him there."

"I appreciate that, Seth. What are you doing here, not that I mind, but weren't you on duty?"

"Change of shift."

She leaned closer. "Did you see Chris?"

He frowned. "I thought he was here?"

He must still be in the office, she thought.

"I came to deliver this." He offered a telegram and shrugged. "Hell if I know what it means."

She took it, an uneasy feeling rippling over her spine.

Chris jimmied the lock and the drawer sprung. He searched carefully, but found nothing, replaced each article as it was and went to the bedroom. He dug beneath the mattress, then retucked it. He opened every drawer, shoving his hand beneath crisp folded clothes, then frustrated, he turned to the wardrobe. He quietly pulled items out of the cabinet—the carefully placed boots ranging in colors, the clothes nattily pressed and hooked. He accidently jolted against the door and stilled, listening for sounds from upstairs, from the girls. The saloon was empty, closed for the afternoon and Chris moved more cautiously. Running his hand along the seams of the wood, he felt for a loose spot, a crack or a break. It was a gut feeling, and he pressed his fingers against the wood.

Then he felt it, the give, the spring and with his knife he pried up the edge. A fractured sound pierced the quiet like a bone breaking before he slid his hand beneath. His fingers touched cloth, the firmness of a book spine and he grabbed the journal, removing it and immediately turned toward the light. He flipped to the last entry, a quick glance telling him he'd rather not read the details of so many deaths, and let his gaze scan the perfectly formed writing.

I can honestly say I am annoyed that the lawmen are doing nothing to find me. It takes the joy from the kill. Almost. None would know I didn't mean to take Velvet. But I was beyond need then, that ugly feasting in my head pushing me over the edge. I wept for her. It was the one time I regretted.

But as he read on, Chris felt the color leave his face.

There is something defiant in her, in her eyes, in they way she deals with these soppingly docile folk. Like me, she does not belong. And I love her so deeply I will go mad if I cannot take her with me.

Chris felt the blood rush to his feet, then skate up to his heart. It beat loudly in his ears.

His prey was selected.

And it was Tori.

Victoria looked down at the telegram, but the writing was faint in the dimming light and she moved closer to a torch. It was addressed to Chris.

Have followed up on cases specified. STOP. *Found three more.* STOP. *Similarities are concurrent.* STOP. *Dates of crimes begin over three years prior.* STOP.

The sender listed date after date, the victims names and occupation. Wife and mother.

Her hands shook. Sudden perspiration dripped down her temples.

He's been here before.

Somebody slammed into her, jolting her from her thoughts

and she swallowed, sinking to one knee and forcing a smile for Lucky.

"See what I won! See!" He waved a fat blue ribbon in her face.

"Way to go, pal!" she said automatically. "Too cool."

Instantly, she felt eyes on her, scraping her face like a knife. In half a heartbeat, she knew she'd made a deadly mistake.

Slowly, she tilted her head and lifted her gaze, staring over the top of Lucky's head. Becket stared back through sharp, narrowed blue eyes from a short distance away.

Time was up.

He knew she was a traveler.

Chapter Thirty-Six

Slowly, she stood.

"Give this to Noble and find Chris. Now, Seth."

Seth recognized her fear and his gaze followed hers to Algenon Becket. The deputy's features tightened and he took the telegram, hesitating to leave her.

"I'll be all right," she murmured quickly. "Go."

He moved off.

Victoria bent and whispered to Lucky. He glanced around, searching the picnickers for Abigale and reluctantly stepped away. Victoria stood still, her breathing regulating into calm. It skipped suddenly as he approached her.

"I wouldn't."

He caught Lucky as he passed, and the boy looked up at Becket, wide-eyed and panicked.

He's hurt him before, she realized. Damn the bastard. So much for her theory about him protecting the kids.

"Let him go or you're dead," she whispered, her hand closing around her gun. "I can put a bullet between those baby blues before you move an inch."

Around them more torches and lanterns were being lit to

stave off the approaching twilight, beer kegs tapped with a cheer and a swarm of thirsty cowboys. Music colored the air with a festive twangy reel, but to the townspeople, who hardly gave them a glance, they appeared to be two people casually conversing.

"Hardly," he said and his gaze dropped meaningfully. And hers followed.

Oh God. His arm was slung around Lucky's shoulder yet in the broadness of his palm was a small knife, tucked close enough to the boy's throat to scare her.

Lucky didn't even realize it, looking up at her trustingly. From the angle of their bodies, not a soul could see it, but her.

She forced a smile to her face.

"Let him go."

"Lift your hand out," he said softly. "And give it to me."

She did. She wouldn't risk a mark on Lucky for anything and handed Becket the gun. He slipped it discreetly inside his coat.

Victoria considered screaming, flinging accusations and getting a wall of people to surround him. But that put innocents at risk, and she'd never forgive herself if anyone was hurt.

This was between Becket and herself. No one else.

"Let him go."

He released Lucky and Victoria never took her gaze off the killer as she inclined her head sharply. Lucky ran into the crowd.

"How long?" He stepped closer, touching a hand to the small of her back and urging her around spread blankets and vendors, families and tables laden with food.

"I've been right behind you every step of the way."

Something slipped behind his stiff features, then vanished. "Not close enough."

No, she thought, not enough to keep Velvet alive, but enough to stop him from taking at least one mother from her family.

"Where are we going?"

"To the fall."

She stopped short. "Not a chance in hell." He was so close

she could smell his cologne, see the deadly intent in his eyes, red rimmed with the disease eating at his brain.

"Oh yes," he said smoothly and lifted the cane to his face as if to scratch his chin. With a practice flick, the cane separated at the hilt. "You're mine now, Miss Victoria Mason."

His smile was thin and sinister, showing to everyone who'd look what he hid.

"I'll kill you first," she said with all the anger raging inside her. "And I'll like it."

"Killed many, have you?"

"Not as many as you."

He nodded, as if modest over the accomplishments, then without looking back, as if aware that no one noticed them leave the heaviness of the crowd lingering at the shaded edge of the forest, he caught her arm and pulled her into its denseness.

"He won't make it, you know," he said when she looked at her watch. "He won't have time. We'll be gone, forever."

Absolute terror spirited through her. Not for her life, but for the certainty in his eyes. She tried not to let her fear show, in her voice, her expression. She'd done it a hundred times without failure, why was she losing it now?

Because he knows what you'll risk.

"Go then, I won't stop you."

He glanced beyond her, to the crowd, checking again to see if anyone noticed them. Obviously satisfied, he met her gaze, his perfect lips curled in a soft snarl. He flicked the cane and the casing slid effortlessly free, revealing the blade, the blade that had ended over twenty lives.

"You'll never stop me. No one can."

He smiled that cheesy, thin smile that made her want to do him right there, now, then he pulled her by the shoulder deeper into the forest.

He was taking her back.

He loosened his string tie to bind her hands tightly behind her. She fought and lost but the scratches on his face and a nasty bruise on his lip were worth the back-handed smack across the jaw. But a gun and the stiletto curbed her temper and she waited for another opening, feeling helpless without her hands, without a weapon. She hadn't strapped her knife to her leg as usual, never believing she'd screw things up this bad. Twentieth century slang got her, she mulled disgustedly, wiggling her fingers, trying to stimulate the circulation she was losing to numbness.

They traipsed through the woods, Victoria comfortable and Becket definitely out of sorts. He was used to luxury. And killing. She was aware of the cane, its position behind and to her right, unsheathed and gleaming like a miniature sabre. He could cut her throat with one flick of his wrist, pierce her jugular with a small poke. He could drive it straight to her heart and she'd be helpless to fight him.

She hated the feel of his hands on her shoulder, dirty bloody hands guiding her, even though they were clean and manicured. She tried to move faster and he pulled her back against him. He was aroused and fear crushed through her again and again. He was getting off on holding her hostage. And Victoria knew that she'd endure rape, if it would give it her the opportunity to wound him or get away.

How ironic, she thought, that he'd be the one escorting her through time and not the other way around. Her only comfort was that she suspected there was a lot more on the other side of that sheen of water than he thought.

Or did he?

Would it take him elsewhere? Did *he* have some control over it that she didn't? She needed to know.

Chris shoved the diary into the safe in his office and was about to close the heavy door when he stilled, his gaze on her backpack. She'd asked him to put it in there, the only safe place they agreed, so no one would open it and destroy history. A history, she said would be irrevocably changed with her existence. An unnamed instinct made him grab it and he was about to pull the slide when he heard the steady rapid thunder of hooves.

Someone called his name and before he reached the door, Seth was there.

"Hurry. I think he's going to hurt her."

Chris was on Caesar in an instant, riding hell bent to the end of town, to the fair. The heavy pack hooked over the pommel smacked against Caesar's side and the animal did his ancestors justice as he charged down the wide street. People scattered when they saw him coming. Noble race up, huffing.

"I didn't see her. No one saw her."

Lucky ran to him, crying. "She gone!"

"No, son. No. I'll find her." Chris scooped him up, riding through the crowd. As best he could Lucky told him what happen and Chris could see the blame he was feeling.

"It's not your fault, son."

"But she give him her gun!" Lucky wailed. "So I could go."

Panic skated through Chris, then settled. "And I'd have done it for you too, Luck. She had to. Now I have to go help her."

He assured Lucky he'd bring her back before depositing the boy in Abigale's arms. When he was clear, he jabbed his heels into Caesar's side and the black stallion surged into the forest.

She's still alive, he thought, I can feel her.

"That was your burial ground, wasn't it? For *souvenirs.*"

He gave her a disgusted look and shoved her ahead.

"The stockyard," she prodded.

His smirk said twenty questions wasn't going to make her the light of his life.

"You mean where I killed your man?"

Her insides twisted with rage.

"How did that feel, Victoria?"

She hated the sound of her name on his lips, close to her ear. "About as sickening as your touch."

Angrily, he pushed her.

"You'll never make it, Becket." She caught her balance,

refusing to show a shred of weakness for him to prey on. "I'll see to it."

His sly glance said he doubted. "But I can't leave you here," he said, as if he were telling her it was a lovely evening. "For when I return."

"Chris will kill you on sight."

Becket scoffed, his expression condescending. "He hasn't a clue."

She stopped, casting him a half-lidded stare and gaging his reaction. "He knows everything."

Becket's eyes flared and he dragged her against him. "You stupid *bitch!*" he raged.

"With all that education, I figure you could come up with something better than bitch." She couldn't believe she was so calm and wondered why. "Of course, I told him. How's the leg, by-the-way? Bullet pass through?" He glared down at her, eyes hard and cobalt blue as night. "Scars are imperfections, Algenon."

And if she wanted him to be a powder keg about to explode, she got it.

Viciousness contorted his features, and the stiletto rose slowly as if by a ghostly hand, touching her side, pricking her skin. His fingers dug deeply into her arm as he propelled her forward, but Victoria refused to step further, the distant rumble on the earth coming to her.

Algenon Becket knew he didn't have much time—at least, not in this century. The marshal would kill him if he got close enough, and Becket regretted underestimating the half-breed. He counted that as a minor miscalculation and adjusted his thinking. If she was a cop, then why didn't she approach him before? And when did she tell the marshal her secret? Was she lying? He disregarded the questions to her incessant chattering. Her words were like needles poking in his brain, finding the soft tender spots and gouging him. He tried to block them out and forced her to move. But she was stronger than he imagined, solid, and he had to drag her. His muscles strained.

"Give it up."

"Never." He hated not planning, not having everything choreographed like an intricate dance. And his mind played scenario after scenario. He could kill her now and leave, but he knew time ceased to move on the other side. And he couldn't risk entering the cavern without a plan or protection.

He couldn't think clearly. If only he could just get this bitch to shut up.

"Mommy wouldn't be happy to see her little boy like this." She gave a quick glance at his rumpled clothes, torn where branches had caught. "But, then, she never liked you, did she?"

"Shut up."

"No one likes you."

"I'm going to *enjoy* killing you, Victoria."

Victoria pushed aside the feral pleasure she saw in his face and said, "Not even Vel did. Or Dee. She just wanted to be first lady."

"She loved me, they all did! Even that mouse Clara—"

"*I'm* Clara Murphy, asshole."

Rage scurried up his body, and she could feel it, in the tightening of his grip on his precious weapon, in the flexing of muscles in his too pretty face. She made him look like a fool, even if it was only to himself.

He's going to kill me now, she thought, just as she hoped that rumbling was Caesar.

She needed just one moment . . .

He grabbed her against him, his breath foul and his eyes wide with impatient fury. "Killing you is easier than taking you with me."

"Do it."

He didn't answer.

"Sort of a twist, huh, Ivy League? You need me for a hostage."

He grinned suddenly. "On both sides."

A shield against Chris and a shield against the FBI, she

realized. "Never happen. I'm just one person. Weigh that against the destruction you've caused—" She shrugged, not feeling as confident as she sounded "And I'm an acceptable loss."

His gaze flicked to the forest, then to her and the hoofbeats grew louder, making him tense.

She arched a brow. "Time's up."

"We'll see."

The rustle of branches and underbrush came seconds before Caesar's black head appeared. And in that instant, Victoria drove her knee up into his groin. He flinched and grunted, but didn't fold, and his hold on her arm kept her from losing her balance, kept her from doing any more than turning away.

"Cheating, Victoria?" He used her to steady himself, his face inches from her ear. "I'd have thought you more skilled than that." His voice was a gasp, even as he slung his arm around her neck, slamming her back against his chest. She arched to the pressure in her shoulders.

The horse halted, riderless and simply stared at the pair, a hoof stomping. Becket's head shifted, his gaze straining in the hazy twilight, but he couldn't see the marshal.

But he felt his presence.

Becket tightened his grip, forcing her neck to twist and exposing her throat.

"Shoot him, Chris," she called in a calm voice. "Between the eyes, so it's a clean kill."

"Shut up!" Becket growled, jerking his human shield. "He'll have to shoot through you to do it."

"Don't count on it." She'd die before she let him kill Chris.

"It hardly matters, now does it? You'll be dead before the shot reaches me."

That was true. She could feel the sharpness of the blade on the skin of her throat.

"Hey, Tonto?" Victoria called out, wishing she knew what Chris was planning.

"If you say another word, I'll cut you wide open."

"You know, Ivy League? You're a waste of human tissue."

''He's in the trees,'' Becket said more to himself, then shoved her aside, withdrawing her gun from inside his coat. ''Less clean, but efficient.''

''No!'' Victoria dove.

An arrow whizzed through the air, imbedding in Becket's shoulder, the gun firing as her body caught Becket at the knees. The bullet ripped through her upper arm, the stiletto flying from his grip as he fell.

Becket arched and howled, clutching the wound. Her hands bound, Victoria rolled to her knees, grappling for purchase as he tried to stand. He kicked out, his boot connecting with her jaw. Darkness draped her vision.

Chris dropped from the trees, hitting the ground in a run.

Becket was gone, lost in the shadows of dusk.

Chris slid to his knees and cut the ties at her wrists, then drew her into his arms. ''Tori, Tori?'' Her blood soaked his shirt. ''Talk to me, sweetheart.'' He checked her wound, tearing her sleeve and binding it. His heart didn't start beating until she stirred against him.

''Stop him—'' she gripped his arm. ''He's going to the fall,'' she gasped, shaking off the haze and sitting up.

''He won't get there, not with an arrow in his shoulder.''

She smiled. ''Nice going, Tonto.'' He drew her to her feet. She staggered. ''No, I'm fine.'' He was examining her wound again, a graze really. ''Got a gun?''

Only one and he gave it to her. ''Got this?'' He held up the murder weapon.

Her eyes flared, gleaming. ''We have to hurry. No, not with Caesar. It's rougher there.''

There. The wall of time. It terrified Chris more than catching Becket.

She saw the pack and ran. ''Oh good, good.'' She pulled the head mics out and gave him one, started to zip the bag closed, then took her knife, NVG's and the micro camera out, jamming the latter in her pocket.

She handed him the night vision goggles. ''Here's your

chance to be high tech.'' Chris nodded, having tried them out weeks before.

They tested the mics—clear, but weak. ''They won't last long, so let's go.'' Chris held the murder weapon and on foot they moved, separating and talking to each other, speaking their love and how the hell they were going to explain this to anyone. But they moved quickly.

''Take left flank, Tori. I have the right.''

She hesitated, then agreed. That would put him there first. ''Remember what I said about bright light in your face,'' she warned, unsure if Becket knew he could blind Chris with just a match.

They ran, Victoria slower and Chris racing like a deer, faster with the NVG's. She could hear him breathe, measured and smooth.

''I see him.''

Her heart jolted. ''Careful, honey.''

''I love you, Tori.''

''Then marry me in the morning.''

''I will.'' A pause, his breathing nearly silent.

''Chris?'' She tapped the receiver in her ear. She quickened her pace, blood staining her bandage and running down her arm. Lightheaded, she tripped, righted herself and ran. Then she saw them. Becket was scrambling up the incline, Chris behind him. Clutching his shoulder, the arrow shaft snapped off, Becket turned and fired, missing, then taking aim.

''No!'' she screamed as Chris kicked the gun from his grip, pain vibrating up Becket's arm. With a growl of rage, Chris was on him, driving him back against the stone wall.

''I'll be free,'' Becket gasped and shifted toward the cavern.

''You'll be dead.''

Chris raised his arm, the silver winking in his fist before he drove the stiletto into Becket's chest.

Becket stared into his eyes, stunned and the moment seemed frozen as his gaze shifted to the blade. His horror was satisfying.

Chris stepped back, mesmerized by the sight of the silver-blue glow coming from the tiny cave. Becket groped for the edge, his back scraping against the stone as he tried to escape.

Chris didn't see Victoria until it was too late. "Tori, no!" He reached.

Victoria lunged, hitting the stiletto, driving it deeper. Becket wrenched in pain and she slammed a black rectangle into his open mouth and shoved him. The wall swallowed Algenon Becket like a pebble dropped into mud, a shimmer of thick silvery liquid.

He was gone.

Bent at the waist, Victoria gasped for air, her hands braced on her thighs and Chris climbed to his feet.

But he touched air, horrified as Becket's arm appeared through the liquid rock, slapping around her throat and pulling her with him.

The wall shivered, then went still as a pond.

Chris blinked, his gaze rapidly searching over the cavern. His heart beat ceased, slamming against the wall of his chest. And slamming. And slamming.

Oh Jesus.

Immediately he hit the stone, seeking a soft spot, but it wouldn't give him entry, shifting and swirling as if smoke beneath glass, but solid to his touch.

And he knew. He knew!

She was trapped in her time.

He gaped at the sealed wall, his breath coming in hard shallow breaths and as the realization hit him, he dropped to his knees, his gaze ripping over the rock, believing and not believing that she was beyond his touch, beyond his help.

Yet he could hear noise, the whirling, muffled voices.

The silver, slow moving and thick like syrup, vibrated, and before his eyes, it solidified.

He would never get her back—never. And the agony of it burst in him with the force of lightning, striking him down to his bones. He threw his head back and he screamed her name, a raw agonizing howl, a wounded cry of neverending pain.

* * *

"Didn't you see her? I saw her movin' around here. Where did she go?"

"Can't trust bounty hunters!"

"Find her. I want a clue or a body!" Federal Marshal Mark Daniels shouted and men scampered, searching the area they'd searched three times already. The tracks ended here, at the stream.

Daniels' frown remained in place, harsher than ever as his gaze shifted between the horse, the saddle bags, then the blood trail. The confusion and noise of a hundred lawmen combing the terrain went on around him. Choppers circled overhead.

Yet his gaze followed the still tacky splatters of blood. He'd retraced it a half dozen times already. His attention shifted briefly to the police wading hip deep in the stream. One man shook his head. No sign of tracks on the other side.

It was like she evaporated right here, he thought, turning toward the heavier blood stains and stepping carefully over the boulders. His craggy face was creased in a deep scowl and only those close to him knew it hid his fear. She'd vanished. And that son of a bitch with her.

He braced his hand on the misty rock, adjusting his feet, his head bowed. Janey was going to be upset about this, he thought briefly.

Suddenly, he flinched, jolting back and slipping on the rocks when something burst from the fall. The plop and splash of water drenched him and men turned.

He wiped his face and the moment seemed frozen as everyone stared, confused, wary, guns out and aimed, until the body bobbed to the surface.

"Jesus!" a cop said, wading across to the man floating face down. He turned it over.

"Well, what do you know!" Wondering, stunned.

Daniels' gaze ripped between the drizzling fall and Becket before he moved quickly down to the bank. Uniformed men hauled him onto the shore.

"He's still alive," a county sherrif said.

"Not for long," Daniels remarked coldly, almost happily. He squatted and flicked the silver spike sticking out of Becket's chest and the man moaned. "That has to be the murder weapon."

"Christ! Is that an arrow tip?" A sherrif said, mercilessly prodding the bleeding wound.

"Let the coroner find out," Daniels said and shifted closer. Though Becket's breathing was rapid and hissing, Daniels forced his fingers between tightly clenched teeth and pried open his mouth. "What have we here?"

He pulled out the micro camera, wiping it on his pant leg, then holding it up to the sun. "It's Mason's." He pointed to the triple lines that always marked her personal gear.

"Then where the hell is she?" Kyle said, patting the horse's neck and wishing the animal could tell them something.

"Hell if I know." She'd sworn she wasn't coming back, but that she'd deliver. Victoria was always good on her word. At what price?

Daniels looked to the fall.

The water had stopped.

Victoria felt the denseness of the passage grow heavier and heavier, casting out sound, sealing off her movements. She could hardly move, each shift more difficult, straining her muscles, her breathing. It felt like gel, sliding softly, but rapidly hardening. And she knew she was dying in here. Her lungs stiffened.

Then she heard his voice. She turned her head, the effort nearly killing her and as if looking through a dirty mirror, she saw Chris.

Dizzy with sorrow, Chris pounded the stone, begging it to give her back, offering his life and his heart.

"Tori, come back! I love you!"

After several useless moments, he fell back on his haunches again. Tears wet his cheeks, mixing with the blood on his chest, her blood, and he dropped his head forward, staring at nothing, his scraped fists clenching and clenching. His shoulders shook violently, but no sound came. He couldn't breathe, he couldn't move. His heart shattered, each piece breaking away like a part of the earth into the sea. The eerie thought of her trapped in stone forever was just too much to bear. A tomb, a grave. He prayed she'd found her way out, at least.

If she didn't?

His throat swelled, the physical pain of losing her, never knowing if she survived, moved through his blood like gravel. It burned, and he welcomed it. It gouged and scrapped, and he deserved it. He should never have left her side.

He should have shot Becket and been done with him.

He couldn't look at the wall, the rock that encased his dreams.

Caesar approached a few yards down hill, his hooves clicking against broken stone.

Chris swore, the sound bringing reality. And sheer agony again.

Through the haze of his mourning, he sensed movement, heard a wet sucking sound before he lifted his gaze.

Abruptly, a hand thrust through the rock, dripping, fingers flexing, struggling to reach and Chris grabbed it and pulled. His grip slipped and he tightened it, nearly crushing the bones, clasping her elbow. He heaved. And Victoria popped through the silvery darkness like a babe from the womb, stumbling, groping for him. His arms crushed around her and they sank to the ground, sliding in the dirt and stones.

"Oh Jesus, Tori. Thank God, thank God!" His hands charged roughly over her, assuring him she was here. "I thought I'd lost you."

She was covered in something slimy and wet, but he didn't care and his hands trembled as he brushed her slick hair off her face. He kissed her and kissed her. She gasped for air, every breath a struggle.

"I heard . . . them. There . . . in my time. The police."

''You're here,'' he said in wonder. ''You're here.'' He couldn't touch her enough and fell back, draping himself with her.

''Yes, yes.'' It was finished, and she sobbed happily against his throat, smelling the masculine scents she needed, clinging to the man she loved. ''I'm home, Tonto. Now you really have to marry me.''

Epilogue

Victoria leaned against the stucco wall of the garden courtyard, smiling at the man rolling in the dirt, children climbing on him like eager puppies. Love, so pure and sweet, bloomed in her heart she didn't think she had room for more. Then she heard their wild laughter and another morsel crept in.

Her gaze lingered on Chris as he suffered the poke of boney elbows and misplaced knees, then shifted to the lone figure curled on a stone bench tucked in the corner. Lucky. Lucky Swift. That always made her smile. He was reading, his glasses sliding down his nose. He glanced at his brothers, amused, and she smothered her laugh when he rolled his eyes, as if their antics were too childish for him. After a thoughtful moment, he removed his glasses, set his book aside, then launched into the pile with a dark growl. The ruckus started all over again, with Chris pleading for mercy.

Victoria decided it was time to show him some.

"Hey, guys." She spoke softly and four dark heads popped up like toast.

"Momma's home!" they squealed and raced toward her.

Chris fell back on his rear, catching his breath and watching his wife as she crouched, opening her arms and letting their little bodies crash into her.

"Whoa, boys, take it easy," Chris said, but they ignored him and her smile brightened.

Victoria tickled her sons, raining wet, smacky kisses over their dirt-smudged faces.

"Aw Mom, yuck." This came from Cole, even as he leaned in for another.

"You kissed him more than me," her three year old peeped, pouting. Victoria cupped Cain's chubby little face and gave him a noisy one. She brushed her mouth over the top of Lucky's head, as she always did, and his hug tightened.

Closing her eyes, she savored the scent and feel of them wrapped around her. She talked with them, listening intently to every detail of their day, then sensed their restlessness. "Abigale said she made cookies," she whispered like a secret.

"What kind?"

"Hey, do I look like I can cook?" They laughed and scrambled off the floor and into the house. "Wash up first!" Their griping filtered to her as she leaned her head back against the wall, staring at her husband.

"Hi, boss."

His lips quirked at that. She was his hunter now.

"Got any of those kisses left for me?" He moved toward her, his gate rolling and sexy, doing things to her she couldn't control. The star on his chest winked in the afternoon light.

"Tons. And a few other tricks."

He offered her a hand up, and she leaned into his long body. He kissed her deep and slowly and their bodies fused tightly with need.

"Tough hunt?"

She unbuckled her holster, and let it drop to the ground. "The usual." She shrugged, looping her arms around his neck. His hands on her trim hips, Chris anticipated the feel of her fingers in his hair and when it came and he moaned like a tired lion.

"They whipped the tar out of me."

"You're such a marshmallow."

He grinned, knowing it was true. "I've grown to like seeing you in jeans," he said with a glance down. There was no mistaking her for woman in those, he thought, as his hands moved over her waist, up her back, massaging and shaping her firm body.

"My rear hurts."

He rubbed there, too.

"God, I missed you," he breathed into the curve of her throat.

"Me too." She tilted her head, staring at his mouth. "I'm not going out again."

"You wanted to work, Tori."

"I know. But even if it's once in a while, it's too much. Cole lost a tooth, Cain wrote his name, and Lucky, Christ, he's reading Shakespere! My babies aren't babies anymore, and I'm missing all the good stuff."

The roar of a fight starting had them peering around the edge of the door jam. Abigale shrieked for Victoria's help.

He arched a brow in her direction. "You sure?"

"No more hunting." She plucked the star off her vest and handed it to him, inclining her head toward the house. "They're the only bounty I'm after."

Chris watched her go, loving her long legged walk, loving Tori and thankful as hell that she took a hunt through dangerous waters—to find him.

ABOUT THE AUTHOR

Amy J. Fetzer lives with her family in South Carolina. She is the author of four other historical and time-travel romances published by Zebra Books, including MY TIMESWEPT HEART, THUNDER IN THE HEART, LION HEART and TIMESWEPT ROGUE. Amy loves to hear from readers and you can write to her at P.O. Box 9241, Beaufort, South Carolina, 29904-9241. Please include a self-addressed, stamped envelope if you wish a response. You can also visit Amy's web site. The address is http://www.apayne.come/amyfetzer.